Captain Grimes

Unreconstructed

John T. Wayne

Grandson of the old Oke!

John T. Wayne

Part I

The New Standard in Western Folklore

Captain Grimes

Unreconstructed

John T. Wayne

Part I

The New Standard in Western Folklore

Mockingbird Lane Press

Captain Grimes (Unreconstructed)
Copyright © 2016 John T. Wayne

Mockingbird Lane Press—Maynard, Arkansas

ISBN: 978-1-9445415-4-5

Library of Congress Control Number: 20115920171

0 9 8 7 6 5 4 3 2 1

www.mockingbirdlanepress.com

Cover art: Gary Lucy
Cover graphics: Jamie Johnson

THE GASLIGHT BOYS

From 1861 – 1865 a storm rolled through our nation and in its wake left behind a path of death and destruction. Over 100,000 children lost everything they had come to know including both parents. This tragedy took place during the Civil War and sadly for years after; during a period known as Reconstruction. What became of those children? How were they instrumental in shaping the future of our society? These questions are answered in my series of books called, "The Gaslight Boys." Charles Dickens is credited with being the original Gaslight Boy, but there were many other Gaslight Children created by the war. The Gaslight Boys series brings to life the hardships, the conditions and individual struggles buried and /or forgotten by time.

These are the stories of the young men and women who grew up to become great in their own right, men and women of the great society. Some of them became great, some became outlaws, and some died short of the chance. The Gaslight Boy novels are their stories.

---John T. Wayne

For the silent masses who know deep down in their heart, the Federal Government is no longer ensuring our freedom, but taking our beloved freedom from us one unconstitutional law at a time.

---John T. Wayne

I personally never judge a book by its cover, though it might cause me to take a second look, and I never personally judge a man by the skin he inherited from his father and mother. I judge him for who he is, not from where he came or what color his skin might be. There is no room for racism in the 21st Century!

In America today we are in danger of losing our history, our identity, our sacred past. I do not believe that we should sensor our history, remove flags or dig up the dead to move them no matter how brutal our past may appear. If you are sheltered from the truth, or if you lie to yourself to keep from knowing the truth, it is a foregone conclusion you will fall prey to the wiles of those who do know the truth and will use it to keep you under foot every time. This is a tool used by the few to get masses to chase their cause without justification. As a nation, we need to grow up and learn to discuss our past like adults. For this reason I did not change the history I found in Captain Grimes memoirs, nor should I.

A gun is neither good or evil, but a human being makes it so.

---John T. Wayne

Cause and effect; these two principles must be considered when one tries to determine the cause of the Civil War, yet for the most part they have been completely forgotten or ignored by historians. The canon fire at Fort Sumpter was not the first salvo of the Civil War, it wasn't even close. The first shot fired was the book *Uncle Tom's Cabin* which was written in Jacksonville, Florida by Harriett Beacher Stowe, released in 1850 which unwittingly created the position of no retreat for both the north and south. This book was the catalyst for the war, the canon fire at Fort Sumpter was only the visible effect of it, ergo cause and effect.

Still, it was not slavery which began the war, but unfair taxation on the plantation owners in the south. Once Congress determined the slaves to be a taxable asset the line was drawn in the sand between the north and the south, the issue of freeing the slaves didn't come into being until Lincoln delivered his Emancipation Proclamation two years into the war, a move he had to make in 1863 in order to get his soldiers to fight.

For over ten years from 1850 to 1860 the country divided itself into one mindset or the other. It was *Uncle Tom's Cabin* which caused most northerners to believe that all southern plantations were filled with evil slave masters, a work of fiction taken as fact.

The country stewed over the words written by Harriett Beacher Stowe, until finally the canons at Fort Sumter fired. So, was the war started by canon fire? Not hardly: it was started by the inflammatory words written by Harriet Beacher Stowe in a place called Mandarin on the south bank of the St. Johns River. Had she never penned her story which was made up fiction, the north and south would likely have never gone to war with one another.

During the first two years of the war Lincoln could not get his soldiers to fight with any heart, not until he took the concepts directly from Harriet Beacher Stowe's work and created his

Emancipation Proclamation. Everyone was trading slaves, not just whites, but blacks, Indians and Mexicans engaged in the commerce. Lincoln was reluctant to destroy the entire profitable industry of slavery, but at last in 1863 having no success against the lesser armed Rebels he had no choice. He had come to realize if the north was to win he had to get his soldiers to fight. Up until then he had been losing badly. Lincoln needed the slaves on his side. Prior to the Emancipation Proclamation the president had not been very successful at recruiting them. Once he declared freedom for the slaves with this emancipation document they came in droves and the north finally began to fight with heart.

---John T. Wayne

Credits

This book is based upon the memoirs of Captain Absalom Grimes, the Confederate mail runner for the south. A majority of the dialog had to be filled in, otherwise the circumstance and the story itself is directly from Captain Grimes detailed account of the Civil War. There should be a place in our history for men such as Absalom Grimes who was Mark Twain's best friend when war broke out, and was also a riverboat pilot from Hannibal, Missouri, but as they say; "To the victor go the spoils."

This novel is the work of John T. Wayne and could not have been written without the aid of the original publishing of Captain Grimes's memoirs by New Haven, Yale University Press in 1926. So sit back and read a colorful account of what really went on during the Civil War.

Chapter 1

By the age of twenty-six, I was a riverboat pilot on leave. The year was 1861. My necessary credentials known to all as a pilot's commission had expired and I was needful of replacing the document, however not before I had a few weeks of vacation from the steamer *Sunshine*.

I was fortunate enough to be a steamboat pilot and captain due largely to my father who had insisted that I follow in his footsteps and become a well-trained navigator and pilot on the upper Missouri and lower Mississippi Rivers. Simply stated, he wanted the upper Missouri to himself. I didn't have the wherewithal in my youth to school my father on the fact there were over a hundred other steamboats on the upper Missouri River at any given time, nor did I care to, as I never seemed able to win an argument with the old man anyway.

The thing that rubbed me wrong was the fact my father had done everything in his power to determine my future, leaving little or no decision making powers to me, and after all, my destiny was my business, was it not? I couldn't understand why he insisted on making it his.

Unknown to me at the time, my destiny had been forged when I was born in Kentucky and purposefully named after a good friend of the family. Enter my father's meddling at birth. In fact, my father's boss had been Absalom Carlisle who was also my mother's uncle. Absalom Carlisle was a man's man, the type to give orders. He would back up for no reason once his mind was made up. He was a big domineering overgrown gorilla of a man at six foot six, and with such a presence he had never to my knowledge taken any guff from anyone. The thing was he was smarter than folks figured him for. If you were not intimidated by his mammoth size you soon would be intimidated by his ability to think and reason beyond that of most men.

Absalom Carlisle had been on the *New Orleans* when she made her maiden voyage down the Ohio River into the Mississippi and on to New Orleans all the way from Pittsburg. While he had not up to that point been the pilot or the captain, he eventually became both. In short Uncle Ab was well respected wherever he went and was especially respected within the family. He was quite simply a living legend.

By naming me after Uncle Absalom, my father had intuitively sought to give me a head start in life assuming I would inherit the old man's steady sure-handed presence and demeanor. In this matter my father was most assuredly disappointed as I picked up none of Absalom Carlisle's steady-handed conviction or his ability to handle men. I believed no such poppycock of myself in my early teens or in my mid-twenties for that matter. I was in fact, a happy-go-lucky daredevil who, for reasons I didn't fully understand, could not let a challenge or dare go unanswered.

At the age of two my family transplanted me to Missouri, a move which sealed my fate. In my early days while attending school in Hannibal, Missouri, I was often disciplined for ignoring Miss Mary Bell Rutherford's instructions and inserting my own classroom curriculum. Teacher Rutherford would put me into the corner to consider my unwarranted and ill-timed misbehavior such as turning lizards, frogs, bugs, and snakes loose in the classroom.

One particular morning I found myself covered in honey after raiding a bee hive down by the river. Although I was severely chided for my action before school, I was allowed to stay so as not to miss the important upcoming lesson of the day. Miss Mary

Bell must have believed the fact I was still covered in honey would be an embarrassment to me, when in fact, I wore the slimy sticky sweetener as a badge of honor.

Just before noon recess we heard scratching on the door of the school building and Miss Mary Bell opened the door to find a black bear licking honey off the door handle. As the hungry bear tried to force his way into the schoolhouse, she managed to push the door closed. Our entire class was held hostage until late in the afternoon when one of the young lady's father arrived to see why his daughter had not yet arrived home. Alfred Trudeau shot the black bear and freed the nineteen hostages inside the building while I received a quite fashionable escort to the Grimes residence, flanked by half the town.

I wasn't, however, the only one causing trouble for I had a bosom buddy. Samuel Clemens was all the more fraught with what the teacher called untimely interference or obstruction of instruction. In any case, I was not the steady hand everyone in the family had been expecting, although my world was about to change into something very different as the United States had an awful tear in its fabric. A tear which was about to rip wide open.

What is it about minding one's own business or setting out to enjoy a fine day which always seems to invite trouble? Whilst shoeing my old mare Betsey one morning in early spring 1861, a telegram arrived at my doorstep. My close friend and bosom buddy, Samuel Clemens, had been visiting me for the last few days and the unanticipated messenger had a telegram for him as well.

I knew the boy messenger for what he was simply because in the year of 1851 at the tender ripe age of sixteen, I had been in the employee of the Morse Telegraph Company for one year. Their only competition in the St. Louis area was the O'Rilley Telegraph Company. I had the dubious distinction, along with

Esrom Pickering of being among the first telegraph messenger boys in St. Louis, so when I looked up and saw the young messenger, I knew exactly who he was, and I reminisced.

This placement early in life had been my father's decision, insisting if I wouldn't settle down and focus on my schooling, I had better go to work.

As I looked at the messenger, I remembered the day I had occasion to deliver a telegram to Miss Jenny Lind, the famous "Swedish Nightingale." Under the bequest of P.T. Barnum I was to deliver the message to the old Wyman hall where she was giving a concert later that evening. When I delivered the telegram she made of me her personal guest. That evening I was nothing less than the proudest young man in St. Louis. The grand treatment I received from this star of unimaginable magnitude was a favorite memory of mine that I had played over and over in my head for several years. As a boy of sixteen, I was dining with the most famous singer in the country without a solitary clue I was being used to keep men from calling on the young maiden's table. Ah, the blessing associated with being a naïve youth.

Now ten years later, the year was 1861 and many were fearful our fair country was about to go to war. Federal supremacy was something I wasn't sure I agreed with, and neither did my good friend and neighbor Samuel Clemens. The fact we believed in state's rights declared by state sovereignty and the solemn right of the individual, was most assuredly to our detriment. But the catalyst for the upcoming dispute had been a book called *Uncle Tom's Cabin*.

A beautiful spring day had unfolded before our eyes as the dogwoods were in full bloom. Sam, having just lit his pipe settled back against the old walnut tree to read his telegram, which is exactly what I was doing, minus the pipe simply because I did not smoke. Not yet anyway. What I read was not what I had in mind for my near or distant future. I was just finishing my Yankee draft notice when Samuel interrupted the serene morning silence.

"Why I never! What makes them Union fellows think for one minute I would pilot one of their boats up and down the river for them?" Sam shouted from the stump at the base of the tree.

"The fact they want you I can believe. However, they want me too."

"Mine says to report to General John B. Grey at Jefferson Barracks in St. Louis immediately for assignment," Sam said.

"Mine says the exact same thing."

Sam's face turned bright red. "Lord Almighty, my mother would come up out of her grave and get me if she knew I was going to be piloting a riverboat for the North!"

"My mother is still alive and she doesn't have any such barriers to overcome."

"It says here the penalty for disobeying this order to report is up to and including imprisonment for treason."

I held up my hand to stop his rant. "Now let's study upon this for a moment, my good friend. The wording in mine says I must report to the general at Jefferson Barracks immediately or suffer the consequences. It doesn't say I must actually do anything beyond report to General John Grey. They hint at what they want me to do for them, but the order doesn't specifically say I must actually pilot their steamboat. Only that they want to question me to ascertain my skill and knowledge of the river. I must report but, beyond reporting all is left open. How does yours read?"

"I'd say mine was no doubt written at the same time by the same incorrigible character."

"So you see Sam, all we have to do to prevent adverse consequences is report to General John Grey, not necessarily anything after that."

"Abe, you worry me sometimes. Why, to think of such a low-down trick."

"It's no trick." I said defending my honor. "There's nothing in this dispatch which says we have to actually join the Union Army or do anything other than report to the post commander. When we do report we may be able to get away clean and never have to honor another order. We'd have to be mighty fetching riverboat pilots to please those fellows. Why the Mississippi is the river I know best, and they want to ascertain our ability to pilot a boat on the Missouri it says here."

"I see what you mean. Well, it's about two days by road or one by steamboat, and it'll take you a good hour to finish what you're doing. Why don't I get my things ready for traveling and we can ponder what we are going to actually do while we're riding."

"We'll get shut of these orders before sunup on Monday," I said.

Riding together the three miles to Hannibal in my old buckboard, we hopped aboard the steamer *Rosebud*. My Betsy could have used the exercise, but I left her with the hostler in Hannibal and we set sail, reporting at Jefferson Barracks by three-thirty Saturday afternoon. When we checked in at the Jefferson Barracks gate, the guard looked at our summons and informed us we were in the wrong place.

From what I could see there was new housing going up for the new Federal recruits, and tents covered the parade grounds for as far as the eye could see. The only conclusion I drew from such a presence of soldiers was how difficult drilling would be.

The parade grounds were so full it would be impossible for any platoon to drill, although I had nothing to worry about for I had an especially allergic reaction to drilling. If I was made to drill on a parade ground, I would be apt to run. I didn't want anything to do with the silly activity which I had witnessed many other soldiers engaging in.

Presently the gate guard returned with a senior sergeant who looked as if he'd spent his entire life in the military. He was wearing three stripes and two rockers below them. This fellow proceeded to remove his glasses and explain to us the error of our ways.

"You fellows will have to go downtown," the sergeant instructed. "General Grey has been placed in charge of the entire district of St. Louis. He has taken up new quarters away from Jefferson Barracks at the Oak Hall building. Shall I draw you a map?"

I shook my head. "No need. I know exactly the building you're referring to."

"Me too," Sam said.

As our pilot's license had just expired we were both desirous to renew our livelihood. We headed to the office of the United States Inspector for the purpose of having the document reinstated prior to reporting to General Grey. Now, renewing our license was one thing, but reporting to a Yankee general was quite another. I was having misgivings about the whole idea of working for the Federals. Something about the way the federal government was forcing its will on the people didn't set right with me. Government was supposed to be limited for the sake of individual freedom. It seemed to me that the Feds were swinging a rather wide loop over too much territory, but then what did I know about government? I knew of the Force Bill of 1833 which empowered a president to use armed force against any state which nullified any act passed by the federal government, but for me to really understand what was happening would take another forty years.

Sam Bowen, another friend of mine, had been sitting on unpacked cargo near the gate where we had entered Jefferson Barracks and decided to see what the two of us were up to. He met us as we were exiting the front gate. Both my friends at that point decided to go along with me to the inspector's office as we all seemed to be lacking our proper updated credentials. The office of the United States Inspector happened to be on our way.

May God pity the youngster who has no father to prepare his path, I thought to myself.

On our arrival we were not greeted by Inspector Monty Churchill whom I fully expected to see, but a disagreeable looking lush of a German who could not help but spit as he spoke. I suspected immediately the man before us had gained his position in some disgraceful fashion. Through political pull or under the table chicanery most likely.

"We're here to renew our license as riverboat pilots," I stated.

"De tree uv you et once?"

The German opened his drawer as if in answer to his own question and placed three statements on his desk which I had never seen before, titled, "Oath of Allegiance." Then he placed a pen on each one and stepped back.

"Fill deez out an I will atminister de oat."

As steamboat pilots we had to renew our license annually and upon renewal it was common to take an oath to abide by the regulations governing pilots, engineers, mates and captains, but to my knowledge such a thing as inducing a man who was born and raised in the United States to swear an oath of allegiance to the United States of America entered uncharted waters. Studying the document I could see nothing which indicated a departure from normal protocol other than the title so the three of us filled in all the blanks. But the title of the document locked horns with my conscience by the time I finished and the term oath of allegiance bothered me. It seemed to me the title change had altered the document's meaning entirely so I inquired of the man as to its intent.

"What exactly do you mean? Oath of Allegiance," I finally asked.

"The "sucsesh" are t'dying to dist'rupt de Union an andyone who wants a pilodt licen mus take de oat of alleadgiant to de Fedral Government." He said as his spittle landed all over the place in his attempt to muster this most disgraceful attempt at the English language.

"Sir," I said as I finished inking my signature on the document. "I was born in this country as were my father and grandfather before me. I have no objection to taking an oath of allegiance to America, but when I do so it will not be from a beer-soaked wretch of a German who cannot even speak the language!"

I then tore up my application and dropped the newly shredded document on the alien's floor and exited the suddenly red-faced man's office. My two companions quickly followed my example by ripping up their own "Oaths of Allegiance," and fled the office behind me post-haste.

"What do you think fellows," I asked as my friends stepped out onto the street behind me.

"I believe if we just go home and relax for a few days all of this talk of a succession will die down and we can go about our business as usual," Bo said.

Bo was the name we used for Sam Bowen when the three of us went anywhere together, simply for the sake of less confusion. All three of us had been raised in Hannibal under the tutelage of Miss Mary Bell Rutherford and we had a habit of teasing Samuel Clemens by insisting his name didn't add up to anything at all anyway. Little did we know how well he would make up for this unwarranted declaration during his later years as the writer Mark Twain.

Without wasting any more time in St. Louis we hastened back up river on the steamer *Hannibal City* and began our unexpected short vacation. Since none among us were married men as yet, we decided to idle about and watch the comings and goings of the steamers at the dock each morning. We listened to the news and rumors of war which reverberated up and down the wharf figuring if we only waited a few days the matter would be settled and the three of us could go and obtain our license in the usual manner without taking the oath of allegiance to the Federal Union. A rather nice fantasy, but it wasn't long before reality set in.

We had left St. Louis on Saturday afternoon without delay and without taking the oath of allegiance to the Federal Government. Four days later about nine in the morning we watched the *Hannibal City* as she docked on the wharf with her regular Keokuk packets. On this morning the three of us were lounging on a stack of skids about two hundred yards south of the landing, discussing the winds of war and where we were headed as a nation, how the issue at hand could be solved without an actual war and so on.

"I believe in a states right to sovereignty," Clemens was saying, "but the book that woman wrote may make the question mute. A lot of folks seem to be divided over the issue of slavery now and if Stowe has her way, all slaves will become free men, even in the south."

Bowen laughed. "That'll be the day. Why I bet she employs slaves herself. How else could a woman like Harriett Beacher Stowe know so much about them?"

"Them Yankee's are biting off an awful big piece of American pie. I just hope they can swallow it," I added. "Take a look yonder my friends."

Suddenly there appeared on the deck of the steamer an officer and four privates. We watched in earnest as the young lieutenant and his men walked down the plank onto the dock. Something warned me these soldiers were not on a field trip as we had no garrison in Hannibal and no office to represent the Union Army shy of St. Louis. After exchanging a few words with Jerry Yancey, the local boat agent and dock supervisor, the five soldiers turned and walked directly toward our vacation spot atop the stack of skids.

An aura of silence had overtaken our assembly by this point and where there had been jovial laughter only minutes before, long and indecisive faces were all which was left to greet the lieutenant and his entourage upon their arrival.

"Good morning gentlemen. My name is Lieutenant Larkin. I understand that the three of you are Bowen, Clemens and Grimes. Am I correct?"

As the four accompanying privates adjusted their loaded rifles to cover us, I had the sudden premonition there was little use in arguing the point. Lieutenant Larkin had obviously been told by Yancey who we were and if we denied the fact now we'd be tempting unnecessary grief and anguish for no reason. Not to mention the fact we could be shot. All four guns were loaded and trained on us while I had the dubious distinctions of attracting two of them for myself.

"I'm Grimes," I offered up.

"And I'm Clemens," Samuel added.

"Then you must be Bowen," the lieutenant said as he looked Bowen up and down.

We could hardly deny our identity as the three of us wore our captain's blouse to guard ourselves from the chilly morning air.

Pausing the lieutenant continued. "I have an order from General John B. Grey, commander of the district of St. Louis to escort you three gentlemen to his headquarters immediately."

"All three of us?" I asked.

"All three of you, and if you don't come willingly we are to have you placed in irons and escorted as traitors to the Myrtle Street jail where you will sit until the general decides what he should to do with you."

"Ab, I fear you shouldn't have told that German off like you did," Bo said.

I accepted Bo's statement as a cue to begin reasoning with the officer and his entourage. "Lieutenant, having been born and raised in the United States of America would you be willing to take an oath of allegiance to your country from a hideous beer-soaked alien who can't even speak good English?"

"I would take the oath," he avowed, although I thought dishonestly.

"But the fellow isn't even an American!"

"He is an American. He recently settled in the German settlement of Hermann, Missouri and although his English is broken and lacking, at least he," Lieutenant Larkin emphasized, "took the oath of allegiance."

We decided then to cause no further trouble for the dutiful lieutenant and the three of us went with him and his men to St. Louis by way of the returning steamboat *Harry Johnson*. We were allowed to gather our things from our homes before we left Hannibal as we all lived in the vicinity. My parents had their farm outside of town a ways and since moving onto their new land I had taken up residence in the old house on the outskirts of our little settlement, one which had begun life as a landing for the ever present steamers traveling up and down the Mississippi.

I had watched closely while heading downriver and several times I could have slipped from the grasp of our guards, but now was not the time for such evasive maneuvers. While I wanted to be somewhere else, I found myself studying their military bearing with interest. Anyone who wanted could escape from these soldiers just about any time they wished. I studied them with earnest for something told me such knowledge would come in handy.

By late afternoon we docked at the wharf in St. Louis and Lieutenant Larkin escorted the three of us under rifle barrel to the office building of General John B. Grey. We were ushered in to the commanding officer who had taken up residence at The Oak Hall building on the northeast corner of Fourth Street and Washington Avenue. Lieutenant Larkin escorted us into the general's upstairs office personally and introduced us by reading the exact order and summons we had received only a week prior.

"Lieutenant, you may be excused," General Grey said and our escort departed for other more pressing duties. Pausing for a good look at the three of us the general rubbed his bearded jowl and searched for the proper words with which to begin.

"Gentlemen I understand the three of you are experienced riverboat pilots and that you were in Hannibal on vacation. It seems nearly all pilots are "sucsesh" these days and difficult to obtain at best. I have it in my mind to send the lot of you upriver carrying troops. I intend to land them near Boonville on the Missouri river provided the three of you do not object."

"Sir, we are not Missouri River boat pilots, the Mississippi is the river we know," Samuel said.

"Why I've never been on the Missouri," Bowen added.

13

"You can't follow another boat up river if she were piloted by a Missouri River boat pilot?"

"Well sir, when put in those terms I suppose we could," I admitted begrudgingly while witnessing the unexpected silence of my two companions.

"Gentlemen, that is all I shall require of you," the general explained.

At that moment two very fashionable young ladies appeared at the office door and interrupted our conference with the general by first knocking.

"Sir, we beg your pardon, but we have urgent business to discuss with you as soon as you are finished here."

"If you will ladies, please wait in the office across the hall. I'll be with you momentarily."

These two fishers of men retreated to the office across the hall and the general suddenly decided the two young ladies were a more interesting distraction. He had us duty bound and corralled in his office, and we weren't going anywhere at all, or so he thought.

"Wait right here gentlemen, I'll be back in a moment," he said as he closed his office door on the way out.

We had been allowed to bring some clothes from home like I said and we had come along willingly so as to cause us little or no bodily injury by the soldiers who had been sent to abduct us, but as soon as the general was out of sight we fondled our carpetbags and set our aim on the back door which opened to a back set of stairs into the alley. Whatever his intentions were with the overdressed ladies we had no idea, but the three of us were glad they had arrived in the nick of time.

The general had been strikingly correct in his assumption nearly all riverboat pilots were "sucsesh," because the man had quite adequately described the three of us without knowing how accurate he had been. While not one of us were cast in a Confederate yoke just yet, only a small nudge or miss-step by the Federals would be needed to cement our unwavering loyalty on the side of Confederate opposition.

We knew the folly of interrupting a commanding general amidst such adult games as General Grey was likely now engaged in with his lady guests, so we took the agreed upon action and summarily dismissed ourselves from the general's office altogether.

"What do you think Ab?" Samuel asked.

"I believe these Yankee fellows are taking a lot for granted. They've never once asked me where I stood on the subject of States rights."

Indecision flitted across Bo's face. "What about our orders? I don't want to go to jail or be hung for treason."

"In order to commit treason you must have a change of mind and then switch sides. We haven't picked sides yet so how can any of us be guilty of treason," I reasoned for my friends. There was more to the argument, but I was naturally inclined to hit the nail on the head or offer more argument when necessary. This was part of my family inheritance; however I did not recognize or view my personal habit as such just yet. Although I had heard the statement "the apple doesn't fall too far from the tree," I didn't really understand just how this would begin to play itself out in my own life.

"Unless that door is locked and bolted fast from the outside I'm going out the back door down the stairs and back to Hannibal. You fellows can come with me or you can stay, but I'm leaving," Samuel said as he picked up his carpetbag.

The door opened easily under Samuel's efforts and the two of us followed him out the door and down the stairs looking in all directions as we went. It would not be a good sign to be caught leaving the general's office by the back way which is why we proceeded with caution.

Under the long staircase was a Union Troll. A soldier placed to guard against any comings or goings. As we reached the bottom of the stairs he stepped out from his hiding place beneath and leveled his gun at our midsection.

"And where do you think you are going?"

In my quickest vernacular I responded and hoped my ploy would work. "General Grey instructed us to tell you to wait for him in his office. He has an errand for you to run post haste." I nodded at the door and stepped down the alley way as if I were doing so naturally. My friends stepped out with me and we made no effort to run or look back. Eventually we heard the office door open and knew the soldier had reached the top of the staircase. Then I heard it close and I chanced a look back. The troll was gone. We scrambled for the end of the street turned the corner and then made our way down to the wharf.

Discussing amongst ourselves what our next course of action should be, the three of us grabbed a packet back to Hannibal where we suspected the Feds would now leave us alone, but we were in for yet another surprise. As we returned to Ralls County I dispensed any idea of stopping by my house and went farther west for twelve miles having decided to visit my mother on the new homestead and family farm. I no longer considered my residence on the outskirts of Hannibal to be a safe place to relax. If the Feds wanted me they were going to have to hike a ways.

Upon arriving at my parents' ranch I found the house had been searched inside out and my mother was nowhere to be found. There was, however, a note lying on her bed which explained everything. This note was addressed to me from General John B. Grey.

Captain Grimes,

Your mother will be held in Federal custody until you return to St. Louis and pilot one of our boats. I regret we must take such action, but I find these tactics both necessary and most effectual at the present time.

Gen: John B. Grey

"Well that tears it! You Yankee Blue Bellies just made up my mind," I said to no one in particular. I wanted their throat in my hands choking the life out of them. Any army that would stoop to the level necessary to arrest a man's mother in order to get him to work for them was no army of mine. This little move on their part infuriated me. My mother locked up as if she were a common criminal! How dare they take such action against an innocent woman? They were scoundrels, criminals in uniform. My mother of all people! Next they would be locking up orphans they themselves were creating for not having a home and widows for no longer having a husband.

I straightened up the house the best I could and put everything which belonged to my parents back in order, but I couldn't escape the feeling I was being watched. This little chore took all of two hours. If they had to take my mother, why had they found it necessary to make such a mess of the house, to cause my mother to cooperate? No, this had been intended to break my spirit. The ultimate cooperation of Captain Grimes had to be the answer, but if they hurt my mother in any way I was going to make them pay. Still, how had the Yankee's gotten here ahead of me? They had to have left St. Louis at almost the same hour as my friends and I. The soldiers had to be on horseback because nothing else could bypass the current on the Mississippi River and make better time of the travel.

My father was running the Missouri river between Alton, Illinois and Omaha, Nebraska, and wouldn't be home for another four months. I had to get word to him somehow about what had happened. Not that I would have any problem doing so, for we had enough friends on the river to develop our own underground railroad if necessary, only I wouldn't be sneaking slaves anywhere. If I could get my mother out of jail I would send her off by way of steamboat to be with my father. I could first leave a message at the dock in Hannibal and then send a message upriver by boat.

Two days later as I had settled into the swing on my parent's front porch I saw someone in the distance, navigating the small creek which ran across our pasture. The gentleman was no doubt Arthur West a crippled old man who never went anywhere without his walking stick. I watched as he made his way nearer the house. As he ascended the front porch he drew to a halt.

"Good morning, Captain Grimes," he greeted me.

"Good morning. What brings you out this way, Mr. West?"

"I was looking for you. I thought the two of us might talk."

Mom was still in the custody of my Yankee adversaries so I invited the old man to have a seat in the bitter chair across from me. "What would you like to talk about?"

Before I go on with my story let me explain; we called that particular chair the bitter chair because whenever my mother would gather persimmons for persimmon pie she would sit in yonder chair and de-seed them. I don't know if you have ever tasted a raw persimmon or not, but if you have you'll understand why the term bitter was so enthusiastically used by my father to coin mother's old armchair.

"I was wishful to let you know that you have friends gathering together this very morning to assemble a brigade of troops for the southern cause."

"Friends of mine," I stammered in surprise, but I shouldn't have been.

"They are over at Matson's farm near New London preparing for what they believe to be an inevitable upcoming engagement with the Federals," he informed me.

"So my friends are southern sympathizers." I had developed quite an enthusiasm for the southern cause since finding the note left by General John B. Grey which I now carried in my pocket as a reminder. West's assessment of troops gathering intrigued me, I had no idea there were so many southern minded gentlemen this far north of St. Louis; enough to form a brigade that is. We talked and I quizzed him on the matter of troops, mounts, weapons and other such elements necessary for fighting a war.

Satisfied with the old man's answers I excused myself from any further chores about the farm. Mr. West agreed to watch over the place until someone returned, so I gathered my things and prepared to ride. Walking out to the barn I saddled my favorite horse, Napoleon. Napoleon was a palomino of good breeding and stood about fifteen hands and he had come to me by way of my parents on my eighteenth birthday. He had come from a long line of studs used for breeding, but father had bought him cheap because all he wanted to do was fight. My saddle was a dragoon with rifle scabbard attached and the old saddle rested easy on the back of my horse. When I finished cinching the saddle tight I walked back to the house and retrieved my shotgun. I then mounted and rode for Matson's farm.

I found upon my arrival the southern "Brigade" being assembled was only slightly short handed with a total accompaniment of ten regulars who had not yet taken an oath. I watched as my friends, (yes these grown men were my friends), argued and struggled over who should be in charge, much as we had done as school children picking sides for a tug of war, a game or any other sporting event. I was surrounded by such notable young men as Charley Mills, Samuel Clemens, Jack Coulter, Edward Stephens, Sam Bowen, Tom Lyon, Asa Fuqua and three others outside our circle of influence which we later had the fortitude to assign as privates.

Watching supposedly grown men who have been raised up together and who have known each other their entire lives attempting to determine who was who and what was what can ignite the flames of ones funny bone. Sitting there, my big smile eventually drew the attention of my well-meaning friends and we all had a good hardy laugh. I hadn't laughed since finding the note left in mother's house and with the sudden return of my mother's memory I stopped laughing and concern once again wrestled control over my emotions.

Undetermined as to what destructive mode we should first adopt as a well trained fighting force, I suggested we find out where my mother was and set her free. Then and only then I found out they had acquired Sam Bowen's mother in the same fashion along with Samuel Clemens' sister. Samuel's sister along with our two mothers having been abducted seemed to be enough of a catalyst to generate all the necessary support and sympathy we would need from our fellow companions.

As yet no two of us dressed alike, which meant we needn't worry about how we were outfitted to go to town, the river port of St. Louis to be specific. There were only a few places they could be keeping the women, and we in our wisdom determined to set them free at all costs. We decided the first requirement would be learning of their whereabouts. Only then could we plan the necessary jail break.

Breaking three women out of jail required the added ingredient that we couldn't put the ladies at risk of being shot. If our mothers or Samuel's sister were shot during escape, our plan would be useless. Whatever action we took to free our family would have to appear normal and within the confines of the prison's daily operation. This meant we would have to study the habits of the Yankee troops guarding them, but first we needed to know where to find them.

We needed to know which jail they were in and if they were being held together. One jail break would be much easier than three separate ones. Asa rode ahead and made inquiries as to the whereabouts of our loved ones and brought news back to us they were being held in the Gratiot Street prison in the same cell. This eased my conscience for this news revealed a lackadaisical attitude on the part of the Yankee's. If they had separated them, our circumstance would have been much worse. As things now stood, I felt we had a good chance of releasing them without causing much of a ruckus.

St. Louis had become a cauldron of spies lately, necessitating the fact we be careful and not seen. At this point no one knew who was a spy and who was a friend. Anything we planned must be done with a sharp eye and even more caution.

As things stood, this would be the first test of such well-trained men as the Ralls County Rangers. Although as yet we had not chosen a name for our brigade, I had heard the title and liked it. Other names were being bantered about in jest, but I liked the one which had our home county at the beginning.

My own mind was off on an information gathering venture. We needed information, and the questions I could not answer for myself I posed to my companions, men who were capable with the correct answers. We had to get this mission right. We could not come away with tragedy. If anything happened to our family members or us it would be the end of our lives as we knew them. Horse play was fine up to a point, but play time was now over.

For a small contingent of men from Hannibal Missouri, the war had already begun.

Chapter 2

Two days later our untested brigade of eleven was in St. Louis plotting and planning, filling in the blanks where information had been vacant. Wherever we could manage clothing or a piece of Yankee uniform we snatched it, but we were having such a hard time finding the necessary attire, we enlisted the help of orphans who had been showing up on the streets. We placed a bounty on the clothing and sent word out among them we would pay two dollars for each and every uniform item, up to a point, they could deliver into our hands.

As of yet there was no official war, but war had been declared for us by the actions the Yankee general had taken against our families. I want to make a point here before I go on, there were only two orphanages in St. Louis prior to the war and those two orphanages housed nearly fifteen hundred children, mostly unfortunate youngsters who had lost their parents to the border war between Missouri and Kansas which had been going on for the last six years. In the last year the orphan population in the city had more than doubled, now standing at a whopping three thousand plus. Both the Mullanphy Orphanage and the St. Louis Protestant Orphan Asylum had been around for more than thirty years. However strains were now being put on them which had folks looking for ways to ease this unexpected pain and unanticipated growth in the orphan population.

Although the orphanages were doing a noteworthy job with the resources at hand there were still untold numbers of children fending for themselves on the street. As these children were destitute and in need of help we offered up two dollars per garment or item and we soon had the necessary uniforms in hand while they all got enough to eat for a few days.

Not wanting to leave ourselves exposed to the possible larceny money tempted in a young and fertile mind, once we had the necessary garments we immediately retreated to a new location lest one of the little beggars sell us out to our Yankee counterparts.

Our new quarters was an old cow barn two blocks from the Gratoit Street jail. We spent the night in the loft, brain storming and plotting, but nothing we came up with made a dabble of sense. No matter the plan, someone always played the Devil's Advocate and spoiled our dreams of grandeur and rescue before we could wrap up.

Early the next morning, unable to sleep, I went for a walk knowing how my mother was suffering. As I walked, the sun was not yet on the horizon, but the fresh air did wonders for my attitude and my fertile young mind. We would never rescue the women as long as someone offered up a pessimistic answer for each equation. An idea dawned on me that this was a mission for a lone operator. This jail break would take nerves of steel and no mistakes, a convincing demeanor and unwavering courage. I would have to think on my feet to warn the women ahead of time so they would not give me away as I knew all three of them and they knew me. Unknown circumstances would dictate the outcome, but so would a sharp presence and a vigorous awareness, yet would such awareness be enough to overcome the unknown circumstances?

From my lapel, I pulled General Grey's note which had been left for me at Mothers and signed by the general. I looked the document over and suddenly knew what I needed to free the ladies. I hastened back to the barn and under the glow of a lantern I forged my own note ordering the release of the prisoners into the custody of the guard bearing the note, whereby they would be delivered to the office of General John B. Grey for questioning. As a youngster working for the Morse Telegraph Company I had whimsically forged every signature I could on a message that I received over the telegraph wire. I had a grand imagination as a youngster and duly used my mind's eye to the fullest extent of my ability. I would imagine for a moment what someone's signature might look like and then I would hasten to apply my interpretation to the particular message in question. Sometimes this got me in trouble with the recipient, but most times they had no problem with a young boy sprouting his wings and making use of his fertile imagination. On this morning however, I had an example of the man's signature in my pocket so little imagination was needed, all I had to do was duplicate his scribble and this I did with glee.

Once I had my note sufficiently crafted I turned the lamp back down and looked across at Samuel Clemens who had awakened.

"What are you doing Ab?"

"I have an errand to run. I'll be back in less than an hour," I offered quietly.

Samuel seemed satisfied and let me go. Had he began to talk I believe the others would have awakened and I would have never gotten out of the barn without an argument.

It was in my mind to handle this prior to daybreak just before the guards changed shifts. They would be the most tired and less prone to suspect deceit and chicanery. I had to work fast and with confidence. Sam didn't miss the fact that when I left the barn I was in full Yankee attire. I could see the caution in his eyes, but he never said another word.

In complete Yankee dress and bearing a rifle I entered the jail on Gratoit Street to find the majority of the guards sleeping. One lone guard sat behind a desk nursing his alertness in an attempt to overcome his sleepiness. I walked directly to him and laid down my hand written forgery from General John B. Grey.

"The general wants these three prisoners in his office for questioning when he arrives later this morning," I informed the guard.

The corporal fumbled with the note for a moment and then looked up at me. He seemed unsure or suspicious about something, but he never vocalized his concerns. Eventually he gave up whatever it was he was about to say and said, "Last cell on the left down the hall."

"Which hall?"

"That one," he said pointing to the east wing. "You'll need the keys. Just make sure you leave them here on your way out."

Picking up the keys I started down the darkened hallway moving slowly and quietly. I picked up a lantern from a small table halfway down the hall and carried it with me. When I reached their cell I put the key in the lock and turned it over. The door moved, squeaking as it opened under my left hand. I sat my rifle down in the hallway and put my forefinger to my lips.

"Shhhh," I said. "We're going to walk out of here, but you have to look somber and displeased, so wipe the smiles off your faces until we are on the street. Otherwise I'll be joining you."

I'll give them credit, I did not have to repeat myself. The closer we came to the entrance the more somber they looked. I placed my lantern back on the table and when we entered the room where the guards had been sleeping two more of them were now scratching their eyes awake, but of no mind to challenge a fellow soldier.

I placed the keys on the table in front of the corporal and pushed my mother softly in the back. "Come on now, move it. We don't want to keep General Grey waiting."

All three ladies stepped outside and halted as I pulled the door closed. Before they could engage me in any idle conversation which might give me away, I intervened.

"Head toward the riverfront," I ordered loudly as the general's office was in the same direction. If the Yankee's were watching I didn't want to give them any reason to suspect anything wrong so we headed south and east. Samuel's sister started to say something but I cut her off.

"No talking," I hastily ordered and she got the hint. I didn't want anything to give us away at this point, not when we were so close to safety.

Steadily, I walked the women toward the wharf and when we were five blocks from the riverfront I walked them around the corner and soon we started west on Salisbury Street. This was the long way around but thirty minutes later as the sun was coming up in the east I opened the barn door and the women stepped inside to be greeted by a throng of jubilant supporters. Samuel Clemens studied me with an upturned eye wondering what I had done to free them and I knew in due time I would have to tell him.

Fatigue washed over me like a bucket of cold water. I had not slept in two days, so leaving the ladies to my companions, I crawled into the back of the barn and laid my head on the hay.

I had just learned a valuable lesson; committees were a good thing if you didn't want a decision. If a man by himself believes he can pull something off, he can likely do so, but a committee would likely stifle any good idea and still be arguing any possible outcome long after one good focused individual had completed the mission. Having justified my individual action with resounding success I was out faster than you could turn down a lantern and say goodnight.

While Mark and Bo stood watch over me in the barn the others made arrangements, assuring the women had safe passage out of town on the *Natchez* where they would soon meet up with my father upriver on the *Omaha*. I would like to have had a few precious words with my mother, but the urgency of the situation dictated otherwise. When I awoke the women were gone and all was dark outside. My companions had returned and were snoozing lightly in the last hours before midnight. I milled around for an hour or so and went back to sleep.

Before sunup we mounted up and rode out returning to Matson's farm the following day. That is precisely when arguing amongst ourselves we first decided to cut our hair to resemble military correctness, although we had no Confederate uniforms and no idea where to obtain such an item. Tom Lyon volunteered to be our barber and produced a set of sheep-sheers. By the time Tom had finished with us, every man in our so-called Brigade had suffered his first battle wound.

Rather than looking like a tight knit military unit we now resembled wounded veterans and the war not yet begun. The wounds we would now have to carry into battle evoked a great deal of sympathy from nearby neighbors who had heard about the recruiting efforts and stopped by to see how things were progressing. Within a few hours each of us were outfitted properly with better horses, canteens, weapons, and ammunition donated from nearby farms. I kept Napoleon under me and concentrated on other hardware such as might be necessary for war.

As the day progressed we learned that Union forces would be landing in nearby Hannibal on the *Hannibal City* and that we stood a good chance of being captured if we dallied about, so we decided to head west. Whether they were after us in retaliation for the prison break or some other reason we had no way of knowing. We decided if we were to become more organized and well-honed troops with sharpened skills, we should drill a bit before we met up with the more experienced, highly motivated Yankee troops who were trampling through our area.

Saddling up, we took inventory of arms, ammunition, food stock, and water along with other tools necessary for our survival. I had learned early in life that any lies or deceit and shortcomings can be properly exposed through the use of mathematics. Not on my own, but at my father's insistence. I now made use of my math skills and something was telling me we were a few apples short of a bushel.

How can I possibly describe our brigade of eleven? No one man matched another, other than the fact each and every man sat a horse and wore some type of bandage to cover his cropped and bleeding head. No two dungarees matched. Our shirts were all of a different color and the only commonality among us seemed to be our captain's blouses of which six men wore dutifully. Our gun belts were hit and miss along with our weapons. If one of us could even hit a target with his weapon I was unaware of the fact.

Paintbrush is the only animal worth mentioning here other than Napoleon simply because the rest were run of the mill stock. Samuel Clemens' mount was a blond colored mule with its tail hair sheered off all the way to the last remaining ten inches or so and when running it lifted straight out behind resembling the artist tool. Sam's war horse was frisky as a jack-rabbit and upon this trusted steed sat the newly coined Mark Twain with his feet dragging the ground on either side. One valise, one carpetbag, a pair of gray blankets, one home-made quilt, a frying pan, an old fashioned Kentucky squirrel rifle, twenty yards of sea-grass rope for tying up prisoners we intended to capture, along with one umbrella was tied tightly to the mule's rump.

"Mark," I said as we rode west toward my parents' farm, "You'll have to paint that mule another color or we'll have to leave him behind when traveling during a night raid under a full moon like we are now."

"Be careful will you? He's sensitive. If he overhears what you're saying I'll not be able to get him to do anything. He's still sore at Tom for clipping his tail."

"I'll do my best not to upset his feelings."

As we neared the eastern most fence line on my parents' place I rode ahead and opened the gate for my friends an exercise Napoleon had helped me accomplish many times. After our brigade had ambled safely through I refastened the rope used to hold the gate in place and trotted my horse back up to the point. I had done all of this without stepping down from my saddle. I took the lead and guided our eleven man army across friendly pastures lest we succumb to trigger happy neighbors or Mr. West.

We rode for about thirty minutes across the farm and came to the neighboring fence line adjacent to the Grimes place. From here we proceeded west until we found the house of Colonel Bill Swain where we ate supper and settled in for the evening. The colonel's young daughters, (I say young but they were all of marrying age) catered to our self-inflicted head wounds while Mother Swain supervised their actions and a merry evening was enjoyed by all.

Dinner was a shoulder of beef from a cow Colonel Swain had butchered earlier in the day. His wife and the girls put together a batch of potatoes, carrots, green beans, corn, and tomatoes to whip up a large pot of beef stew. Then we set about for hours to come up with the moniker Ralls County Rangers, a fetching name I thought, notwithstanding.

The following morning Colonel John Ralls appeared and we took his presence as an omen. He joined us for breakfast and when we had finished he gave us a lecture on the importance of State's Sovereignty and our mission. When he completed his speech he added, "Gentlemen I am duly authorized by Governor Jackson to enroll recruits into the Southern army. I can swear you all in now if you so please."

This caused a flurry of Confederate sympathy and immediately after taking the oath I realized we were all one step deeper into serious trouble. Mounting up, our brigade headed for Goodwin's Mill located on a branch of the Salt River. On our arrival we discovered another brigade of young volunteers headed our way, known only as the Salt River Tigers and we trembled with fear at first sight of them. These boys were ready for war to our way of thinking. Just their appearance was enough to cause us to quake in our boots. Each and every man was armed to the teeth and ready for battle. Then we realized we were on the same side and things simmered down a bit. Remember, as yet no one had a Confederate uniform or knew how to come by such a thing if the south even had one. When we saw armed men floating about, we believed whole heartedly the Yankee's could be suffering from lack of uniforms as well. We soon learned this was not the case as the Yankee's controlled the industrial north and uniform making was their strong suit.

While sitting in camp their lieutenant made a roll call and suddenly we Ralls County Rangers realized we had no command structure and had placed no officer in charge. We did however have seven senior officers. This was only a temporary snag and soon the comedy which had played itself out at Matson's Farm unfolded once more, only now there were numerous witnesses. For the sake of shortening the sequence here all I'll say is we elected seven chiefs and the remaining three men were assigned duty as privates. Mark Twain was given temporary assignment as second lieutenant, meaning he would do the most work and accept most of the responsibility concerning the underlings.

Then Mother Nature unleashed a flurry of rain. There are swamps in Missouri, but when it rains for any length of time the entire state becomes a swamp, a dreadful nuisance which seems to leave its mark on everyone and everything. Two days into that dreadful downpour in which the skies had opened up we heard a rumor that the Yankee's had landed in Hannibal and that a force of several hundred regulars were headed our way. Knowing our own ability as we did the Yankee's superior numbers did not unsettle us in the least; they had simply given us more targets at which to shoot and we thanked the good Lord for such a setting of the table. The thought we were outnumbered twenty five to one never occurred to us. Then I counted my ammunition.

"Lieutenant," I said to my best friend. "I can shoot seven Yankee's and then I'll have to run."

"What are you talking about, Ab?"

"I have seven shells and with a double barrel shotgun I figure I can shoot three and one half times before I have to tuck tail and make my getaway."

This was the signal for my esteemed companions to count their ammunition rations and circumstances did not favor the Ralls County Rangers, or the Salt River Tigers for that matter. While we all brandished the latest weapons of human destruction, we had little ammunition to load them with. Most had been used shooting at rabbits and squirrels intended for supper.

We were miserable, tired, wet, and hungry by this point, yet we honored our duty and posted guards as we had no intention of disappointing the Yankee's. How much unnecessary work does a man create for himself when he strays unknowingly far from the truth? Those wasted hours and movements shall never be tallied or known, for first they must be recognized.

Sam Bowen, Ed Stephens and yours truly were secured for the night watch as we were all boat pilots and could keep awake better than most of the others save for Mark Twain, Asa Fuqua and Jack Coulter, also riverboat pilots, but Mark was placed in charge of said picket guards.

Our morsel of information had the federal troops going to Monroe City and turning south so we headed up the lane to where the road forked and waited, knowing the Yankee troops would have to come down that particular pike. If they came at all they would be coming from the north. Back away from the road and opposite the lane were several trees and bushes so we chose to tie and picket our mounts there. Then we shook several coins in a hat to see who would stand watch and when. Being the sharp young men we were, we saw no necessity in the four of us staying up all night long. I replaced Sam Bowen at eleven in the evening and was scheduled to stay on duty until three, however a little after midnight, certain I heard the enemy moving in our direction I decided I had better wake the others.

Mark Twain straddled Paintbrush immediately and held the reins of our horses after we had saddled. Then the three of us eased back up the lane in the direction the soldiers were coming. I was in the lead and the most awake so I commanded the best view when I saw the enemy column swaying as they came over the hill. First they swerved left and then right as if in answer to a marching command which I never heard because I unloaded my double barrel shotgun into both flanks.

Having just emptied both barrels of my model 1858 Smith Sporting muzzle-loading shotgun, I had the immediate revelation that I was no longer armed. However, I did suddenly and completely feel rather naked. My weapon was now empty and those Yankee's, several hundred of them were still coming, only now they knew of our presence. This piece of information was not lost on my companions who had already turned and taken out at a dead run.

At moments like these the human mind is incredible. As if all the information is fed into your conscience at the same time, over-stimulation, if you will, the human body is suddenly able to outrun anything on four legs. At such a moment I didn't wait around to see how many men I had left dead or dying in the lane. I completed my about-face landing on my feet in an all out dash headed for the horses with my two companions directly ahead of me, men who had not fired or backed me up, but were sprinting quite valiantly in the opposite direction. I did my best to catch them, but to no avail. When we got back to where our mounts should have been we saw Mark headed for greener pastures with Napoleon and the other animals in tow.

Bo screamed at him, "Stop now or I'll shoot!" This no doubt alerted the Federal troops as to what direction we had taken. Bo didn't stop his yelling, but increased his vulgar tirade as we drew nearer our mounted but now stationary lieutenant. Without waiting to see what kind of a hornet's nest we had stirred up, we continued running in the direction of our evasive mounts, weapons flailing in the air. When we reached the spot where our lieutenant was waiting for us we each swore at him and mounted up. The mule Mark was astride, the one called Paintbrush had been outrunning our horses it seemed.

"He got spooked and I couldn't hold him," Mark offered in self-defense.

"Had you not stopped when you did I would have been carving your headstone come morning," Bo advised our lieutenant.

"I told you Bo, I wasn't able to hold him."

"No I guess not, not with your hand slapping his rump like it was doing. It may be dark, but I'm not blind."

At that point the air had thickened so a man could feel no distance between himself and those surrounding him so we spurred our horses and headed back for our camp, effectively leaving Mark behind with his mule that was suddenly unable to keep up. We then hailed our camp as we neared to make sure our new found friends, the Salt River Tigers, didn't mistake us for the Yank's and blow us out of the saddle.

"What happened," Asa asked upon our arrival.

"We found the Yankee's about four miles north of here at the fork in the road where you go either to Hannibal or Monroe City," Bo said.

"How many were there?" Asa wanted to know.

My companion's eyes settled on me then and everyone focused on me waiting for my answer. "I don't know. I didn't have time to order up a review and count them."

"Part of your mission was to discover the enemy's strength and number."

"We'll need broad daylight if you want an accurate accounting," I said.

"Since you fellows already know what the enemy looks like, you can stand guard until sunup," Asa, the lead captain among us concluded.

Well, I couldn't sleep anyway, not now. I had just encountered a brush with death in the form of Yankee soldiers and my senses were now all a'fright. I sat down beside the fire and reloaded my shotgun. Once I had my weapon recharged I took my post on the outer perimeter of our camp on the Salt River and waited for the retaliatory assault that was certain to come our way.

I settled in to do some thinking then and wondered why our fragile numbers still hadn't equaled the numbers I had witnessed setting up at Jefferson Barracks. The evidence was that the Federals were having no trouble acquiring recruits of all kinds, while southern recruits seemed to be in mighty short supply. Maybe it was just the part of the country we were in, or maybe we were going about things differently. Still I couldn't help but wonder how outnumbered we were.

Everyone in our camp knew why I had fired my weapon and they knew the Yankee's were near as everyone settled back into the confines of their blankets. As a result no one in our camp, save for Asa, tried to sleep as we were waiting breathlessly for the enemy to surround and capture us.

Then in the distance we heard the lone clatter of running hoofs and the inevitable order was given.

"All right gentlemen, make ready your weapons," Bo said as we placed our guns in firing position.

"Hold your fire," I called to the men, realizing Mark hadn't been able to keep up. "The lieutenant and Paintbrush are still out."

Just then the blond colored mule came roaring into camp with Lieutenant Mark Twain in tow. He didn't stop or slow down until the animal reached the far end of our camp and then you well know his picket guards heard from him. Mark, as we had now agreed to call him, was unleashing a special diatribe of abuse for his guard detail which caused him to loose his religion and didn't stop until he had blamed the loss of his new hat on us. When things quieted down we got back into our positions around camp and waited on the enemy which never appeared. Finally at dawn we felt safe enough to sleep.

There had been no Yankee charge, no scouting party, nothing with which to say the Yankee's were just across the next field or a few miles away. There was however an eerie silence which overtook our unit and caused us to pause and consider just what we were doing.

If the Yankee troops had taken any kind of casualties they would have sent a detachment after us. They would not rest until they had the culprit in hand and once they had taken us prisoners, what then? Would they even take prisoners? I was encountering a highly complex problem as the day wore on. What if I hadn't shot at the Yankee's at all, what if they had been a figment of my imagination?

Chapter 3

At noon we all gathered about our humble campfire in the steady drizzle to fix what little we had left for breakfast which was warmed over biscuits with no gravy. If we didn't find a supply train pretty soon our brigade was going to succumb to starvation and we would have fought the shortest war in the annals of history which by all accounts had not officially started yet.

Once we had finished such a meager meal I got Sam Bowen aside and convinced him to return with me to the spot of our engagement the night before.

"Maybe we can find the missing hat along the way," I suggested.

"It would be best if we did. The lieutenant is none too happy with us right now."

We mounted up, said our goodbyes knowing full well we may never be seen alive again, not if we ran into those Yankee's in broad daylight. We eased our horses out of camp and stayed well back in the tree line so as not to be seen by any advance scouts. About two miles away from camp I saw the lieutenant's hat lying in the middle of Schrader's field. I pointed towards the spot and Bo took a good long look in that direction.

"What do you think," he asked.

"I think we leave the hat lay until we know where the enemy is. There's no sense getting ourselves killed over a hat."

"I'm with you. If we live, we'll pick his cover up on the way back. It would be just like the Yankee's to leave the hat laying there as bait. They're probably sitting in the woods yonder right this minute just waiting for us to ride out and pick it up."

Nudging Napoleon, Bo and I ambled on through the woods for another hour moving cautiously. Several times we stopped to check and listen, yet we heard and saw nothing which might indicate Yankee troops in the area. The steady downpour of the last few days had not relented and everything we owned was wet. I wanted nothing right then but a nice warm fire and some shelter.

As we neared the crossroads where the action had taken place only a few hours before, I wilted. Cautiously I approached the fenced corner and viewed the field of battle in the daylight. There was no sign of any Yankee troops, no evidence they had ever existed and then I saw the mullein stalks swaying in the breeze and almost choked on my own fear, fear that I had fired on the stalks, mistaking them for Yankee troop movements.

"I don't see any sign of Yankee's in the roadway," Bo observed.

"Nope, I don't either. Maybe the steady rain has washed out the tracks."

"No, with all the rain we've been having they would have sunk mighty deep into the roadway if they had passed by here."

"Bo, I believe I ought to come clean, but you must swear never to tell anyone what happened." He looked at me for a minute and then I said, "I'm serious. You must promise me you'll never tell a soul as long as you live."

"All right I swear," he said as he crossed his heart. "Cross my heart and hope to die."

"Do you see those tall mullein stalks swaying on the side of that hill yonder? Well, last night the wind blew and I could have sworn they were Federals on horseback."

Bo looked at me then as he was seeing me for the first time. "You played hell, didn't you?"

"You might say."

He stared at me, then at the stalks and back at me. Slowly he turned his horse down the lane and began to whistle, satisfied that there were no Yankee's within a hundred miles of our position. We stopped in Schrader's field on the way back and picked up Mark's hat. Then we had us a good laugh.

"I was ready to shoot him in the back last night if he hadn't stopped," Bo chuckled as he lifted the lieutenant's hat from the ground.

"Me too, only my gun was empty by then."

When we returned to camp I was not surprised at Bo's first words.

"Guess what Grimes took a shot at last night," Bo shouted to gain everyone's attention. Immediately every pair of eyes in our camp was trained on me as Bo began to tell the story.

"He was shooting at mullein stalks waving in the wind!"

"So much for promising never to say anything," I accused.

"All bets are off when the laughter to be had exceeds the value of sworn secrecy," Bo assured me and I knew him to be correct.

"Grimes, I don't guess you'll be standing guard tonight, not in my camp," Captain Asa decreed.

"Thank you sir, I do believe I could use the rest."

The laughter and puns continued the rest of the day around our wet and miserable camp, and I was the brunt of all jokes. I kept looking at my friend wondering how I could get even with him, but the good Lord has a way of taking care of things like that if you let him. I had the need to learn patience and later that evening my need for learning such patience was remarkably demonstrated. Sometimes God's justice is better than anything a man can extract on his own. This I had yet to learn and that night I learned it just so.

A young fellow by the name of Dave Young who was one of the Salt River Tigers had been posted on the early watch and the rest of our camp had gone to sleep. Dave had a tendency to take a swig from his hidden stash of liquor when no one was looking, which he kept in a flask inside his lapel. As the posted guard he had ample opportunity to reach for his reserve while standing watch. During the latter part of the evening several of us heard trampling and then Dave yelled, "Halt or I'll shoot! Are you going to halt and give a password or take a bullet?"

As Dave's order to halt was ignored I noticed several of the boys were not hesitating to pick up their arms and get into a less vulnerable position so I joined them out of a need for self-preservation.

"I said halt or I will fire," Dave repeated.

As the commotion in camp had now awakened everyone, Dave let go with both barrels of his shotgun and the rest of the men jumped, ready for the Yankee rush which never came. We heard a thud and groan coming from the bushes, so we knew the night guard had hit his target. Cautiously we rushed to Dave's side to find him looking over his own buckshot riddled steed lying on the ground kicking in the throes of death. We descended on Dave in the dark standing over his agonizing horse looking mighty dejected.

The entire camp burst into laughter and I received an instant reprieve from my friends. However, I knew better than to say anything for fear I would be dragged right back into the center of attention. Dave's vial of courage was found by Captain Asa Fuqua who proceeded to deposit the remainder of Dave's drink onto the wet ground.

"But captain, have a heart," the young private said.

"You just killed your own horse, Private Young. What if you had shot one of my men? I'd have the unpleasant duty of hanging you. From now on you'll stand your watch without this devil's brew."

I was sympathetic with the young soldier's plight for inside I knew if I joined my throng of friends I would no doubt find myself a party to the camp laughter again, and I, in no way, wanted to be an unwilling participant in their gaiety. In the last few hours I had taken enough of their ridicule. Granted their actions were grounded in fun, but a man does have a limit to what he can endure. I had a reprieve and I took it.

The following morning when we awoke we found our camp had been visited by an uninvited guest in the middle of the night. Mark Twain had become afflicted with a nasty boil while everyone slept and it was immediately apparent the visitor was of much discomfort to our friend. There was no chair or stool for him to rest his carcass on and this became a constant source of pain for the up and coming writer who had not yet taken pen in hand.

We tried placing Mark in a bed of straw, but although he spent his time lying on his side and wondering at the patience of Job in the Old Testament the boil persisted and grew. Over the next few days the lieutenant was the new source of attention and fun for everyone. Still, I held onto a loathsome desire to get even with Bo for outing me over the misidentification of mullein stalks for Yankee troops.

Our entire unit was disengaged because of one little visitor and I began to wonder what would happen if we encountered a real battle. Although our first wounds, the ones created by the cutting of our hair, were for the most part now forgotten, what would happen if we received new ones? If a boil could make our unit this ineffectual and dysfunctional, what chance did we have in a real crisis? I called the captain over and brought this to his attention.

"Don't you think, sir, that we should put in some kind of first aid supplies?"

"That's a good idea, Grimes. What do you have in mind?"

"Well sir, I could go about the neighbors and gather some of the necessary trimmings, but if we go into battle like we're now equipped, we'll die from any wounds we receive, life threatening or not."

"See if you can find something to give our lieutenant some relief while you're at it. I need him up and about."

"Can I make a suggestion, sir?"

"I wouldn't turn one down."

"Move the men over to Schrader's barn and get them out of the weather before they all get sick."

"Colonel McPherson told us to wait here until he returned," Asa insisted.

"Sir, he can track you. If you don't get the men out of the rain we'll all be sick and Mark's condition will be the least of your worries."

"If you see him while you are out, tell him we've moved."

"I'll do that, sir."

I threw my dragoon saddle on Napoleon, slipping my shotgun into the scabbard and rode out. The first place I headed was home. I knew Mother had supplies stored which would help us and plenty of white sheets which could be cut into bandages.

As I rode I began to think. We'd had an easy time so far, but with the Yankee's ramping up something fierce; recruiting like they were doing, I had the notion that war would soon be the word of the day. As of yet war had not been declared, but in my estimation I was fearful of the worst. Our new president had no intention of letting the southern states secede from the Union without a fight. He had the bully pulpit and he was not disposed to remain silent on any issue. He had a way of talking down to anyone and everyone he encountered. He was not a man who would easily let go of an issue. In fact it seemed that every issue brought before him was tailor made for him to use as an excuse for going to war.

When I arrived at the old homestead I found Mr. West busily cleaning the windows. At this I felt ashamed because for the last several years I had been doing this chore for Mother whenever I was home. Home to me was still the old house in Hannibal.

"What are you doing, Mr. West," I asked as I entered the house.

"I'm window cleaning, at least on the inside."

"Why don't you leave that to me?"

"Fine, but I had no idea you were coming back this way so soon."

Tossing me his rag he hopped down and went to sweeping the floor.

"What are you up to these days," he inquired.

"I was going after first aid supplies. We don't have any in our camp."

"Dad gum, has the war started already?"

"No, but we do have a few injuries just the same."

"I guess I hadn't thought of war causing injuries before it even got under way."

"You're not by yourself on that account, we didn't think of such things either."

"Well, I can help you put a few things together, and your mother does have some old sheets we can cut into patches, but how will you carry the stuff without getting everything wet?"

"I hadn't thought of that."

"We'll figure something out," West said. What he figured out was to melt candle wax onto the outside of the valise which held the gathered supplies and this kept the rain from soaking everything.

I picked up what I could at our place, including a good meal, that I knew my friends back at camp wouldn't begrudge me, then Napoleon and I headed towards the retirement home of our neighbor Colonel William "Bill" Swain. Here I was given more medical supplies and asked to stay the night which I did without complaint. I knew that in my neighbor's home where I had spent a few nights growing up, I would at least have a warm bed out of the rain.

At sunrise I hurried to the breakfast table where I shared an unlikely banquet with Bill, his three daughters, and Mrs. Swain. I knew them well and had been to church with them in my younger days, but now things were different. Although none of the young ladies were married, I was spoken for and all of the Swain girls knew of my engagement to Miss Lucy Glasscock. This turned out to be a blessing as the conversation at the table settled on more lighthearted subjects such as war, death and dying.

When I returned to our camp later that morning, I was outfitted with enough bandages to handle a good battle, but the main thing was the medical supplies I had in tow for Mark. He was most grateful for the salve I had in my saddlebags and the bandages I carried with me, the udder cream and other things. I had doctor's tools that I had no idea how to use and many other items with instructions on how to distribute proper amounts of medicine. No one in our outfit was a doctor, but no one would go without medical supplies.

My fellow soldiers had moved to Schrader's barn and made themselves comfortable. They were getting dry and had a glowing fire going in the middle of the floor to keep warm. I made their day when I produced sacks of beans and rice ready for the kettle. The problem was we had no kettle. Sam Bowen rode out saying he'd be right back. When he returned about ten minutes later he had a kettle with him and we placed it on the perch we had assembled for the purpose of cooking.

We had a grand time then, but Mark was still in the throes of pain created by the boil on his posterior. No one wanted to volunteer as company surgeon, so our lieutenant was doomed to wait for someone qualified to use the doctor's tools correctly. Although we had the medicine needed to complete the surgery, no one felt accomplished enough or capable enough to go carving on the lieutenant's behind which would no doubt cause him to lose his religion once again.

When it became obvious his inept, incapable friends would not volunteer to give him the much desired relief, even with the proper medical supplies at hand, Mark began to emit such slanderous verbal tirades at us that I can still hear them all these years later. They're not something I can repeat nor would I dare try for they were very unbecoming of any man, let alone an officer in the Confederate Army. He was in severe pain so he had an excuse, but had it been me, I would not have carried on so. No good could come from letting your men see you in such a disgraceful position. Since Mark was my friend, I never saw fit to hold this shortcoming against him.

We proceeded to make him as comfortable as possible by stacking hay in a trough where he could lay in a soft bed. Our efforts proved fruitless however, and his condition worsened throughout the night and I feared his religion would leave us for good.

Two days more we waited out of the rain and then decided our colonel wasn't coming back. It was our guess that he had no taste for war and that he had spirited himself away, although we were mistaken. He had in fact taken sick and was holed up at Matson's farm trying to recover from a bought of pneumonia.

During that spell we talked of what we might do to disrupt the Yankee's efforts in our area. We talked of blowing up trains, sinking riverboats loaded with troops, stealing supplies the Yankee's needed, setting fire to General John Grey's headquarters, you name it we were wishful to extract a price from the Yankee soldiers.

"I sure would like to shoot me some Yankee's," Tom Lyons said.

"You've already wounded more soldiers than anyone in camp. You'll have to wait your turn," Captain Asa warned.

"We could tear up some railroad tracks. If they can't get from Hannibal to St. Joe by rail that would slow them down," Bo suggested.

Colonel McPherson helped to build those tracks. He won't be of the mind to tear up such infrastructure," Asa said.

"What if we ambush the train as it's going by, firing into the cars carrying Yankee's. By the time they get the train stopped we'll be gone," this was Bo once again.

I surmised while listening that sometimes a man needs a cause in order to overcome his personal fears and self-imposed limitations.

"We'll wait boys," Asa said. "General Harris has been appointed to command the troops in this section and he'll be here soon to lead us to victory or death, whichever the Good Lord sees fit."

It was quiet then as each of us stewed over our thin fare at sunup. As quiet as things were, the silence which settled over our camp became an eerie one.

Then Private Evans spoke up. "General Harris has been a guest at Clay Price's house for the last two weeks."

"How do you know that, private?"

"I was just over there yesterday, but I didn't know he had anything to do with us. He's living in the lap of luxury and staying out of the rain."

"How far is it to the Clay Price farm from here?"

"Two miles straight south," Evans answered.

"Do you mean to tell me we've been eating beans, rice, side-meat and corn bread while he gets fed like a king?" This was Lieutenant Owens of the Salt River Tigers.

"Calm down, lieutenant. We don't know all of the circumstances."

"I know my circumstances damn well, captain and if he's been not two miles away dry and warm I'll be hanged if I follow him," Owens swore.

"That settles matters for me too," I said.

"Me too," Mark put in.

"I'm going to pack up and head for Monroe City. That's where the Yankee's are supposed to be holed up and I'm ready for some action," Bo added.

"Now hold on fellows, I'm sure if I ride over and see the general I can get a sufficient answer which will explain his absence," Asa offered.

"You find out what you've a mind to, we're going with them," Owens said.

Throughout all of this Mark had been laying in his soft bed wracked with pain from the boil on his hind side. As we broke camp we showed no signs of military discipline even after all of our hard training and effort.

As we were about to depart the premises, Mark rose up on one elbow and suggested, "Ab if you'll saddle up Paintbrush for me I'll join you fellows and come along."

48

Can you imagine Riding a
Mule with a boil on your ass ?
John T. Wayne

Knowing my friend's condition hadn't gotten any better, I grabbed his saddle and got his mule ready. I placed his gear in front of and behind the saddle then led Paintbrush over to the trough where Mark had been resting. Taking his hand I helped him up and into the saddle. We then left Captain Asa to find out the answers on his own behalf.

The Salt River had been right outside the barn within a short distance all along, but once out of the barn and back in the rain Paintbrush refused to set one hoof into the running stream. It was now swift and full to the banks as rain had been falling nonstop for more than a week. Instead of being waist deep, the stream ran ten feet deep or more and the river was now twenty yards wide instead of the usual five feet. I think the old mule knew the situation and wanted nothing to do with crossing what appeared to him a raging river; with or without a passenger on board.

"Ab, you'll have to throw a rope on this mangy old mule, he won't go into the water for me," Mark said.

The rest of our crew had navigated the swollen river, then turned about, waiting on the other side for us to make our crossing. Saddled with my friend I stepped down and shook out a loop with my rope. I tied one end around the mule's neck good and tight, then stepped back into the saddle and tied the other end off on the pommel. I eased Napoleon up to the river's edge and waited for the stubborn mule to come alongside. When he did, he leaned down as if to sniff the water. I took up the slack in the rope, wrapped the hemp twice around my pommel and then put spurs to Napoleon and leapt way out into the stream taking the stubborn mule and Mark with me.

The riverbank where we had stood was at best a foot above the water and once in the swift current we found it to be eight or ten feet deep and moving fast. As my horse swam valiantly for the other bank the wet rope slipped a couple of times causing me to

49

look over my shoulder. To my horror I saw nothing of my friend or his mule, but the rope was still pulled tight so I knew I would at least pull the mule from the raging water when I reached the other side. Worried sick with fear for my friend, Napoleon finally caught his footing on the other bank and lifted us from the water. I didn't stop him at the water's edge because there was still so sign of Mark or Paintbrush, so we continued to pull the mule, and hopefully Mark, from the water.

Noting the peril, Lieutenant Mark Twain was in, some of the men had jumped down from their mounts and made their way to the river's edge where the taut rope disappeared into the water, grabbed hold of the line and began to pull. To everyone's surprise Mark's hat appeared, then Mark still attached to the mule. As Paintbrush waddled from the water Mark rolled off onto the ground spitting up muddy liquid, trying to catch his breath. The mule weaved helplessly from side to side for a moment until he got his feet back under him. Suddenly, the animal regurgitated buckets of muddy water directly on the lieutenant who lay on the ground beneath him. *Ridiculous!*

In his slow southern drawl, Mark said, "Ab, that infernal mule waded every step of the way across the river bottom!" He wrung out his handkerchief and began to wipe his face.

"Are you going to be all right?" I asked.

"If I'm not I want you to promise me you'll shoot that dad-blamed mule."

"You have my word on it," I said as I stepped down and offered my friend a hand up.

Mark was going to step back into his saddle before all the onlookers, but the mule had a look of pure evil in his eye and Mark hesitated. He took the occasion to look the mule in the eye and tell the animal what for before he settled back onto his mount.

Stepping back into leather the rest of us had intended to evacuate the area but we were unexpectedly met by our Commanding General, Tom Harris, who was returning from the Price farm with Asa. Evidently our fiasco at the river had consumed more time than we had imagined.

"Gentlemen," he greeted us. "Where are you going?"

Well, we just glared at the darned fool. Here was a man most of us had never met and judging from what we knew so far we didn't want to know. Harris was answered by unwavering silence.

"I'm ordering you to return to your camp this moment," he said, but we just grinned at his assuming authority over the likes of our well-trained fighting outfit.

"Gentlemen, you will obey my orders and return to camp."

"We're going to get some real breakfast sir," Owens said, nudging his horse.

The rest of us followed and where we ended up was Clay Price's farm. A good breakfast was set for everyone and when the general returned, he was none too happy we had invaded his sovereign territory and disobeyed his orders all before noon.

After we stuffed ourselves we mounted up and rode out leaving the general in command of no one. We headed east from Price's farm and about three in the afternoon the rain began to clear off, the sun came out and we were once again tired, still wet and hungry. Mark was complaining of his boil and we all needed a rest.

"There's a farm house up ahead, maybe we can get fed there," I suggested. If anyone knew who lived on the farm no one said anything.

Twenty of us rode into the yard and dismounted, tied our horses to the hitching rails and went up the stairs to the front door. The door was open so I hollered through the screen, "Anybody home?"

There was no answer so I opened the door and stepped into the house with Mark filling my shadow. Presently several of the other men stepped into the room and took a seat while others loitered about the front porch and in the yard. A few moments later a tall thin woman with cold grey eyes and light hair combed back tightly entered the living room from another part of the house.

"What do you men want?"

As Mark had the most humble face among us he was our spokesman. "Madam, there's about twenty of us and we're tired and hungry. We were wondering if you could fix us something to eat."

She peeked out the window and I know all she saw was rabble, which translated meant Rebel. She took a moment to look at those of us occupying her living quarters. "Something to eat is it? You'll not get it here."

"We're willing to pay for a meal," Mark said.

"Pay nothing! Get yourselves and your truck out of here and make it quick."

At this point the lady produced a large hickory stick used to fluff her feather beds and pillows no doubt and she started for Mark.

"Hold on madam, don't be so hasty. We're gentlemen and intend to pay for whatever you serve."

"Do you think for one moment I would feed a bunch of Rebels and my husband a colonel in the Union Army?"

"But there is no war, not yet. We're all still just Americans," Mark said.

Suddenly the room cleared behind us leaving me and Lieutenant Mark Twain to deal with the riled housewife. I held my position just behind Mark as he slowly backed his way to the front door, fearing no doubt to expose his boil to the woman with the branch. She began striking at his shins keeping him at bay while herding us toward the front door.

"You get out of my house!"

Taking another swipe at Mark she whacked him on the thigh, "And don't come back."

"But madam, there's no war," Mark said.

"Then what are ye all gathered up for? Now git!" she said as she struck again.

"Madam, we're just tired and hungry."

"You can be tired and hungry somewhere else," she shouted as she made another swipe at Mark's knees.

By now the rest of the men were mounted and laughing at the spectacle of Lieutenant Mark Twain getting manhandled by this skeleton of a woman. I stepped into my saddle and turned Napoleon around to watch Mark descend the steps backwards in order to protect his tender posterior while at the same time dodging the lady's spiteful jabs.

As we rode away I asked him, "Why didn't you slide your sword and handle that Yankee properly?"

"Do you think I would disgrace my weapon by spilling the blood of a woman?"

"I was thinking of her more as a Yankee the way she manhandled you."

"Shut up!" Mark said.

We both laughed and rode down the lane. As we caught up with the remainder of our unit the fellows were still roaring with laughter. Our lieutenant had lost his first battle with a Yankee and a woman no less.

We came upon a neighbor walking down the road leading an old plough mule. He was in overalls and a straw hat with a lasso in one hand and the mule reins in the other.

"Sir, would you be kind enough to tell us who lives in yonder house," I begged as we sat our mounts.

"That house is owned by Colonel Tinker who has been with the Union army about three months if I am not mistaken."

"Ya, but who was that woman," Mark wanted to know.

"That was Mrs. Tinker," the local explained. "She's the general at home."

"I'm of a mind to believe you mister," Mark said as he nudged old Paintbrush and headed down the lane.

I watched the old man smile big as he took note of Mark's transportation and the way his feet dangled and drug the road bed. He shook his head and I nudged my own horse forward to catch my lieutenant. We rode on, headed for the Swain farm. This was a place the lot of us knew we could get a good meal and the girls would be of comfort to the men, even if none of us were ready to marry.

We witnessed the witching hour pass us by before we reached the Swain farm and because of the late hour we did nothing to wake or notify the family. We put our horses and mule away in the barn and fed them with Swain's oats like good farm boys would, then crawled into the loft to go to sleep. Everyone searched for and found the right spot for sleeping comfortable. Mark set up in a soft bed of hay near the gable end of the open barn door.

This turned out to be a short slumber as someone yelled "fire" just as I was nodding off to sleep. Everyone jumped straight up knowing we were sleeping in a barn filled with hundreds of bales of hay. Instantly awake and seemingly in the middle of the flames Mark rolled over about three times and disappeared out the loft door some twenty feet above the ground outside. He had evidently fallen asleep with his pipe lit and turned his bed made of hay into a bed of flames.

It would have been Loose Hay Not Bales at that time.

54

As the fire seemed to be localized near the open door Bo and I grabbed a couple of nearby pitchforks and rolled the burning hay out of the open gable end of the barn. We didn't think about Mark still lying on the ground just below with a sprained ankle. We shoveled and pushed without looking until we had the fire out the door and on the ground below. The pile of burning hay began to move to and fro all over the barnyard and we instantly knew our error.

The fall from the loft had sprained Mark's ankle and he was sitting on the ground rubbing his boil with one hand and his ankle with the other when the burning hay we threw out the door landed directly on top of him. This was no small amount of hay as we wanted to be certain we had removed any chance of fire from the second story loft.

It's important here to note that in an instant our lieutenant had received his third and fourth wound in just a few days. His head was still somewhat sore from the clipping, although like the rest of us that wound had mostly healed. His boil was bothering him to no end and now he had a sprained ankle and was literally being burned alive. Oh yes, and he had almost drowned in the river and had narrowly escaped being beaten half to death by a Yankee woman, and the war not yet started.

When we looked down at the sight of the fire moving around haphazardly my friends wondered what could be causing such a commotion and our companions began to laugh at Mark's expense. As the fire dissipated and Mark was revealed, he turned to us with language I can't repeat here and threatened us to no end.

Mark would not come back up to the loft no matter how we tried and finally we gave up our efforts to sway him and went to sleep. Mark insisted he would be just fine with the horses down below and went about to make another bed of fresh hay out in the corral. Now Mr. Swain was a light sleeper and with shotgun in hand, was suddenly present to see what was happening. Taking charge of the situation he escorted Mark to the house and ordered the rest of us to bed.

"And no smoking in my barn!"

It occurred to me that evening as I lay in my section of the loft; there was a reason why some of us men were riverboat pilots. We were surefooted on the deck of a boat, while our ability on fertile ground was proving less than adequate. We were prone to stumbling and falling, except on the deck of a good paddlewheel.

I felt mighty responsible for my friend about then and determined on awaking later that morning to help him overcome his wounds. I wasn't sure how, but I was going to see to his recovery one way or another. I had been the first to shovel burning hay down on top of him so I was obligated.

One of the girls entered the barn just before sunup and startled us from our slumber. Nancy took in the situation at a glance and knew the score immediately. We went to the house for a hardy breakfast and a good visit. Our fare consisted of biscuits and gravy, eggs to order and fried potatoes. There was fresh milk for all who wanted a glass and a good time was had by all.

By eight-thirty we were in the saddle again headed east. We rode all day until we reached Matson's farm where we had received our butchering at the hands of Tom two weeks prior. Welcomed with open arms we had dinner that evening, but Mark's wounds were getting the better of him by then and there was evidence of burns on his back, neck, legs, arms, face and hands to which Mrs. Matson ordered him upstairs to bed immediately. He was given refuge in a room across from Colonel McPherson and she went to work on him. The next time I saw him he was completely wrapped up in bandages, languishing in the big bed.

The following morning the lady of the house came out on the front porch. "Ab, I want you to collect some mullein stalks for me."

"Mullein stalks ma'am?" I trembled.

"There's some kind of healing agent in them, vitamin E and aloe I believe. I'm not sure why but the Indians have used them for many years. Now go and get me some."

I saddled Napoleon wondering if this wasn't poetic justice and rode out after, of all things, mullein stalks, and I knew just where to get them. When I reached the crossroads a chill ran down my spine, for although the mullein stalks were there, so were the Yankee troops. I halted and stopped well short of the soldiers who were marching to God knows where. These men were foot soldiers and could not catch my horse, but a bullet could sure enough outrun me. Kneeling beside my horse and covering his nostrils I waited for them to pass.

I held to the woods beside the road and waited until I had seen the last man was well clear of the intersection before I stood to examine my surroundings again. I waited a few minutes more and then eased my horse out of the woods looking both ways. There was nothing to see but mullein stalks so I cut several of them and tied a bundle together for Mrs. Matson. The Yankee's may have come and gone but I was still feeling their presence in the air.

I rode back to the farm and delivered the stalks to Mrs. Matson. Then I turned to the boys and told them what I saw.

"How many of them were there?"

"About seventy-five would be my guess. I tried to count them by two's."

"We can handle that many," Lieutenant Owens assured his men.

"Then what's your plan," I asked.

"We just ride in and start shooting."

"You can," I said. "But I'm staying right here with Mark."

"You'll take your orders from me, Grimes."

"I'm not even part of your unit, Owens. I'm a captain and I'll not go with you. Neither will my men," I added.

"You've been itching for a fight since the beginning," the lieutenant accused.

"Lieutenant, I'll not start the war and as far as I know there has been no war declared as yet."

With a creeping realization the lieutenant gleaned the idea I might be correct. There was no war at present so why be the blame for starting one? If he went looking for those Yankee's now and engaged them in battle, it would light the fuse of a war nobody wanted.

"You think it's better to wait here until they find us?"

"No, but think about what you're doing. If you go after them now the war will be started right here on our home ground. Our farms and families will take the first punches of a war nobody wants. If we lose our homes and families, what are we fighting for?" I paused then added. "Keep an eye on them, learn what you can, study them, but don't engage them until war becomes absolutely necessary."

"That makes good sense, Grimes. But what about Asa and General Harris? From what you say those Yankee's are headed straight for the Price place."

"They are, and they'll have to handle the situation on their own. We've got enough to worry about. McPherson isn't even up and about yet."

"All right, you've made your point. We're going to go take a look though. Maybe we can learn something about them."

"Do that lieutenant, but be careful. We have no idea what their orders are."

"Mount up!" Lieutenant Owens ordered of his men. None of the Ralls County Rangers moved. We watched as the Salt River Tigers rode for the Price farm and waved goodbye.

"Well captain, I guess we'd better find a way to make ourselves scarce," Bo announced.

"Why? If anything happens those boys will be back here like a bolt of lightning. We'll be warned well ahead of time."

"Shall we put up in the barn then?"

"Get everyone in the barn and take care of the Matson's stock. If we're going to be here for a few days I want to look like working farm hands."

"Yes sir. You sure found those mullein stalks handy like," Bo teased.

"If you don't shut up and mind your own business I'm going to send you on your own reconnaissance mission."

"Yes sir, we'll get the barn in tip-top shape," Bo saluted in jest.

There was a little colored boy the Matson's took care of named Clancy who was recently orphaned and I called him to me now.

"Listen Clancy, I want you to go down to the end of the road and sit there. We'll bring food down to you, but if you observe any Yankee soldiers coming our way I want you to come yelling, the Yankee's are coming! Do you get my meaning?"

"Yes sir, iff'n I see's Yankee's I come a hollerin'."

"Good, now go down there and keep your eyes open. I already saw some today and I don't want to see any more."

"Yes sir, I's goes now."

Clancy took off, heading down to the end of the lane. From that far away we'd have plenty of warning if the Yankee's did show up. Such a warning we wanted and needed. I still wasn't sure if I would run or fight, but I was thinking and hoping the correct solution would avail itself soon. My men were depending on me for the time being, and I didn't like being in charge. If I made a mistake I had no one else to blame.

Determined to have my men looking more like farm hands, I set about getting them assigned duties. There was little objection to this as we were finally scheduled to engage in regular meals. The fact Mrs. Matson was a great cook didn't go unnoticed by the men either. We stayed for a few days, but Mark appeared none the better for his care. My friend was suffering and from all accounts very little of it was his own fault.

I later learned that Mark healed rather well and the vitamin E kept him from receiving any type of scaring from the fire. Not only did he heal without scars, but he healed quickly. This was amazing. A miracle if you will.

I saw Mark after he was on fire and he had no hair, his eyebrows was singed off and his face was a hideous mangled mess of flesh. His right ear seemed melted into a grotesque shape and his lips were burned and swollen. I believed he would never look the same again, but then I didn't know the things Mrs. Matson knew. Today, I'm still in awe of her ability to bring about such perfect healing.

I don't pretend to know why doctors to this day discount the healing powers of vitamin E, but I assure you it has many healing attributes. Having since been in a fire of my own, I saw no other alternative. Either my life was over as I knew it, or the substance in the vitamin would heal me. I had seen the cure work on Mark so I tried it myself years later. I'll never know if it was the vitamin or my faith in God, along with my prayers, but I'm here to tell you I was miraculously healed. I have no burn scars and my skin is as normal as anyone's, but that's another story all by itself.

Chapter 4

The last I saw of Mark for a time was him propped up in bed with wrapping from head to foot. The proportions of his wrapping offered up visions of a baby elephant if one looked closely enough.

"Are you going to be all right," I asked from the doorway.

"I'll be just fine as long as you fellows are somewhere else."

"Well, we're moving out, breaking up the unit and going home."

"The Rangers are dismantling?"

"I think it's a good idea, don't you? If war does come we know where to find one another."

We were shrouded by silence for a moment, then I added. "Sam, are you sure you want to be called Mark Twain?"

"What are you getting at, Ab?"

"Ever since you took that handle look what's happened to you. You're lucky to be alive."

"And you think changing my name has something to do with it?"

"Don't you?"

"I hadn't really thought about it."

"You were just fine right up to the point you changed your handle, then all hell broke loose. It's my feeling that the good Lord is trying to tell you something."

"I hadn't really thought about it Ab, but what you say does bear study."

"I wish you would change back. I think you'll live longer."

"I think I'll keep the name for now, but if anything else happens I'll be convinced to take a much closer look."

"If anything else happens you could be too late. What if you turn up dead?"

"Your point is not without merit, but what if I'm just supposed to be on the water? I think I'll get back on the river once I'm well and everything will be just fine."

"You mean you'll have your feet back under you once you're back in familiar surroundings?"

"That's where I'm headed, old friend."

"Well don't forget those Yankee's will be stopping every boat on the river if the war starts."

"I won't forget, Ab."

"Take care, Mark. I'll return for you in a week or so," I said as I saluted him and retreated back downstairs. Mrs. Matson had prepared a good meal for us and before anyone left that day we partook of her gracious table setting. In the Matson home we were treated like royalty.

Mark seemed somewhat safe in bed so the rest of us disbanded and went our separate ways before anyone else had their life threatened. Clancy was left on watch to warn Mark of any impending Yankee soldiers, and the Ralls County Rangers departed on friendly terms knowing we might be reassembled on any given day.

A week later I returned to recover my friend and was astounded at the way in which he had completely healed, but Paintbrush was nowhere to be found. We loaded Mark in the wagon and I headed home with my friend in tow.

As we traveled along the lane staring at the back side of my old mare, Betsy, our conversation naturally drifted to the next part of our game plan. I was surprised to hear myself mutter such words, but not too surprised once I considered my immediate future and my eight year background as a riverboat pilot.

"My dear Mark, I believe I know what I'm to do."

"You have a plan, Ab?"

"Somewhat. I think I'll carry mail to the Missouri troops in the southern part of Dixie. The Federals will take Missouri so fast our boys that signed up for the Confederacy to the south will find it a hard thing getting news to and from home. Strikes me they'll want news, and the folks back home will want to hear from them as well."

"You know the first thing the Yankee's and Confederate's will do is blockade the Mississippi. You won't be able to get a toothpick up or down that river once the first shot is fired."

"I figure you're right. But you can always slip through the lines somehow. All you have to do is use your head."

"If they catch you, that's the first thing you'll lose, your head," Mark said.

"Ah, I have no intention of letting them get their hands on me, but if they do, there are means of escape they've never thought of."

"A means of escape providing they don't hang you or shoot you on the spot."

"There's always such a possibility, but I'll go unarmed and never fire a shot for or against one side or the other. All I intend to do is transport mail to and from the Confederate troops."

"Have you thought about how you might go about collecting such specific parcels for the Confederate troops? No one has ever attempted such a thing before to my knowledge."

"Mine neither. It'll require a good deal of study and planning."

"How will you have the mail carried to any collection point, and where will that collection point be?"

"There's the old hollowed out oak tree just south of the Lemay Ferry near the old river cemetery. A place seldom visited by anyone but widows."

"That's how you do it old boy, the widows!" Mark almost startled old Betsy into a run when he slapped his knee with excitement. "No soldier in his right mind would bother a helpless and grieving widow, young or old. They could carry the mail under their petticoats and bring the letters right to you. They can sew in reverse pockets for carrying the letters and no one would be the wiser."

"I tell you, there were never two more jolly fellows thrown together in the bucket of life. If we don't get some separation real soon, there's reason to believe we'll both outwit ourselves and come to no good at all," I said.

"I deem you may be right, but I've had a lot of time to think and the boldness along with the audacity of what you propose intrigues me greatly. If you should manage to pull this off and not get yourself killed, I think I'll write a book about your exploits."

"If I survive, I'll write the book. If I don't, you have my permission to proceed."

"Now I think of it, how could I proceed with none of the facts relating to your actual story?" Mark asked.

"You already have the basis of all fact. You already know the plot. All you have to do is fill in the rest with your grand imagination. I know you to possess one of those."

"Yes, yes I see what you mean. Do me a favor, live to write the story yourself. I would rather have my friend return alive and well."

"I'll do my best, but what of you? Where do you intend to go from here?"

"I believe I'll do as ordered and pilot a river boat."

"You know I think the Confederate troops have blockaded the Mississippi River already," I said.

"Somewhere just north of Hickman, Kentucky I believe."

"Everything north of that point is in the hands of Federal troops if I am not mistaken."

"What do you think I am? I'll run up and down the Mississippi for the Confederacy, or go west with my brother."

Turning old Betsey into the long drive above my quaint Hannibal cabin I headed us down the path toward home. What lay ahead was going to be a night of brainstorming and lots of coffee. We would, like so many times before, discuss the many possibilities unto infinite exhaustion which would occur at about sunrise. Then we would pass out for a few hours and rest a short time, and if we weren't finished, we'd brainstorm some more, leaving no stone unturned. Such was the relationship I had with Mark Twain.

For the next three days we exercised our intellect, planning and plotting the routes, speculating where we might find success. My success as it were was tied to Mr. Twain stopping in St. Louis to make contact with a certain widow by the name of Caroline Webster. The widow of Daniel Webster now devoted her talents to educating young ladies about the finer things southern living had to offer, although St. Louis, Missouri was not so far south. She ran a finishing school of sorts, the best west of Boston itself and it was a hot bed of Confederate sympathies which were only kept under control by the head schoolmistress. Widow Webster would be the perfect ally if I were to find any ally at all in my endeavors. While her husband had been known as a staunch Federalist, she was a Southern Belle in every meaning of the word having been born and raised in North Carolina.

Waving goodbye to my friend at noon on the third day, I entered my abode and no longer thought of my small residence on the outskirts of Hannibal as home. I still enjoyed it, but my new home would be one of self-imposed exile if war came, and I was under no illusions of grandeur. My life would be on the line from the moment the first shot rang out.

We didn't have long to wait Mark and I. Less than a week passed and the cannons roared at Fort Sumter, an island off Charleston, South Carolina. The first cannons fired at the fort ignited a war, although the only casualty had been a colonel's horse. I packed my things knowing my future was scribed before me. The burden of war was heavy down the centuries now to be borne by Captain Grimes. I would take no orders and give none, fire no weapons nor carry one. My mission was peaceful even during a time of great uncertainty. I had my duty assigned by none other than God himself and I would not be dissuaded from my mission by anyone.

There are those who'd swear me a traitor, but I was not, for my sympathies had always been with the southern cause. I had never agreed with the Federals or what I felt were their contrary ways. Given what they wanted they would soon let women and the Negro slave's vote, which would be the end of our grand nation as I saw things. For when you have people going to the polls and voting their pocketbooks or lack there of, or not understanding the issues at hand, then they will inevitably vote in the wrong way in mass. No good could come from such a thing except chaos. Mass chaos would end any level-headed rule put in place by the founding fathers. The constitution would be shredded by ignorant voters and congressmen alike, folks who had never read or studied the founding documents.

My feeling was, if you don't know the foundation of government and you couldn't understand the basic rule of law, you had no business voting. My point being, I was no traitor because everyone who knew me knew how I felt and I still believed in old glory, only I didn't agree with what the Federals were trying to shove down the throat of southerners. If the north won, it would be the beginning of federal rule, the end of State Sovereignty, not just for the south, but for the north as well. They would not stop until they had all power mustered in Washington and the ability to tax the people into bankruptcy, telling them one thing while doing another, which they were already beginning to do through newspapers. When a government can shape public opinion knowing what the outcome will be, it's only a matter of time before that government makes a miscalculation and falls prey to its own errors. "They shall be caught up in their own craftiness," or so the Bible says, and I believed every word.

Then I remembered the founders, the constitution was actually a contract with God. That was the meaning of the word Federal. Maybe they had been smarter than folks gave them credit for. They had each one fulfilled their end of the contract. Did anyone honestly believe God would not honor his end of the bargain? It seemed to me no matter what the Yankee's did they would not be able to shred that contract.

Down the centuries man has always strived to better himself, yet in no country do the criminals sleep. They are always plotting and planning how they can steal and take from the poor and fatten their pockets. The poor are often criminals too, but they are the simple ones, they who steal for a morsel to eat or to covet another man's property. They never figured out the place to be is in uniform or elected office. The most excellent criminals have known for centuries how the appearance of the uniform or the position which commands respect can hide even the most horrendous of crooks, but usually only until their intentions are revealed. Once they have been exposed, they often become killers, striking out at anyone who opposes them whether their victims are one or many.

When common crooks are voted into the halls of government, when those who represent us don't know the constitution or care to understand it, when party's plot and scheme for the sake of political power we're doomed, for those men have no idea what they're actually dealing with. This war, which must now be fought, was only the beginning of folly.

If we now free the black man, those uneducated destitute heathens, where will the insanity end? You can dress a heathen in the finest clothes and teach him anything, but his tendency's as a heathen are still his foundation. Most of them would starve, die from disease or succumb to their lack of any ability to care for themselves or one another. Many more would die with gun in hand. 'Tis a cruel sentence those northern rascals would be placing on the black man and the fine southern gentlemen would get the blame as would be reported in the newspapers, not the man who rightfully deserves the blame, Abraham Lincoln.

My mail idea was put on hold for the time being as I unexpectedly joined forces with Captain Theodore Brace. Not long after I attached myself to Brace and his company of soldiers, Porter and Green came down from northern Missouri and we met up with them in the town of Shelbina. There we were obliged to engage in our first battle with the Yankee forces and several in our company were badly wounded in the fight while we were engaged in tearing up the tracks of the Hannibal & St. Joe Railroad. This was the spring of 1861. Napoleon and I traveled with Brace well into the summer, my initial well-laid plans but a vacant memory in my mind.

Before I go on, let me explain. In this, our first battle, the Yankee's had filled the boxcars of the trains and steamed out onto the tracks we were dismantling. They were so far away several of our boys went down before we heard the report of the rifles or had any idea they were onboard shooting at us.

We had by then developed unique shotgun ammo which we molded with the use of sewing thimbles donated by the ladies in our area of Missouri. While the lead was still hot, a sharp rod would be thrust into the thimble shaping it in the form of a mini ball which was a perfect fit for our shotguns and could shoot through a boxcar from three hundred yards away. We killed four Federals and wounded several in retaliation and then departed for the backwoods where we hid and regrouped. *I doubt that!*

Our command with Porter and Green now numbered several thousand men so we started west and took up residence near Glasgow later that evening. The following morning we awoke to a steamer coming down river from St. Joe and the commanders had the presence of mind to place three cannons on the levee, forcing the boat to heave to. It was my old companion the *Sunshine*.

This was the last boat I had piloted on the Mississippi and Missouri before joining the Ralls County Rangers. We boarded the boat to find two Yankee officers and twelve regulars contaminating her decks. These men were locked up and their stars and stripes were hauled down. I then raised the Confederate flag with the help of two others and we had our transportation for crossing the Missouri River.

Our Confederate army had immediately taken possession of the boat and began to ferry troops, stock, and supplies across the Missouri River. Reed and Vickers were piloting the steamer and were good men I had known. They didn't want this war any more than any one else, but the war was upon us now and we deemed our situation better to be doing something than to stand by and do nothing. I crossed with the first shipment having been designated as the officer to inspect the ship for stowaways and settled into a good rest.

In the middle of the night I was awakened by a gentleman named Captain Brent to take charge of the wheel. Although I knew them to be good men it seemed that Vickers and Reed had deserted the helm and could no longer be found. As I had piloted the boat and my superiors knew of my experience, they selected me to complete the crossing of the troops. I guided Napoleon back on board, not wanting to lose such a friend to chance or circumstance and set about to complete the crossing.

Putting my experience to work I got the crew together and made sure what I was working with. The fellows were all men I knew. The engineer was named Gibson. He was a big man of six feet four inches and all of three hundred pounds. The meat and muscle on his bones was deceptive. He didn't look all that heavy, but he was.

The mates were all men I had worked with so I discerned no problem here.

"Fellows, I'll make this short and simple. I don't want to cause any more commotion than necessary to get the job done. Let's just pretend it's the old days and we'll be out of your hair as soon as these men get across the river. I'll return the boat as soon as the commanders say we're finished and no one will get hurt. Agreed?"

"Agreed," they all said.

"All right then, take your post gentlemen and let's get this done."

I took the wheel and we began crossing the remainder of the troops. I started at one in the morning and didn't finish until late in the afternoon the following day. I was exhausted. I had been moving troops across the river for nearly thirty-four hours. This was an undertaking I could have used some help with, but where the Ralls County Rangers had been smitten with pilots only a few short weeks ago, I was now the only one in the company of thousands of troops who knew how to pilot a riverboat.

As the army headed north after the crossing at Glasgow I went to the captain's quarters and went to sleep. I wasn't worried about the Yankee's overpowering me, as the men on board were my friends and would never allow such a thing. Besides I was the only one left on board who knew how to pilot the steamer.

My orders were to head back upriver and keep the boat in a state of readiness just in case the army needed to cross the river farther upstream. This required more wood or coal as the area called for, but like I said, I went to sleep.

Later the following day after I had gotten some well needed rest I headed the boat back upstream as ordered, apologizing to the crewman for their extended duty. They took the situation well and we had no problems navigating our way toward Kansas City. As night fell we docked at Cambridge and soon discovered the Yankee's were on the other side of the river.

Captain Brent had remained aboard with a small troop of soldiers, about thirty men in all, so I had plenty of company when the Yankee bullets began to aerate the steamer giving her the ventilation she needed for taking on more oxygen and muddy water. After ten minutes of this unexpected hostility, Captain Brent ordered me and the troops, now joined by the mates, and engineer to depart the boat with our horses and unlock the door for the Yankee soldiers.

This I did myself because I wanted to ensure they received their share of rifle fire from their mates across the river. In this matter they were summarily on their own. All they had to do was find their flag and hoist the colors in place of the Confederate stars and bars, but they'd have a beggars time producing the red white and blue. I had thrown the Yankee flag overboard the day before and the colors were probably nearing St. Louis by now, figuratively speaking. Being a riverboat pilot and captain I was certain the Union flag would never surface as it was most likely hung on a sawyer in the river (a tree stump or a snag as they were called), but I held onto my endearing illusion of the flag floating past the docks on the wharf in downtown St. Louis and the Federal troops watching their colors float helplessly by.

We rode our horses off the boat and headed for Lexington to meet up with the other troops. When we arrived late in the morning we found our companions hunkered down below a long hill. The Yankee's were high on a bluff and dug in with an elaborate array of trenches. They had cannons staring down our throats, and they were ready. Their position couldn't have been better as they surrounded the Lexington Ladies College. Our forces were positioned between them and the river.

"Captain, there's a warehouse down the road. I believe we should see if there's anything we can use which might aid our assault on the hill before we move," I suggested.

"That's good thinking Grimes, take some men and see what you can find."

Gibson went with me and the mates from the steamer *Sunshine*. The warehouse was full of cotton bales and rope so we began to move the large bales back to our position by the wagon. Behind them we could assault the hill and protect ourselves from most of the enemy bullets. Cotton bales wouldn't stop a cannon ball but cannons were not an accurate aiming device when pointed downhill as these cannons were.

We took all the rope we could find as a hedge against any future situation which might rear its head. Reporting back to the captain I took my men and we made ready for battle. Behind fourteen bales of cotton we began to push forward. Bullets began to pepper the bales, but the square bales were so thick none could get through. Then the cannons began to fire. Although they raised the fear in all of us, they were as expected, ineffectual.

One large coil of rope was knocked loose from its position near the top of the ridge by one of our own guns. This had been a Yankee rope of some size and the large coil began rolling downhill picking up speed as it went. The rope I'm describing must have weighed in the neighborhood of one hundred fifty to two hundred pounds, maybe even more. When Captain Brace stepped out from behind his bale to corral the wild hemp it struck him dead in the chest and face on a good bounce at nearly forty miles an hour. Whatever had possessed him to try and tackle the runaway coil of rope is beyond me, but we all turned to watch as the rope took our captain and bounded down the long hill, tossing him in an unimaginable fashion. Captain Brace and the runaway rope finally came to a rest at the bottom of the hill.

For Captain Brace we all said our prayers because no man could have lived through such a horrendous entanglement and beating. Our suspicions were confirmed as he laid lifeless down below. We then turned and started back uphill as the bullets were absorbed by our oversize squares of cotton. Advancing five feet at a time we continued to roll uphill. It wasn't long before we were too close for the cannons to aim in on us at all. We had gotten under the rim of the hill so to speak. Here we hunkered down and waited for darkness.

From time to time we gave the Yankee's a hat or a boot to shoot at but we made sure they were empty when exposed to gunfire.

Gibson stuck his finger through the hole in his new hat. "My hat's not going to be worth a plugged nickel by the time we finish taking this hill."

"My boots neither," Calhoun said.

Trying to find a more comfortable position, I muttered to neither in particular. "We all have to make sacrifices. At least it's not your head."

This tactic allowed us to deplete the Yankee ammunition supply over time or so we believed and gave other Confederate troops time to surround the entire hillside fortification. On the third day of the siege they surrendered, for they were cut off from any help, giving us possession of a good deal of ammunition, cannons, wagons, and horses. Had they continued the siege the Yankee's would not have eaten. They were out of food.

The Yankee troops under the command of Colonel Mulligan were paroled at once, and later Mulligan himself was paroled for the simple reason we didn't want the inconvenience of caring for and feeding prisoners. We didn't have any more food than our enemies, and prisoners would have to be guarded, fed, and so on. So far as we could tell, our army was eating everything in the area that was edible and couldn't handle the additional mouths to feed.

For two weeks we settled in and ate everything we could get our hands on. But the food ran out so we headed west then south where our food supply became non-existent. The corn we found was too hard to eat although when ground it made bread and good grain for the horses. We attacked a smithy in Johnstown and had him make some grating for us so we could turn the farmer's corn into corn meal properly. We then grated our corn, mixed the fare with water and flour baking a much better cornbread. The ensuing bread along with any side meat we could forage was all we ate for the next week as we moved farther south.

By this time almost all our stock had come down with a contagious disease known as "grease heel," forcing us to walk our mounts instead of riding them. Napoleon was one of the first to get this inconvenient disease. Such circumstance made for a column which was spread out for many miles. Then one day there was no more food to be had, though we kept walking, hoping to find something. Corporal Jimmy Hayes was beside me each and every day walking his mount which was afflicted the same as mine. He was good company and I was glad to have him. Gibson and crew had checked out after taking the hill and returned to their boat.

When we stopped for the evening we picketed our horses together beside the road and lay our worn out carcasses down beside them. Then Jimmy rose up on one shoulder and said, "I hear music."

Listening, I heard nothing. "You're imagining things, Jimmy."

"I hear music I tell you."

"What you are hearing is your stomach."

"No captain, listen."

I lifted up on one elbow like he was doing and I heard what he was referring to. "You're right, I hear music."

We had been stretching our legs from sunup until nine in the evening by which time we were staggering without the benefit of a meal and we knew what the word exhaustion meant. Everyone had spread out on the edge of the road at the base of a long prairie and the rest of the troops were likely already asleep by the time we caught them. I immediately rolled out of bed and said, "Come on."

Jimmy and I untied our horses and led them in the direction of the music. After only a few minutes a light came into view on the porch of a home about a mile away. We made for the light and then as we neared, it began to sound like a party was going on. As we closed in we realized the musicians were a Confederate band.

As we neared the dwelling I turned to my companion. "Thank God for your good hearing, Jimmy."

We made for the light with haste and found General Slack's headquarters' band which had been on their way to join our army, but had no idea the army was so close. We were welcomed with open arms, fed, wined, and dined.

While downing our fair share of treats, a bewildered old farmer that was three sheets to the wind, stumbled up to the door. Looking around the room he said, "Where'd you fellows come from? Have you seen my nigger, Jim?"

"Who are you?" one of the band members asked.

"John Jacob Asbury. My horse threw me and Jim ought to be coming after me with my carriage by now." He slobbered down his shirt front.

"Crazy old coot," one band member said.

Getting up from the table I took Mr. Asbury by the arm and walked back out the door with him. "Sir, where do you live?" I asked.

"I live yonder," he pointed farther west.

"About how far is it?"

"Three miles or so as the crow flies, four by road."

"Are you hungry, I could fix you a plate."

"Thank you young man, I'd be obliged."

"Would your Jim come here?"

"He most certainly will."

Have a seat in yonder chair then, I'll fix you something to eat and we'll wait on him."

"Thank you, son, I could use a bite."

I went back into the house and although I was tired, I fixed the man some food and took it to him. John ate most of what I had put on his plate and then fell asleep in the old corner chair. I took our dishes inside and went back to sit on the front porch swing and enjoy the breeze drifting across the fields. In the background I could hear the noise of the party drifting through the window pane. About midnight as I was about to pass out myself, a big black fellow showed up in a carriage and stepped down.

"Is you see'd anything of Maass'a John?" he asked.

This inquiry aroused his master and John cursed him for taking so long.

"But, massa, I started as soon as ol' Lucifer pranced into de yard."

"Young man," John addressed me. "Will you be here come morning?"

"Yes sir."

"I'll send you all a good breakfast first thing then," he said as he stumbled down to the wagon. "Let's go home, Jim."

The carriage of John Jacob Asbury was drawn by two of the finest horses I had ever seen and the carriage itself spoke of elegance seldom witnessed on the frontier. I say frontier because anything west of St. Louis was still considered the open wilds at that time. Missouri was quite unsettled because of the border war with Kansas which had lasted the last six years or so and now the Civil war was making Missouri a very dangerous place to navigate. There were still Indians to contend with as well, but most of the ones left behind in Missouri were friendly. The area we were in now was inhabited by the Osage tribe.

Certain residents from Missouri were known to shoot on sight and ask questions later in the area we now were traveling through, so we cautiously headed south the following morning. Mostly they were just tired of being set upon when minding their own business.

Since 1849 when gold was found at Sutter's Mill the wagons had cut deep ruts into the earth from St. Louis to St. Joe and Kansas City. If you couldn't make the two hundred mile trek from St. Louis or you found the trip difficult, you were best advised to settle where you were and many pioneer families had done just that. Missouri was well populated by 1861 for that very reason. Countless adventurers had stopped right where they were when supplies ran out and put down roots along the fertile ground. The Pony Express had come and gone with little fanfare, bankrupt in just over a year. They had used orphans for several reasons, they were lightweight, they had no family, and if they never returned no one would miss them.

When breakfast arrived the following morning, as we were preparing to leave, you can rest assured our respect for John Jacob Asbury stretched upward a notch or two. He sent us enough breakfast to last a platoon for two days and the meal lacked nothing. The gravy was still hot in the kettle, biscuits and ham with all the eggs a man could eat.

"Massa said take it wit ya."

"Tell Master John we offer many thanks," I said.

We hung out on the porch after breakfast for our bellies were stuffed. No telling when we might get our next meal so Jimmy and I horded and packed away all we could. We weren't much in the mood for sharing and the band didn't seem to care a lick, so we took all we could carry. No doubt the boys with instruments hadn't done any starving of late, but our experience with famine was quite recent and well marked in our memories. Those boys will get along fine I told myself as Jimmy and I saddled our horses, which couldn't yet carry us.

We walked away leading our horses, waving our goodbyes to the gracious host, a host who I never actually met. Jimmy had met them, but the couple had gone to bed early and I had sat on the porch most of the night with John Jacob Asbury looking at the stars wondering what it all meant.

Chapter 5

Jimmy and I left a little later with the band in tow trying to overtake our unit which had moved on southward at sunup. Of course we didn't move too fast for we were carrying food which would be taken from us as soon as we arrived, so we held back just enough to make sure we ate a good lunch and supper before we caught up with our army of insufficient provisions. I don't know if that was the correct thing to do or not, but the move certainly felt like the right one.

As we walked, it began to rain once again. At first it was just a slow drizzle, but soon enough the skies opened up and began to pour, so we knew misery once more. Luckily we had the food wrapped properly enough to keep the fare dry, but for ourselves we were drenched.

For weeks we sauntered around Missouri like the children of Israel looking for food and shelter from the elements, only instead of dry desert air we had a rainy season that just wouldn't quit. Thunderstorms and lightning was the usual evening fare. Many of the troops became ill, too sick to fight and several times we ate horse meat to keep from starving. Wet and cold, little to no food and poor shelter if any, the summer of 1861 passed us by so fast I didn't know where the season went and autumn had begun to settle in.

We sojourned in St. Clair County for a good while and by the time I left the area I was part of Company K of the first Missouri Calvary under Colonel Elijah Gates, a man I considered nothing short of noble and brave.

Upon his orders we began to move south and Gates understood something my other commanders had not; soldiers had to eat.

I won't admit we had the best of food, but we never went hungry in Gates command. For two weeks we moved south and eventually settled in near Springfield. South was where the soldiers wanted to be because seasons change and we now looked at the upcoming December. Yankee soldiers, our targets dressed in blue, had been scarce since leaving Lexington, but I was quite accepting of the idea. I was growing weary of travel and less excited as the leaves of fall surrendered their green and trickled to the ground.

On December 23, 1861 I encountered a reprieve from the drudgery of several months travel. As had been the case for several weeks I was assigned to round up some cornmeal or whatever I could get my hands on to feed our unit. There was a mill on the outskirts of Springfield where I had encountered luck several times before so I took my helpers to the stone mill at Glidewell flanked by a couple of extra mules and wagons to acquire the needed rations. Our unit packed up on supplies once again offered by the ever gracious Mr. Keener and headed south to rendezvous with General Price's division in the Ozark hills.

Once the wagons and mules were stocked I sent the unit on ahead because the army would have need of those supplies. I stayed behind and spent the night with my helper Sergeant Hurst. Price's army was somewhere about twenty or twenty-five miles to the south of our location on the outskirts of Greene County.

I believe I should explain here that this General Price was not the same man whom the Ralls County Rangers encountered in Ralls County months before.

After a good breakfast the following morning which had been my purpose for delay all along, Sergeant Hurst and I saddled up and rode out. Our quarters that evening had been a small farm house on the road from Springfield to Cassville. Sometime after breakfast on our trek to rejoin our unit we came to a main road where several horses were tied to the hitch rails in front of a big farm house.

Having not seen a Yankee in several months we had no idea they were in the area. Our curiosity along with the sin of gluttony got the better of us and we figured to have another breakfast as we knew not when we might get our next meal. Supposing the horses belonged to some of our own outfit we bounded up the stairs opened the door without knocking and waltzed right into the enemy's clutches.

A dozen soldiers were gathered around the dining room table eating, only these men wore the wrong uniform. Their uniform was dark blue.

"Well, what have we here," the lieutenant asked as he slipped his pistol from his holster and trained the weapon on the two of us.

"Looks like Johnny reb's," another snickered from behind.

Before we could move or respond, our guns were taken from us by two guards who had moved in behind to corral us at which time we were invited to join our captors.

"Damn the luck," Hurst objected.

"Have a seat, gentlemen," the lieutenant motioned, "we were just discussing your whereabouts. Maybe you can shed some light on the subject for us. Go ahead, have a seat, I beg you."

We took possession of the two chairs which had been emptied by the men who took our weapons and settled in to dine with a room full of Yankee's. There was no telling what kind of meals we might get from here on, so we tried eating once again although our appetite was fairly consumed by our situation. The room had become utterly silent until the lady of the house placed a couple of fresh plates on the table before us.

"Eat, gentlemen. I insist," the lieutenant commanded.

I picked up a fork and began to nibble at my food, Hurst doing the same across from me. Every bite I took was one which I forced, my appetite having flown the coup.

"Captain, surely the food is satisfactory," the lieutenant said.

"The food is fine," I said.

"Surely you know that your presence here is most timely captain. How should I address you?"

"The name is Captain Grimes."

"Captain Grimes and you are with what outfit?"

"I decline to say."

"Maybe the sergeant can tell us, and your name is?"

"Hurst. Sergeant Hurst."

"Well, Sergeant Hurst, what unit are you with?"

I stared at my companion across the table forbidding him to disclose the information requested by the unknown lieutenant sitting at the far end of the table.

"Gentlemen, gentlemen, this is no way to treat your host. I'm feeding you a good hot meal. The least you can do is offer up a morsel of information."

"Information trading is considered treason," I said.

"So is taking up arms against the Federal government," the lieutenant said in a more serious tone. "Sergeant O'Donnell, I want you to escort these two prisoners to their new quarters in the prison at Springfield."

"Yes sir." The sergeant saluted.

"Gentlemen, I bid you good day as you do not appear to be hungry or cooperative," the lieutenant said. At gunpoint we were escorted out of the house and back to Springfield where my favorite horse was taken from me, never to be seen again, or so I believed at the time. I watched in abject horror as the sergeant escorted Napoleon toward another Yankee encampment, dragoon saddle and all.

Sergeant Hurst and I were introduced to the structure known as Yankee manor which had been converted into a soldier barracks and temporary prison. The upper rooms were used to confine the Rebel prisoners and the downstairs was used for troop quarters. This building was about twenty-four feet wide and two hundred or more feet in length paralleling the railroad tracks. Only one half of the structure was finished and as we watched, I noticed the guards didn't pay too much attention to the comings and goings of prisoners. A telegraph was directly below our quarters so I sent for a diary and began to immediately scribble down all incoming messages in cipher. The important ones which could not wait got shipped out immediately.

Let me explain. Within a couple of days Hurst and I agreed that we could probably vacate our quarters with nobody the wiser. As our luck turned favorable, the guards below placed two drunken Union soldiers in our cell later that very evening.

"I'll get this man's cap and gown and we'll be half outfitted," I said.

I gathered what clothes I needed from our new cellmates while they lay on the floor in a drunken stupor. At the foot of the stairs in the lower room I picked up a gun and eased back up to our room. This rifle had been left behind by a soldier who was off duty at the time. None of our cell doors had been locked so we could visit whomever we wanted among our Rebel friends as long as we returned to our own rooms, and as long as we didn't go downstairs. This was highlighted by the fact we were escorted out to a well outside the grounds whenever requested. The only place the Yankee's had guards posted was the doorway leading into the yard.

"Jacobs and Wilson, you guys go down and get some water. I'm going to find out how sharp these fellows are," I ordered.

The two men went down and told the guards they needed water and promptly the detail marched away leaving the opening unattended just as I had expected. Whenever we sent out for water those two guards would vacate their post and escort the prisoners lest they escape. There was no wall around our building and once out of the yard you were free. There were a few other guards posted at the corners of the building, but we were unsure of their attention to duty so we set about to test them.

We were about five steps out the door with me leading my prisoner when a guard yelled, "Halt!"

"I'm just escorting a prisoner to water," I said to the invisible voice.

"Go ahead, I just had to make sure," the invisible voice responded in a much more courteous tone.

I never turned to look and neither did Hurst, we just kept walking until we were out of sight and headed down the street. In the dark the extra guard had obviously mistook me for one of them and permitted us passage. Knowing that the Yankee's were all about us we kept up the prisoner charade until we were well on the outskirts of town.

Here on an old road we found a lighted house and after surveying the surrounding area properly, we walked up to the front door and knocked. The door was opened by a "pert young lass" by the name of Logan and her sister. Sergeant Hurst and I were invited in and once we knew we were in no danger we settled down to visit.

This lasted no more than ten minutes and there was another knock on the front door. The girls jumped up and led us to the back room where we could hide, and went to answer the door once again. Hurst and I could hear voices in the other room and after a few minutes the youngest Logan came to warn us.

"There are two Yankee gentlemen in the parlor and they are growing suspicious. You gentlemen had better leave," she said.

"Can you help us out the back door," I asked.

"Take off your boots. They'll hear you," she whispered.

We sat down and took off our boots and then followed the young maiden to the back door. Here she opened the back way out and as we each went through the door she grabbed us by the arm and kissed us on the cheek one at a time. "Be careful," she whispered.

"Yes ma'am," I whispered in return.

"I wouldn't mind doing that again," Hurst said.

"Me neither, but we've got to get out of here."

Dropping to the steps we slipped our boots back on. As we rounded the corner of the house we were greeted by two of the finest horses in the state, both of which were Missouri Fox Trotters. The officers had left their cartridge belts hanging around the pommel of their saddles and their rifles were in the scabbards. We were immediately armed with Colt navy pistols and two fine Henry repeating rifles.

"What do you think, captain?"

"I think those fellows owe us a couple of very good horses," I answered.

Hurst let me have my pick and we stepped into the saddle. We sat there for a long minute wondering at our fun having been displaced by the Yankee officers.

"Come on, captain, those girls are trouble."

"How do you know?"

"Any girl that pretty knows her place and she'll be more trouble than a graveyard full of black cats." Pausing Hurst added. "You're spoken for anyway."

Nudging my new horse we rode quietly away.

"Are you saying beauty isn't worth having?"

"No sir, not at all, just too much beauty. Beauty is a good thing, but when a woman looks like a goddess, whoever marries her will live in servitude for the rest of his life."

"Hurst, remind me to keep you around. I seem to have a wandering mind and although I love my fiancé, I also love the ladies, but I need someone to help keep me in check from time to time."

"Yes sir, I'll do my best to keep you honest."

The two of us rode most of the night and headed south discarding our Yankee duds as we went. We passed Ozark and continued on. Just before sunup we saw a barn and helped ourselves to the loft. It was then I realized I had left my cipher book under my mattress back at the prison. Near mid-day we awoke and climbed down. Saddling our new mounts we rode out and kept heading south knowing our unit was somewhere in these Ozark hills. With the cold of old man winter setting in, the farther south we went the better I liked the weather.

We had just spent Christmas in the Springfield jail, and now we were coming on to New Years. I suspected the weather wasn't going to get any warmer. We pulled our jackets tighter and continued on southward. Near sundown we made camp in a small ravine hidden on all sides by the rising hills about us and built a good fire to keep warm.

Late the following day as we neared the Arkansas line we discovered by way of returning Confederated troops that General Price was returning to the north to engage the Federal troops at or near Springfield. This pleased us immensely and we made another camp deep in the woods much like the day before and settled into wait.

"Where are General Price's troops," I asked them.

"They're riding back north to engage the Federals. We've been sent in advance to scout the enemy."

"Five of you, that's an odd number," I said.

"We were just picked, captain, we didn't ask why," one of them said.

The men gathered about our fire and settled in to get warm, tossing on more sticks and getting the flame hotter. The biggest of them was about six foot six and heavily bearded, although he was young. Another fellow looked a lot like him only a bit smaller. Then there were two other young men and an older man who was also bearded. They settled down around our fire as if they were waiting for something.

I had assumed and believed that the troops we'd run into were advance reconnaissance troops who would eventually report back to General Price and his army but Hurst got me aside near our horses.

"Captain, I don't think these fellows are our friends, I think they're deserting. Watch yourself. They're looking at our horses like they've never seen the like."

I looked around at the five of them and I knew suddenly that Hurst was correct in his assessment. They were looking at us with suspicious eyes. I turned around and walked back to the fire, picked up my coffee cup and filled it. Down in the ravine like we were, offered us shelter from the wind, but if bullets started flying there would be nothing but exposure. There was nowhere to hide, not for them, not for us.

I slowly walked over to my saddle and sat down with my back to a tree. Warming my hands on my coffee cup I reached down and slid my new found rifle from the scabbard. I checked the load and cocked it, ejecting one unspent shell. It wasn't just our horses these men wanted. They also desired our more modern weapons, unwillingly given to us by our Yankee friends. I tilted the rifle to cover them and studied their eyes.

"You fella's remember you're gentlemen and you'll live longer," I said picking up the ejected shell.

At that point Hurst returned from the horses and added. "We've enough loads to wipe out the lot of you four maybe five times before we have to reload. I hope you fellows will keep that in mind."

As Hurst knelt down to pick up his coffee cup the youngest of the men made a wild lunge for him from across the fire. Hurst shucked his pistol so fast the teenager almost landed face first in the flames, but instead caught himself and backed off slowly. I waved my rifle covering them and said, "We're going to bid you gentlemen good day. Now get around on the other side of the fire and huddle together where we can keep an eye on you."

"Easy, captain, we're on your side," the biggest one said.

"I'm not so sure. What are your names," I asked as if who they were made any difference.

"I'm Cole Younger, this is my brother, Bobby. The others are Frank James and Bill Doolin."

"There's one more," I counted.

"You mean Quantrell? He's harmless unless you're a Kansas Red Leg. Then he's as mean as all git out."

"How come?"

"They killed his brother and left him for dead. Took everything the two men owned. He's got him a list and he's crossing the names off as he eliminates them." Pausing Cole added. "Why don't you join us, captain? We're surely going to give them Yankee's fits and we could use a couple of good sharp men like y'all."

"I'm not into revenge, Cole. Personally I believe it's the lowest form of human behavior on the planet."

"If that's how you feel, you'd better ride then. It would never work out."

"I believe you're right, Cole. I believe we'll ride and leave you boys to do what you will, but do us a favor will you?"

"What's that, captain?"

"Don't do anything to hurt the honest hardworking Confederate's in this state and don't attack Confederate soldiers. We're good people. Confine your battles to fighting with the Yankee's and we'll all be better off."

"We'll take that under advisement, captain."

"Let's go Hurst," I said as we began to ease our way back toward our horses.

"Before you go, captain, may I ask where you come by such fine weapons."

"We got them from Yankee officers, Cole. Good day now," I said as I walked backward to where my horse was being saddled by Hurst. We stepped into our saddle's, keeping our casual companions covered. As we rode out we kept an eye on the gang which was later to become known as Quantrell's Raiders although their numbers certainly grew from when we met that day.

We didn't know them from Adam at the time, but not long after, we heard about their raids and how they conducted themselves and I have thanked my lucky stars many times over I had Sergeant Hurst with me that evening.

We were not happy about deserting our fire, however we delighted in the information we had about Price's army. They were close which meant we wouldn't have to ride very far to meet up with them again. We turned our mounts west and found our army engaged in the "Battle of Pea Ridge."

Our first problem was getting on the proper side of the battlefield. The way we came into the theatre of battle had us positioned behind enemy lines. I motioned for Hurst to follow me and we began to circle in a wide sweeping arch. We headed east into the woods. Within an hour we were back on our side of things and proceeded to help in the engagement.

Near the end of the battle later that day I had run out of my Yankee ammunition and took a rifle butt to my forehead while engaged in hand to hand combat. When I regained my senses my brow was being bathed by a Yankee soldier with a bloody wet rag.

"Well, there you are," he said. "I guess you won't try that again."

My youthful desire to engage in the fire of battle had been quenched.

I didn't have the wherewithal to tell the darn fool I had no idea what he was referring to. Something had happened, but what I had no idea. What had I tried? Looking around I searched for Hurst, hoping I wouldn't find him among the many Confederate soldiers that lay dead.

"Come on, get up soldier," he said as he helped lift me from my sitting position against a tree. From here he led me to a long line of about one hundred Rebels who had been captured on the field of battle and from there back to my former cell at Yankee manor just in time for New Year's Eve.

As I settled back into my quarters in Springfield I determined I had better things to do than try and escape. Word was that Gate's outfit, under orders from Price, had been routed and was fleeing back in the direction of St. Louis. I knew this because I had ears for the Morse code that the Yankee's were using to communicate. I thought I would wait until they transferred us by train back to St. Louis and then I would escape making my job much easier, allowing me to re-unite with General Price.

Knowing this would take several weeks, I began to develop a "grapevine escape route for those who wished to leave." This was no easy undertaking, but the Federal troops guarding us really had no idea what was going on right under their noses. I set out to find my almost blank diary which still rested beneath my old mattress. As the Federals saw no harm in the practice of writing daily, I soon had my notebook in good order and I began to take notes of all the messages coming across the wire. In cipher of course.

I began by cutting a hole in the wall behind my bed that was big enough for a man to crawl through. When it was finished, I went downstairs to the unfinished and unused portion of the building. I was able to do so as my room was butted up against the portion still under construction. Here I found a key to the back door loosely guarded and stuck it in my pocket. I went back through my hole to my cell and waited for the right moment. I passed the word to see if any of my companions wanted to escape. Discovering ten volunteers among them to include Hurst, I sent them to bed and waited.

Later that evening after the hour of six had passed I gathered the men and led them through my hole and downstairs, giving them three dispatches to carry to the Rebel commanders in the field. These dispatches were nothing more than Yankee troop movements and intentions taken off the wire, but the kind of information a field commander would love to know. There were no guards posted in the large unfinished confinement room so we managed this part without any undue risk. I led them through the long vacant building downstairs to the back door and opened the solid wood aperture with my key. Then I led my willing protégés across the open yard in the dark where they went their merry way.

Hurst, who had returned with me, suggested we visit the Logan girls for old time sake. I was desirous of having some young lady sew me a special pocket into my pants which would allow me to carry my cipher scribbles in a hidden location which the Yankee's would never dare search.

"I thought you said they were trouble," I said.

"Yes sir, but trouble isn't half bad fun sometimes."

"I wouldn't mind seeing the girls. I have a special request to make of them."

When we arrived at the Logan home we found the girls inside preparing to dine. We were welcomed in and my head wound was pontificated over so that Hurst became jealous of all the attention being paid to me by both ladies. When the older of the two women brought me a blanket to wrap myself in and asked me for my pants, I thought Hurst was going to loose his mind, but once the actual reason was explained my subordinate settled down.

When we left later in the evening he said, "I'll never suggest we do that again."

"But you said…"

"I know what I said, captain, and I need to listen to my own advice."

"You mean the fact those girls are trouble?"

"That's exactly what I mean."

"They are certainly trouble, but boy, what beautiful trouble they are."

We let ourselves into jail the way we had come once we returned, with no one the wiser. My "grapevine" escape route had worked. The fact was more prisoners were being thrown in with us every day and the Yankee guards had no idea how many men were supposed to be in prison. I observed that the guards couldn't even do a proper roll call if we didn't want them to.

After the first round of escapees had departed the grounds we found it necessary to answer for the missing men, but the guards had no idea if someone was repeating or not. So it was that whenever roll was called someone was always assigned to answer for the escaped confederates in order to douse any suspicion.

For the next several weeks Hurst and I led the prisoners who wanted to go out and then we went to visit our lady friends at the Logan house. A fine evening was had by all accounts and then one Monday about noon Hurst and I were ordered to report to Lieutenant Baker Young, Commander of the prison at Springfield.

Two guards escorted us by gunpoint to Young's office and then stood outside.

"Have a seat, gentlemen."

"Thank you, sir."

"I hear tell you gentlemen have been out in town," he said.

"Sir?"

"Come clean Grimes, you've been seen by more than one person," he said.

"We go in and out whenever we want to," I stated cautiously.

"Just how do you get by my guards?"

"I can't disclose my secrets sir, but I would be more than happy to call on you one evening later this week if you don't mind."

"You mean you'll come here to my quarters," the lieutenant asked.

"Why not, you do want to see for yourself, don't you?"

"That would be just fine, captain. I'll look forward to dining with you."

"What time is best, sir?"

"Any evening about six-thirty will be fine."

"Did you want us for anything else, lieutenant?"

"No Captain Grimes, I believe that will be quite sufficient."

The guards reappeared as if on cue and led us back to our cell. We had some planning to do, but I didn't hesitate to let the prisoners know that if they wanted out they had better go on

Wednesday night. It was Monday and I suspect the lieutenant had been referring to our night on the town the previous Saturday.

Upon returning to our quarters I learned of a man named Martin who had been sentenced to be shot and his time was growing short. I learned many things by listening to the chatter coming across the telegraph wire as the Yankee's had not yet discovered the necessity of not letting the prisoners overhear the Morse code going on below. I knew what the Yankee's were up to just by keeping my ears open to the wire downstairs.

The difficulty of springing the man who was sentenced to be shot lay in the fact that he was in the county jail downtown, not in prison with us. I began to picture in my mind how I might be able to help him escape and an idea came to me, although I was uncertain if I could muster the courage to see the thing through.

Without second guessing myself I grabbed my Union soldier garb and a rifle which the soldiers had not hidden from us and left the prison by the back door on a mission.

I didn't know Mr. Martin personally, but I felt great sympathy for the man.

There was a burden placed upon my heart for him. I did not know the circumstances surrounding his case or if he was actually guilty. I only knew I wanted to set him free. Tomorrow he was to be loaded onto a train to Savannah, Missouri and disposed of. I had all I knew of the man from the local paper and other than what I had read I knew nothing.

Upon leaving my confines at sundown I happened onto a small hardware store where the owner was just closing up shop and I bought a pen and paper, money being something prisoners were allowed to keep. Then I proceeded to write out a release for Martin and forged the document by Colonel Mills. This statement was no more than a bogus order, but I was hoping the city jailer wouldn't notice the paper or look too closely.

Upon my arrival at the jail I handed the note to the jailer and he looked at me a bit funny. "I wish you Federals would make up your mind what you want."

"The colonel wants to question him before he leaves in the morning."

"Wait here, I'll be right back."

The clock on the wall ticked the seconds away as I watched three minutes of my life evaporate before my eyes. The jailer returned with a man in handcuffs and pushed him over to me.

"Please remove the cuffs," I said.

"What if he tries to run," the jailer said.

"If he tries anything his death sentence will be carried out immediately."

Momentarily the jailer opened his drawer and pulled out a set of skeleton keys. Stepping over to Martin he removed the handcuffs.

"I hope you know what you're doing," he said.

"If he tries anything he'll be dead before he hits the ground," I promised.

We left the building and I marched my prisoner down the street toward the western edge of town.

"Where are you taking me? Why are we going this way," he asked.

"Just shut up and walk," I said.

"You're going to kill me now aren't you?"

"Mr. Martin I'm here to set you free, now keep walking and don't turn around. Otherwise you'll blow my cover."

"But who are you, why are you freeing me," he asked as he walked.

"You'd rather be shot or hanged?"

"Well no, but....."

"Just be quiet and keep walking."

About thirty minutes later when we reached the edge of town, I told him to halt.

"I think we're clear now. Here, take this gun and get out of here."

When Martin turned around he had tears streaming down his cheeks as if he'd been crying for some time.

"Who am I to thank," he asked.

"Absalom Grimes, now get moving before they figure out what I've done."

I watched the prisoner leave town running and stumbling, never looking back. I suddenly felt my spirit lifted and headed back for town where my warm cell was waiting. I let myself back into the prison and went to sleep in my bed with no one the wiser. The only thing missing was the rifle and I wasn't going to be around to hear about that, not if everything went off as planned.

Tuesday evening thirty-three prisoners departed the premises and on Wednesday morning when roll call was given the guards were onto us. More than sixty prisoners had left through the "grapevine" route with no one suspecting until now. There was a big to-do about the whole ordeal, so that evening Hurst and I prepared to have dinner with Lieutenant Baker Young.

Hurst commandeered a pair of bayonets from the rifles at the bottom of the stairs fearing the missing rifles would be noticed more easily and proceeded to tie them onto the end of two broomsticks which we used to keep our quarters swept out and clean. We only had to resort to such tactics because the Yankee's were onto us. They were watching us more closely as they had determined that sixty-seven men had disappeared without a trace and they were taking bets that Hurst and I could not get to the lieutenant's house without being caught.

Lieutenant Young's home was about five blocks from the prison and we were not recognized as we walked straight to his house and knocked. A maid opened the front door for us and allowed us in. The lieutenant was just sitting down to dinner for the evening and said, "Come in, gentlemen, I've been wondering if you were taking my invitation seriously."

"A good meal is nothing to trifle over, lieutenant," I said.

"No, I guess it wouldn't be. Tell me, did you honestly get by my guards by using those?" He asked pointing to the brooms we had stood near his front door.

"We could have gotten a couple of rifles, but we thought they would be missed, so Hurst here made us a couple of dummies."

"And the uniforms?"

"Your men leave them laying about the prison. It's no effort to pick up what we need here and there."

The lieutenant was entertaining several ladies and gentlemen who were now choking back laughter. At this point, Lieutenant Young introduced us to his friends and insisted we would be joining them for the evening. One of the couples at the table with us was Mr. and Mrs. Rodgers who were in town from their farm about twenty miles east.

"Captain," Rodgers asked from across the table. "You must be a very observant man to fool the guards even when they're on the lookout for you."

"It's not hard at all. Anyone can do so." There was more laughter and while I had everyone's attention, I added. "I know Lieutenant Young that you plan to move all of the prisoners to Rolla next week by wagon, and then place us on a train to St. Louis. I hope you won't delay as I am looking forward to returning home soon."

This brought abject silence and a slight snicker. The lieutenant asked, "How in God's name can you know that? I only received the telegram an hour ago!"

"When I was a youngster, lieutenant, and before I became a riverboat pilot I operated the telegraph for the Morse Telegraph Company in St. Louis."

Slowly the smiles vacated the faces of those around me as realization dawned on the lieutenant and his guests that his telegraph wire was housed in the same building with his Rebel prisoners.

"I see. Well, captain that is a situation I shall rectify immediately. I take it you've been sending word of Federal troop movements along with your escapee's."

"Among other things."

The lieutenant looked on in horror, realizing the full extent of my handiwork.

We finished our supper and retired to the parlor where all of the furniture had been moved away from the middle of the room to make way for dancing.

As the night wore on Lieutenant Young pulled me aside and said, "Listen Grimes, I have no doubt you'll return to your cell tonight, but I want to see you go through the front door with your fake guns while the guard is watching. I want to see how you do it."

When we left the house that evening, Lieutenant Baker Young was walking beside us. Our gig was up so I didn't mind showing him a thing or two. As we approached the jail he stepped aside and watched from the corner of the nearest building. We were almost at the front of the prison at that point so he couldn't help but see the results.

Hurst entered first and I followed behind with my Yankee overcoat thrown over the broom portion of my dummy rifle.

Both of us had our bayonets in full sight when the German on guard at the front door jumped up and yelled, "Dang-nab-it, those rascals have been out in town again!"

This brought the rest of the guards running and we were escorted back to our warm cell promptly. Our Yankee uniforms and bayonet's were taken from us immediately and we were locked down for the evening. The following morning things began to change. First the telegraph wire was pulled out of the building and placed across the street. The guards who had been on duty were arrested and placed in custody for dereliction of duty and a search was made for our escape route until our means of gaining freedom was discovered. This didn't happen until I was personally searched, at which point they found my key to the back door and my note ordering the release of Mr. Martin that the jailer had given back to me two nights before.

"Sergeant, go find out if Martin is still in custody. I want to know this moment."

"I can save you the trouble, lieutenant. I released him two nights ago."

"Grimes, you are a menace, but I think I shall keep you around."

"Thank you for the compliment, sir."

"Sergeant, I want these two men placed in irons. I want the hole in the wall sealed up and I want them watched at all times night and day."

"There's no need to go to all that trouble, Lieutenant Young. We're not going anywhere. If we wanted to escape we'd have left with the others.

"You don't understand, Grimes. I am short sixty-seven...no make that sixty-eight prisoners including Mr. Martin and I can't afford to lose any more. That means you must be confined with no possible capacity with which to aid your Rebel comrades."

"Well, we've had a fine time of things anyway," I said.

"That we have, captain. I have learned a lot from you. I hope you won't hold it against me if I take what I've learned and apply it accordingly."

"Touché, lieutenant, I hope you don't mind if we do likewise."

"I would expect nothing less from you, Grimes."

Chapter 6

By late January wagons were made ready and the prisoners in Springfield were assembled for an official roll call. At this particular point in time the Federal troops determined the actual count of men who had left through my grapevine route to be actually sixty-nine. Lieutenant Young appeared along with Colonel Mills, the commander of the district, and they came over to Hurst and I to inspect us personally.

"Sergeant, why aren't these men in irons like I ordered," Lieutenant Young asked.

"Well sir, they were placed in irons but they got out of them somehow. After three attempts to secure them I felt the exercise useless."

"How do they get out of their irons, sergeant?"

"I don't know sir, but they do."

"Grimes, you are the scoundrel who forged my name and freed Martin?" Colonel Mills asked.

I could see right away the man didn't like me and considered me a derelict. I was not of course, but I would never convince him.

Colonel Mills was a small taciturn man with an over-active ego. He did posses the skills of a well-rounded soldier, but I felt he would dispense with them anytime he considered an opportune moment and stoop to some type of degradation. There were soldiers you could count on, like Lieutenant Young to always honor their duty by the book and then there were the others like Colonel Mills who would go to any level they could get away with to accomplish a military objective. His type didn't seem to understand the fact things would always go easier if you stuck to the rules of military leadership. Although this seemed to warrant their intervention they never understood they only made things harder on themselves.

"You didn't catch him again did you, sir?"

"No! And Grimes you will wear irons on this trip!"

At his order, a blacksmith was brought up to place Hurst and myself in irons that took a good bit of time, causing an unexpected delay. The day was cold and blustery and everyone stood by freezing as they watched the shackle operation taking place to the satisfaction of Colonel Mills.

When the colonel left, I called Lieutenant Young over to me and said, "Look here, Lieutenant Young. You know very well that I could have escaped prison twenty times had I wanted to do so. If you insist on keeping us in irons I will make certain that as many prisoners as possible escape on the way to Rolla and St. Louis, including myself. If, on the other hand, you'll conduct yourself as a gentleman and remove these barbaric restraints, I'll give you my solemn word none will escape en route. I'll personally guarantee that everyone arrives in St. Louis as scheduled. Otherwise, your guards are going to play hell."

"Smithy, hold on," Young said as the blacksmith was finishing up. The lieutenant walked down the street to Colonel Mill's headquarters for a short consultation and returned a few minutes later.

"Remove the restraints, Olson."

"Are you sure? I don't want to do this again."

"Do as you are told. You'll be paid."

"Yes sir."

"Thank you lieutenant, you have made a wise decision."

"Captain Grimes," he said holding out his hand. "I hope this war finds you alive and well when all is said and done. You're a most worthy adversary."

"And you as well, Lieutenant Young," I said as I gripped his hand.

He left and went back to Colonel Mill's headquarters and disappeared into the brick office building on Main Street. I was wishful to get into the wagons which were set to hold ten men apiece. The trip to Rolla was one hundred and twenty miles and the air would be much warmer inside the wagons where wind-chilled bodies could find solace.

About ten thirty the same morning we rolled out of Springfield with ten wagon loads of one hundred Rebel prisoners. The Yankee guard detachment was seventeen in all and could have been easily overthrown but for my promise to Lieutenant Young. We closed the curtains front and back as the day offered no sunshine. Gray cloud cover threatened snow as we made our way up country toward the railroad depot at Rolla.

That evening we camped near a creek in a low ravine out of the wind. We drew straws to see who got to sleep in the wagons, which offered only two sleeping positions each. Hurst and I had no luck in this endeavor and had to sleep on the cold hard ground. We had our coats and a military blanket, but that was all. The sleeping arrangement was very inadequate considering the time of year and the cold frigid weather conditions. We couldn't build fires big enough to keep us warm as we risked the wind spreading wildfires, hence our first night out was a miserable one.

The next day went better and we made twenty miles, but the air grew colder and that evening snowflakes began to fall. A light flurry appeared at first, yet by ten that evening you couldn't see more than twenty yards through the white blanket. Eight men huddled below the wagon with our blankets shielding us, which

Why didn't they all sleep sitting up in the wagons?

made for staying warmer, but there was no way to get comfortable. Leaning and dozing on one another's shoulder is how we endured the second night and by morning all were exhausted from lack of sleep.

At sunup there was two feet of snow on the ground and we had a time getting the wagons hitched up and rolling again. For this endeavor the prisoners were unwittingly enlisted as volunteers while the guards supervised the detail. With no ready firewood visible we climbed into the back of the wagons with our blankets and ate a cold ration while the wagons began rolling.

At times the soldiers driving couldn't see where the road entered a field or where the road departed. At noon we stopped to make sure they were still on the road to Rolla, and after finding our way, continued on. At three in the afternoon we stopped for a break and ate another ration.

"Grimes, we want you up front with us," Sergeant Walker said.

"Whatever for?" I asked.

"You know how to navigate. With the snow drifts we're encountering, we'd feel better if you were leading us through. You'll recognize the creeks and such which are covered up now."

"If Hurst can join me," I said.

"As you wish, captain. We're concerned about missing our mark and ending up somewhere none of us want to be."

"I'll see you get to Rolla, Sergeant Walker."

"Thank you, captain."

"We already seem to be off course, but in time we'll manage to recover."

When we resumed our journey, Hurst and I were in the lead wagon, reins in hands. From this point Rebels drove the wagons and the guards rode shotgun or in back with the prisoners where the riding was warmer. Snow continued to fall in smaller quantities, but continued to hamper our travels. When we arrived at the Gasconade River where we knew there to be a bridge, we couldn't find the crossing. Scouts were sent north and south along the river and an hour later we learned we had missed our mark by about a mile. Not wanting to tackle the move back to the north after traveling all day, we settled in to camp right on the banks of the Gasconade. Obviously the Yankee's had lost the road before asking me to lead them on.

The following morning we began our trek to the north and this wasn't easy. We had to navigate through the thick woods along the river on the west side. Several times we had to chop down trees in order to clear a path wide enough for the wagons. Here we also chopped up firewood for later in the day or that evening and carried the fuel inside the wagons with us.

This one mile voyage through a thick wooded area was quite draining. Hurst went on ahead searching out the best path and I followed in the lead wagon. By the time the wagons reached the wooden bridge our day was shot, so we crossed over and made camp on the east bank of the Gasconade and built several good hot fires to warm our bones.

Five more days were required to reach the Rolla train depot and by then we had missed our train. The railroad had left behind the transport cars for us though, and we took to them like ducks in water because they were full of hay with which the prisoners could use to keep warm. When the next train arrived the following afternoon, our boxcars were hooked up and soon we were rumbling along the tracks toward St. Louis.

When we arrived in St. Louis, Hurst and I were placed in the Myrtle Street prison which was known formerly as Lynch's Negro pen where slaves used to be held and auctioned prior to the outbreak of war. This was the same prison which I had had the necessary duty of freeing my own mother and two others. The old slave market made a perfect prison and the Yankee's had commandeered the old slave grounds for just such a purpose. About half of us were placed in this prison and the rest of our group were placed in the Gratoit Street prison which had been the McDowell Medical College at the corner of Eighth and Gratoit prior to the war.

The first person to visit me in my new confines was Miss Lizzie Pickering, Esrom Pickering's sister. Esrom had been the young man with whom I had been one of the first two telegraph operators in St. Louis. Miss Lizzie brought me news of a sort which sprung my brain into action. The ladies in the city had set up a network of mail collection several months ago, but they had no one to deliver their post. The Yankee's had blockaded everything between St. Louis and New Orleans on the Mississippi River and no mail could get to their loved ones down south in Mississippi and vise-versa.

"My dear Lizzie, I'll study on the matter to see what might be done."

"If anyone knows how to get this done, I believe you can, Ab."

"I had made plans for carrying the mail, but I somehow got sidetracked."

"We have no idea what has become of Esrom. All communication has been cut off with the Confederate troops down south."

"Thank you for the food and clothing, Miss Lizzie. I had already put a great deal of thought to this matter, but for some reason I went west when the war started. I feel I let you down. Forgive me."

She left then and the wheels began to turn in my head. My commission could not be undertaken behind cell walls. How could one go about moving the mail to the troops down south?

Most of the boys from Missouri were now in Mississippi. The river was blockaded by a Confederate chain and gunboats. Moving freely through the lines would not be easy, but hadn't I just done so back in Springfield? I had come and gone from my confines at will. How hard could running a blockade be? I knew the river better than the Yankee's so I reasoned the risk to be minimal.

For the next few weeks I was visited on a regular basis by many of my friends and acquaintances, not the least of which was my fiancée, Lucy Glascock. I tell you she was a sight for sore eyes. She had brought one of mother's persimmon pies from home having baked this one on her own and I devoured half of it before sharing the remainder with Hurst.

"How are you being treated, Ab?"

"Oh honey, I'm fine. Ask Hurst here, these fellows treat us just fine."

"That they do ma'am," Hurst confirmed.

"When will you get out of here?"

"I can leave anytime I'm good and ready."

"What do you mean when you're ready?"

"We can escape any time we want to, but I'm gathering information and planning my escape as we speak."

"But won't they shoot you?"

"They have to see me first."

"Ab, I don't understand you."

"I know, dear. I'll be fine and so will Sergeant Hurst. We came here voluntarily."

"You did what?"

"I don't expect you to understand, but I have a purpose for being in the Myrtle Street jail just now."

"Ab, you don't make a lick of sense sometimes. What am I supposed to tell your mother when I see her? Your son is in prison where he's supposed to be. Oh, that will go over like a funeral on Christmas day."

"Here, take a note to her for me. She'll understand the meaning of it, but you'll have to send it upriver to the *Omaha*."

I sat down and wrote out a note for my mother telling her what I had in mind and I wasn't kidding about sending the note upriver. Mother was on the *Omaha* with my father until the war settled down or ended. When Lucy departed I was pretty sure my time in the Myrtle Street jail was drawing short. Just then Hurst produced a small file.

"Where on earth did you come by such a thing?" I asked.

"It was concealed in my half of the persimmon pie." He smiled.

On March 30th the guards gathered about thirty prisoners from the Myrtle Street pen and about two hundred or so from Gratoit Street. After merging the two groups they marched us down to the wharf where we waited for the steamer *Alton* destined for the penitentiary in Alton, Illinois. The Yankee's had seen fit to convert the Alton facility into a military prison. As we waited on the waterfront to board the boat, I noticed old friends of mine everywhere.

One of these men was Jim Montgomery, pilot of the *Alton*. Another was Leonard Pike the pilot of the *Henry Clay*. Leonard was waiting for his boat to come back downriver and pick him up on the wharf. He looked at me kind of strange and then went back to reading his paper.

Unaware of how many friends I had on the wharf that morning, my esteemed colleagues began a procession to where I sat and shook my hand, bid me well and so forth until the Yankee guards finally put an end to the unauthorized visits.

I met Brigadier General Stone who was a prisoner along with me and we were soon after loaded onto the steamboat. The two of us were placed on the lower deck with a compliment of ten guards with more than one hundred rebels for them to mind, so we began to speak freely.

"Sir, with only ten guards per deck we can overpower them and run our boat south," I suggested.

"Who would pilot the boat?"

"Sir, Captain Grimes at your service," I offered my hand.

"You're a riverboat pilot?" he asked.

"Yes sir, and one of the best."

"Well then, we might try something."

"I'll need to investigate to see how many Federal troops are on board."

"How might you do such a thing?"

"Lieutenant Grissom," I called out.

"What is it, Grimes?"

Lieutenant Grissom was the Yankee lieutenant in charge of the prisoner transfer. I had known of him before the war as he had been a boat pilot on the river as well, although he was only learning when the war broke out. What I didn't know and dearly wanted to was if he remembered me.

"Would you mind if I go up to the wheelhouse and visit my good friend Jim Montgomery for a few minutes? I just want to say hello."

"Very well, come with me."

I was then escorted to the wheelhouse. When we arrived at the door the lieutenant turned to me. "My duties force me below. I want you to promise me that you'll not try to escape. I want your word on it, Ab."

"I give you my word, lieutenant."

"You stay here until I come back for you."

"I'll be right here with Jim."

Lieutenant Grissom left me, and Jim insisted I take the wheel.

"You haven't forgotten where to put the bow have you?"

"Not hardly."

"Good, I need a rest. Take the wheel while I eat something would you, Ab?"

So it was that our plan was foiled. The lieutenant never came back to the pilot house for me until we could see the dock at Alton, Illinois. This little hiccup prevented me from working out the prisoner escape with Brigadier General Stone and the escape attempt was forfeited because we had simply run out of time.

As we neared the dock, Lieutenant Grissom guided me downstairs and deposited me back where I had began the trip, sitting next to General Stone. He left me there to lick my wounded pride and it was then I saw the foot-locker beside one of the engineers who was yet another friend of mine. I sat down beside him on the box, incognito for I had found a civilian coat and began to visit as the rest of the prisoners were escorted onto the dock.

As the last of the men walked down the plank onto the dock I surmised I was home free, but just then a mean looking German sergeant spotted me and we locked eyes.

"D'you come down'd f'dom dere," he ordered, another German with a poor grasp on English speaking skills.

I held my position and pondered my chances of diving into the frigid river. The water still had ice in it and was much too cold for swimming. Where could I escape to? He began to move and walked back up the plank onto the deck of the boat once again.

"I have nothing to do with those men," I protested.

"D'you know you are a prisoner! I saw'd you on de wharf't in St. Louis."

The sergeant continued to walk in my direction. Dusk had settled in and night was coming on fast. Just then the *Henry Clay* swung around as she passed the stern and began to chug back toward the dock causing a bright light to pin me and the sergeant to the deck.

"Fire!" I yelled and started aft.

The sergeant sensing his duty to overtake me ran headlong into the light and sprawled over the rail, falling brutally into the churning wheel. As the engine was still turning the wheel in the water below the sergeant landed directly on the uprising paddles. The wheel lifted him up and around and then he was drowned and caught before the pilot could bring her to a stop. I had not intended that the man should die, only that he be refrained from taking me prisoner. Unfortunately, his poor eyesight or lack thereof became his undoing.

Looking back at the shoreline I saw more soldiers returning so I removed my borrowed civilian coat and rolled up my sleeves. At that very moment Mr. Lovett appeared. He was the engineer on the boat.

"Ab, my fireman, an old negro saw that trick you pulled on the sergeant. You'd better look out because the guards always come back and make one last sweep to see if they've left any prisoners on the boat."

"Give him this five dollar gold piece and tell him to keep his mouth shut," I said. This was a coin I had been given by Lizzie Pickering. Grabbing the oil can used to oil the pump and a wrench I greased myself up. I was oiling the "doctor" (a pump engine used in conjunction with the boiler) up good when two soldiers appeared at my side.

"Have you seen any prisoners still aboard?"

"You must have got them all," I responded, trying to sound uneducated.

They continued to search the boat, but all they found was their unfortunate sergeant's mangled body in the stern wheel and within a few minutes the distraught guards went ashore. Lovett returned to stand beside me and watch as the boat churned idly in the water and lifted the gangplank, but only after having recovered the mangled soldier and giving the body to his comrades.

"My fireman said thanks boss, but the soldiers don't belong to me," Lovett said as he handed me back my five dollar coin.

"Well, how do you like that?"

"Looks to me like you found your freedom, captain, what do you plan to do with it?"

"I'm going underground with the mail. I've been pondering such a mission for some time."

"Do yourself a favor. Don't let them Yankee's capture you anymore."

"That's the general idea. If I'm running the mail I won't be on the battlefield getting shot at."

"Wanna bet?"

"No, I don't think I will, Mr. Lovett."

"Smart man. You know you're bound to lose."

"You might be right, but I sure don't want to think about such things."

By morning I had made my way back down river and gotten off at St. Louis where I looked up some old friends. Friends who could help me get the mail running. I visited with Walt Davies who was the captain of the *City of St. Louis*. If anyone knew the lay of the land here it would be Walt Davies. Once in his office he asked me to take a seat and we talked of old times prior to the war and what the Yankee's were up to now.

He told me that Fort Henry and Donnellson had been captured by Federal forces and they were testing the blockade chain across the river at Columbus and Belmont. Presently, I came to the reason for my visit.

"Captain I was wondering if you could do me a favor."

"What will it be, Grimes?"

"I wonder if you might get in touch with Widow Webster for me."

"You're referring, of course, to the widow of Daniel Webster."

"Yes. She's been contacted but that was almost a year ago. I've been severely delayed in my original plans, however I'm now ready to follow through with them. Could you get a message to her?"

"She's been made very anxious because of your delay, captain."

"You know of my plans?"

"The entire Confederate State of Missouri knows of your plan via your friend Mark and we're anxious to have you begin. Mail has not been anywhere near regular since the beginning of the war, and the only plan which seemed feasible has been delayed simply because the plan's mastermind, the one person who can pull this off, has been missing in action."

I sat in my chair stunned. I had that many people counting on me? There was nothing I could say at the moment. My mind sped into all sorts of thoughts as to how I had been letting folks down. Was the word of Captain Grimes good, or wasn't it?

"Captain Grimes, take a boat home and I'll start things moving here. I'll send you a message by the end of the week if I have been successful with the arrangements. You should know you're not alone by any stretch of the imagination. Most of what you proposed has been put into place. Your lady mail carriers were only waiting for you to reappear."

I walked out of Walt's office in a state of shock. All this time others had been counting on me and I, Captain Absalom Grimes, had let them down. Well no more. I was going to run the mail south or die trying. I weaved in and out between people on the busy street of Washington Avenue watching for any unexpected Yankee's who might recognize me and made my way to the Pickering's home. There I found Lizzie and she eagerly ushered me into the parlor after our initial greeting to let me see my old friend Samuel Clemens, now known as Mark Twain.

Lizzie turned to face me. "It is so good to see you, captain. You're finally free. So, the Yankee's let you go?"

"Not exactly."

"You mean you've escaped?"

"Now you're getting the lay of things. I was looking for a place to get off the street until I could catch the boat home later this evening. I wouldn't want to be recognized by a Yankee guard unexpectedly, I would henceforth be returned to prison."

"You may visit with me, until such a time as you need to leave." Taking me by the arm Lizzie guided me down the corridor and into the parlor where Mark was sitting beneath a window with his foot propped up holding a cane in one hand and a paper in the other.

"Absalom Grimes, I was beginning to believe you would be incarcerated until the end of the war," Mark said.

"I could no longer remain in prison anymore than I could make a deal with the devil and you know it."

"Yes, yes, well I don't suppose you have come to the realization that you were never intended to be a regular."

"As a matter of fact, I have rather abruptly and recently come to just such a conclusion."

Turning to Lizzie who was dressed in a blue and green plaid dress with a white lace trim, I asked, "Have you heard from your brother?"

"I haven't heard from Esrom since he went south to fight for the Confederacy."

"I see. Do you know what unit he's with?"

"No I haven't heard a thing. Mother's worried and so is father, but they have traveled to San Francisco on business."

"I'm going to be headed south soon, I'll see if I can pick up his trail."

"Oh, Ab, that would be wonderful. You don't know how much that would mean to the entire family."

"I'm beginning to get the idea the Pickering's are not the only ones hungry for news from relatives. What's happening is terrible and you need to hear from him. I'll see what can be done."

"So you have decided to run the blockades," Mark said.

"I'll get us some tea," Lizzie said as she departed the room.

I glanced down at the newspaper lying on the coffee table and began to read, although what I read was nothing I should be concerned with, yet I couldn't help myself.

COLONEL LEIGHTON TO WED

Early that morning I had been the guest of Captain Arthur Matson of the Matson farm and I had dined with him at breakfast in the wheelhouse aboard the *Hannibal City*. I had told him of my "parole" as he brought me back downriver from Alton and that I was returning to St. Louis. Unbeknownst to me at the time two detectives that had been sitting outside the captain's cabin overheard my conversation with Arthur Matson and called upon the office of the provost marshal upon our return to St. Louis, telling him of my statement which they had doubted. The provost marshal corrected the two gentlemen and told them to return at once to the boat, apprehend me and bring me to his office. Before they returned however, I had left the steamboat and walked to Walt's office. Now I was sitting in Lizzie Pickering's parlor with Mark, looking for amusement to pass the time. I needn't look too far.

When Lizzie reappeared she brought with her a young lady named Mrs. Welsh. Her husband edited the St. Louis paper. She was a friend of the family and a former acquaintance of mine as well. Mark and I greeted her cordially and the four of us shared a cup of tea while I told them of my escape and how I had pulled it off.

"I dare say, captain that's the most amazing story," Mrs. Welsh said.

"I'll tell you what's more amazing. I'm going to a wedding this evening. Lizzie, will you accompany me?"

"You wouldn't dare!" Mrs. Welsh argued.

"Oh, yes I would. I would be less noticeable if I had a partner. How about it, Lizzie?"

"Ab, it's simply a stupendous idea."

"Stupid is more like it. The two of you are absolutely crazy," Mark chimed in.

"No, the experience will be that of a lifetime. I'm willing to bet the last thing Colonel Leighton will do is cause a scene or allow one to be caused at his own wedding or the reception. Why, Lizzie and I will dine on the colonel's finest wares and have the jolliest of times."

"You may have something there, captain. Such a position as the colonel would be in, never occurred to me, but he will surely have the guard lay in wait for you when you leave."

"I can't believe I didn't receive an invitation anyway," Lizzie complained.

"I didn't receive one either," Mrs. Welsh said.

"Mrs. Welsh, why don't you and your husband join us tonight? You can witness first hand an act of bravery and wit. Crashing the Leighton wedding will give your husband a fabulous story for the papers next run."

"Ab, what if the guards should lay for you?" Mark asked.

I paused for a moment and straightway I knew.

"I know just what to do. I'll need one of the children who have taken up residence down at the wharf. Lizzie, could you find one of them for me and bring the young man here? I shall need one of the older boys."

"You mean one of the orphans who have taken to robbing passersby? Ab, what are you thinking?"

"I'm thinking the one I need should be able to lead. I'll need him to orchestrate and coordinate a diversion with the help of other boys. I'll pay them, but I need the leader of the bunch."

"Ab, there must be over a hundred boys living down there by now. How will I find the one who's capable of leading the rest?"

"Ask. Just stop and ask the first one you see. Work your way up the line until you have him."

"I don't suppose you would care to escort me on this venture."

"Lizzie, you're a big girl. You won't need any help from me."

"Lest you forget, Absalom Grimes, The Cauldron has become the worst place on the riverfront. Not even the police will go into the Gaslight district without fear for their lives and you expect me to go down there alone?"

"All you have to do is pretend you're gathering orphans for the St. Louis Protestant Orphan Asylum and no one will bother you, you can come and go at will."

I glanced over at Mark, and the look on his face said, are you really going to send an innocent young maiden down into The Cauldron at risk of her very life just for your own pleasure and folly?

"Lizzie, I've got to go and tell Dutch. He'll want as much advance notice as he can receive prior to our engagement this evening," Mrs. Welsh said.

"Very well, we'll wait for your eminent return before we proceed."

"I'll muster a carriage so that we may arrive in vogue," Mrs. Welsh said.

I stood and bowed to the ladies as they left the room then retook my seat and smiled. I was going to have a grand time this evening, but still I had a few wrinkles to iron out. What if I were caught and thrust back into prison? What if I was arrested and placed in irons because I offended the good colonel?

Lizzie returned and smiled. "Well, Ab, I can see why you're said to be so dangerous."

"Dangerous?"

"Yes, even Lucy says you're dangerous."

"I have never thought of myself as dangerous, why truth be known, I'm harmless."

"Just the same, I believe she's correct. Mrs. Welsh said if she's not here by seven that we should go on without her, but if I know her at all she'll not be late."

"What a wonderful evening the two of you'll have," Mark said.

"Yes, a wonderful evening. Now, I must be going, if I'm to find this young man who can lead other young men to unspecified, certain mischief!"

Mark took a step toward her. "Not so fast, Lizzie. The captain and I have decided to go instead. Sending the likes of Lizzie Pickering down into The Cauldron would never lay off my conscience, nor would Ab be able to live with himself."

Chapter 7

Mark and I returned by three in the afternoon from doing business with a young man named Nolan Richards. He was a smart looking and fetching young man except for his clothing that was literally worn to a frazzle. His pants were unwashed and full of holes, his shirt not much better and he was barefoot with feet too big for shoes no doubt. He wore a straw hat which had seen better days and his only possession seemed to be a pocket knife that had belonged to his father.

This was the part of town where even a riverboat captain needed to watch his step. The riverfront was lined with gambling houses, bordello's and every kind of shyster managed a business here. I spotted the young man lounging on a bale of cotton next to the roustabouts and called him over to us. I had borrowed Mr. Pickering's lasso and Mark was armed with a pistol and his cane. The cane was only necessary because his ankle had not healed properly from the year before.

"Young man, I have twenty dollars in gold for you if you'll guard my exit this evening at a wedding which Miss Lizzie and I must attend."

"How do I guard your exit?"

"You'll need some help from your friends. If you see any soldiers in the area I want you to create a distraction and detain them when Miss Lizzie and I walk out of the church building."

"You're talking about Federal troops," Nolan said.

"Now you are catching on."

"I'll have to promise the boys something. That'll take money and I don't have any."

"What about the twenty dollars I've promised you?"

The boy just stood and looked at me as if I was some kind of idiot. "Mister, if I use that money to lure my friends, there won't be anything left for me when the job's finished."

"How many friends will twenty dollars buy?"

"Ten, maybe twelve give or take a few, but I want twenty dollars for myself."

"All right kid, you win. Here's twenty so you can muster your troops. Meet me at the Pickering house which I'll show you later this evening when the wedding is over and I'll give you another twenty."

"You have yourself a deal, mister."

"The name is Captain Grimes and there's one other thing. If I somehow get detained, I want you boys to create enough of a diversion so I can get away."

"Yes sir, captain."

Nolan walked with us back to the Pickering household and I introduced him to Lizzie. After the boy left Lizzie began to fret over my appearance. First she noted how unbecoming it would be for me to appear in my captain's coat and fitted me with her father things. Mr. Pickering was on a business trip to San Francisco and wouldn't miss a thing, she insisted. His tuxedo fit rather smartly and she slipped me into a top hat and gold watch with chain which had a carving of Mt. Rainier inlaid on the bezel. When she thought she had me properly outfitted, she turned her attentions to herself.

"There, now I'd better get myself ready or you'll be off without me."

"I shan't move an inch without you on my arm, dear."

Lizzie blushed red and disappeared upstairs for a good while. When she came back down, the clock struck a quarter of seven. She'd transformed herself into the perfect accessory. Her dress was full and wide as the liberty bell. The color was peach and her shoulders were laid bare. The V in the front of her dress did nothing to hide the voluptuous curves of womanhood. She did a complete turn around at the bottom of the stairs and revealed a very low cut back, something I had never witnessed before.

She wore a pearl necklace and earrings to heighten the color of the dress and an ostrich feather of white tucked into her blond French twist.

"My God, but you're stunning," I said.

"You don't think it's too much or too little?"

"I believe you've found the perfect accent for the evening, Lizzie. You'll turn heads and be the envy of all men.

"You mind your manners and remember you're engaged to Lucy Glascock."

"You may have to remind me of that a few times."

"If your behavior requires it, I won't hesitate."

"I want nothing more than to be the perfect gentlemen this evening."

"With Miss Lizzie on your arm, you'll be the perfect gentlemen, but you can't go as Ab Grimes, riverboat pilot. Have you thought about what you will do at introduction?" Mark asked.

"I have, but I'm not sure if I should go as Mr. Shively from Louisville or Mr. Howard Lawrence from Indianapolis. Both are fictitious names but very close to people I have explicit knowledge of."

"And what do you do for a living, captain," Mark asked.

"I'm a boat builder, much the same as James Eads."

"That's perfect, Mr. Shively. And what is your first name?" Lizzie asked.

"Harvey, Harvey Shively, my dear, and I've just signed a contract with the U.S. Navy to build a fleet of ironclad gunboats to be used in the open seas to enforce Federal rule."

"Oh, Ab, I must be a fool to let you talk me into this, but the prospect is so exciting. I can't believe I didn't get an invitation. I've known Jennie since we were three years old," Lizzie said.

"As I recall it took all of two seconds for you to climb aboard this plan of gay veracity, my dear Lizzie. I've talked you into nothing, and what do you mean, you can't believe you weren't invited?"

"Mr. Shively, you must allow a young lady her illusions and remember that she's never wrong in public or private. I've known Jennie virtually my entire life, and she has somehow failed to invite me."

Just then we heard the carriage pull up out front with only three minutes to spare. Mark opened the door for my bewitching ornament and she stepped out on the front porch and descended the stairs as the coachman held the door and placed a stoop on the street for her. The colored man stumbled and bumbled as he tried to complete his task without taking his eyes off of Miss Lizzie.

"Get a'hold of yourself, Garner and quit floundering," I heard Mrs. Welsh say from inside the carriage.

"Yes ma'am."

Once Miss Lizzie was seated properly I stepped into the carriage and waved goodbye to Mark who was still gracing the front porch with his presence.

"Harvey Shively is the name. I'm a ship builder from Louisville," I managed.

"You are indeed. My name is Dutch Welsh and I understand you've already met my wife."

"Yes, the pleasure has all been mine," I said.

Garner boarded the coach seat up front and swept us down the street. As we rode I wondered if the boy named Nolan was going to be there at the proper time to defer any interest the Yankee's might have in me.

Before I continue I must explain. Dutch Welsh was the newspaper editor for the *St. Louis Post* and I had known him half my life. We first met while I was in the employee of the Morse Telegraph Company. Many a time I delivered a message fresh off the wire to his office. In short, we had met before.

"Captain."

"Sir, if you are going to refer to me as captain that's fine, but remember I'm a ship builder named Harvey Shively from Louisville."

"Captain Harvey Shively, just what kind of story are you looking to create for my paper this evening?"

"One of daring and wit. You may write anything you want for your paper, but in short I want it known the escaped prisoner Captain Grimes attended the wedding of one Colonel Leighton, dined on his wares and danced on his floor, maybe even with his lovely bride if I can pull such a thing off."

"Are you sure you want me to print that?" Welsh asked.

"Oh, this is so exciting," Mrs. Welsh chimed in.

"Dutch, I plan to be a thorn in the Yankee's side for the remainder of the war. You can print that if you like. The Yankee's don't seem to know who's coming or going and for that very reason we'll be able to enjoy the evening without worry."

"I sure hope you're correct, captain," Dutch said.

The carriage pulled up in front of the church on the corner of Washington and Eleventh Street and we waited in line to debark as there seemed to be a procession of carriages in front of us. Within a few minutes there were just as many horse drawn carriages behind us, the occupants waiting their turn to step onto the red carpet spread out on the church steps.

Finally time was for us to exit the coach. Garner stepped down and placed the stoop at the door for the ladies. Dutch exited the coach first with me directly behind him. Then we gentlemen tended our ladies one on either side of the stoop.

This was a long practiced tradition to prevent a fall. With such cumbersome dresses to deal with oftentimes a young lady would become entangled in her hoops or undergarments and fall headlong out of the coach, sprawling on the ground in plain sight of everyone. As gentlemen, we could not permit such an embarrassing state of affairs to unfold. Our luck held and neither of our ladies stumbled from the coach.

Garner, who was dressed as nice as Harvey Shively and Dutch Welsh with his claw hammer tail tuxedo, picked up the stoop with his white gloved hands and proceeded to guide the coach down the street and into the park where the servant waiting area was cordoned off. Here was where the coach drivers waited until their party was ready to leave.

We entered the chapel and took up our planned residence on the back pew which caused all sorts of consternation with the crowd on both sides of the aisle. The women kept looking over their shoulders to see the best dressed lady enter the church. A lady who could have been engaged in her own wedding the way she was dressed, and before long their men were stretching their necks to get a glimpse. While many of them knew Lizzie, many of them didn't.

As the wedding began, Colonel Leighton did not let Lizzie go unnoticed either. Whether this was because he spied her on his own or because he followed everyone else's gaze I don't know. He began to stare in my direction as if he couldn't figure something out, as if he had the necessity to solve some problem before proceeding with his own wedding. I wondered if my game wasn't up, but the ceremony continued, and the colonel said his vows with marked attention to his bride and Miss Jennie Beach missed not a beat in the saying of her own.

Miss Beach had seen to things in the church, or someone had handled the decorating for her and every candle stand was adorned with a bow of ivory and pearl. Each pew had in the center aisle the same garnishing along with a single red rose tucked between lavender, giving off the most amazing aroma. The bride and groom were surrounded by all types of flowers and lace.

We four marshaled our will power and stayed the course on our back seat perch chosen for its proximity to the only escape route. As the service concluded everyone was invited downstairs for the reception and here my resolve began to fluctuate. The colonel stared my way so much I was certain he knew Ab Grimes, Confederate escapee, was in the chapel.

"Come on Harvey, let's go downstairs," Lizzie was saying.

I sat frozen stiff. My self-assured confidence had all but left me.

"You don't think the colonel recognized me?"

"How could he? He has no idea who you are," Lizzie assured me. "He was staring at me, not you silly."

"Are you sure?"

"I'm positive. He's trying to figure out who I am. He could care less about the bearded man I'm with."

"I hope you're correct, my lady, otherwise my neck is going to be exposed above the shoulders."

"Come on you two, before they begin to get suspicious," Dutch insisted.

We got up and made our way to the stairs at the front of the chapel. There was still a line and when we reached it, the girls acted as if they had known the bride for years, which they had. In fact, what I had learned on the ride over was that both of them had known the bride since childhood. Although they hadn't been invited, both ladies were eagerly welcomed.

As we reached the bottom of the stairs their welcome became quite evident. The bride and groom were waiting in eager anticipation to see who had crashed their wedding.

"Dutch Welsh, I should have known it was you," the colonel said.

"You don't think I would miss the biggest wedding in this town in forty years, do you? The newspaper would fire me!"

"You scoundrel, you're not about to fire yourself," Colonel Leighton corrected.

"Well no, that would be quite impractical wouldn't it," he said as everyone laughed.

"Lizzie and Daphne, I can't believe I forgot the two of you in my invite! Can you ever forgive me?" the new Mrs. Leighton cooed.

"You are already forgiven, my dear," Lizzie insisted. "We were rather hoping you would forgive us for taking it upon ourselves to attend your wedding."

"Don't be silly, I've known the two of you since I learned to walk. Daphne, I know your husband, but who is this gentlemen with Lizzie?"

"This is Captain," Daphne paused for effect, "Harvey Shively from Louisville, he was in town on business and we insisted that he come along."

"From Louisville. May I ask what side of the war you support, captain," Colonel Leighton said.

"Darling, that's a most improper thing to ask the gentlemen. This is our wedding!" Jennie insisted.

"It's quite all right," I broke in. "The colonel has a right to know. I'm building ships for the United States Navy, sir. My contract is to deliver gunboats for the open seas," here I lied and prayed forgiveness at the same time, for my own mother would slit my throat if she knew how easily I could lie for the Confederate cause.

"Then it's a pleasure to meet you, captain," he said as he shoved his gloved hand into mine. "You're welcome to remain and enjoy the festivities of the evening."

"Thank you sir, your hospitality is most gracious," I said.

Colonel Leighton was dressed in his best uniform as were several other officers who were present, but to my knowledge I knew none of them so we stayed on and began to dance the evening away. Everyone seemed to want to dance with Lizzie, including Colonel Leighton, so I took the opportunity to dance with his lovely bride, Jennie.

"It was a lovely wedding, Mrs. Leighton."

"Thank you, and you captain, I don't see a ring on your finger."

"That is because I'm not married. Not yet," I said as we danced.

"Do you have anyone in mind?"

I continued to dance and then remembered who I was with and the question my dance partner had asked of me. "I do have someone back home, but I find the fair maidens of St. Louis most inviting."

"Miss Lizzie Pickering would make such a fine wife. I'm surprised she is yet unmarried."

"She is fetching."

"She's more than just fetching, captain. She's a complete woman in every way except one. She has yet to find her beloved man."

"I'm not sure I understand your meaning."

"I'm sorry, captain, I didn't mean to confuse your choices."

"I see, and you think I could fill those shoes for her."

"Quite handsomely."

I glanced over at Lizzie and studied her graceful moves on the dance floor and my dance partner did nothing to block my view. Quite the contrary, she did all she could to aid me in keeping my eyes on Miss Lizzie.

"You make an interesting dance partner," she said taking my hand. "I guess many things happen in life which we have no control over. Not even my own wedding is exempt from the revilement others will make of it."

"How true my dear lady, how true. I hope you'll forgive my audacity, Mrs. Leighton, for you have no idea the extent of my depravity."

She stepped back and looked into my eyes as if she hadn't really seen me at all, yet we continued to grace the dance floor with our most polished and best moves.

"I have always known Lizzie Pickering to be a dare-devil, Captain Grimes, but I believe she has outdone herself this time. As for the depths of depravity, I assure you if you cause a scene at my wedding, I can equally surpass any performance you have in mind."

My dancing stopped and I froze in place looking directly into the preying eyes of the beautiful Mrs. Leighton.

"I've known who you were from the moment you descended the stairs. If I thought you were up to anything really dastardly, I would have my husband arrest you, but I like a challenge, and this is my wedding. I just wonder what my husband will say when he discovers your true identity?"

"You're going to tell him?"

"No, Dutch will do that in the Saturday morning edition of the *Post*. That's why he's here, isn't it?"

"Mrs. Leighton, I don't believe I had better place you in the same category with any other women I might ever have met."

"Captain Grimes, I always look at the sunny side of things. Shall we continue our dance?"

Glancing Lizzie's way I was certain the colonel wasn't yet ready to relinquish her company, but the room was beginning to get a might too hot for one Confederate soldier named Captain Grimes.

"You go ahead and dance with Lizzie during the next set. You're secret is safe with me. I'm more than curious to see how my husband handles the news when he reads about you in the Saturday morning edition than I am in seeing you caught."

For a moment our eyes locked. "You're a more cunning bride than I ever expected to meet."

"And you, captain are a more cunning Confederate soldier than I ever expected to meet," she whispered. "Now you go on to Lizzie before she becomes jealous and blows your fragile cover."

I bowed to the bride for the music had ended and we made our way over to Lizzie and Colonel Leighton. Lizzie took up my hand and the colonel took that of his bride. We continued to dance throughout the evening.

"Captain, you are an amazing partner."

"My dear, I assure you I did not come by my adaptability intentionally."

"No, but you do adapt quite naturally."

"I only intended to attend the colonel's wedding so the story of my presence could be broadcast in the Saturday morning *Post*. Dutch is here to see to it the complete story is written for the benefit of Colonel Leighton."

"What if the colonel figures out who you are?"

"I don't have a thing to worry about," I promised, although I really didn't know anything for certain. Now that he was dancing with his wife my confidence was rapidly deteriorating.

"You don't have…why, captain I don't believe you have considered what they'll do to you if they find out who you really are."

"Mrs. Jennie Leighton already knows who I am," I whispered into Lizzie's ear.

She stepped back and looked into my eyes. "Don't you think we should be going?"

"Yes, my dear, but not just yet. If we leave too soon we're liable to garner even greater suspicion."

Taking Lizzie back into my grasp the two of us continued to dance. We slipped silently around the room while Lizzie, deep in thought tried to absorb exactly what was happening.

"I wonder if I'll ever really know you." Lizzie said out of the blue, her warm soft palms resting in my own larger masculine hands.

"Only time will tell Miss Lizzie, only time will tell."

"How much time, Ab?"

"Shhhhhh, I'm Captain Harvey Shively from Louisville."

It was then I saw the messenger boy descend the stairs and look about the room. He was the same telegraph boy who had delivered the summons to me last spring which stated I must report to General Grey at Jefferson Barracks. Did he recognize me? If so, he had no way of knowing I had joined the other side. Spying Colonel Leighton the young man hopped down the remaining stairs and went straight to him. Opening the dispatch the colonel looked around the room and then his eyes settled on me.

"May I have your attention please?"

Immediately a silence fell over the room and the colonel continued.

"This is for the benefit of the officers in the room. General Grant has taken the Columbus-Belmont position on the Mississippi river. The blockade chain has been taken from the Confederates and we now control the blockade."

A cheer went up and the colonel walked to where I stood with Miss Lizzie. I must have looked a bit shocked and pale, but gathering my composure quickly I stood my ground.

"Surely, captain as a boat builder you can appreciate the significance of such a matter," the colonel gestured. "Are you all right?"

"Just fine, thank you." Pausing I began to sell my position on a grand scale. "I assure you sir that the consequence of the blockade changing hands is not lost on me. Of all men in this room I know the importance of the position you are referring to and the major role the event will play in the days to come."

"As my guest, would you care to share a drink with me?"

"Certainly, Colonel Leighton, it would be my pleasure."

"If you ladies will excuse us, I want to speak with the captain," Colonel Leighton said.

Turning on his heel I followed him to the drink table. This part of the Catholic wedding had always befuddled me. I believed as Benjamin Franklin that all things should be done in moderation, especially drinking. I thought the idea was to refrain, abstain, to withhold one's self from such folly in lieu of judgment day.

The colonel handed me my drink and looked me in the eye. "I wonder if your ships will be able to navigate the river and avoid such an obstruction as the chain," he asked.

"Not at all. You see I'm building open seagoing vessels, not the river kind like those down on the wharf. There are striking differences between the two. If you were to steer an open sea ship up the Mississippi it would be grounded in the first five miles, run aground simply because she sits too low in the water. By the same token a riverboat with little draft would not fare well on the open seas."

"No doubt you're going to pocket a good deal of Federal money. When this war is over I may have need of your services."

"Sir." My hand shook, rattling the ice in my drink.

"I may need a job. When the war is over there will be little need of so many officers in the service of the war department."

"Ah yes, I hadn't understood your meaning. If such a thing becomes necessary, Colonel Leighton, I would be more than happy to consider you."

Just then a bevy of young ladies arrived at the drink table wanting to dance.

"Captain," the colonel offered.

"After the groom," I insisted.

He chose the young lady he wanted for a dance partner and away they went. I grabbed another and left three standing awaiting their turn. When the music finished we changed partners and began anew. The ladies wanted to dance and after more than thirty minutes of feminine folly I found myself dancing once again with Lizzie Pickering.

"I am beginning to wonder if you aren't having too much fun, captain."

"There's no such thing as too much fun," I assured her.

"I hope you're correct. Dutch has enough fodder to flip St. Louis upside down and all because of you," she said.

"I've never tried walking upside down," my comment was immediately abandoned in favor of what was on Lizzie's mind.

"If you and Lucy don't get married for some reason, come calling. I believe you would create no end of joy in my life."

"My dear Lizzie, if such tragedy were to become my lot I wouldn't hesitate to visit you, but I can't picture any circumstance undoing what must be." As I said this I remembered my meeting with Mrs. Foster and realized suddenly how my loyalties were all screwed up.

"Just the same, you may visit me any time, darling."

"You are supposed to be keeping me honest, remember?"

"I remember, but I never anticipated such feelings," she said.

"Lizzie, I must remain true to my fiancé."

"I know that. But you have corrupted me."

"I have?"

"Yes you have. I would not accuse you if it weren't so."

"We haven't done anything, how could I have corrupted you?"

"Lucy Glascock is my friend, but I could not withhold myself from you if you so desired to have me," Lizzie whispered into my ear.

I stopped dead still on the dance floor and looked down into Lizzie Pickering's luscious blue eyes. Good Lord, did she really mean what she was saying, knowing I had to go home with her for the evening?

"You have vexed me, captain, and I cannot withhold my feelings."

"We must refrain," I said as we eased back into the dancing.

"Must we?"

"Yes, Lizzie, we must."

I looked across the room to see Colonel Leighton sipping a glass of wine and visiting with Mr. and Mrs. Welsh. Mrs. Welsh glanced my way and waved daintily with her handkerchief in hand. I was dancing with one of my long time friends, yet in my mind I knew it was time to go. I had to get away from these women before I became weakened by my pent up lust. I belonged on the river mastering her current. No man knew how to master a woman, let alone several at one time.

Mark would be waiting for our return to the Pickering residence. His curiosity was such he wouldn't leave until he knew what had transpired. He would likely be waiting on the front porch swing anticipating the return of the horse drawn carriage. Mr. and Mrs. Pickering were not due back from San Francisco for several months. My suspicions were Lizzie's parents would vacation there until the war was decided one way or another. Were they aware of the comings and goings in their home while they were away? Somehow I suspected they knew about the leanings of their daughter. They would know of her alignment with the Confederacy and support her. Esrom was somewhere south fighting for the Confederacy and his parents knew well what he was doing down there.

Chapter 8

Colonel Leighton awoke Saturday morning to coffee and breakfast on the veranda that ran the full length of the house and overlooked the garden out back. His home was situated near Jefferson Barracks in an old neighborhood surrounded by other Victorian houses of the time. It was made of stone and rose above most of the others in the neighborhood. Jennie had prepared an ample breakfast to include apple cider, French toast and eggs and she had made certain the Saturday morning *Post* was laying face up on the table when the colonel took his seat.

The front page story did not go unnoticed by the newlywed as he picked up the current edition and began to read.

INSOLENT NERVE

The wedding of Colonel Leighton to Miss Jennie Beach was attended by none other than Captain Absalom Grimes who had only recently escaped from custody while being transferred from Myrtle Street prison to Alton, Illinois.

The captain danced with Miss Beach after the ceremonies and many other young ladies who were present. At one point he shared a drink with the colonel and discussed future possibilities such as the colonel working for the captain when the war is concluded.

As luck would have it the captain is going to be running the blockades put in place by the Yankee's to deliver mail to the troops in Mississippi as soon as next week. He would not elaborate as to how the mail is being gathered or transported, but insisted that he would have no trouble moving back and forth between enemy lines. If his presence at Colonel Leighton's wedding is any indication of the captain's prowess, the Yankee's won't even know he is anywhere in the area.

Miss Lizzie Pickering was escorted by the captain upon this foray and impressed the crowd with her dress. It was peach in color accented by pearls and a single white ostrich feather adorned her hair. The effect was quite stunning as it took the colonel's attention off Grimes and placed his attention squarely on the young lady as it did with everyone in attendance. What effect this had on the bride is yet unknown.

Others in attendance included the mayor, Colonel Leighton's command and nearly seventy-five civilian guests, most of them friends of the bride. It will be interesting to see what affect, if any, such news will have upon the colonel.

"Captain Grime's was at our wedding!" the colonel exclaimed as he dropped the paper back onto the table.

"Yes dear, I saw the news."

His wife's reaction caught the colonel by surprise and he looked up at her.

"I take it you knew this was coming."

"I recognized the captain soon after he descended the stairs to join our reception, my dear."

"You mean you knew a Confederate captain, a wanted man was at our wedding and you didn't say anything?"

"Our wedding was not the place, nor the time to create an unpredictable commotion. I can't believe you would expect me to endure such embarrassment."

"So instead I'm to be embarrassed in front of the whole world," the colonel stated, sweeping his right arm in a wide ark.

"You are a colonel in the United States Army, and if you can't carry such a small bit of embarrassment upon those mighty shoulders then maybe I have misjudged you," Jennie smiled.

"But why, who was he? Shively! He pretended to be Captain Harvey Shively."

"That's very good, my dear. You have rightly guessed."

"How could you knowingly embarrass me like this?"

"My dear, I have friends who sympathize with the south, and I have friends who believe the north is right. This war will be decided one way or another someday but my friends shall remain my friends no matter the side their men have chosen. We women are not fighting, only you men. Now you may go fight your war, but leave me and my friends out of it."

"I am not going to ignore people who blatantly oppose the law."

"Your law, as you call it, is something a lot of folks around here don't agree with and I wouldn't worry about enforcing it until and unless you are able to win the war. If you manage victory, then you can impose your laws. Until then you have other fish to fry, my darling."

"I should have asked this long ago, but where do your sympathies lay?"

Jennie turned to face the colonel, staring at him with her hands on her hips and clippers in her right hand. Clippers she used to make an arrangement for the day. Flower arrangements were something she placed about the house with daily devotion. Blooms were her way of dealing with the world, as it could always change the mood or the setting of the day. Her face was suddenly as red as the roses in her hand.

"My sympathies lay with you, colonel. I don't side with either the south or the north. I'll have to live in this city no matter who wins this stupid war. My husband is my concern and I don't want him to go off half cocked making a fool of himself."

"I have just been made a fool of my dear, and I don't like it."

"Colonel, I want you to promise me that you'll not harm any of my friends whether they be man or woman, north or south. I want your word."

"What?"

"You heard me. I want your word that you'll not allow any harm to come to my friends. If you hurt them in any way our marriage is going to become a long drawn out tedious affair that you will find very uncomfortable for the rest of our lives. I want you to confine your war to fighting soldiers."

"My dear, I have to obey orders just as any other man in the army. It's not my decision."

"Yes it is. You have the power to see to it nothing happens to my friends. I want your word on it."

"My daring Jennie, I'll see to it that no harm comes to your friends, but I must fight this war and sometimes circumstance gets in the way."

"I don't want any excuses, I want your word."

"All right, I'll do my best to avoid any conflict with them and if any situation rears its ugly head I'll defer."

"Captain Grimes is off limits too!"

"What?"

"I don't want you to take revenge on him."

"He's a soldier! He's a Confederate soldier and he's wanted besides."

"I don't care. What he did the other night was a lark, he meant no harm by it and I don't want my husband stooping to the level required for revenge."

"You know, my dear, I'm beginning to believe I don't really know you."

"You don't know the half of me colonel," Mrs. Leighton confirmed.

Returning to his paper Colonel Leighton began to tackle his breakfast and read. Jennie returned to her task of making the flower arrangement for the day and the morning air calmed. The colonel read about the various battles under way and who was expected to win, the battles already won and noted troop movements as best he could. It appeared that the battle for Shiloh was underway in Tennessee. He noted with knitted brow that he wasn't going to be master in his own home, but subservient to the woman he loved.

Jennie Leighton made too much sense to be ignored, although she was five years younger and that was one of the reasons he had married her. She was way beyond her years in ethics and always above reproach, whether instinct or training he wasn't sure, but she was quite capable. So the town would have a laugh, but being married to Jennie would ensure the last laugh was that of Colonel Leighton.

"My dear, I don't have the slightest clue how I can maintain my promise to you, but I'll endeavor to do so," the colonel stated as he took another drink from his cup of cider.

"Often times when one begins he can not see the way, but as time goes on the road becomes clear. I have no doubt that you'll be able to maintain your promise to me, colonel," Jennie said as she clipped another rose and placed it on her cutting table next to the waiting vase.

"I had it in mind to go straight to the Pickering residence and apprehend the scoundrel, but that will never do."

"Colonel, why don't we invite him to supper? Maybe you could learn something from such a slippery character."

"Invite him to supper? We could never do that. The only reason I haven't been reprimanded for what happened at our wedding is because I was unaware and not enough time has lapsed. If we invite him here then I would have to arrest him or surely face the consequences."

"Then we mustn't," Jennie said.

"My dearest Jennie, I must consider just what I'm going to tell General Grey. He'll certainly want to know how this happened without my knowing."

"You can tell him the truth, dear. I stand behind my position. As long as we women of this fair city do not pick up arms, I insist on hands off treatment by both sides. There are two women in the Myrtle street jail this very moment, young ladies I went to school with. I want them released."

"I believe I'm beginning to understand the depths to which a woman will go to obtain what she wants."

"You had better take that back, colonel. After the last three blissful evenings and days which we have spent together you cannot honestly believe that."

"I'm sorry dear, I was speaking out of turn. Of course you never planned this."

"I would never have thought of such a thing had Captain Grimes not graced us with his presence the other night."

"I believe I understand. One can not turn back the clock once the sun has risen."

"I love you. You must never question that," Jennie said.

"I know you do, and I love you too. You make me a complete man."

"I make my man complete as every woman is expected. I'll do no less than tell you what I need," Jennie said placing her newly crafted flower arrangement on the table and took her seat.

"You will have to forgive me, I'm in uncharted territory."

"You should always go as far as you can see, and when you get there you'll always be able to see a little farther," Jennie said.

Colonel Leighton looked into the eyes of his wife, and smiled. "You're very good at laying an ambush. If I could figure out how you do that one thing, I would be a general in charge of this United States Army in no time."

"Men of all ages and rank are open to manipulation and exploitation by women. All we have to do is coo properly and bat our eyelashes in his direction and the male will be helpless and feeble if she so chooses. But for a strong man like you things must be handled differently, delicately for you must remain strong."

"Your insight is staggering."

"You will soon discover, colonel that I expect great things from my husband and I'll not allow him to become misguided or marred by disgrace no matter the situation. Not if I can help it."

"So I'm to understand that you feel war is disgraceful?"

"The handling of this war can become so if history offers us any guide. I don't want my husband or my new name dragged down into the abyss of a living hell simply because you let your animal instincts take over your decision making process in the heat of any given moment."

"Where did you say you were educated?"

"You know very well I was educated right here in St. Louis. My father insisted on my knowing how to run my own ship, but the only ship I intend to run is that of my own home. Blanche Leathers may enjoy running a riverboat up and down the Mississippi, but I prefer to keep my feet on solid ground."

"Blanche Leathers? Who in God's name is she?"

"We went to school together and she now pilots the *Natchez* up and down the Mississippi," Jennie said as she sipped hot coffee. "Had I hung around with her, my manners and ladylike eloquence would have been completely overshadowed, destroyed, buried asunder by her overbearing attitude towards all other women and men alike."

The couple's servant stepped out onto the patio and poured fresh coffee. Corinne was a black servant, a former slave and yet the colonel only saw it necessary to provide her room and board plus five dollars a month for her services. In Colonel Leighton's manner of thinking she was being paid all she was worth, but Jennie hadn't gotten a good hold of him on the matter yet.

Corinne was middle-aged and had three children at home who were, for the most part, raising themselves because their mother worked seventeen hours a day catering to the Leightons. As Jennie saw things this was little more than slavery itself. Corinne was slim by the standards of the time and she wore a black and white checkered dress with an apron. The apron was covered with smudges here and there because she had been preparing breakfast that morning and nothing ever went perfect in her kitchen. She did her laundry along with the Leighton's because it was simply the only time she could get hers done. In the evenings she would hurry home to feed her children, who always seemed to be starving. Corinne had no husband, having been killed many years earlier. Her children were now the ages of ten, twelve and thirteen, all of them boys.

"Corinne, why don't you go on home when you've finished the laundry. I can handle things about the house this evening," Jennie said.

"Yes ma'am."

Corinne gathered the dirty dishes and went back inside.

"You're giving her the rest of the day off?" the colonel asked.

"If you plan on making love to me this afternoon, I suggest we empty the house."

Colonel Leighton had brought his fresh coffee to his lips and now he halted the cup so quickly he spilled some of the hot java on his fresh shirt. He drew the cup away and looked at his wife. He felt her unexpected bare foot seeking the only area beneath the table which left no doubt as to what she had on her mind. He jumped at her touch and spilled the rest of his coffee.

The tablecloth hung so low that if anyone were present no one could have seen what she was doing to torment her husband, but Jennie knew this and continued to tease him.

Their eyes met across the table and the colonel knew it was only a matter of time before they were frolicking in bed once again. Did the woman have no limit? Corinne had been on a virtual paid vacation since their wedding night. His back was beginning to ache from all the extra curricular activities and she wasn't in the least bit satisfied or so it seemed. Good Lord, he couldn't spend his entire life in bed.

"Naturally, you're joking," he said.

"Colonel Leighton I've never been more serious," she stated as she aroused him further beneath the confines of the tablecloth.

Jennie retrieved her foot and placed it back into her slipper, got up and went back to her cutting table to prepare a fresh flower arrangement.

"You are the very devil, my dear Jennie."

"You know that's not true. Anything goes between husband and wife as long as both agree on the activity. There's nothing sinful about making love to one another once you're married," Jennie said.

"You have me all wound up and ready to go, but we must wait until Corinne has left the premises."

"You could expedite matters if you so choose."

"And let the help off scott free?"

"If Corinne were help on a plantation she would at least have her children present where she could set an example. The way you have her employed, she cannot give them any guidance at all."

"You think I should send her on home then?"

"That's up to you. If you want to wait, I can wait, but with the whole day to ourselves, I think we'll have infinite more fun."

"You're going to drive me crazy," Colonel Leighton said.

"No I won't, but I'll make sure you treat all people properly, including Corinne."

"Corinne!" the colonel yelled into the back door.

Momentarily the hired help appeared and stood in the doorway.

"You may have the rest of the day off. I'll not dock your pay and tell your children I'll be around to see them tomorrow.

"Sir?"

"I want to make sure they have what they need in the way of clothes and so on," the colonel said as he eyed his wife.

"Yesir, you's want's me to goes home now?"

"Yes Corinne, go on home to your children. We won't need you anymore on this day."

"Yesir, I's gone," Corinne said as she backed through the door.

"Now my dear, where do we go from here," the colonel asked.

"I was thinking the garden."

"The what?"

"I want to make love in the garden. I'll get some blankets and meet you there," Jennie stated flatly as she disappeared into the house behind Corinne.

Colonel Leighton looked around the grounds of their new home and thought to himself what a wonderful life the two of them would have together, providing the war didn't disrupt their plans.

Chapter 9

If I was going to carry the mail now was the time to begin. I had conceived the idea and put the wheels in motion a year ago and the time was nearly past to execute my plan. With this in mind, I enlisted the help of several ladies, Mrs. Marion Wall Vail, Mrs. Deborah Wilson, Mrs. Reanna Loughridge, and Miss Louise Venable, along with Lizzie Pickering. All of these young ladies reported to the Widow Caroline Webster, and because of her status in the community, she was unable to offer any further services, but organized the ladies and sent them about to collect the mail.

Widow Webster knew her husband's hand still reached down and directed her destiny in many matters and as he had been a staunch Federalist she did not want to occasion anything which might betray him or upset the applecart. Mrs. Webster stated that she could offer advice only; she could not be engaged in moving or collecting the mail, insisting that her position lay in the shadows, so the other ladies heeded her advice and took to the streets while I returned to Hannibal for a few days to gather my horse and buggy and visit Lucy.

I found Lucy at home so we took a seat on her front porch swing and I began to tell my fiancée what I was about to do.

"You keep your head low, Ab. You've already got one scar on your forehead."

"I'll do my best. I don't want another blow like that one."

"How did it happen?"

"Hurst and I were moving onto the battlefield at Pea Ridge when several soldiers overran our position. After emptying my weapon we turned to hand to hand combat. I lost, taking a gun butt directly between the eyes."

"You're lucky to be alive."

"I can't take another blow like that one, that's why I plan to go unarmed."

"You don't intend to defend yourself?"

"No. Putting up a fight is what got me this scar."

"I have five copies of the Saturday morning *Post*," she said changing the subject. "You certainly know how to anger the Yankee's."

"Let's hope I don't anger them too much," I said.

"When are we going to get married, Ab? Can't we set a date?"

"As soon as this war is over. I certainly don't want to turn you into a widow."

"I don't care about that."

"You should. I insist you must."

"But I'll never love anyone else but you."

"Be that as it may, we must wait."

"I read you were with Lizzie Pickering at the Leighton wedding."

"Lizzie was handy, and she did an excellent job of not betraying my identity."

"I could have done as well. I find it difficult to swallow some of the things you do, Mr. Grimes."

"Yes dear, you would have done fine, and now you're jealous?"

"I am, but I don't know why I should be. Lizzie has always been a good friend and shall always be."

I had reason to believe Lizzie might not be the friend Lucy believed her to be, but I was not going to say or do anything to fertilize the idea in either woman's mind. Lucy set me up with my favorite persimmon pie as we said our goodbyes and shortly thereafter I rode away in my wagon. I spent two days with Mark who was thinking about going west, before I headed back south. His brother had invited him out west to assist with converting the Arizona territory into a state.

Late in the week I guided old Betsey toward the river cemetery where the old oak tree stood and was surprised to find a note neatly placed inside the old tree trunk.

Absalom,

I am now laying the groundwork for your underground mail route. Several things have happened in the last few days which serve to hasten my efforts. Samuel was adamant that you receive mail at this location by way of certain local widows. I tend to agree with him, and even as I write, the weaving of the mail pouches into the back side of our skirts is being undertaken. The mail will be dropped into the tree on the first day of each month and on the fifteenth hereto known as our days of mourning.

This will take several months to sort out and develop fully, but what you're undertaking is heroic. One or more of my lady friends, all of them widows, will be there with the mail no sooner and no later. If it becomes necessary we'll enlist the help of local orphans. To leave mail exposed to the elements even inside of your tree would be frightful. Nothing will ever be said in passing or in common from this moment on, only your mail bag will grow as the war goes on. Many are hungry for news already. Please be careful and God Bless You.

P.S. Burn after reading.

C. Webster

There was no turning back now. The wheels had been set in motion and I would do what was expected of me. I would run the

Yankee blockades and deliver mail to the Confederates. Missouri was well in the hands of the Federals already, noting the fact so many of our good men had headed south to join up with the Johnny Rebs. Such a void was filled almost instantly with nary a shot being fired by either side. By the time I finished reading Caroline's letter, Missouri was under control of Union forces from St. Louis all the way to Kansas City and south to Carthage. I found myself having to cloak my movements as well as myself with no chance of returning home. The Yankees had taken Missouri post haste last year and set about to block off all supply lines to the rebels in the south.

I sat under the oak tree, holding the match to Widow Webster's note making sure the paper was burned thoroughly to ashes. I contemplated the position of most Yankee troops in the area, relishing my wait. Two days from now the mail would be delivered into my hands at this very location. How much was anyone's guess, but I should not be here when the parcel arrived. These grounds could not be allowed to look like a regular meeting place. Suddenly my dark side wondered what would happen if I had a small door built to open and close covering the hollow point in the tree. As quickly as I thought of it I dismissed the crazy idea altogether. Such a door would be a dead giveaway.

When I finished burning the evidence I hopped into my wagon and turned Betsey down the lane toward Bellefontaine Neighbors where I would seek to stay the night with a long time friend and his wife. Three miles north of town I heard men coming before I saw them, a troop of Yankee horse soldiers riding south for St. Louis no doubt. I tugged on my reins and headed Betsey off into the woods and brought her to a halt behind scrub brush on the west side of the lane. I could see them as they rounded the bend to the north and eased myself down from my wagon. If I were spotted, no good would come of it because Federal troops were controlling traffic in and out of town. I eased myself back into the woods and squatted down keeping an eye on Betsey, hoping she would stand quiet.

She didn't. She snorted and shook her trace chains, rattling them something fierce. I heard the horse soldiers draw to a stop but I didn't wait around to see what might happen next. I took off running through the brush as quickly and as quietly as I could, deeper into the woods hoping not to be seen or followed. Wouldn't you know it? One of those fellows was half Indian or part bloodhound and with little to no warning I was running for my life. Those fellows being on horseback I knew it was only a matter of time before I was overtaken, but suddenly the ground beneath me fell away and down I went into a deep ravine filled with water. I ran south a ways and then struggled up the other embankment, grabbing handfuls of roots as I went. With my feet back under me atop the other side I ran once again, my breath coming in gasps. I would never be able to hide from them, not with the noise I was making as I struggled for air.

Ahead I heard what sounded like a waterfall. The creek I had just waded had circled around and headed me off, so I focused on the direction of the water and soon found the culprit. Diving into the pool of water I startled a snake that had been swimming from one side to the other. He now turned back for the far bank and left me to my business. Pulling myself up on the rocks beneath the waterfall I climbed in behind the veil of water and huddled behind a large bolder. Here was the only place I could catch my breath and recover from my foray without being spotted or heard. I watched intently as two Federal horsemen rode up to the bank only seconds after I had hidden.

"What do you think, Skip?"

"I think he's hiding behind the waterfall, but I'm not going in there after him. Be my guest," the fellow doing the talking gestured to the other.

"Not today I'm not," the other soldier answered.

"We better get back to the others, and report what happened here."

"What did happen here?"

"He got away!"

"That sounds good to me." As suddenly as they had arrived, my pursuers departed the area.

When I finally crawled out from behind the waterfall I was shivering cold and wet. I needed a good warm fire but was too scared to chance one with the Union troops in the area so I began to walk. I knew the country and my surroundings probably better than the soldiers did, but I had yet to get my bearings after running wildly as I had.

Around midnight I spotted a cabin I recognized near Quail Creek which belonged to a Mr. and Mrs. Foster. Smoke rolled lightly from their chimney as I made my way to the door. I tapped lightly and a feminine voice called from behind the threshold.

"Who's there?"

"Absalom Grimes, ma'am. I'm sorry to be calling on you at this late hour but I'm wet and have need of your fire to dry myself out."

Slowly the cabin door creaked open and Mrs. Foster stood in the doorway.

"Are you by yourself?"

"Yes ma'am."

"Then you may enter, but please be quiet or you'll wake the children."

"Thank you. I'll be as quiet as possible."

Opening the door the rest of the way I entered the small two room cabin and made my way to the fireplace.

"There's more wood by the front door if you need to stoke the fire. I'll fix you a place where you can bed down in front of the fireplace and get warm. You must be freezing on a night like this."

"Quite so ma'am, quite so."

In no time Mrs. Foster had prepared a pallet for me in front of the warm fire and scurried off to bed. I didn't bother to ask where her husband was. I was happy just to have a warm fire to huddle near and get dry.

What kind of foolishness was I engaging in anyway? Those Yankee's had my rig and my persimmon pie. Here I was risking my life, and for what? No one cared one wit about Absalom Grimes except for Lucy Glascock. I had no wife to fret over me although Lucy was begging me to marry her. My mother and father were always busy nowadays and the only real friend I had ever acquired had been the friendship of Mark Twain. Who was I kidding? No one was going to loose any sleep over me if I died, yet I kept telling myself there was a greater purpose being served with my undertaking. I would be doing something which mattered. No doubt my suffering had only begun. I now had no horse and buggy in which to travel, unless those soldiers let Betsey roam, which they wouldn't. She was contraband. She would no doubt be confiscated for service in the Union Army to be used as they pleased. She was as good as dead to me. Betsey was working for the Federals and so was my rig.

As I lay before the fireplace thinking of my next move I began to wonder how my friend Mark Twain was getting along, if he had made his way back home to Hannibal. Mark was the best of friend to me, and I would surely miss him, but there was no reason to involve him any further by meeting with him, for he already knew what I knew. If we both survived we would have some interesting stories to pass onto our grandchildren.

The Yankee's had Missouri under their gun. I would do good to realize that although I was in my home state, I was now operating behind enemy lines. Movement would be more difficult and the Federals were making things unpleasant in these quarters. I knew whatever I did must be done on foot until I could acquire another rig. I could depend on nothing and no one.

The mission required I be able to handle any situation without intrusion from the outside. Time would be needed to get used to the idea, yet there could be no other way. I would be a man alone. The rest of my story would prove me wrong on that count, but at the time I could see things no other way.

When I finally passed out, I really passed out. I awoke the following morning to see two little carpetbaggers staring at me from the dining room table. I say dining room but the main part of the cabin seemed all one room with a table in one corner. There were sleeping quarters upstairs in the loft and curtains behind the table, leading to a back room. Other than the table I could discover no real furniture. There was a large crate in the near corner tucked nicely into place which was stamped New Orleans, St. Louis, and Omaha, the type of crate which was used to ship store goods, a crate such as I had hauled on steamboats up and down the river. As I gathered myself, I noticed more. There were pegs near the door for a man to hang his hat, although there was no hat presently. The pegs were occupied by women's clothes and a small boy's jacket.

Mrs. Foster had indoor plumbing with a small hand pump off to one side of her sink which occupied the far corner of the room. She had yellow curtains with bluebirds perched on branches to help break up the cabin's rough textured interior. There were old-fashioned muskets hanging above the fireplace.

The Foster children had awakened to see a strange man occupying the space in front of their fireplace; hence I was holding up their breakfast. Having no children of my own, I didn't understand how egregious a situation my presence had spawned in their little minds.

"Mommy, that man is awake now," the little girl chimed as she looked into my eyes.

"Good morning. I trust you were able to get dry and stay warm."

"Yes ma'am. I did in fact rest very well," I said slipping from under a buffalo blanket she had placed over me sometime in the middle of the night.

"If you'll gather some firewood, I'll fix breakfast."

It was when she said breakfast I understood how I was making her children late for their morning slop. I usually didn't eat so early most days, but when offered a good meal I hastened to accept. The wood pile was appallingly inept, for what firewood was left would not last out the week. I grabbed the necessary handful and went back to the cabin. Mrs. Foster was prepping the embers from the overnight fire to receive the fuel I was packing. Gingerly she placed the kindling first and then the logs. In no time the breakfast fire was going and the children appeared relieved.

I ate my fill as Mrs. Foster egged me on. Finally I pushed back from the table in what must have been Mr. Foster's chair and rubbed my belly.

"Where's Mr. Foster if I may be so bold as to ask?"

"He's gone off to fight the Yankee's."

"Ma'am, he's got no wood set by, and you're out of hay for your milk cow."

"I know. He said he couldn't do everything before he left or he'd never be able to go."

"I'll gather wood for you. I may have need of your services again before this fiasco is over. It's the least I can do."

"Thank you. I'm ashamed to even be in such a position."

"You won't be when I'm through." Getting up from my chair I walked out the cabin door and took a look around. There was more fixing needed here than I had time, but I could leave them in much better shape than they were currently. First I turned the milk cow out to graze and forage for good springtime grass as there would be no hay available until late July or early August.

Grabbing a length of rope I began to repair the corral. The gate needed mending and the axe sharpened on the wheel stone, but once I had a sharp edge I went to work clearing logs Mr. Foster had left fallen. He had cut several trees and begun to strip them, but I guess the war was calling. I never understood a man who would leave a mess for others to clean up, or a job incomplete. It was a good thing he wasn't around because I'd naturally have to read to him from the good book if he were.

By mid-afternoon I had two cords stacked beside the cabin under the makeshift awning and sat down to take a breather. Much of the wood had already been chopped by the man of the house so all I'd had to do was gather it into some kind of order. Mrs. Foster had certainly kept the kids from bothering me. I've found a man gets more done in the first few hours of the day than he generally gets done in an entire week when folks are about bothering him. Mrs. Foster evidently knew of the distraction her kids might cause for they never came out of the house while I was working.

I was winded by noon when she opened the door and asked me if I would like a piece of apple pie. Well, I was up in no time. I soon found Mrs. Foster could bake a grand apple pie.

"Mrs. Foster that's the best apple pie I ever sank my teeth into," I said.

"I'm glad you liked it. I would make apple pie more often but I've been short of jars for canning. If I could get more mason jars and lids I'd be able to make them year round."

"Well now, that does beat all. It just so happens I have dozens of jars and new lids to go with them. You may have them for I'm afraid duty calls me, and I'll have no further need for such instruments."

"Mr. Grimes, why would you have such an array of household goods?"

"My dear lady, I've want of the finer things too, although I've no wife to share them with as yet. My father was trained at West Point and one thing the army teaches is the want for finer things in life. One must plan if one wants to ascend to the heavens, or if you just want to live a little better. I doubt I'll have any use for them now. As soon as I can find a way, I'll bring them to you, provided you'll bake me an apple pie whenever I visit."

"You have a deal."

"I'll get back to work and bring more wood up from the creek. If you don't mind, I'd like to stay a couple of days in which I'll earn my keep, but then I must be about my mission."

"Your mission?"

"Yes ma'am, I can't tell you just yet, but in due time you'll come to know."

"Your honor is safe with me, Mr. Grimes."

"Even so, I must insist on secrecy for now."

"Well, I won't be nosy. You do whatever you've a mind to, and I'll see to the feeding of you."

"Thank you, ma'am. I had best get back to work."

As I stepped outside I noticed instantly that her children, although they had been sitting at the table with us, hadn't uttered a word. Either I scared the poor mongrels to death with my presence or they were very well disciplined. And one other thing,

Mrs. Foster seemed to know something she was not obliged to tell me. What secret she was hiding I wish she'd have said something before I made a complete fool of myself.

I worked the rest of the day down by the creek clearing a picturesque view from the cabin. I could see what Mr. Foster had in mind and continued along the same vein. It might not be exactly the view he was after, but he'd have to settle for what he got considering the condition in which he had left his family. I had never met the man, although I knew of him and had seen him in Hannibal from time to time. In my mind, a real man would have never deserted his family in such a time of need. He should have at the least tended things around the cabin before marching off to join the Confederacy.

As darkness fell, Mrs. Foster came out to tell me supper was ready. I washed my hands the best I could and headed up to the cabin where she had laid out a towel for me. I could smell the food from outside, but when I stepped into the cabin I was almost brought to tears by the aroma coming from the table. When I bit into my first taste of her beef stew I knew I was in love, but I had a problem. I was already engaged and Mrs. Foster was another man's wife.

I ate, keeping my thoughts to myself, but wretched thoughts they were. I wondered such damnable things as would her husband be eliminated by the war and free her from the bonds of her present marriage, allowing me to court her and take her as my wife? Would I kill him if we ever met? What might become of such treachery? And, who's to say if she cooked for anyone other than me what would happen? Would other men who partook of her fry pan cast about the same dreadful thoughts I was engaging?

Suddenly I found my entire Christian upbringing a thing challenged by the most sinful of thoughts. What could come of such dastardly plans? A man who coveted another man's wife was for all intents and purposes a coward and an adulterer and the worst type of scoundrel. I looked into the eyes of her children and wondered what they might think if I became their mother's husband. Surely they would not approve if I had anything to do with the killing of their father, but then neither would Mrs. Grimes…I mean Foster. Good Lord, what was happening to me? I had never encountered such despicable thoughts my entire life. I continued to down my allotment of her stew and then glanced her way. I had been afraid to make eye contact for fear my intentions might well be plastered all over my face. When I did make eye contact my worst fears were confirmed. I could not hide my feelings, now or ever.

"Mr. Grimes, I was wondering, how is your stew?"

I could not answer her. I was dumbfounded and unable to respond.

"It's not that bad, is it," she asked.

"My dear Mrs. Gr—Foster." My tongue had betrayed me. "There has never been a better meal prepared for any man."

"Did you almost call me Mrs. Grimes?

"Purely an innocent mistake, ma'am." I tried to cover my suddenly exposed day-dreaming.

"A man's tongue shall likewise betray what is in his mind."

"Am I that obvious?"

"A rabid wolf could not slobber over his tongue the way you're doing. I would thank you to withhold your thoughts and try to think of something else. I am a happily married woman, sir."

"You are married, no doubt, but are you happy?"

"Mr. Grimes, my children shall not be subject to such conversation. Please excuse yourself until the children have been put to bed."

"I apologize, Mrs. Foster, I had no idea they would understand at so young an age."

"Children do understand if there is any unrest in the home. They feed off of my forbearance, and I'll not have an unhappy home."

"May I take my stew outside with me?"

"You may have more, and yes, you may take your food outside."

I sat on the front porch stoop thinking what a fool I must have made of myself and doubted she would have anything to do with me whatsoever. What kind of evil was in me that I should have designs on a married woman? When I finished my stew, I leaned back to contemplate my next move for I was still thinking of Mrs. Foster and her flowing hair, her curved body and light smooth complexion. What of Lucy? Didn't I still possess love for my fiancée?"

The cabin door opened and my tormentor stepped out onto the porch, closing the door behind her whispering skirt. I tensed at what was to come, but my reaction was unfounded.

"I'm accustomed to being the object of another man's lust. I can't help the fact I was blessed with beauty and portions. However, I'm not accustomed to being made a whore in my own home and I'll not allow it."

"I'm ashamed of my own wretched thoughts, ma'am."

"You ought to be. I've seen men look at me before, but not with such overwhelming lust in their eyes. I can certainly maintain myself, but I insist you do likewise. I can in no way have thoughts of any other man as long as my Shelby lives."

"Your Shelby is a very lucky man. How he could leave you for any reason is beyond me."

All was dark outside as we spoke. The frogs and crickets had begun their evening serenade. Nothing moved except a slight breeze coming in from the south tossing the upper tree limbs to and fro in a dance long practiced.

"My husband should not be judged so egregiously. He has his honor."

"I'm no judge of men I've never met. I just don't see his way of thinking, that's all."

"I've made your bed for you in front of the fireplace although tonight I doubt we'll have need of a fire now that my cooking is finished."

"Thank you ma'am, and again I'm sorry for disturbing you. I guess it's what becomes of a man who has been so long a bachelor."

The following morning I was up before the dawn, though I don't know how, for I got little to no sleep. Not wanting to disturb my host, I made as little noise as possible until they had proven to me they were up and about. I turned to my wood cutting and lay in more wood for the household. There were other things which needed tending, but they could wait, for without wood the Foster family would soon be in a dire way.

Before long there was a plate of flapjacks placed on the front porch for me, along with a fresh glass of milk. I was truly getting what I deserved. I was being locked out of the house. I guess I had earned my distinction.

Maybe she just didn't want me eating in front of the children, not knowing if my sinful thoughts would betray themselves. Certainly, that must be the cause of my new station here at the Foster cabin. Mrs. Foster was too gracious a host to throw me out for no good reason although she had every reason. She had said as much the night before. Something about not subjecting the children to what might be my intentions. She would protect them as any mother would.

I went back to work and found each stroke of the axe rewarding, although I couldn't keep my mind from wondering what could happen, what might happen to allow me to garner her favor. I couldn't shake the feelings she had uncovered in me, and I wasn't sure I wanted to. I had never felt like this in my life. Never had any woman excited me the way she had, not even my Lucy. Was it her cooking, or was it something more? Clearly there was more. She was a rare beauty and she could cook.

At noon she brought a basket lunch down to the creek where I was working to clear a better view of the fields. I had no reason to suspect she wanted to dine with me, but dine with me she did. A blanket was laid out on the ground in full view of the cabin, but far enough away to give us verbal privacy. Then she pulled out her wares and once again I was smitten. This time she had outdone herself by preparing a cool smorgasbord of meats and cheeses along with condiments I hadn't thought about in ages, topped with a glass of wine.

"Dig in, but rest assured I'm only interested in conversation."

"I would never believe anything but."

"My husband has in a way shelved his responsibilities to his children and his wife to go fight a war, but that's not an open door invitation for to you to fill his shoes. You do have your own mission, do you not," she said.

"My assignment is not that big a deal ma'am, but I've got to follow through for my heart tells me so."

"And does your heart tell you to make a fool of yourself in front of me and my children?"

"Quite especially my lady, for I can't withhold my feelings in your presence."

"My Shelby would never understand, and neither shall I. Your work is of the utmost character and shall be rewarded as such, but any advances toward me shall be dealt with severely. I cannot condone such behavior."

"I understand Mrs. Foster, and I shall have no need of your first name, for I'll keep our relationship purely on a business level." I told her then of my mission. "I fully intend to run the Yankee blockades, ma'am."

"Whatever for?" she asked.

I don't know what divine presence made me spill the beans, but I blurted out the entire mission, trying to impress the lady. "I intend to deliver mail to and from home for the Confederate soldiers from Missouri."

"Good Lord, you'll be hanged if the Federals catch you."

"It's a good bet, but I have contingency plans."

"For a hanging…and I thought Shelby was a fool!"

"May the providence of God Almighty favor the foolish, Mrs. Foster," I said extending my wine glass.

"I have heard of dunderheaded commissions before, but this one takes the cake," she said as we tipped our goblets.

"I'm not commissioned to do so ma'am, I only intend to."

"You mean to tell me you haven't even been saddled with any such orders?"

"I'm in the Confederate Army, but currently I'm without a unit. My mission, as I have chosen will be completely voluntary."

"Cheers to the foolish man who thinks only of others," she said as she again lifted her glass of wine.

"Cheers to the foolish," I allowed and we drank again.

"Just when do you plan to begin this little escapade of yours? I'd like to know so I might have time to plan your burial."

"Day after tomorrow if all goes well. I could begin tomorrow, but then I might run the risk of bumping into my mail carriers and I think it best if they never see me nor I them."

"I see. So you'll be leaving us the day after tomorrow?"

"Yes, ma'am, but I'll stop by and check on you whenever I'm in the area. That should be at least once a month. I'll do things around the cabin to get you set for a spell each time I'm here then I'll be off again."

"Can you take a letter to my Shelby?"

"Most certainly, I wouldn't miss such an opportunity."

"You consider my mail an opportunity to do what?"

"To meet your husband, and serve," I answered.

I finished my third sandwich and lay back on the blanket to nap. The sun was high overhead but the shade where she had placed the blanket never moved. She left sometime while I was snoozing, and I awoke to hear the children playing. Looking up I saw Mrs. Foster hanging her laundry and keeping an eye on her little ones at the same time. If she noticed I was awake she never let on. Not until the axe thundered into the wood I intended to cut that afternoon did she notice I was up and about.

When I finished cutting wood for the evening my supper had been placed on the front porch once again. While picking up my plate I realized my pallet had been moved to the front porch as well. As I was about to finish my supper, Mrs. Foster stepped out to check on me.

"How is your banquet this evening?" she asked.

"Like no banquet I've ever tasted before."

"Is that good or bad?"

"Quite good, Mrs. Foster, quite good indeed."

"I took the liberty of putting the children to bed early so we might have a chance to talk."

"Anything particular on your mind?"

"Yes. You don't seem to be outfitted properly for your mission. You came here with no weapons, no guns."

"Mrs. Foster, a peaceful mission does not require weapons of any sort. A fertile mind is all I'll need."

"Do you intend to run the Yankee blockades with no weapon of any sort with which to defend yourself?"

"Ma'am, my only weapons shall be my strength of body and my tongue and my wit. If I were to be caught with a weapon, I would not be considered a peaceful man. If caught with no weapon, I have the benefit of the doubt and won't be considered an enemy combatant. Not immediately anyway."

"I see, so you think not going armed in the middle of a war where everyone is packing weaponry is a positive thing."

"I've thought my strategy through quite well ma'am. If I'm captured I'll not be guarded as heavily as if I were armed. If I insist my mission is a peaceful one, I may at least have a chance of escape, maybe even be released."

"You really do not intend to fight?"

"No ma'am, not in the least. I tried fighting once at Pea Ridge and got my fool head knocked off. I could change my mind I know, but I plan to deliver mail to and from the soldiers who hail from Missouri and that's all."

"What if you are set upon by Union Soldiers? You must defend yourself."

"No ma'am, that's the last thing I must do. You see, I've some experience dealing with the Yankee's already. They held me in prison in Springfield for several months. I escaped and was captured on the field of battle then decided against another attempt at escape until they transferred me to St. Louis. I have an idea what they will do if I'm captured, and I'll be just fine."

"I must say, your plan is rather intriguing. Just how do you plan to get past the blockades on the Mississippi River?"

"I'm sorry ma'am, but I must not discuss that with anyone. Not even my best friend Mark Twain knows how I'll do that. Not that I don't trust you, but I wouldn't want such a thing known, for a simple slip of the tongue could ruin everything. How I travel up and down the river or through the Yankee lines is a matter which I must be at least flexible. No doubt each trip will present a different set of circumstances."

"Then I'll respect your secrecy and bother you no more. I believe in what you're doing. What you propose is a good thing and will help a good many folk sleep at night knowing their loved ones are alive and safe."

"To include you ma'am. I'll not hesitate to bring you news of your husband's well being and get a taste of your good home cooking."

"As a daughter of the Confederacy, I'll consider cooking for you an honor."

"Mrs. Foster what will you do if the war comes this way?"

"I have no earthly idea."

"And, if the Yankee's should show up on your doorstep some day?"

"I hadn't thought much about such a thing."

"Don't ever tell them your husband is fighting for the Confederacy ma'am. They'll destroy everything in sight and no telling what will happen to you and the children. Tell them your husband went off to sign up for the Union and you haven't seen or heard from him since. In that way they'll have little reason to question you about your husband's unit."

"Do you really think they would dishonor my home?"

"They'll do more than dishonor your home given half an excuse."

"You seem to have many presupposed opinions of war Mr. Grimes."

"Because I studied at my father's request ma'am and I have a bit of experience to date. War is not pretty. Some men are at their best, some at their worst. The worst always bear watching."

"I see. You believe they would violate me."

"They wouldn't hesitate with a woman as pretty as you ma'am, kids or no kids. However, if they thought your husband was a commissioned officer in the service of the Union they would do nothing for fear of hurting one of their own and retribution if found out."

"So you think I should lie," she stated flatly.

"Ma'am, evil hates the truth, especially when the truth is on the side of right. You don't have to lie one wit, but you'd better be prepared to deal with vile and evil men if you choose not to."

"You're welcome here any time, Mr. Grimes. Would you like some more dinner?"

"Yes, indeed I would."

Taking my plate she entered the house and checked on her children as any mother would. I only hoped I was giving the lady appropriate advice. All I had to go on was what had happened down through history in other wars. It would be nice if we Americans would fight one another with more dignity than other countries, but I had my doubts. One side or the other always seemed willing to bend to the devil's ways eventually and usually it was the side which was losing. Knowing the Confederate beliefs as I did, I wasn't worried about the south falling into that trap, although I had no way of knowing at that time that's exactly what took place.

Mark and I had discussed the mission carefully, and had decided on several factors before he headed to St. Louis to see Widow Webster and then return home. First of all, I would not go armed. A gun of any kind meant instant death if caught. There would be no trial as to my innocence or guilt, hence no delay. Once captured, time would mean everything. Time would be needed to formulate a plan of escape.

If capture became eminent I was to throw the mail bag into the river and let it sink. For this I would require rocks in the bag along with the mail. If I wasn't on the river, I should always have a place in mind where I could stow the letters until such a time as I could return. I would travel incognito as often as possible to avoid anyone recognizing me. This would require a travel partner at times, a child perhaps.

The streets of St. Louis were becoming overrun with children of late who had been orphaned by the early stages of the war, not to mention the Kansas and Missouri Compromise of 1854. The compromise had been legislation designed to relieve tension between the two states, and all it had done was escalate matters, fanning the fires of war. The fact Bloody Bill Quantrell and his raiders even existed was evidence enough. Thinking back to that day Hurst and I had met him I thanked my lucky stars once again.

Quantrell's Raiders was a group of renegade soldiers who took no prisoners. If women were involved, they were usually raped until the raiders tired of playing with them and then they were murdered. No army seemed to be able to corner the bunch. The men we'd met said that Bloody Bill had a vendetta against a bunch of Kansas Red Legs for the murder of his brother and he carried with him a list of names. Those names he would mark off one by one as he killed the men involved, some thirty-two in all, but then the country was full of such crazy stories. The one about Bloody Bill though, seemed to bear out some semblance of truth as the newspapers often recounted his dastardly deeds. I was quite surprised to discover that he and his men were riding for the southern cause. No one seemed to know who his men were, but I knew of four and so did Hurst.

Mrs. Foster returned with my plate and handed it to me. She had also refilled my glass of tea and set it down beside me.

"There now. Is there anything else you require?"

"Ma'am, you sure know how to set a table, even if it's on the front porch."

"Why thank you, and I must say you sure know how to stock a wood pile. I hope you won't be too long delayed in coming back. I may have need of more wood."

"I won't be gone too long. I sure wouldn't want to miss out on the vittles."

"There is on my mind a feeling I should tell you what I believe."

"Ma'am," I said with sudden anticipation.

"I believe one day we shall all stand before the Lord and good or bad we shall have to tell him our story. In the end, all we have is our story. Nothing we own here on earth will back us up, earthly goods shall be as if they had never been, but our story will either confirm us or deny us. I have never told that to anyone, not even my Shelby, but now you know me, and I'll do nothing which will place embarrassment upon myself or my family."

"I have rarely thought of what my moment of death should summon, but if you don't mind ma'am, I'll adopt your opinion of the matter for my own. I believe you to be a very wise and capable woman and you've not come to such a conclusion haphazardly."

"Thank you. But I assure you I did not tell you to earn favor. My reason for telling you is this; you are about to embark on a very dangerous mission, one which will no doubt have you exposed to the possibility of capture, torture and death more so than the average soldier. I want you to always remember your story, be true to that and don't do anything you'll have trouble explaining to the Lord on Judgment Day. If you do that, I'll be proud to call you my friend, and if you should ever need a safe harbor in which to light, please do not hesitate to come here. My door shall always welcome you, even if my husband should be present."

"Your motherly wit is astonishing, Mrs. Foster, and forevermore I'll consider your home a haven of rest for as long as I live."

"Thank you. I'll be praying for you every day, asking the Lord to aid and guide you in your mission and keep you safe on your journey.'

Suddenly she pulled an envelope from her skirt and handed a letter to me addressed to Shelby Foster of the 1st Missouri. I took the letter and placed it inside of my left hand lapel pocket where the correspondence fit perfectly.

"Ma'am, it'll be my pleasure to deliver this letter personally."

"Thank you. Are you finished eating?"

"Yes ma'am."

"Then I'll take your plate, sir."

"I may be gone by morning. I need to get an early start, and I should have trouble leaving this blessed home on time if I see your face again."

"I understand, but you needn't worry, I'll fix up a bundle of goodies for you and place them right outside the front door in a carpetbag. I've been working on such for two days now without your knowledge. Where you're going there'll be no chow hall, no hot and ready meals to speak of. I hope you find what I have prepared worthy of your mission."

"I had no idea."

"No sir, you didn't, but I'll not send you off without proper sustenance."

"My lady fair, you are truly a rare and capable beauty."

"Maybe so. There are many women who feel as I do and who would do no less. In fact, Lucy could do as well for you given half a chance and she is no less a beauty."

"I reckon so ma'am but..." I stumbled over my words. "You know Lucy," I asked in sudden shock.

"Lucy Glascock and I are old school mates, and best of friends. I didn't dance with you last week but I was present at Jennie Leighton's wedding. I just sort of put two and two together and came up with you. No one else could possibly fit Lucy's description. You're exactly everything she described to me."

"Goodnight ma'am," I said as I dispatched my hat.

"Goodnight."

As she entered the cabin I got up from my perch on the front porch and took a stroll down to the creek where I had cleared off the trees. There I stood listening to the water trickle over the rocks. A small levy of large stepping stones I had placed in the creek would allow Mrs. Foster and the children a place to cross without getting their feet wet if they so desired. In only a few days I had enjoyed some of the best memories of my life. Memories I couldn't imagine I could replace in any way, but I didn't understand at that time how a war I had not wanted could create incredible memories of its own, both good and bad.

My sentiments turned to Lucy, my childhood sweetheart, my fiancée and I realized suddenly who Mrs. Foster was. Lucy had always referred to her as Evelyn. To have played such a fool was one thing, but to have done so with Lucy's best friend was even more deeply troubling. Would Mrs. Foster tell of my weakness to Lucy? Thinking about her and what little I knew of her I was quite certain she would never reveal my childish reaction to her beauty and cooking. Evelyn Foster was a woman who could do many things, but ratting out a friend was not one of them.

Chapter 10

At three in the morning I was awakened by the front door of the cabin opening and closing. I raised up from my blankets and realized Mrs. Foster had just placed my food outside the cabin door in a well made bag. I lay there for a few more minutes wishing I hadn't any reason to go, but in the end I got up and made ready for travel. I bathed in the washtub at the corner of the house and dried myself off, picked up my bounty and headed off down the long hills.

After stepping across the stones I had so carefully placed in the creek I walked east across the long field. As the gray of dawn began to illuminate the sky I took one last look back at the cabin for I was about to enter the tree line two miles away. I couldn't tell for sure, but it looked as though Mrs. Foster was standing in her doorway watching me. I waved not knowing if she was really there and to my surprise she waved back. I knew then she could see me much better than I could see her.

Ducking into the woods I was on my way, but I had a problem. There was so much food in my carpetbag I could hardly carry it, so I devised a way to hang the bag over my shoulder and struggled on with the bulky and cumbersome thing. I walked another two miles until I came to a small stream and sat down on the edge of the bank. Pealing open the bag, I found fresh baked pastries wrapped individually in paper. I ate the first one and gave thought to turning around right then and forgetting my silly mission, but then I felt the letter in my lapel and remembered she was another man's wife and Lucy's best friend.

I ate a half dozen of her pastries hoping I might lighten my load a bit. If I made any progress in that department I sure couldn't tell. The bag was just as heavy as ever with apples, dried beef, salt pork, several sandwiches, and four different kinds of pie, along with a lot of biscuits. My only consolation was I knew in my mind the carpetbag was lighter, but I couldn't tell by the feel of it.

I made the graveyard at Lemay Ferry around noon and sure enough there was a bundle of letters for me to deliver to the boys down in Mississippi. I sat under the old oak tree and partook of a readymade lunch that Mrs. Foster had prepared. She had a way of separating the fare in stages as it should be eaten. If I ate what was on top first the food on bottom would still be good.

After consuming my lunch, I picked up the food bag and the mail bag wondering just what I had gotten myself into. I now had two bags to carry and only two arms, which meant no rest for either side and neither horse or buggy to aid me.

"Captain Grimes, when you set out to do things up, you really do them up good," I said aloud to hear the chastising I so richly deserved. Had I known the long months ahead would be so lonely, I would have never began this madness, but you see I was uniquely suited to the self-prescribed mission.

I knew most of the riverboat pilots on the Mississippi, a fact I was hoping the Federals had overlooked. I knew the locations of all the landings on the river from New Orleans to Omaha, and the men who ran them. If anyone could run the Yankee blockades on the Mississippi it was yours truly, Captain Absalom Grimes.

I was under no illusions. The grand prize in this Civil War would be the Mississippi river and its commerce. The river itself was already running red with blood from Yankees and Confederates alike when I walked out of the woods three days later at Nealy's Landing sixty miles south of St. Louis. The life-blood of the Confederacy was at stake. To control the movements of supplies up and down the Mississippi was to control the war and its outcome.

Were the South to loose the main artery of transportation offered by the Mississippi River it would mean a split force. The South would become divided and hence easier to conquer.

The Federals had quickly seized New Orleans to the south and St. Louis to the north, but everything in between was a gamut of Confederate sympathy for the moment, and this is where Grant was now concentrating his efforts. This was where I had to travel and except for the chain across the river from Columbus to Belmont, I was in friendly territory, or had the Federals dismantled the apparatus?

There was one small problem. The Yankees had seized more land than I suspected and the chain across the river a good ways north of Hickman Kentucky was no longer in place. They had fortified ground on the hill where they had reinforced their move with twelve pound guns added to the ones left behind by my friends. Any riverboat captain wanting to make the turn around the horn from or for New Madrid would find himself backpedaling his steamer under the watchful eyes of the Federals and their cannons. The same guns abandoned by Confederate forces when Grant moved in. This was the beginning of the blockade they had placed on the river. If I planned to deliver my mail to the Missouri fighters in Mississippi, this was the blockade I would have to run.

Pierce Hogan was the first to see me as I sauntered down to the dock at Nealy's landing and he was the instrument by which I heard the news.

"Captain Grimes! By joe it's good to see you. Where you headed?"

"Corinth, Mississippi," I said.

"I do say, have you lost your mind?"

"Not in the least Hogan. I'm delivering mail to the boys down there."

"I see. You sure you're not crazy? There's a dozen Yankee ironclads on the river between here and there and no boat is getting past them without being boarded, seized or blown out of the water."

"Hogan, I'll deliver the mail and I'll return."

"If you say so, but how're you going to pull it off?"

"I'm working on that."

"You're working on it? If you manage to survive, do me a favor."

"What's that?"

"Come by here regular-like and bless my dock with your presence will you? Because if you should manage to make the trip down and back, you're most certainly a blessed man or a lucky one, and either way I want some of your voodoo to rub off."

"Okay, as you wish. Who's the young fellow sitting on the edge of the dock with the cane pole?"

The boy was dressed in overalls and a white shirt turned yellow by days of wear without washing. His skin was a bit red from the sun, but that was laid over a darker tan which he had already developed.

"Don't have any idea. The boy drifted in here a couple of days ago and won't say nothing at all. I can't even get a name out of him."

"Watch my bags will you?"

"I never saw a bag with legs." Hogan insisted as he went about his business.

I walked over to where the boy was sitting and dropped down beside him noticing he had no shoes.

"Nice day for fishing," I said.

No response.

"What are you using for bait?"

Again no response.

"You after catfish or carp."

"I'm after anything I can cook," the young man insisted in an irritated manner.

"Well now, I take it you're a might hungry. I've got some vittles in my bag what would make a blue ribbon cook cry. You come with me and we'll have some lunch, and then we'll see if we can't drag an old catfish out of the river for supper. How's that sound?"

"I don't want to depend on others, mister. I've got to learn to fend for myself."

"Well, I can see you're not a beggar, but son when a meal is offered a man should never refuse on account he might offend the person doing the offering."

Slapping the boy on the knee I said, "Come on, lad. Let's eat. I've even got enough for Mr. Hogan to join us if he likes," I added as we got up.

"You don't have to feed me. I've got my own grub," Hogan insisted.

"I've been walking for three days carrying the best food a man could get into his mouth, and I can't take that much of it with me where I'm going. I would be disappointed if you and this young man here don't help me lighten my load so that I can at least carry my bag. The weight of the thing is plumb wearing me out."

"In that case I'll help you eliminate your excess baggage," Hogan said.

Pulling up a small card table and three chairs, Hogan had us in fine shape for a good lunch while his workers took our move as a cue to eat their own. I started pulling out my wares and sharing all I could. I had no idea what had become of the boy's family, but it seemed to me he was in dire need of sustenance.

"Now son, I don't share my table with just anybody," I said. "My name is Captain Grimes and we both know who Mr. Hogan is. What's your name?" I asked while dangling the food in front of him.

"My name is Bobby Louden."

"How old are you son?"

"I'm sixteen."

"What are you doing on the river?"

"I was a volunteer fireman down to St. Louis but the captain said for me to git. He said I was a pyromaniac, whatever that means. I tried to sign up for the Pony Express last year because they were advertising for orphans, but they said I was too big already."

"Pyromaniac means you like playing with fire."

"That's not so, I was only trying to understand how fire works."

"If you know about such things you've found a partner right now. I'll show you how you can put your skills to work."

"Doing what?"

"Oh, I don't know, blowing up steamboats and what not, just the ones transporting Federal troops, mind you."

Hogan looked at me with a funny eye and then said, "Hell of a thing to be teaching a youngster."

He dug in then and so did we.

"Look at him. He's got facial hair already. He'll work out as well as any man once we have him shaved proper," I added.

"That is a lot of peach fuzz," Hogan tossed in.

"We'll fix the young man up proper first chance we get."

I kept shoving food at them for although I loved Mrs. Foster's wares, I couldn't carry them anymore. We feasted on all I could pull from the bag.

"Go ahead, eat up. I can't take my spoils with me. Besides there'll be food on the boat."

"Which boat are you waiting on?" Hogan asked.

"Whichever is the first one headed south," I said.

"That would be the *Natchez*. She'll dock about eight-thirty to take on wood."

"Captain Blanche Leathers on her husband's boat," I slapped my knee. "Boy howdy, I can't believe my luck. Why she'd hide me anywhere on that old crate to get me past the Federal gunboats. How about it, son? You want to take a ride down the Mississippi with Blanche Leathers on the *Natchez*?"

"What would I do?"

"You'd keep me from getting my fool head blown off, that's all. You see, with a boy along, I could make like a traveling man where I would never be suspected of being in the service of the Confederacy. If you don't mind traveling that is."

Bobby looked at the last fragments of his sandwich and said, "If you'll feed me, I'll do whatever you ask, long as I don't get killed."

"Put her there, partner," I said as I stuck out my hand. We shook and I handed him another sandwich.

"Hogan?"

"Don't mind if I do," he answered. "You don't want to carry all that food aboard the *Natchez* anyway. Why, if Blanche or old Bowling Leathers ever got a taste of this stuff, they'd forever be firing their cook and hiring a new one until they found the like. That wouldn't be any good at all, now would it?"

"No sir, it wouldn't," Bobby piped in with a smile.

"Eat up young man. There's more where that came from."
Pausing I added, "Why haven't you got a hat, Bobby?"

"Never had one. Pa never got around to buying me one, and when ma died I never thought about needing a hat, though I suppose such a thing would be good to have."

"Life ain't worth living until you've selected your first hat, son. My own father told me that. He said a man doesn't know who he is until he slaps on his first hat, and then life gets good."

Hogan leaned over then added, "That's true enough."

We ate our fill, and did our best to finish off my carpetbag of food, but we were under no illusions. Our endeavor would take time. I had eaten from it for three days and now I had shared with two others, and I still hadn't uncovered the bottom. There was no mistake about it, Mrs. Foster had fixed me up proper, only I needed a mule to carry the goods for me. A mule, now there was an idea.

Just before sundown we tore into my food stores again and this time we found the bottom, although that didn't mean we were able to clear it. We got there, but by no means did we devour the foundation. Carefully we stacked what was left in Mr. Hogan's cupboard and prepared ourselves to board the *Natchez*.

Bobby and I sat on the dock watching the river roll by while Hogan directed the unloading of the wagons which had arrived with wood for the steamer. Bobby no longer needed his cane pole, but I told him he should bring it with us anyway. We might have need of it later.

We backed off and napped until we heard the boat chugging downriver. Hogan had his lanterns lit and properly placed so the pilot could identify the landing. With aid from that light the stern wheeler pulled up along the dock and tied off. Dropping the left plank, men began to move wood aboard then down to the engine room. I kept out of the way until they were done and when old

Bowling Leathers came out to pay Hogan for the wood, I introduced myself.

"Captain Grimes, you old renegade, how are you?"

"You have no idea how appropriate a name you just called me."

"Renegade? Why you've always been a man who navigates into the wind. How else would I recognize you?"

"How about blockade runner," I smiled.

"See what I mean?" Leathers laughed.

"Young Bobby here and I need passage aboard your boat. I have mail for the Missouri troops down at Corinth."

"The 1st Missouri?"

"Exactly. Bobby here is going to help me get through the lines."

"Blanche will sure be glad to see you, but once she finds out what for, I'm not so sure. If we get caught with that mail on the boat we'll be decommissioned and placed under arrest our own selves. Them Yankee's ain't letting any of the normal mail runs through."

"I won't let that happen. I already have several stones in the bag which will aid its descent to the bottom of the river should the Federals stop us for any reason."

"Okay, but the boy's money is no good. You've passage any time you need and the Federals be damned."

"Thanks, Leathers. I won't let anything happen."

"You'd better stop by the wheelhouse and say hello to the wife. She'll chide me good if'n you don't."

"You know I wouldn't miss a chance to say hello to Blanche," I said as Bobby and I boarded the steamer.

The roustabouts were still busy loading wood into the engine room when I ascended the stairs to the wheelhouse. Blanche recognized me at once and threw her arms around me.

"What brings Captain Grimes out on such a night as this?"

"A dastardly calling, my lady. I'm taking mail to the 1st Missouri down at Corinth Mississippi."

"I could have guessed as much. Put yourselves in the first room next to the engine room. I know it's noisy, but if'n we should be boarded for inspection such as they have been doing of late, you need to be near there because that's where you'll hide, making as if you are one of the mates. Young man, you do whatever the captain says, he knows what he's doing. That mail bag, we'll have to look for a good hiding place."

"I think I know of one, but I'll check first to make sure."

"Be on with you now. I've got a boat to debark."

"Have you got any hats in your ship's store, Blanche? We need one for Bobby."

"I reckon there's a few. Look them over and let me know if you find one what fits. There might be a pair of boots if he can find a pair to fit."

"Thanks, Blanche."

Taking young Bobby along with me we went down to the engine room and looked in. The men were there and working steadily to keep the boilers stoked.

"Get up a good head of steam, Saul, we're pulling out." I could hear Blanche command through the megaphone.

"Come on, we'll check into our room and get comfortable." Opening the door I pushed in and showed Bobby his bunk.

"This is right handy. If we're set on by a gunboat during our travels, we'll run into the engine room and get dirty real fast. We'll look like we belong there. That way they won't recognize me, and they don't know you."

"No sir, they don't."

Setting the mail bag aside we went to the ship's store and looked for Bobby a hat. The one we found was just what we needed and fit him perfectly. The hat was a tan leather affair with an extra wide brim and sported a darker tan leather trim about the base. He also found a good pair of comfortable boots. I gave him twenty dollars and told him to pay Blanche for his new belongings while I got settled in our room.

"We might as well get some rest while we can. There'll be little warning if we come upon a Yankee ironclad. I'll be in our room waiting on you."

"Yes, sir."

Bobby returned a few minutes later and we went to sleep. Along about four-thirty in the morning there was a loud banging on our door. It was Captain Bowling Leathers.

"Captain, you'd better make ready. We've gone as far as we can go. We're seven miles upstream from the Columbus Belmont. Cairo landing is in view and we're heading back north from here," he shouted through the door.

I was up quickly and opened the door to look at old Leathers.

"Belmont is just ahead, we'll have to give you a skiff and turn about. Otherwise they'll cut the *Natchez* in two with their gunboats."

"Have the mates prepare the skiff and we'll meet you at the bow," I answered.

Grabbing my bags, Bobby and I got ready for debarking. We made our way to the front of the boat. I knew what was down river and wanted no truck with those fellows, but I figured we could kill two birds at once if I could report on the Yankee progress. I wanted to spy on them short of drawing their attention to us.

Once we rounded the bend at Cairo there was no cover on the Mississippi to hide a large boat like the *Natchez*, but a skiff like we would be taking might get through. If we could lay still and cover it with enough branches from deadfalls we might go unnoticed.

"Captain, a present for you," Old Leathers said as he handed me an old pistol.

"You'd better keep the weapon, Bowling. I'm on a peaceful mission," I said shoving the weapon back into his hand.

"You mean you're going to do this completely unarmed," Leathers wheezed.

"That's exactly how I intend to operate. If I'm caught with a weapon, I risk instant retribution. If I go unarmed at least I have a chance if captured."

"You're positioning in this matter is striking, captain. You may have the boat and Blanche and I bid you the best of luck."

"Thank you, Leathers. Tell Blanche I'll see her again soon."

We lowered the skiff and put into shore where we tied on leaves and branches to cover the white paint on the boat so we would look like a log jamb floating downriver. Back in the water we began to row our way past the Yankee gun boats.

Bobby had experience rowing and it showed. We went to the near side of the river directly under the guns they had placed on the cliffs. It would be impossible for them to shoot at us in a straight down fashion. If we had taken the west side they could have blown us to smithereens if spotted.

We quit rowing as we neared the Yankee encampment and ducked down into the skiff just in case they had soldiers on the river bank below. We drifted quietly by on a dark moon night.

The current took us around the horn where we would be visible from up on the cliff if there was enough light, but on this night there was a low hanging mist which blocked the view of any watchers from on high. The river turned east and north for about two miles before New Madrid and we were carried across to the other side by the mighty current. We could see the Yankee work camp in the middle of the field to the west and I surmised they would have cut their channel by week's end, bypassing the Confederate guns located on Island Number Ten. Then the river snaked southward again and we rowed swiftly past three ironclads tied off on tower rock a ways below Belmont. The crew was obviously sleeping on the small island desiring the release from the confines of the gunboats they operated. Somehow the Yankee's had managed to get one of their boats by the Island Number Ten, but only one and he didn't seem to be in any hurry to return.

Those gunboats were great as to what they were designed for, but James Eads had never really thought them out to the point of placing room on board for the soldiers to rest. And if the ship was doing battle, it made such a racket nothing within five miles could sleep.

Once the rock was out of sight we relaxed and drifted for a while. I watched for snags or floating logs, which was always a possibility on the Mississippi. Bobby slept as the sky began to gray and I donned my old uniform. I was after all, a riverboat captain.

We drifted downriver for most of the day and put in at Butcher's landing just north of Memphis, tied the skiff off and went ashore. Riley was there ordering his roustabout's up and down the dock, getting ready for the next boat. He was preparing his dock for the sale of wood to the steamers which were taking more and more risk just to stay on the river.

"How's business, Riley?"

"Slow. Them Federal boys have things so bottled up a boat can't get up or down the river without getting shelled, shot at or boarded."

"I just came down from St. Louis with no problem," I stated.

"You don't say. Well now, will you be heading back?"

"Just as soon as I deliver my mail to the 1st Missouri."

"Is that what you're carrying?"

"That and nothing else," I said as I now had my mail bag inside my carpetbag.

Riley had a pair of good horses and he let Bobby and I use them and dry docked our boat for us. It was a two day ride to Corinth, Mississippi by horse and then we held mail call. I had never seen such a look on men's faces as the look of astonishment I received from the men of the 1st Missouri. I knew my reward then, and I was certain I would never desert my mission or betray these men. My men wore the gray uniform of the south and they were all my brothers at that moment.

Then I remembered the letter I had for Shelby.

"Shelby Foster," I called out last of all.

Presently a lone man of about thirty walked up to me. He looked disheveled and worn. His uniform was dirtier than most and he hadn't shaved any time recently.

"You have something for me?"

"Yes I do," I said handing him the letter from his wife.

"From Evelyn?"

"I have never known her as anyone other than Mrs. Foster and a fine lady she is, but the letter is from your wife," I said. "She and the children were fine when I last saw them six days ago."

"Thank you, captain," he said and saluted me. "I'll never accept a letter from you without saluting. I have the utmost respect for your prowess, sir. You've delivered the mail intact from behind enemy lines. No one else could have managed such a feat."

"Thank you, Mr. Foster. I'll remember your charity."

"How is she?"

"Your wife is doing well under the circumstances. She has food stores for a while and wood too."

"I was worried about the small amount of wood I left when I signed up."

"You needn't worry, Private Foster. I finished clearing the dead fall trees and other wood from the creek and stocked the wood pile next to the cabin. She's in good shape. Some of the wood is a mite green, but she'll be fine."

"I thank you, captain for what you've done and if you need a volunteer for anything, you look me up. I'll be the first at your service," he said.

"It seems that your wife and my Lucy know one another," I tested.

"Lucy Glascock? Why, captain I had no idea. They are the best of friends. Then you are Absalom, Absalom Grimes the riverboat pilot."

"I am, and I had no idea either, but your wife seemed to know who I was from the get go. I figure she knew from the beginning," I added humbly.

Turning away, Private Foster began to open and read his mail. We ate with the troops that day and passed out pen and paper for the men to write return letters. We remained in camp three days and every log, stump, box, and keg was used as a writing desk while the men wrote letters home. The fourth morning my bag was full of exchange mail ready for delivery to Widow Webster at Lemay Ferry so we began our return trip. The Foster family letter was once again safe inside my lapel.

With transportation provided by Riley we were back at Butcher's landing within twenty-six hours of our departure from Corinth. Now we had a return trip to make and a lot of rowing to do. My thought was to wait for a steamer going upriver and pile on board with our skiff, to be let down well upriver. This was our plan and the ploy worked rather well. The *Tecumseh*, the original mail packet from St. Louis to New Orleans, was making her way upriver, although she carried no mail now. They took us aboard, along with our skiff, ready to be dropped at a moments notice. Captain Leo Bryce was the pilot and a man I knew well. Again we were not charged for passage, a common courtesy extended from one riverboat pilot to another or one captain to another. In my case it was both.

Leo's pilot was back downriver at Memphis and as such asked if I wouldn't mind taking the wheel so he could get some rest. I did so gladly with Bobby looking on in astonishment. All Leo wanted me to do was keep the boat hidden upstream from Memphis until morning. Bobby was keen to everything happening around him, wanting to learn all he could about piloting such a monstrosity up and down the river. He helped me watch for snags and big logs. For seven hours we held her upstream, then backed down the power, and when once again in sight of Memphis, I began to call out instructions to the engineer below in the engine room.

"Back one third," I yelled into the megaphone.

"Back one third," he repeated.

"Steady as she goes."

"Steady as she goes."

I took to my wheel and steered the *Tecumseh* in toward the dock.

"Cut all power," I yelled.

"Cut all power."

As the ship drifted up next to the dock just at the point the current was about to take her in the other direction, I yelled to the roughnecks on deck. "Tie her off!" and they tossed their lines to the roustabouts waiting on the dock.

They pulled us in and I called down, "Lower the plank."

The next thing I heard was Bobby behind me. "Wow, I never dreamed such a thing could be so easy. Can you teach me how to dock a boat?"

"In due time young man, in due time. We've got a lot of traveling to do and the winds of war will surely catch up to us. I'll teach you what I can if you'll stick with me and do as I ask."

"You've got a deal," Bobby said.

At the dock we took on wood and Leo's missing pilot. The latter was nursing a hangover. He said he could handle the boat, but Leo told him to go to bed and he would take her on upriver as far as New Madrid. We steamed out of Memphis about ten o'clock that morning and again Bobby was in the wheelhouse watching in awe as the captain made his departure.

Going upriver takes a little longer than coming down, the boat fighting against the current every step of the way. Bobby stayed with me at the wheelhouse. Near sunset Captain Leo's pilot appeared and took over. I believed at this point Bobby would come to rest in our cabin, but I had underestimated the young man's level of excitement. He stayed at the ship's helm watching every move the pilot made, asking questions and being a general annoyance. I wasn't about to stop the lad. He had found something he could learn, and I had no intentions of dousing his spirit.

I lay down for a nap and when I awoke, the boy was in his bunk. He had to be tired, so I let him sleep until two in the morning. I went with him to the galley, and we ate in peace and quiet having been late for any meal.

"Well, did you learn anything," I asked.

"I've learned a lot, captain. I hope we'll travel many times by riverboat."

"If I can use my rank and stature to make travel for us easier, I'll not hesitate. But as you can see, riverboat pilots help one another regardless of the circumstances."

"Yes sir, and I want to be a member of that group one day," he replied.

"And so you shall Bobby, indeed you shall."

We enjoyed a new form of beef stew, compliments of the chef. Now cooks on riverboats were not considered chef's, but this guy was a former chef from New York and proud of his work. He might not be in the spotlight on Fifth Avenue anymore, but he was an artist just the same.

He waited on us personally and introduced himself as Antonio McGuire. He served us desert and wine, making certain we were well taken care of despite the late hour. I offered my thanks and we bid him good evening. I continued to think though, something was amiss. I had done nothing heroic. In my mind I didn't deserve such fare or treatment. I was only doing a job I thought would be necessary for the morale of the troops in Mississippi.

We bid goodbye to the *Tecumseh* and her crew the following morning just below New Madrid. She dropped our skiff on the dock for us to worry about. The *Tecumseh* was headed back downriver where there was less chance of any Yankee cannons putting a hole in the wheel house or splitting her deck asunder. I spoke with an old Negro who seemed to be watching over several boxes of goods which had just arrived via the *Tecumseh* and asked if he knew how we might get the old skiff back upriver over land.

"U's a pilot, sah?" he inquired.

"Yes, and I need to get that skiff upriver."

"How's fah?"

"To the Cape."

"Jobe and Mick'll get her there by this time tomorrow for five dolla's."

"Can we ride along?" I asked. If they could get the boat there that quick they'd beat me and Bobby by two days walking.

"He'll charge a dolla extry for each rider if'n I know's anything," the Negro said.

"That'll be fine. When will Jobe be here?"

"'Bout a howa."

"We'll be making this trip about once a month if he wants the job."

"Oh, he'll be want'n the job. Money's get'n so's a man can't find none." The old fellow smiled.

"I'll pay regular, if he moves us and the boat, we'll be ever most grateful."

"Yous don't go nowhere and iz fetch Jobe as soon as he rides in."

Chapter 11

New Madrid was out of sight of the Yankee guns, and seemed to be completely unmolested. If the Federal troops had wanted her they'd have treed the town by now. They were digging a trench around Island Number Ten, which was only eight miles from New Madrid. It was all well and good for me if they didn't realize the significance of the hamlet's location. We needed a good landing like the one just below New Madrid and Island Number Ten. The less we had to travel by land the better.

We sat down on the dock at Engler's Landing and waited for Jobe. Bobby wanted to talk so we talked of things like how to get around the troops, what to do if caught and so on, and then he asked me about the New Madrid fault line and what it was. The best way I could explain it was to tell him a story so that's what I did.

"Do you know the name of the first steamboat to ever navigate the Mississippi?" I asked.

"The *Mississippi Queen*?" Bobby said.

"Exactly fifty years ago, a man named Robert Fulton had an idea, and he had money, and when you put the two together they naturally create something. Steam engines had been around for a couple of years by then and he figured if they could run a sawmill, why couldn't they power a boat? He believed his idea had enormous commercial capabilities and he was correct.

"He had a partner named Robert Livingston and they were already operating steamboats on the Hudson River around New York, but the Hudson is a calm river compared to the Mississippi and when they began to build their boat in Pittsburg,

Pennsylvania everybody laughed and scoffed at them saying it would never work. They had no doubt the boat could go downriver, but to overcome such a swift current upstream as that of the Ohio, the Mississippi and the Missouri, why they were considered crazy."

"He called it the *Fulton*," Bobby said.

"In 1809 Robert Fulton commissioned Nicholas Roosevelt and he took his wife Lydia on a flatboat down the river all the way to Natchez Under the Hill, and then took a rowboat the rest of the way downriver to New Orleans."

"He called the boat *New Orleans*," Bobby guessed again.

"With absolutely no evidence to support your theory, you have rightly guessed the name of the first steamboat on the Mississippi," I announced.

"The third time's a charm."

"Anyway, the trip was made so the company could survey the river and know the low spots where a boat might run aground, sand bars, tributaries, and places he might be able to dock such a large cumbersome boat. They stopped here and there and asked questions of all sorts of folks so they could get a better lay of the land, or the river if you will."

"What's all of this got to do with New Madrid?" Bobby asked.

"Just hold on, I'm coming to that. I believe that on this trip Mr. Roosevelt got his wife pregnant or soon thereafter. I can't swear to it, but things seem to point in that direction. They arrived in New Orleans the beginning of December and immediately took passage on another boat for the return trip back to New York. Yellow fever was aboard the boat with them and as soon as they could they jumped ship and took a stage the rest of the way to New York.

"He reported his findings to Fulton and Livingston and insisted they should build the steamer at once. The Roosevelt's took up residence in Pittsburg that following spring as work began to get under way on the boat. A storm of controversy arose over the fact that the good-natured Roosevelt was going to take his very pregnant wife along on the ship's maiden voyage, but he quelled much of the controversy by hiring two women servants to wait on his wife's every need. Finally in September 1811 the boat was christened and readied for her first trial run.

"After several turns on the river, the date was set and the boat was loaded with captain and crew. The river banks were lined for the maiden voyage with doubters and believers alike for all wanted to see the great boat wheel down the river. At Roosevelt's signal the anchor was pulled up and the big wheel began to turn. Slowly it moved away from the shore and then picked up speed and was soon out of sight.

"Now 1811 was a very strange year, things were about to happen that no man had control over and the boat was soon in peril. As they made their way downriver the sun began to turn red instead of bright orange and a haze settled on the waters day and night, making travel almost impossible. But for his log book and the sounding of depths as they went, Roosevelt would have no idea where he actually was, but because he had recorded everything meticulously and noted every change in the river he knew exactly where he was even though he could see nothing."

"He must have been really smart," Bobby said.

"He was the smartest man I've ever known."

"You know him?"

"Who do you think taught me how to navigate the river? My father tried, but it was Roosevelt who really got me to understand what I was doing."

"You learned from him?"

"Everything I know about the old Muddy. Anyway, like I was saying, 1811 was a very strange year. There was a comet overhead at night which could be seen for days on end as it sped by. On the night of October first, that comet was still in the sky but it couldn't yet be seen and the sun was setting in the west and the color of it was blood red. The moon was coming up in the east and the color of it was also blood red, and if a person didn't know which direction he was looking he might mistake the moon for the sun or visa versa. All of this was going on the night the boat reached Louisville, Kentucky. Now imagine you've never heard a steam engine in your life, you're looking at both the sun and the moon. Somewhere there's a comet you can no longer see because the sun hadn't fully set and a haze had settled on the land. Then you hear the whistle and the engine as she lets off her steam. Why those people ran down to the river to see where the comet had landed and you know what they found? The *New Orleans* setting pretty as you please on their landing.

"The next day when Mr. Roosevelt had invited guests from town to dine on the boat, he was bothered they didn't believe it capable of going back upriver. So while they ate, he cast off, blew the whistle, and took them for a ride. His guests ran from their places in the dining room to look out on deck and what did they find? They were headed downstream. Now the next thing that happened was the Ohio Falls."

"There's falls on the Ohio River?"

"Yes there are falls, and those men had to get the boat over them or through them, but the water level on the river was too low for the *New Orleans*. She had a draft of twelve feet. When they left Louisville several of the town's citizens had waved goodbye and farewell never expecting to see the boat again. You see, they knew about the falls, and they also knew if the boat ever got to them, the current would be too strong for the boat to overcome.

But, since the boat couldn't navigate the falls yet, Roosevelt turned it back upstream and went all the way back to Cincinnati, sailing right past Louisville waving as they went.

"While in port at Cincinnati, Mrs. Roosevelt gave birth to her baby and because of recent rains upstream the river began to rise. Without delay Roosevelt loaded his new family on board and took off for the Ohio falls. At Louisville they had another delay. The weather had brought no change and no rain to the region, yet the river was still rising. The sun shown through the mist like a "globe of red hot iron," and the moon followed in the east. Everyone was so stunned at the sight the ship's captain was afraid to move. What did it mean? Everything was still, and not even the animals which frequented the river for a drink would go near it.

"Day after day the scene repeated itself and people were praying to God to deliver them, believing the world was at an end. Then in the last week of November, Roosevelt made the decision to go on while the water was up, although his crew thought he was crazy. The mist which covered the land made navigating the falls impossible. They steamed away once again and this time for good."

"You mean they perished?"

"You'll know soon enough what happened. Well, no matter what Mother Earth was doing, they had to make an attempt at a run around the falls. Mrs. Roosevelt had refused to stay ashore and stood near the stern watching. She knew her husband and she was putting her life and the life of their newborn son in his hands. Now, the only way you can steer a boat downstream is if the paddle wheels are turning and the boat is going faster than the current. When they reached the falls, they had to be perfect, almost wouldn't do and they couldn't see. If they made one wrong move the boat would end up a wreck and a failure by any man's measure. As they approached the falls the boat was going nearly twice the speed of the water in the river, but speed is just what they needed. They were able to steer the huge behemoth of a ship and drove it right through the narrow gap and around the boat went of its own volition, caught up in the current beneath the falls. Shouting quick orders down to the engine room got them quickly out of harms way. Had they not worked quickly enough, the current would have pulled them in under the falls and destroyed the boat. With the new family dog sitting beside Mrs. Roosevelt the vessel was once again under way.

"Soon the boat turned into the Mississippi and that's when tragedy struck. That night, just as the men had put out the anchor for the evening the earth began to heave and shake, trees were uprooted, ground where a person stood just fell away and great holes were made in the earth's surface. The riverbanks shook and suddenly the big boat became a little toy in the hands of Mother Nature."

"Is that why none of the animals went near the river?"

"I'm afraid so."

"Gosh, how did they know?"

"I don't know the answer to that son, but they do know. I'm certain of it."

"Was the moon and the sun still red?"

"Now that I don't know, but let's pretend it was."

"I wish I could have seen it."

"It all happened right where you're sitting. It was called the great earthquake of 1811 and rightly so. New Madrid sits on a fault line of some sort and that night she gave way. The Mississippi river used to run straight south, but now because of the earthquake she swirls around in all sorts of directions. It's twice as far to go downriver as it used to be. There's not a straight stretch on it south of here.

"December 6ᵗʰ, 1811 in Charleston, South Carolina the cold winter night was shattered by a sudden ringing of the bells at St. Phillips' church. The entire town awakened to feel the ground moving beneath them. In Boston they felt it too, New York and all the way to Maine. Later in February, 1812 came a hard shock which finished the backwash now known as Reelfoot Lake. The earthquake of 1811 and 1812 was felt over the entire United States.

"Anyway the waters of the old river began to rush from one bank to another, pitching the little boat to and fro like a ship on the ocean. And then suddenly they decided to pull up anchor and head downriver where things would be much better. They were wrong. South of here where the river flowed backwards they got caught in the current which was stronger than any normal current. All they could do was throw anchor and hope it held. They watched as whole trees rushed by and treetops which were now under water raised back up, then fell again. Mother Earth was not done. For two days they were caught right there and the river flowed backwards all that time filling up a great cavity which had opened up in Tennessee. Had the river run backwards any longer they might not have made it, but as things were, they survived to tell their story. They had a few holes to patch here and there but the *New Orleans* never sank and soon they made their way downriver toward Natchez to make repairs.

"The Mississippi river was no longer in the same shape as when Roosevelt had recorded his soundings two years before. The earthquake had changed everything. As they sailed south toward Natchez they passed New Madrid, Hayti, and Caruthersville and had to ignore the plight of the destitute people on shore. Everything had been toppled wrong side up, torn from their very grasp in some cases. Only when the boat reached Natchez Under the Hill did the crew learn the extent of what had happened from the people in that part of the country, and reports were still coming in.

"Entire farms had disappeared, people vanished without a trace, and animals were gone. If you can name it, no doubt it disappeared during that disaster. For two days flocks of birds blackened the horizon not wanting to settle anywhere for fear the earth would move again. Many wild animals and people were drowned in the river and began to wash up on shore. Indians were terrified and tried to get away to anywhere, but ended up going nowhere. People up and down the river begged Roosevelt to take them aboard, though he steadfastly refused to give into their fear. Indians at times shouted war whoops and several times they tried to attack the smoke belching monster they believed had turned their world upside down. It was during one of these attacks the boat caught fire.

"One of Mrs. Roosevelt's servants had placed some wood too near the stove in her forward cabin. With great undertaking, the fire was extinguished and the boat was once again saved.

"As they sailed south the earthquake was by no means finished. Whole islands in the river disappeared before their very eyes. Still the ground shook, the river groaned and the boat was tossed from side to side as the crew sailed south. When the boat next put in to take on wood it was learned that the Indians were calling the boat *"Penelore."* To the local Indians it was a sign of the devil or the Devil's Canoe.

"New threats to the boat and its occupants occurred almost daily to the point no one could sleep. The boat would have to navigate over the tops of completely engulfed forests, watch a new channel develop and take it to who knew where. Trees were everywhere in the water, floating downstream, still standing erect only fifty feet below the water's surface threatening to entangle the boat and still standing ashore as if nothing at all had happened."

"Wow, is all of that true?"

"I wouldn't have told you if it wasn't. Look son, this old river is not for the faint of heart. It will kill you if you aren't careful. I'm telling you these things so that you might one day be able to handle whatever comes your way, just like Roosevelt and his crew did."

"Is that important?"

"What is important is the fact a man can never quit. Once you know what you're about, and where you're going, you must go. Don't wait around for someone else to make a decision, it'll never happen. You do what you know to do and head where you know you're headed and everything else will fall into place."

Our transportation arrived and we quickly made haste to settle the skiff into position on the wagon. We had so much trouble with that little step I determined to develop an easier way of hauling the thing from now on. As we bounced along the road to Cape Girardeau, I let my thoughts turn to just how I could make our traveling better.

A man likes his comfort, young or old he has things he's used to and I was putting myself into more and more uncomfortable positions all the time. I wanted to rest and I did. My so-called thoughts came to nothing and when I awoke we had stopped to eat. The four of us sat around a small fire and ate a couple of recently killed rabbits.

Jobe and Mick would never be the cook Mrs. Foster was, but then how could they be? I had half of one rabbit and Bobby was glad for half of one. There was nothing else to eat so we fairly cleaned those rabbit bones.

Sitting around the fire like we were I naturally began to talk, telling Bobby of things on the river. The two old Negro's listened.

"It is better to hasten danger than to linger in the shadows, from a saying of Captain T. P. Leathers."

"The captain of the *Natchez*?"

"Not the folks you met, but Bowling's father. He pilots a riverboat too."

"Wow, no wonder they're so good."

"Sort of runs in the family. Anyway, he's right. If I wasn't hastening danger I would be at greater risk with less control over the outcome."

"So it's better to go headlong into a situation rather than standing about debating what might happen?"

"You catch on quick, son. That's exactly what I'm saying. Most times if you wait, the opportunity is lost."

"Is that what we're doing?"

"Yes it is. We're going to dive in head first and if we're lucky we'll be past the Federals before they know it."

"They got's no reason to come dis way," our chaperone said.

"Bobby, the *Natchez* was sporting a pair of antlers hanging high above the wheelhouse between the two stacks. Did you happen to see them?"

"I sure did. What are they for?"

"Those antlers represent speed and supremacy. They mean there's no other boat on the river at the moment that can outrun the *Natchez*. They're a badge of honor, but one day they'll be taken away by a newer, faster boat just as the *Natchez* took them from the *Princess*."

"You mean she'll lose them?"

"More than likely. There are new boats being built almost weekly now, even though the war is afoot. The war won't stop river travel, and in fact, will probably only increase it, but navigation will become more difficult and dangerous."

"What would happen if we found a couple of old axles with wheels and attached them to the boat upside down and put a harness neck on it? Could we pull it by horse or mule then?"

"Bobby, you're a genius. That would work perfectly, and we wouldn't even have to take the wheels off, just flip it over and roll it down into the river. Those wheels would make things much easier when it comes to tying on tree limbs and branches so that we only look like a tangle of logs floating down stream. If we paint the boat black inside and out the Yank's will never spot us."

"Will we still get to travel on the riverboats?"

"Of course, but mostly upstream. We can catch a ride downriver from time to time, but upstream is where we'll need the help."

"Good, I was afraid I might have outsmarted myself. I like riding on the big boats."

"We'll do our share of riding them son, no need to worry about that."

At the town of Cape Girardeau, Missouri we slid our skiff off of the back of the wagon in front of the Smithy's. He took one look at the boat and said, "I don't work on boats. I'm no boat builder."

"Old timer, I wouldn't have come to you, but I know you're capable of repairing an axle on a wagon or the wagon wheels, is that correct?"

"Generally, but this boat isn't a wagon."

"It will be. I want you to cut two holes right here on either side of the craft and insert two axles, one fore and one aft and I want wagon wheels at all four corners."

"And what are you planning to do with such a misfit?"

"What I plan to do with it is my own business. Can you do the job?"

"I can do it, but it will cost you."

"How much?"

"Hold on now, I need to know a few things. Do the front wheels need to turn and pivot like the wheels on a wagon?"

"I hadn't thought of that, but yes."

"Will it need a tongue like a wagon?"

"Yes, but can you make it removable so we can carry it in the boat while we're in the river?"

"The wheels will need to be rather large to keep the boat from dragging while you're on land, or we'll need to figure out a way to seal the boat if we locate the axle lower down."

"I can see I've come to the right man. How much do you figure your expertise will cost us?"

"I reckon about a hundred dollars. Fifty in Yankee green backs and fifty in Confederate notes," the old chiseller stated.

"Why such a strange request, smithy?"

"'Tis no more strange of a request than you asking me to outfit your skiff with wheels. One side or the other is going to lose this war and the side what loses won't have any good currency. Therefore, I want to collect half from either side. In such a way I can reduce my risk should my soldiers lose the war.

"Why, you ought to be in the state house. You make more sense than anything I've heard lately."

"And sir you ought to be in the nut house. I'll build your boat, but if you get blown to smithereens on the river it shan't be my fault. I'll have a clear conscience all the way to the bank."

"How long will it take you to complete the work?"

"About two weeks if I work late every night. I won't shun my other responsibilities just to take care of you."

"Two weeks will have to do. What's your name good man?"

"The name is Tuck Dyer and I'll need some type of payment up front."

"Tuck stands for Tucker I take it?"

"It does."

"Well Tucker, sixty five in Confederate notes is all I have on me. The Yankee green backs I'll have to acquire."

"Fifty in Confederate is fine, be sure the rest comes in the color of green. Is the boy with you?"

"Yes, his name is Bobby Louden and I'm Captain Grimes."

"Pleasure to meet you, Bobby," he said shaking the kid's hand. "The riverboat pilot Captain Grimes?"

"You have me pegged."

"All right, for you it will be forty and forty. That's the best I can do."

"Sounds like a deal."

Taking out my wallet I paid the man his first forty in Confederate notes and saved the rest for our adventure. Up the street we found a place to eat and milled about listening to the talk of war. It was in my mind to find someone who could help us with the boat whenever we might need help. Without question, I would need stock to pull such a contraption past the Yankee's and horse stock would need to be at Engler's Landing for each return trip. We would be bringing the stock upriver while pulling our boat, but the animals would need to be returned to the south.

"What do we do now?" Bobby asked.

"We find someone who can return our stock to this place once we get upriver."

"What stock?"

"The horses or mules we get to pull our boat home. We can get home, but the animals will need to be here whenever we return from Mississippi."

"Where will we get the animals?"

"I'm still thinking on that one, but we're halfway home because of your brilliance. Putting wheels on the boat was a great idea. It will save us both time and money."

"We're halfway home?"

"At least halfway, and now we seek a solution."

"What if we don't find someone?"

"We'll find someone. I'll make the necessary arrangements just like we did with Mr. Dyer." Pausing I added, "Bobby, let's go for a walk. A walk all the way back to St. Louis. We need to get our return mail home and pick up the next batch. We can do that while the boat's being prepared."

"That's a long way to walk, but it will do us good, give us time to think."

Draping my mail bag over my shoulder we started out. We'd had a fine meal, and the town of Cape Girardeau was not offering me the selection of folks I wanted to choose help from. There was Bobby, but I wanted him with me just in case I needed cover.

Now our wagon ride with Jobe had been in the bootheel country of southeast Missouri and up until now the land about us had been the lower river bottom country of the Mississippi. As we left Cape Girardeau the hills rose up before us and we began to climb. From here on we would be in the lower Missouri foothills. Bobby complained not a wit and did his best to keep up with me. It was hot and thirsty work. We spied a small stream and made for it. As we drank deeply, a wagon and team topped over the hill behind us and we waited, knowing the man would probably water his horses in the same creek. We weren't off the road but a few feet, and we stood waiting.

"Good afternoon," the gentleman said as he rolled his wagon to a stop and let his horses drink. I couldn't help notice the rifle on the seat wagon which was pointed in our direction and handy to his right hand. The weapon was one of the best of recent efforts by arms manufactures to improve on the old and tired cap and ball weapons. This rifle was one of Greene's Carbine's and a fine weapon it was. I had handled such a weapon before, but at the time I had no interest in handling the breach loader.

"We could use a ride if you are headed north. We've got to get all the way back to St. Louis this week," I said.

"What's in your bag?"

"Mail. We're hauling mail to and from home for the soldiers."

"Confederate soldiers?" he asked.

"Yes sir, down to Mississippi and back."

"I got a couple of sons down that away. I reckon I'll be glad to find out about your mail run. Wouldn't mind hearing from them. Hop aboard, mister."

"The name is Captain Grimes, and the boy here is Bobby Louden."

"The pleasure is mine. My name is Jacob Renfroze and the Z is silent."

"You have a Z in your name?"

"R E N F R O Z E! Like I said the Z is silent. I can get you as far as the next twenty miles or so, but after that you'll have to depend on someone else. Hop on," he repeated.

We climbed on the back of his wagon and settled in for a lazy afternoon ride. I napped while Bobby peppered Mr. Renfroze with questions. A good part of the afternoon was spent with Bobby guiding the horses and learning from the old man. He had three sons in the war, two on the Confederate side and one down here fighting for the north somewhere, a situation he grumbled about constantly.

"My luck is them boys will kill one another before they recognize each other over the barrel of their guns and they'll leave me no grandchildren at all."

Late in the day we ambled onto the farm of Jacob Renfroze and met his lovely wife who insisted we stay for dinner.

"We've had an empty table of late and it wouldn't be no trouble at all," she said.

"We'd be mighty thankful for the company," Jacob added.

"Well, if you insist," I finally gave in.

"Ma, set those places while the captain and I jaw for a minute."

"Something on your mind?" I asked.

"Can you get mail to my sons, the ones fighting for south?"

"If they're anywhere about, I'll get it to them."

"There's spare bedrooms in the house and I'd take it kindly if you'd stay the night. Give me and Ma a chance to write them, and in the morning I'll give you a ride as far as Bloomsdale."

"That's fifty miles."

"Maybe, but I have kin folk up that way I haven't seen in over a year. Sort of give me a chance to catch up on family matters and see what everyone else is up to."

"Mr. Renfroze, we don't need all this help. You'd just be setting yourself up for trouble if the Yankee's showed up anywhere on the road."

"I can handle any of them Yankee's. In fact, I'm in a unique position to do just that. If for any reason we get stopped we can tell them we are headed north to St. Louis to sign up for the Federals."

"I guess we could at that."

"Darn tootin' we could. This here war is just getting up a good head of steam. They won't give us a second look if we give them that story."

"Come to think of it, I still have my orders to report to Jefferson Barracks. That should be a convincer if anyone doubts our story."

"You have orders to report to Jefferson Barracks?"

"I did have. I reported last year with some friends to the post commander General Grey and he was too busy to see us. We didn't want to get in any trouble and then we walked out," I said fishing in my coat for the orders, touching it to confirm its presence.

"Perfect, I'll get the horses put away and we'll wash up for dinner."

Bobby went with Jacob to tend the horses and I took up soap and water to wash my hands before setting up in the Renfroze household. The lady of the house stepped to the door and invited me in as I finished, so I went with her. She was a small woman in size but for what she lacked in size she made up for in spirit. She chewed tobacco and spit in her spittoon with amazing skill. When I commented on her ability I got my answer.

"If I happen to miss my cup I have to clean up the mess. I don't miss often."

Her long black hair was tied into braids on either side of her head and she wore a blue checked dress while she worked.

"Don't get much company now that the war's started," she commented, her back to me

"I guess it's the same all over. Folks are afraid to move about much."

"You sure seem to be moving about."

"That's because I'm on a fool's errand."

"And what would that be?"

"I plan to deliver mail to the soldiers down in Mississippi who hail from the state of Missouri."

"My goodness, you do have a dangerous errand, and with all them Yankee's nosing about."

"There's Yankee's about?"

"Well, not so much now but a few weeks ago they came over this way from the river looking things over trying to get the lay of the land. Burned the Simpson place to the ground and killed the old man when he told them to get off'n his place. I guess his mistake was all his boys signed with the Confederate army. That and he pulled his shotgun on them."

"You haven't seen any since?"

"No, but they're about. We still hear tell of an incident here or there and none of it good."

"Do yourself a favor and never mention the fact you know me. If my suspicions are correct it won't be long before they figure out who I am and what I'm doing. When they find out what I'm up to, it'll be best if you and your husband have never heard of me."

"Why captain," she said, "I've never even heard of you and you sitting right here at my table, the shame of it all," she said as she began dipping stew.

Just then the front door opened and Jacob returned with Bobby. They took their seats and Mrs. Renfroze began to stack the food on the table in front of us. The old man dug in and motioned for us to do the same while the lady of the house stood watch over the three of us, making sure we were satisfied.

After dinner we men settled down outside on the front porch and began to talk. There were things I needed to consider, so I was doing some thinking at the same time.

The sun was beginning to sink behind the trees to the west when Bobby said, "Mr. Renfroze, is that a wolf chasing your horses across the pasture?"

Without saying a word Renfroze got up from his seat and disappeared into the house. A moment later he emerged with a rifle and leveled it against his shoulder squeezing the trigger. The wolf nose-dived into the ground and Jacob lowered his rifle. The one horse the wolf had cornered trotted off a ways and then turned around to look at his disabled assailant. Winnie, his wife was at the door by then and he handed her the rifle.

"I guess we'll be eating wolf meat for the next few days honey," Jacob said.

"It cooks the same as any other," Winnie replied.

Chapter 12

As things turned out Jacob's home was on the outskirts of Perryville and after riding north we found ourselves near Crystal City. We walked over to Nealy's landing and caught the steamer *Ohio* for St. Louis. From there it was small work to reach Lemay Ferry and put the mail back into the hollow oak tree at the graveyard. Working our way around Jefferson Barracks was a mite tricky, but nothing two healthy fellows like Bobby and I couldn't handle. From there we made our way to the Foster home and I found myself in a state of shock as my fiancée was present.

"Lucy?" I half mumbled under my breath in disbelief.

"Oh Ab, I'm so glad to see you," she said as she ran down to meet me, almost tackling me at the creek.

"What are you doing here?"

"You're not happy to see me?" she said taking a step back.

I pulled her back to me and whispered into her ear, "Darling, you know I'm happy to see you, I just never expected you'd be here."

"Well, wherever else should I be since you and Evelyn figured out our relationship to one another? Evelyn wrote me immediately and asked for me to come. She said I would be of great assistance in helping you with your mission and her with the children."

I looked up the hill to see Evelyn smiling down on our happy reunion and realized she was a woman in a class all her own. We continued to hug one another. I finally pulled back and kissed my fiancée like I should have in the beginning and then I took another measure of the woman I had asked to marry me. Evelyn had been correct, for Lucy was no less beautiful when the two were placed side by side.

"My dear, this young man is Bobby Louden," I said, suddenly aware of the young fellow standing behind me.

"It's a pleasure to meet you, Bobby. My name is Lucy. If you men will come on up to the house, I'm certain we can find the wherewithal to feed the two of you."

Lucy took my hand, and we began to climb the small ridge from the creek to the cabin. As we neared the porch Evelyn spoke up.

"I'm glad to see you've completed your first mail run without encountering any severe trouble, captain."

"So am I. I hope, Mrs. Foster, that you will forgive my current condition. My travels have taken longer than I had originally expected and caused me to neglect my personal hygiene these last few days."

"Under the circumstances, captain I can't complain of your attire or condition. Who might the young man with you be?"

"This young buccaneer is Bobby Louden and a genius he is too. Why if it weren't for him I'd be having no end of trouble."

"Well then I'll see to it he gets an extra piece of my apple pie."

"If you fellows will wash up, I'll help Evelyn get dinner ready," Lucy said.

We stumbled back down to the creek and fairly dove in, knowing we were in the presence of two grand ladies. I had removed my shoes, socks and shirt while Bobby watched. He then followed suit. We were both standing in the shallow pool I had created on my last trip when Lucy appeared with a clean change of clothes for the both of us.

"Evelyn said Bobby could wear some of Shelby's things until we got your clothes clean. I'll leave them on the rock and, gentlemen, no one will be watching."

"Thank you," I said as she turned and walked back to the cabin.

"What did she mean, no one will be looking?"

"I believe they want us to bathe completely and thoroughly young man. As gentlemen we have no alternative but to oblige them."

Bobby was shy at first and uncomfortable about being naked in front of another man, but I assured him it was a common thing among men and women alike, but that it was not common for the two sexes to bathe together. He finally stripped and took up the soap Lucy had delivered with the clothes and began to wash. When we were finished, we dressed in the clean clothes and left our filthy dungarees on top of the rock in a pile. Lord knows we didn't want to get dirt on our hands before we set up to dinner.

We sat down on the front porch, and after a minute Bobby laid his head back and rested while flat on his back. It wasn't long before I was doing the same thing. I must have been bone tired because I awoke to Lucy running a feather under my nostrils. I sat bolt upright from a dead sleep.

"Dinner is ready, my love."

I looked over at Bobby and he was choking back a laugh.

"Is something funny, my young friend?"

"You are."

Before he could finish implicating me I had him pinned against the porch and was tickling him.

"How's this for funny?" I asked as I continued to rack his ribcage. "I'll show you funny."

"Absalom Grimes!" I heard Lucy yell from behind me.

I finally let go and Bobby scrambled up to the porch to get away from me.

"Seems to me everybody here wants to play. I was just joining the fun," I vented.

"Well, dinner is ready. The fun can wait."

"That's easy to say after you have had your fun," I said as I began to stalk my fiancée.

"Absalom Grimes don't you dare tickle me!" she commanded as she backed ever closer to the cabin door for safety.

Suddenly there were the faces of the Foster children grinning in the doorway and I knew if I pursued my love any further she would turn and sprawl on the living room floor as she tripped over the little mongrels. Sparing her the embarrassment of falling over them, I ceased my chase and straightened to a gentlemanly demeanor so she would know my pursuit was over.

"I owe you though," I said as I ascended the porch steps.

Inside I couldn't help but notice the Foster children were looking at me as if they were no longer afraid of me. What had I done, I wondered. I'd had them exactly where I wanted them and now they seemed to have no fear of me. The little monsters had, on the spur of the moment, been unleashed by my own shortsightedness.

Bobby and I took our seats and Evelyn wouldn't let me sit anywhere but the head of the table. The women flanked me with a child on each side and Bobby sat at the far end.

We said grace, and Bobby looked at me as if he hadn't really known me before. I guess I had been neglectful on the trail, but we were home for now and nothing short of grace before a meal would do, especially with such tattletale witnesses as the Foster children present. I knew their kind. They would ask questions which seemed innocent enough, but the questions they asked would all be aimed at getting a man into trouble. I knew they would mean nothing intentional, but troublesome they would be just the same. Kids were not something I tolerated very well and I knew the Foster children would be no different.

I heard a peacock just then and knew my Lucy had brought them from home. She loved peacocks hanging about in the trees, all day scratching here and squawking there. She had brought her banty rooster and other small animals to help her feel more comfortable in a home not her own. Somehow the two women had conspired to make sure I was cared for whenever I returned from one of my mail runs and, the amazing thing was, I understood exactly what they were up to. There would be safety in numbers and in the ability of their minds to work as one.

I could tell we would want for nothing as our care was assured. After dinner, Bobby and I went to work to put up more wood and I learned Bobby was quite adept at swinging an axe and wedge. He said swinging an axe did a young man good, said it put meat on the bones. I had no reason to argue with him for I had swung an axe many a time in my life and the experience had left me with stronger than usual arms. From that day forward, I attributed my large arms to the axe swinging.

We worked along the creek clearing more trees for a better view of the opposing fields which rolled away from the cabin's front porch. It was a time we had figuring just which trees would accent the view and which ones would be a bother. Mrs. Foster offered her expertise later in the evening and when the sun was setting we sat on the front porch and rested from a long day's work. We had a good look at our efforts, and I knew tomorrow we would be removing tree stumps. We had our view, but the stumps along the creek were a distraction.

As darkness descended, Lucy walked with me down to the creek and we talked of the future, our future, and what the war might bring.

"Why didn't you say anything to me about what you planned to do, Ab? You know I would support anything you desire to pursue."

"Everything developed too fast, and I wanted to protect you from suspicion. From the time I last saw you until now, I've been engaged in gathering and delivering the mail. Just the same, I'm glad Evelyn put two and two together and sent for you." I kissed her then and held her close.

"I don't really see what I can do to help you."

"Just be here. If you don't do anything else, please be here whenever I return from one of my trips into Mississippi," I begged. Her presence was a sobering deterrent for my feelings toward Mrs. Foster and rightfully so.

"I'll be here for you, Ab. You just be certain not to get hurt."

"I'm quite possibly the only man qualified to do what I do. Sam might be able to run the Yankee blockades, but I thought of the venture and I believe if done correctly the experience may lead to greater things."

"What kind of things?"

"I don't know, but the postal service of the United States has contracts with T. P. Leathers to run the mail from New Orleans to Vicksburg. I wonder if he's still running his mail now that the war's started."

"What are you thinking?"

"I was just wondering. With the Yankee's in control of St. Louis, New Orleans, and Baton Rouge, if he was able to move upstream from New Orleans to Vicksburg. If the Yankee's are controlling New Orleans the same way they are handling St. Louis, he can't move without risk of being blown out of the water. Vicksburg is in the hands of the Confederate's. Holmes on the *Princess* may have the same trouble."

"You mean the normal channels of mail have stopped?"

"That's exactly what I mean. There's no mail getting in or out of the southern states except for what I'm doing. The question is, how does the mail move now?"

"Well, I think you should concentrate on getting mail to and from the boys who are from Missouri. Let someone else handle the rest of the southern states."

"You don't think I should worry about the rest?"

"If Evelyn and I know anything about the widow Caroline LeRoy Webster, she'll have you loaded down with so much mail you'll need a full team of horses to move it before long."

"You're probably right. I'd be biting off more than I could chew. Her late husband, Daniel was quite the organizer."

Unexpectedly our conversation broke off. The sound of hoof falls greeted my ears and I stiffened. I looked around to see where the sound came from and who was making it. The only reasonable answer I could conceive was Yankee horse soldiers, but my eyes landed on my old friend, Mark who was sitting on the back of a Tennessee stud. I know this because I once owned the horse he was riding.

"Mark, what a pleasure to see you. What brings you over this way?"

"I was looking for an old friend. Somebody said there was word out for a traitor in these parts and I knew they weren't talking about anybody but my old bosom buddy, Absalom Grimes."

"Step down off that old walker and join us up at the cabin. It'll be good to talk with you. How're things up at the home place?"

"Things are just fetching up Hannibal way, its down here I'm worried about."

"What do you mean?"

"The Federals are onto your game already. They're looking for you quite diligently and offering a substantial reward for your capture should someone turn you in."

"That's impossible. How could I be such a wanted man already? The war has barely begun," I protested.

"That's what I believed initially. Here, you'd better have a look at this," he said handing me the document which confirmed his news.

I was confounded. How could I already be wanted and with a reward no less? Someone must have slipped up, but who and where, not to mention how? Immediately my mission took on a bleak and dire consequence. My illusions of grandeur and heroism suddenly evaporated before my eyes and I reached up to rub my neck making sure I still had one.

"I thought you might like to know before you walk into a trap."

"Thanks, old friend. I'm glad you're watching out for me."

Stepping down from his horse, Mark walked over toward my Lucy and introduced himself to Mrs. Foster who had just joined us.

"The name is Mark Twain, ma'am."

"Evelyn Foster."

"I'm sorry, Mark, I should have introduced you right off. I never had the chance to tell you about Evelyn and you know my fiancée Lucy."

"Yes, you've told me of her, but you never mentioned her beauty."

"That's because I didn't want your daydreaming mind worrying about her. As I said, she's my fiancée. And Mrs. Foster is happily married."

"Your words of warning lash at my heart, old friend. I would never betray your trust where a lady is concerned. Nor is there any other reason I could think of."

"That's good to know because I'll be many days on the road thinking of my Lucy and I wouldn't want to have to add worry to my mission."

"Ab," Lucy chided me. "I'm surprised at you carrying on in such a manner."

"Yes, Ab, so am I," Mark responded.

We heard the horses. This time I suspected our luck had run out, for through the trees and following Mark's trail were seven Union horse soldiers. They were looking for someone and my gut told me that someone was Mark.

"Gentlemen, I believe we've found the rabble we were looking for," the lieutenant said as he drew his Colt Dragoon revolver from its holster.

I was immediately wary. Mark had half turned to meet them as they came in and I stepped forward to stand beside him. Might be I couldn't help at all, but I wasn't about to let them have my friend, not if I could prevent it.

"Unbuckle your gun mister," the lieutenant commanded as he brought his mount to a halt only a few feet away.

"Hold on there, young man." I stepped between them. "What's this all about?"

"We've followed this man from a Rebel encampment. He's our prisoner.

I laughed. "Mark is no Rebel soldier. He's been ordered to report to Jefferson Barracks to pilot a riverboat, me along with him." Reaching into my lapel pocket I cautiously withdrew my draft notice which had been doctored, and handed the document up to the soldier. "Mark's reads the same as mine. Show him, Mark."

Mark produced his and I held my breath not knowing if Mark had doctored his in any way. The lieutenant began to lower his pistol.

"We trailed this horse all the way from an enemy camp. I don't suppose you can explain what you were doing there."

"Sir, if I was in the company of the enemy I never knew such. I simply stopped to have a bite to eat. They invited me to their fire and I accepted."

"There was no talk about the war and what they intended to do?"

"If there was talk they said naught in front of me."

"The two of you are riverboat pilots?"

"Yes sir. We grew up on the river and just as soon as we have enough wood set in for the ladies we intend to honor these orders," I spoke up.

The lieutenant looked over toward the woodpile and confirmed what I had told him. The woodpile was not sufficient for the women if their men were about to go off to war.

"Don't deliberate too long, gentlemen. Your orders have nearly expired. I reckon we were on a wild goose chase," he said as he handed our letters back.

I reached back and handed Mark his own orders without diverting my attention from the men in front of me. Suddenly an idea developed in my head so quickly I offered it up without planning.

"Sir, if you wouldn't mind, we'd like you to keep an eye on our home for us if you are going to be assigned to this area. No telling what kind of rabble our womenfolk might have to fend off while we're away."

"It would be my pleasure, captain. The name is Lieutenant Bledsoe of the Cincinnati Fifth."

"If you ever see the wood pile low, lieutenant, the girls can cook, providing you do a few chores around the place. But remember your manners. The ladies do belong to us," I expressed heartily. Mrs. Foster really didn't, but they had no need of knowing one way or the other.

There had been little time to engage in idle leisure. Chores needed doing and the fact the women would be looked after by the concerned Yankee horse soldiers eased my mind a bit. The Federals already held most of Missouri, a fact not likely to change. I considered our young lieutenant an asset and counted the ladies lucky. They would not want while we men were away at war.

Time to make the next run came all too soon, but when one has work to do, he does it. Bobby and I made our way to Lemay Ferry and gathered our mail then skedaddled back around Jefferson Barracks on the south side of town and headed downriver. This time we were on horseback for I had made the necessary arrangements to help us establish our scheme, and I had managed to acquire one hundred dollars in Yankee greenbacks so we could dislodge our vessel from the hands of Tucker Deal in Cape Girardeau.

Warning was riding the wind and Federal troops were all about us as we picked our way carefully southward. They were present in Cape Girardeau when we got there so we swung wide of the town and continued south. Bobby had some concerns about the mail bag being so visible to anyone who might notice two horsemen, and his concerns did nothing to ease my unrest.

I was putting my head on the line and well I knew it. Bobby, too, was at risk of exposure. How on earth were we going to get through the Yankee's this time? The first trip had been all too easy.

After two days ride we were in Arkansas when they saw us. I watched as the horse soldiers made a bee-line in our direction and I turned to Bobby.

"You sit here and act like you don't know me. I'll hide the mail in the swamp somewhere, maybe a tree stump or something, but if they get me it will be up to you to go in and retrieve it and deliver it."

Putting spurs to my horse I rode into the swamp and continued south. I was under no illusions. If caught I would be in serious trouble. I knew the Mississippi and I knew my way around steamboats, but the swamp was something else altogether.

I heard someone shouting where I had left Bobby on higher ground and I gritted my teeth. If they hurt that boy I was going to be plenty sore. A pistol sounded at the same time a tree spat bark into my face. The soldiers were coming and I had to ditch my bag. My only saving grace was that I still wore the trappings of a riverboat captain, hat and all.

I rode through the waist deep water and swung from side to side as I rode, offering no steady target to shoot at. The depth of the swamp water remained knee high but the trees surrounding me were getting thicker and bigger. Soon I was only a shadow moving through the underwater forest. Late in the evening, I spotted a broken off tree with a hollow stump. I stashed the dispatches I was carrying and started making my way back to dry land. For this maneuver I headed toward the Mississippi River.

As I approached the mile wide portion of the Mississippi, I turned back to the north and eventually made my way to where I had last seen Bobby, the point at which the soldiers had began their pursuit. Bobby was not there and neither were they. It was dark now and I had little to go on until I saw tracks on the ground. I pulled off my blanket roll and camped near the spot that night.

In the wee hours of the morning as the sky began to gray and a mist settled into the bottomland near the Mississippi River, I studied the ground in front of me. Looking at horseshoe markings on the ground, I surmised the Yankee's had not taken Bobby at all. He had headed into the swamp behind me once the soldiers were out of sight. There was only one thing to do. Return to the swamp, retrieve Bobby and my mail bag and continue on to Dixie.

Suddenly it dawned on me Bobby had spent the night in the swamp. Not even I wanted to do such a miserable thing, yet Bobby had gone into the murky quarter knowing he would have no other choice. My estimation and stock in the young man had just gone up. Bobby was carrying out assignments grown men would hesitate to perform. He was not making excuses as to why he couldn't go into the swamp; he had tackled the mission without delay.

I stepped into the stirrup, lifted myself aboard my horse and eased back into the swamp, once again following the same path I had navigated the day before. After a half hour in the swamp the trees once again closed in around me and I knew I was in the general vicinity of where I had stashed the mail bag. From time to time I called out for Bobby, but I was greeted by the lonely silence of the swamp.

At noon, I realized I was going in circles and nowhere nearer my mail. I swung wider, still calling out for Bobby from time to time. The silence which greeted me was eerie. I began to doubt Bobby's ability to survive a night in a swamp such as this. I thought back and remembered the cry of wild cats just before dark the night before and feared for my companion.

Just as I was about to give up on finding him or my mail, I heard him yell. The direction was deceiving and another thirty minutes was needed to close the gap between us, but Bobby was there and he was fine.

"I've been looking for the mail all day but I haven't seen where you put it."

"I've been looking for the mail all day and I'm the one who hid it. I'm thinking our mail bag may be lost for good," I said.

"What will we do, captain? We can't lose the mail."

"We may lose a lot of mail before this war is over. Think about it. We may have to drown the correspondence in the river if we encounter Federal troops at the wrong time. We may not have a choice."

"I guess I hadn't really thought of that."

"If they catch you with the mail in your hands you'll go to prison. That's why I should be the only one to actually carry the mail, but sometimes I may not be able to get through where you can."

"Is that why Mrs. Foster said you are on a fool's errand?"

His words slapped me in the face. "That's exactly why she said such a thing."

"I don't think she's right. I think you're doing what needs to be done and no man is better equipped to handle such danger."

"I appreciate that son, but we'd better get out of here unless we want to spend the night in the swamp."

"I wouldn't like staying the night again."

"Didn't figure you would. Come on, let's ride."

Turning our horses we rode west toward the Mississippi River once again. Our mail had been unintentionally misplaced in the Arkansas swamp. We could spend weeks looking for the spot where I had hidden the bag and never find it. We considered our misfortune a lesson learned and counted our lucky stars we were still together. Our second trip south had been altogether different than our first excursion.

When we arrived at the Confederate troops camp in Corinth, Mississippi there was disappointment written all over the soldiers faces when they discovered we had to abandon the mail in a swamp. There would be no mail call this trip, but they felt better after sitting down and writing home. The fact was, Shelby Foster had received the only letter I had managed to hold onto, as I carried it in my lapel. For two days we stayed in camp with the Missouri fighters and when we rode out our saddle bags were full of correspondence for our return trip to St. Louis. I also had a return letter in my lapel pocket for Evelyn.

I had not recognized Shelby Foster right off this time because he had changed. He was no longer the bedraggled looking soldier I'd witnessed on my first trip, but a clean shaven well-groomed sergeant who was in command of a platoon of regulars. Something had changed him. Had it been the mail from home?

As we made our way back to the river, we picked up other mail for the folks back home in Missouri. Twelve units in all had filled our saddlebags to overflowing. At Yazoo City we received a new mail bag and put the mail in it, allowing us to carry food in our saddlebags. At Vicksburg we crossed over by ferry and found ourselves in Louisiana where we floated down the river enjoying the scenery. Soon after skirting the Federal troops in the harbor at Baton Rouge found ourselves near Plantation Bell Grove, a six thousand acre Garden of Eden south of town. The owner was one John Andrews who was away in France on business. William E. Clements was running the plantation in his stead.

Belle Grove was situated on the river below the capitol, some eight or nine hundred miles from St. Louis, I believed. At first I'd had misgivings about traveling so far south, but the Yankee's weren't trying to control the river down here like they were up north, although they did have designs on Baton Rouge.

They were guarding the riverboats, but not making everyone they saw heave to. I wasn't sure exactly what the reason for the difference was, but I was glad for the lack of attention just the same.

Now in this part of the country I could see myself settling down. A few yards from the water's edge there was a road which during high water seemed impassable. The road ran along the levy at times and at others the path led right down to the water. Large oak trees were graced with the presence of purple, pink and white azalea bushes, which blossomed and rose to a height of ten feet tall, blended with the dripping Spanish moss which hung from the limbs of the old oak trees to create the most serene and calm picture I had ever witnessed. At some places folks had lined their property with waist high white picket fences and these fences would follow the river road for miles, offering green grass and an assortment of unlikely flowers for their owners. We could have floated all the way to New Orleans, mesmerized by the stunning beauty of one plantation after another lining the riverfront, but alas duty called.

We docked our boat and sauntered up to the house known as Belle Grove. The jubilant caregiver made certain we were treated like royalty on that night as Mr. Clements saw to our every need. The slaves he had about the place were the best specimens I had ever witnessed. The men were black as coal and stronger than most. The women were gentle and caring in every way. Our baths were the best I had ever encountered and our clothes were cleaned and tended to while we bathed. When we sat up to supper that evening we were outfitted in grand fashion and Bobby had a new set of clothes which actually fit and his first proper shave. I hardly recognized him.

"Captain, you're our guest for as long as you wish, or as often as you wish," the old man said. "Young master Bobby included."

"Thank you, sir, we're gratified beyond measure. Your hospitality is second to none," I replied as I took another bite of boiled crawfish, or mud bugs as he called them.

"Let's talk of the war, captain. Where do you see this nonsense heading?" he asked.

"I really have no idea, sir. If the south wins you shall retain your grand estate. If we succumb to defeat you may forfeit all. I'm doing my part to preserve a way of life which the Lord has seen fit to bless us with."

"Does the state no longer have the right to choose its own destiny?"

'That will be decided by the outcome of the war. For now we are sovereign, but if the south should loose, all sovereignty will be in the hands of the Federal government," I said.

"Damn those Yankee's thinking they can force us to stay in the Union."

"Be that as it may, Sir William, all hinges on the final outcome of the war. The northern states think they are fighting to keep us in the Union, but what they are really doing is creating a monster which no one can deal with, save for God."

I watched Bobby eat in silence as we talked of the war, the majestic grounds surrounding the plantation home and the types of crops Mr. Clements was growing. Mrs. Clements was a lady of grand stature. She filled the room with a calming presence and a sure-handed command of etiquette second to none. She was the sister of John Andrews who had no wife. The Clements children we learned were away at school in London, England. The old man had insisted that the boys get the same splendid education he had acquired from the old school; some place called Cambridge.

As we finished our supper we retreated to the drawing room and lit up a couple of stogies, the finest Cuban tobacco money could buy. I was awash with the idea that I might enjoy a good cigar in good company, although I had never tried one. Bobby joined us and had a bit of trouble trying to get used to the aura of a cigar. William had the windows opened to help the young man out and soon Bobby was doing quite well. Then I noticed he was a little pale and asked to be excused from the room. I pulled cautiously on my stogie, but Bobby had smoked himself sick and we both chuckled at the young man's expense. Tobacco could do that to you the first time you tried it, especially if it was a cigar you were tackling. I was turning a little green around the gills myself, but managed to withhold any evidence which might betray my condition.

"Captain, your cause is a noble one," Clements said. "Still, is there nothing you can do to aid your own army in victory?"

"I am doing just that, sir. The fellows whom I deliver mail to are highly motivated soldiers simply because they can look forward to word from home each month. Without the prospect of communication they would be a group of woebegone men."

"I see your point, captain, but still I believe you can do more."

"I don't quite follow the direction at which you are hinting."

"If you were to carry dispatches for the army you would be in no less danger of stirring the Federals ire towards you. I believe you have incensed them or there would not already be a price on your head. You could do no more damage to your reputation and you might do a great deal of good."

"I see what you mean. Since I'm running the blockades anyway, I should carry dispatches from one Confederate unit to the next."

"It's only a suggestion, yet it's that very kind of thing which might determine the outcome of the war. You are a visionary and with your skill at running the blockades the war could turn on your efforts alone."

"I've never considered such a position, sir. It seems to me that the only visionary in this room is you."

"On the contrary, you also know how to move into the future clearing a path which would benefit you and the ones you love. Is that not what a visionary is?"

"I'll take your word on it."

"Captain, I should like to hire your services. You're already risking your neck, but what I have in mind will endanger your neck no further."

"You have my attention, sir."

"John Andrews owns six thousand acres of land, captain and I should not like to lose an inch of her. I want you to find for me, if you will, a good smith who could chisel a set of plates with which to print Yankee greenbacks. I have a good enough smithy as far as smithy's go but he'll not have the education to produce such a detailed plate with which to print money from."

"Sir, I believe the process calls for four separate plates laid perfectly one over another."

"Now, that's something I didn't know. You're an interesting man, Captain Grimes."

"You sir are no less interesting. You have proven worthy of such a grand estate, one which is the envy of the south no doubt. How you managed to pull off such a grand vision, I have no clue, but my hat is off to the lot of you, sir."

"Vision is exactly the word. A man must first have a vision before he can attain anything. Without first the vision there is nothing to attain. Everything you see on this plantation was first only an idea in someone's head, small at first, but with time it grew more complete and detailed until now you see what lies before you."

Bobby walked back into the room looking a good deal better. His color was back and he had overcome his light-headedness as he told me later. He learned how to smoke a cigar that day, and from then on when offered one he had no trouble disposing of it in a manly fashion.

When we left Belle Grove we had an additional mission which seemed unusual to me, but who was I to judge? I had to find a smith which could make a set of plates for Mr. Clements.

As we made our way north, it was clear the Yankee's had made no meaningful incursion into Louisiana as of yet. The only folks we met were southerners and people of good spirit. They had high hopes for their boys in gray for they knew themselves to be in the right. Our hope that first summer had been anything but grim. Several battles of late had fallen to the southern column for victories and southern morale couldn't have been higher, yet the Yankee's were ever steadily making incursions and hard fought progress into southern territory.

Once into Arkansas we took a route which would let us enter the swamp where we had hidden our mail on the way down. Our hope was to retrieve the bag and carry on. Coming into the swamp from the south was a little tricky because we had never seen the south end of the marsh.

It was there and no mistake about it. The forest laden swamp water was deeper on the southern end. As luck would have it we found our parcel and struck out for the north immediately, not wanting to spend the night in the clutches of the scary bog.

I myself hadn't had much experience with wetlands because I was used to running a packet from St. Louis to St. Paul. Working to gain southern experience, I realized I had much to learn about such devilish places in the heart of Dixie. Notwithstanding,

Bobby was very adept at bringing me up to date on the subject of swamp survival from finding and eating turtle eggs to gathering roots for sassafras tea. I was supposed to be teaching him, but at times our relationship was the other way around.

We arrived back at the Cape to find our skiff outfitted with a new set of wheels and painted black. The inside was a dark red and the oars were slipped into place on the side and affixed permanently so that we wouldn't lose them. Tucker showed me how to dislodge them and put them to use, allowing how to re-secure them where they would not be lost. His engineering skills amazed me. I looked at him and wondered.

"Tucker, could you make a set of plates from these drawings," I said as I spread the papers out in front of him.

"Now captain, where did you come by such a thing?"

"That's a secret, but if we lose the war southerners are going to need money."

"I know, that's why I want to be paid half and half, but to create our own greenbacks; very slippery, captain, very slippery."

"Could you do such a thing?"

"I could, but I must have a press for the molds and that would take a great amount of luck or time, neither of which we can count on."

"What if I told you where to find the press?"

"Go on."

"How do I know you can be trusted with such information?"

"Captain," he smiled. "I have something to show you that will remove all doubt."

Turner walked over to the corner in the shop and pulled out a drawer where a drawer appeared not to be. From this hidden space he removed a burlap bag and opened it. Reaching into the bag he pulled out a piece of rectangular shaped burlap and un-wrapped the first of four plates.

"Now can you trust me? I had the idea months ago, but I still need a press to make it work."

"I'll give you directions to the man who can provide you with what you need. He'll more than gladly give you room and board on the greatest plantation the south has to offer, and Tucker, when you fellows have completely destroyed the Yankee monetary system, don't forget your old friend Captain Grimes."

"I'll never forget you, captain or young Bobby. Why, the two of you are the most fun I've had at my job in years. What do you say we get your boat hitched up and we'll both be on our way?"

We hooked harness to our skiff and tried the detachable seat he had made for the boat when it was being pulled on its wheels. The contraption was of better build than I could account for. If Tucker ever needed a job building steamboats I was certain he was suited to the task.

We got some odd looks when we were leaving town on our contraption, but I knew we had a boat which could serve us for a good while, as long as we didn't get caught while plying her downstream.

When we pulled up to the cabin, the women looked at us as if we'd lost our minds. They had a right, but they were over the initial shock soon enough. They looked at the contraption at first with suspicion, and then with acceptance of the engineering required to design and make such a thing work.

"Oh Absalom, where did you come up with such an idea?"

I looked over at Bobby who was beaming with pride and said, "There'll be no living with you now."

"You don't mean...? Bobby, was this boat your idea?" Lucy asked.

"Yes ma'am." Bobby's face flushed deep red.

"Like I said, there'll be no living with him now."

"But Ab, he deserves recognition. Why, who else would have thought of such a thing?"

"Nobody. Not a living soul," I said.

"And that's exactly why he deserves some credit. Come on up to the house Bobby while Ab puts the boat in the shed," my fiancée said.

I lifted the first saddle from the bow of the boat. "Now hold on just a minute. I might need a little help."

"Well all right, but Bobby gets an extra piece of persimmon pie," Evelyn stated as the women turned toward the cabin.

"How do you like that," I said as I stacked my saddle on the wood chopping stump.

"What?"

"I didn't even get a kiss from my girl."

Bobby didn't say a word because he knew he was the reason. Grabbing the other saddle he placed it beside mine and went to unhitch the horses.

"Hold on a moment, Bobby. It might be easier if we use the horses to back the thing in."

"Can we do that?"

"There's only one way to find out," I said.

Bobby went to the shed and opened the doors. We realized we had some work to do in order to get our boat into the tight fitting shelter. We got busy cleaning and moving things until we had the space we needed and then guided the horse drawn boat around in front of the open doors. Grabbing the horses by the collar I began to back them up, and in short order we had the boat inside the shed, pulled the tongue and closed the doors.

The following morning I took the mail to Lemay Ferry and dropped it into the tree trunk and left. I returned to the Foster cabin and there we stayed for the next two weeks cutting wood for the upcoming winter and helping the women with things around the cabin. I didn't know it, but my life was about to become very dark. By that I mean the Civil War was about to put me into dark and cruel places I never thought I'd see in my lifetime.

I had taken to carrying a lasso and was very good with it. I could strike a fly resting on the table or snap a small tree limb at will. Usually, I gently nudged the horses with it, but such a weapon could do quite a lot of damage to human flesh as I would later discover.

Bobby and I picked up the mail at Lemay Ferry and headed back to the cabin for our skiff. As we neared the place, we had to rein in as the young lieutenant and his men were at the cabin giving the ladies a hand for the day, or so it appeared.

In fact, as I later learned, the lieutenant had recognized my name on a wanted poster and put two and two together. The women no longer felt safe and felt it was time to move into town. They assured us they could handle the move on their own so Bobby and I got ready to leave.

Once we were hooked up and harnessed to the skiff we rolled toward the Mississippi and our destiny. We knew we had to be quiet this close to the Yankee troop movements in and around Jefferson Barracks. At any time we could be spotted, so I stuck to rarely used paths that I knew of. This worked and about midnight we were at the river.

We began immediately to tie tree limbs to the boat and in some cases they draped the hull completely. This maneuver took us two hours, at which time I handed the reins of the horses to Bobby and let him head off south. He was somewhat woebegone and sorrowful for not being allowed to go with me, but somebody had to get the horses south so we could pull the boat back to the St. Louis area.

Once in the river I was on my own. The night was quiet but for the trickling of water as it rushed past the boat and tree limbs. I had quite a ways to go, although we had put the boat in south of Moore's landing. In the last few weeks riverboat traffic on the Mississippi had come to a virtual halt. The Yankee's had blockaded the old river very effectively. Nothing was getting up and down the river between St. Louis and New Orleans unless the Federals wanted it to move. Boats had been commandeered to move troops, guns and ammo, but unless you had permission to be moving on the Mississippi, you were likely to have your carcass blown out of the water.

In my little ship I drifted as a snag would drift. I gave no care in trying to steer the boat, for any motion from me could spell my doom. In the wee hours of the morning as the sky began to turn gray I saw a snag in the river and headed for it. I rowed by it and then reversed my skiff and rowed into the snag having let most of my tree branches free. I gathered new ones about me and settled in to wait until dark once again. I was nowhere near land, but with the fresh limbs I was finding I would never be noticed as anything but part of the snag.

I slept but from time to time I was awakened by boat traffic on the river. I studied the boats as they moved and watched them from my covered position. Two of the boats which passed at noon were ironclads heading south. The last thing I wanted was to meet up with them farther downriver but I had a sick feeling I would see them again.

What is it that possesses a man to buck the odds when he knows his chances of success are little to none? I had set out on a mission, one that could lead to nothing but trouble for me and mine. Collecting the mail wasn't the problem. Moving the mail about on the streets of St. Louis was no problem. Everything that happened once the mail was in my hands became a very knotty point. What possesses a man to do things no other man will do? What does he hope to gain?

I had chosen to run the Yankee blockades and of all the men in the nation, I was the only one stupid enough to risk life and limb to the moving of that mail. Captain Absalom Grimes, an experienced riverboat pilot was dodging troops and seeking cover, and for what? A bullet in my brisket or a hangman's noose? As I watched the *City of Alton* loaded with troops move north, I wondered just what I was doing. Millions of men in this country and I was the only one trying to be a professional mail carrier for the Confederate army. I figured my friend Mark may have chosen a much safer course.

Mark was riding in Missouri with an underground group of Rebels doing whatever he felt like doing. He was giving the orders and if I knew Mark he was dragging his feet if the day had anything to do with armed conflict. He was likely laying under a tree somewhere talking of war, but not really engaging in one.

Finally as the sun began to set in the west I made ready my skiff and pushed off from my mooring. I had managed to pass the day safely by not moving, but darkness was on me and it was time to go.

Drifting downriver once again I was comfortable with my position, yet I was nowhere near any riverboats at the moment. There were no Ironclads in sight and no sternwheelers either. That all changed as soon as I relaxed. Rounding the bend several boats came into view and two of them were the ironclads I had seen going downstream earlier in the day. There were five boats in all and one of them was being boarded by the Yankee's. It was the *Natchez*.

The way the boats were spaced out on the river, I was going to have a time not being seen, for this portion of the river was not wide like it had been earlier, and the narrowness of it worried me.

I continued to drift, not wanting to create any motion which might be seen by a sentry. If I began to drift too close I would have to take my chances. My nerves began to tingle as the current pushed me closer and closer to the armada which besieged the river. My lion heart was growing ever smaller as the distance between us lessened. I had to be crazy to think I could get through without being seen. The lights on board the boats would expose me once I was close enough. Still I refused to stop.

The first boat was the ironclad *Carondelet* and she was tied off to the *Natchez*. I slid quietly by the two and found myself nearing another steamer. This grand boat was the *Louisiana*. I counted my lucky stars as I slipped by in its wake and then I was nearing the last of the steamers. The last steamboat was the *Lucky Lady* and then I had the ironclad, the *St. Louis*.

As I drew near, I stiffened and lowered my head below the hull, for a soldier had just stepped up to the side of the *St. Louis* to relieve himself in the muddy river. I'll never know if he saw me or not, but just then my skiff bumped a snag in the river and came to a halt. The unmistakable thud of the log striking the hull of my boat was deafening in the cool night air.

"What the devil?" I heard the soldier exclaim. "Captain Quigley!" he shouted.

I held cautiously still in the bottom of the boat hoping the craft would dislodge itself, while the fate of my trip rested on the arrival of Captain Quigley. I didn't have long to wait.

"Captain, I think there's a boat in yonder snag." I pictured the young soldier pointing directly at me in my mind, although I was hunkered down in the skiff.

"A boat, huh? Private Hamm what would a boat be doing out on the river this time of night?"

"Running our blockade?"

"Private, one would have to be a hysterical fool to think he could run our blockade. There isn't a man alive who would try it. If there's a boat in yonder snag I suggest it's empty and not worthy of investigation."

"But, captain…"

"Private Hamm, if there was someone in the boat they would have steered around such an obstruction."

"But, captain…"

"There's nothing to see. Do me a favor and return to your post."

"Yes sir."

I remained still as I only heard one set of boots retreating on the deck of the ironclad, which meant the captain was not so sure of his conclusion. He was still standing vigil on the edge of the *St. Louis* listening, waiting to see if there was the smallest chance the private had been correct. I know because I would have done the same thing. The slightest sound from me or my boat would be all the excuse he would need to heave to.

I had to remain perfectly still. I had to outwit this captain. What was it he had said? One would have to be a hysterical fool to try and run their blockades. Well he had me pegged all right. I had to be a fool to try what I was doing.

In the black night on the Mississippi, I suddenly heard the water lapping against the hull of my boat. They were only little trickles of waves at first, but as the weather began to change the little waves grew and began to tell on me. A blind man could hear the waves slapping the hull, but could the captain? He was still there and had been for almost an hour. My only hope was that he thought he was hearing waves slap the hull of his own larger boat. Just as I was about to give in and peek over the gunwales, the captain turned and left, barking orders to prepare his boat and crew for the upcoming storm.

With the sudden commotion aboard the *St. Louis,* I took the occasion to dislodge myself from my unexpected mooring and shoved off. I could hardly tell what branches belonged in the river and what belonged with my boat. It took a couple of minutes, but eventually I was free of the entanglement created by dead tree limbs and tree trunks. Some folks had begun to call them sawyers, but an entanglement was a snag in my book. Had I been aboard any riverboat as skipper I would have been able to see the snag long before I got to it, but down on the water, there was no help. They were something I would have to contend with.

Hours later I neared the Columbus Belmont position on the river and went under the cliff as before, only this time I was by myself. I drifted around the bend and started the long slow turn around Kentucky Island. We riverboat pilots called the tract of land Kentucky Island because the upper point of landfall was considered to be in Kentucky, though anyone who wanted to stand on that fair portion of Kentucky would have to go through Tennessee to get to it.

It was from here and onto points farther south where the Mississippi became the most treacherous. Many dangers lay ahead of me and I began to cut loose my tree limbs for they would only hinder me. The Yankee's had boats on the river, but they weren't anywhere south of the position they had taken from the Confederates. My enemy was now the river itself, and it was unforgiving if you made a mistake. As the sun began to drift through the gray haze of morning, I napped along the riverbank.

I had pulled an all night stretch of duty and I was tired. What lay before me needed my full attention. I dozed until noon that day and then made ready for my trip downriver. I needed no tree branches to hide my skiff. If the Yankee's were this far north it meant they had taken Vicksburg and that had not happened. I was safe to row and head on downriver in the light of day.

Bobby was well ahead of me and probably halfway through Arkansas with the horses by now. My intention was to deliver my mail and head on down to the Clements plantation at Belle Grove to meet up with Bobby. Doing so would put me closer to the Federal troops, but I would also know their whereabouts. Something I'm certain General Moore in Corinth would like to know.

I untied my skiff and shoved off. Picking up the oars I began to row. The sun was high overhead and the day was hot. I rowed off and on until I saw the dock at Butcher's Landing come into view and then I rowed in earnest. As I neared the dock I stood and tossed my lasso to catch one of the steamboat moors and pulled myself in. There I let go my lasso, tied off the skiff and climbed the flatboat ladder. Flatboats were a thing of the past, but the ladders still remained at the docks because once in a while a poor family would show up on one. Dock masters still wanted to accommodate them whenever they showed.

I said hello to Riley and borrowed a horse, a pinto of good breeding. When I rode out he was still staring at my contraption on the dock as I had pulled it free from the river until my return. I had covered it up, but he had seen fit to uncover it.

After expressing my desire that he shouldn't let anyone else see it, I rode away on his stallion. The horse was a good one and helped me make mail call at dusk two days later. I heard the call as it went up.

Chapter 13

"Here comes Grimes!" a sentry had shouted and as I rode into the camp tired and bedraggled soldiers came to life. I was surrounded by the southern brigade from Missouri as I dismounted. One soldier took my mount and another handed back the mail bag. I wanted something to eat, but I could wait until the mail was handed out. I opened my bag, grabbed a handful of letters and called off names.

"Bixby, Owens, Stover, Jackson, Hamilton, Tipton, Sullivan, Rodgers, Ford, Aldrich, Harper, Morgan, Drury, Fitzpatrick, Stewart, Mac Fee, Patton, Horne, Fletcher, and the names went on. For an hour I handed out the mail because I also had the previously lost bag to deliver and when that was done I had a few words for the men so they all gathered around to listen.

"I was almost captured on my last two trips down here. I don't expect going north to get any easier. If you're going to write return mail for me to carry, do yourself a favor and don't mention anything about what you're engaged in or where you're located. If I do get caught, I don't want to give the Yankee's any undue information. That means anything which might give you away. I have to assume they'll open every letter. I wouldn't put it past the Federal troops to drag the river if I dropped my bag overboard, so don't mention your whereabouts or discuss any vital information which the Yankee's could use against you."

I turned away then and met Shelby Foster who was put off by my not calling his name.

"Ah, sergeant, I almost forgot the most important letter I've carried." Reaching into my lapel pocket I withdrew the letter his wife had penned for him.

"I hope you enjoy the reading sir, and I must say the women are doing fine."

"The women?" he asked.

"My fiancée arrived at your cabin and is staying with your wife and children until we return from this dreadful war."

"Lucy is at my home?"

"Lucy was at your home and the children are doing fine," I said.

"Captain, I can't believe we never met until this dreadful war, considering our womenfolk."

"Who's to say, sergeant? My father had gone thirty years without seeing a man and then one day they saw one another and it's as if no time had passed between them. I've been witness to such meetings. Life is funny like that. We might see one another regular during the war and when it's over, not see one another for years."

"I think, sir, I should like to know you better than that. I would be squarely disappointed if I were not able to continue our friendship when this is all over, given how close the women are to one another."

"If we survive this devilish war, sergeant, I should like nothing more than to sit on your front porch and watch the sun rise in the east and go down in the west. I have cleared out the creek bed and you now have a full view on yonder fields."

"Thank you, captain. If there's ever anything I can do to repay you."

"You keep yourself from getting killed. That wife of yours needs you. If you can do that, I won't ask anything else."

"I'll do my best, sir."

Turning about, Shelby was off to read his letter and I found the scraps left over from dinner. I ate my fill and was ushered into the officer's tent for an evening repose. I rested and awoke with the bugle like every other soldier in camp.

I gathered all of my return letters and was about to step into the stirrup when Major Stover called me back to his tent. I was surrounded by officers as I entered, not the least of which was General John C. Moore, and I wondered what was in the wind.

"Captain, I called you over because I have a request to make."

"If ya'll need me to take letters home, all you have to do is prepare them."

"You seem to be able to go wherever you may at will. Being a riverboat captain has no doubt prepared you for carrying the mail like no other profession possibly could. I have a dispatch I need to get to General Matthews at Vicksburg. I was wondering if you might deliver it for me."

"You don't have a courier, sir?"

"I've sent three since you were here last month. None of them have returned, so I'm left with the unfortunate conclusion that they either deserted, or they didn't make it."

"I see. If you believe it will help, I'll be glad to involve myself."

"Captain, why have you not signed up? You still dress in the attire of a riverboat pilot. The army can offer you pay, shelter, three squares, and more," General Moore said.

"The army can't provide three squares where I have to travel and what I must do I do alone or with little help. Also sir, I have signed up as you put it. I have been engaged since last year."

"This is the dispatch I want to get to General Matthews. It's imperative that he gets this."

"Yes sir."

I did an about face and went back to my horse. Sergeant Foster was holding him for me as I mounted up.

"See you soon, captain," he said as he saluted me.

I was not a regular officer in the Confederate States of America, I was my own man, yet suddenly it occurred to me that Shelby must have been behind the recent effort to enlist me. I saluted back and rode out of camp, glad to be moving.

At Butcher's Landing two days later, I gave Riley his horse back in trade for my skiff and started downriver toward Vicksburg. There I gave General Matthews the dispatch I was carrying and waited to take on more mail. If I was going to be coming farther south anyway, I might as well get all the mail I could. The general eyed me suspiciously.

"Captain Grimes is it? Why are you not wearing a Confederate uniform?"

"I must navigate around the Yankee positions, sir."

General Matthews was a stalwart man. He carried a cane and smoked a long cigar. His beard was full and although he walked with a limp, he carried himself with a marked dignity.

"Do you know what's in this dispatch, captain?"

"No, sir. I don't read the mail, I just carry it."

"It is a request that we promote you to Major Grimes. The promotion of course, hinges on your acceptance."

"Sir, I don't know that I'm ready to tackle such a commission."

"According to General Moore you already do. He says you're running the Yankee blockades and doing so effectively. He also insists that you know your way around this part of the country like no other man."

"I know my way up and down the river, sir. I was a riverboat pilot prior to this feud. It's the river I know."

"The Yankee's have seized the chain across the river near Columbus. How may I ask are you getting by them?"

"In the dark sir, with tree limbs tied to my boat to give the illusion of floating debris."

"I have a dispatch for Major Stover and I haven't been able to get a courier through in weeks. I don't know why."

"The Yankee's sir, have made an incursion into Mississippi and I would guess they're between the two posts. I don't know how big the unit is, but I've gotten wind of their presence."

"That's the kind of information that can change the outcome of the war. I hope you'll give some serious thought to carrying more dispatches for the Confederacy."

"I will gladly do anything to aid the cause, sir."

"Very well, captain, I accept your answer. Be careful."

"I will, sir."

I gathered the mail from the soldiers at Vicksburg and the dispatches the general wanted delivered and put back into the river. In a short time I was at Belle Grove landing and tied off to the dock. Plantations along the River Road as most folks had begun to call it had their own docks in order to make loading of crops and whatever else needed to be transported easier. Belle Grove was no different. The grandest plantation in the south, though she was only ten years young, had a dock fit for St. Louis or New Orleans. That would change if the Yankee's managed to get upriver past Port Hudson.

I walked to the house and found Bobby waiting on the porch with another young boy. His name was Mickey Ledbetter. Bobby had taken it on himself to enlist this young man to help with the horses. I discovered he had made the entire trip from Moore's landing south.

"You've been doing some traveling," I commented.

"How did it go?" Bobby asked.

"It was hair-raising there for a bit on the river, but I made it down. Once I got past the chain I was fine. There's no Yankee's coming upriver yet."

"Let's go get the boat out of the water," Bobby said to Mickey and the two boys were off. I reminded myself I was going to have to stop thinking of him as a kid.

I knocked on the big doors using the door bell. Actually the device was a very heavy knocker, but a door bell just the same.

A well-groomed black man opened the door as before and let me into the house. It was going to be a shame if the south lost the war, because places such as Belle Grove would no longer exist. Belle Grove Plantation could do quite well as the White House. Actually the grounds were much nicer and quite a lot bigger. I had been to the White House and seen its grounds and there was nothing in Maryland or Virginia which came close to Belle Grove.

"Master Clements is in the basement, sir and has given me instructions to see you are cared for until dinner."

"Can I get a bath?"

"Most certainly, sir," the butler said.

He led me to the same upstairs guest bedroom and ordered a bath prepared for me. I glanced out the big upstairs window and saw Bobby and his new friend nearing the dock with the horses. He probably knew more than I did when it came to that boat.

At dinner that evening we were a festive party of folks. Tucker Deal was there along with William Clements and his pretty wife, and the two boys Bobby and Mickey.

"I'm sorry I wasn't around all afternoon, captain, but I had important business to attend to."

"You don't have to apologize to me, sir. I'm a guest in your home."

"Still, I don't want to seem rude. Tucker and I, we're knee deep in our little conspiracy."

"So how's it coming?"

"St. Louis is still in the hands of the Federals is it not?"

"Most undoubtedly."

"Try these when you get there. Let's see how well we've done," he said tossing hundreds of dollars in Yankee greenbacks on the table. The boy's eyeballs bulged.

My spoon was in my mouth and held there as I eyed the money lying before me. I knew it to be counterfeit, but for the life of me it looked real as any Yankee currency I'd ever seen. I swallowed my stew and picked the money up, laying my spoon aside.

"This is most unexpected," I gestured.

"You'll find four different denominations there. Once we put our minds together, there was nothing to it," Tucker added.

"Well, I'll find out firsthand how well you did and report back to you."

"Good. In the meantime we'll be printing what we need to survive should we loose the war," Mr. Clements said.

I was ten days getting back to the cabin and I couldn't go near the place. I had to send Bobby to find out what was going on. There was fighting in the fields surrounding the house and the women were nowhere to be seen. Bobby returned with a report which gave me hope.

"The Federals are using the cabin as a command post. According to them the women were moved into St. Louis for safety. First to a refugee camp near Jefferson Barracks, and then to stay with someone in town, but they don't know who."

We rattled our hocks out of there and let them fight. I had not expected such a thing, but the women were probably safer in St. Louis considering the fighting going on across from the cabin.

We soon found ourselves dodging the Yankee troops at every turn. Putting the boat back in the water and covering it up made the most sense so that's what we did. We rode the two horses and came into town just after dark. I didn't want to be seen by anyone who might betray me to the Federals. I was still a wanted man.

There were dives along the riverfront where a man could pick up information and no place for young boys so I gave them a few dollars to get a bite to eat and made my way down to the wharf. There were few places on earth as tough as the riverfront in downtown St. Louis during the war. A man with money was likely to get robbed at any moment so I kept a sharp eye.

I stepped up to the bar in the Gravois and ordered a drink placing the first of my counterfeit money on the counter for the bartender.

"You do accept greenbacks, don't you?" I asked.

"I don't accept nothing else."

"Good, I'll take a rye."

I tossed off my drink and looked around. I knew the kind of situation I had placed myself in. There were men about who would know me, but they wouldn't turn me in. There were men about who didn't know me who would rob me for two cents and they wouldn't hesitate to turn me in if they knew of my status.

I was glad for my lasso. As I looked about I knew I was being watched and I couldn't leave with so much money in hand. They would be waiting for me outside but who, and where, was the question. I had another drink to help me feel better for the fight in which I was about to engage and headed for the door.

I saw the back door slide shut just as I stepped onto the street and knew the game was afoot. I had made a point in my life to stay away from such places, but on this night I was testing the waters. I wanted to see if the money was accepted and I wanted to find out what the Yankee's were up to. I had picked up only a few words here and there as I stood at the bar, but enough to know the Yankee's were spreading out west and south through Missouri. If they succeeded, it was only a matter of time before they made Arkansas and Louisiana.

Two men came out of the alley in front of me, and two men had stepped out of the bar behind me. I was on my own. I could handle one or two men, but four was beyond my ability. Suddenly out of nowhere a group of boys ran up to the two men in front of me and molested them. I mean the boys cleaned their pockets and took off running.

"Hey, now wait a minute!" one of the men yelled as he began to chase the young men back through the alley.

I turned on the men behind me just in time to see them succumb to the same fate and I began to smile. I had quite a team of little helpers I had never met.

That was remedied an hour later as I met up with Bobby and Mickey near Washington Street. All the boys who had participated in the ruse were there, bickering over their newfound funds back in the alley like a bunch of banty roosters fighting over hens.

I learned that many an orphaned youngster was showing up on the streets of St. Louis lately. These fellows were only a few. They were sleeping wherever they could, but as the months drew on they would have to find shelter inside somewhere or freeze to death. I pulled out my wad of cash and dispersed a good bit of it right there.

"Save what you can so you can purchase room and board for the winter months. You're all going to need shelter of some sort," I said.

"Is there any way we can help you gather the mail?" one of the boys asked.

"I don't see how, but maybe something will come up." Pausing I added. "There is something you can do for me. I need to know what the Yankee's are up to, where they're headed next, where they are now and so on. If you can get me that kind of information I can pay you for it."

"That might be hard to do."

"Maybe, but maybe not. You're in Yankee territory already. All you have to do is keep your eyes and ears open and compile what you know. On my return trip, if you have any information worth having I'll know it and I'll pay you well."

"When will you be back?" one of the boys asked.

"In about a month."

"Shazam! That's a long time!"

"It may seem like a long time, but that's how long it takes for me to make a complete trip," I added.

"Captain, you get yourself in trouble and we'll be there. All you have to do is send word," the oldest of them said.

"What's your name, son?"

"Rastus P. Cohen sir, my friends call me Rassie."

"You'll do. If I need assistance I'll do my best to enlist your help."

We parted ways. Bobby and Mickey left with me and we began to search earnestly for the women.

Two days later we found them and a good thing we did for I was running out of time. I had to pick up the mail at Lemay Ferry the next day. They were rooming at a boarding house owned by one Mammie King originally from Kentucky. I introduced myself at the door and she went to get the ladies. A moment later I was welcomed inside for dinner along with my boys. It was a rather late hour, but Mammie set up a quick table and we ate leftovers.

"You must stay the night, captain. It's getting too late to be out. The Federal troops will be enforcing their curfew," Mammie insisted.

"They have a curfew on the streets?"

"Even down on the wharf."

"Then we'll stay the night," I replied.

She put us men up in the parlor and made us as comfortable as possible. There was little talking that evening and soon we were all asleep. I was awakened the following morning by two big eyed children belonging to the Fosters. Ida Mae and Ezekiel were playing with my beard when my eyes opened. My sudden response startled them and they ran from the room.

Mammie King was in the kitchen when I came into the dining room just before daybreak. She was there working with a black woman who did most of the cooking. She was not a slave but worked for her keep. After breakfast Lucy went to the door with me and she was agitated.

"Be careful, Ab. The Federals are everywhere now, and they're looking for you incessantly."

"The less we speak of such things, the better." I shook my head and wagged my forefinger. "Only good thoughts to see us through, my dear. I've been on the river more than just a little."

We said our goodbyes and I lifted my mail bag which was now a makeshift carpetbag and stepped through the door. I was getting accustomed to carrying such weight when the horses or the boat was not around to do it for me. This bag was full of return mail. I still had to get to my hollow oak tree at Lemay Ferry and switch bags before heading downriver.

The first thing I did was take a good look about but I saw no sign that anyone was paying attention at this hour. I told Bobby and Mickey to retrieve the horses from the stables and where to meet me. I headed down the street. Like a ghost in the darkness, I evaded the gaslights which lit the corners, and took to the alleyways. I watched behind me to make certain I was not seen, then turned on Broadway heading south along the river. Occasionally I had to pass under a lit street lamp, but light was beginning to show itself on the eastern horizon. I was less than a mile from Jefferson Barracks and began to wonder if Lemay cemetery had been a good idea. Was there not some better place to make the switch?

I walked on but felt as though the Yankees were looking over my shoulder at every step and my skin began to crawl with fear.

How much farther was it? One, two hundred yards? If the Federals caught me making the switch they would hang me sure. They would have all the evidence needed to convict yours truly. I considered my fate, yet I walked on. I had to succeed. Too many soldiers down in Mississippi were counting on me. I took lighter steps as to make less sound.

I could see my tree through the early morning fog and no one seemed to be near it. I heard them then. I heard them before I realized what the sound meant and hastily I made for my tree. I ran through the grass and ducked behind the oak tree just in time to see a platoon of soldiers headed uptown. I closed my eyes and prayed.

As they disappeared into the early morning fog I ducked around the tree and switched carpetbags then hightailed it back down the street, keeping the soldiers within earshot in front of me. If they stopped or the fog lifted I had to be ready to disappear.

Before we got as far as Chippewa Street I ducked into the woods where I was supposed to meet Bobby and Mickey. They were there waiting for me just as I had asked and I took my first deep breath in a while.

Bobby was the first to notice something was wrong. "What's the matter, captain? You look like you've seen a ghost."

"Aye, my own. Let's get out of here," I said stepping into the saddle.

The two boys rode double. Slowly and carefully we picked our way around Lemay Ferry which was now a hotbed of young recruits looking to make a name for themselves. The pace was slow going because I didn't want to make any noise that might alert the Federals to our presence. The hair on the back of my neck was standing on end until we cleared that section of woodland, (the section of woods now known as Lemay).

As we cleared the area around the south end of Jefferson Barracks, I picked up the pace and the fog began to lift. I wanted in my boat where I had better control of my own movement and I wouldn't be running into Federal troops at every turn.

It was noon when we uncovered the skiff and put it into the river. Bobby was with me and Mickey headed south with the horses. We had taken to calling those animals Judge Walker and Lady Banks, and good horses they were. Bobby had selected a boy who knew horse flesh at an early age. Mickey knew more about horses than the two of us put together.

I wasn't worried about the horses, I was worried about us. "There's an inlet just south of Arnold. We'll put in there until dark. If we're spotted on the river in daylight we'll be dragged somewhere we don't want to be."

We took turns rowing and it didn't take long to get off the river. We paddled our way up the canal out of sight. By late afternoon we had caught a dozen bullfrogs and made a small fire, having frog legs for dinner.

When night fell we had our tree limbs tied into place and we shoved off making our way back out to the Mississippi. We held fast at the mouth of the inlet to let an ironclad pass in the night.

The naval ship *Cincinnati* was headed north and that was fine with me. We were headed south out of the area.

Nighttime was sailing time for the *Jokers Wild*, the name Bobby had given our boat. I didn't care about such things, but apparently naming things was what cut it with these younger boys. They had a name for everything. They even called themselves "The Gaslight Boys." They were making a name for themselves with me. Whatever else they did, they were good kids in my book.

There were small islands in the middle of the river near Cairo and Mound City so that's where we tied off at sunup the following morning. Making sure the boat was well covered, we made our way inland and found a comfortable place to sleep, or so we thought. We were run off the first spot by mosquitoes, more than I had ever encountered in my life. The woods were full of them. We soon found another spot farther up where they weren't so bad and rested through the day. We snacked on food the women had sent with us and rested some more.

At sundown we uncovered *Jokers Wild* and headed downstream. We weren't far from Columbus when we pushed off.[1] The Yankee's had now dug in on top of the easternmost cliffs overlooking the Mississippi and were manning cannons to blow anything that appeared to be a boat out of the water.

As we rounded the bend from Cairo, I noted the seven mile straight stretch ahead of the waiting Yankee blockade. Once again there were shadows on the river eclipsing the entire seven mile stretch between us and the bend.

The moon was up and the ironclads cast an eerie shadow on the waters along with the steamboats they were holding. There seemed to be an army of steamers on the water. For what purpose they were halted on a moonlit night such as this, I had no idea. You could see as well as daylight, only everything appeared in

---

[1] Now known as Columbus Belmont State Park, Kentucky.

black and white, a reflection of the moon. If we got by tonight we were going to be lucky.

The only reason those steamers weren't moving was because the Federals were holding them there. There could be no other reason.

"If we get close to any boat, don't make a sound, and don't move," I warned Bobby.

I rowed the boat into the current making sure it was thrust toward the eastern side of the river as the boats seemed to all be moored on the west bank. Quietly I lifted the oars and laid them in the boat placing them where they couldn't move. Then me and Bobby ducked down and waited.

We waited in silence and it seemed forever. Bobby kept looking at me wondering if he could move yet and each time I had to signal him to lay still. The boy was having trouble holding still for so long, but he wasn't going to move without me saying it was all right.

For more than an hour we drifted downstream with the current. I heard men's voices in the night and then our little boat thudded against the only boat on the east side of the river. It was the *St. Louis*.

I grabbed the bag and dropped it overboard immediately. A moment later there were soldiers everywhere pointing guns at us.

"Don't shoot!" I said, "You'll hit the boy."

"Captain Quigley!" one of the soldiers shouted over his shoulder.

I had us in a pickle now. I looked over at Bobby and he was worried, but not half as much as me. Within moments Captain Quigley arrived on deck and took a look down at us. "Bring them aboard and sink the boat," he ordered.

"Sir, there's something in the water by the boat," one of the soldiers said.

Bobby dove in, disappearing under the skiff. A moment later the carpetbag disappeared and I was stunned by the boy's actions. One of the men lifted his rifle to shoot, at what I don't know. There was simply no target to shoot at except for me and I wasn't moving.

"If that man moves in any direction other than to board the boat, shoot him."

With a dozen rifles trained on me I wasn't moving until told. I climbed aboard as ordered and they shot my boat full of holes and let it drift on downriver never bothering to remove the tree limbs which would keep it afloat. My first thought was to find it and make repairs. There were many reasons to find that boat again.

As I walked under gun to the captain's quarters I noticed a bump on the water a good ways downstream. It was Bobby and the carpetbag. He had made it and was swimming silently around the bend toward New Madrid. A gun shoved me in the back as I hesitated and then I was in the captain's office.

"Have a seat, Captain Grimes."

I was startled he knew my name.

"We've been watching for you, captain. I'm a little surprised to find you coming downriver in such a compromising manner."

"In a compromising manner you say?"

"Captain, we didn't get the mail, but we got you. Your boat had wheels on it. That's pretty ingenious. It was covered with branches for camouflage. That also was well thought out. That boy may have escaped with the mail but you aren't going anywhere but straight to jail for the remainder of the war."

"If you're going to imprison me until this thing is over, could you do me a favor?" I asked.

"I'm not disposed to doing favors for the enemy, captain."

"Of course not, but my fiancée will be…" I trailed off.

"You were saying?"

"Nothing, nothing at all."

"You started to say something about your fiancée."

"It doesn't matter. Do with me what you will."

"Who was the young man who dove into the water after the bag?"

"I decline to answer."

"We'll find out soon enough, Captain Grimes. In the meantime you're going to jail."

Chapter 14

The Myrtle street jail was well fortified with troops and guards, and I was fortunate the Union officers had decided to place me in St. Louis for the time being. The Gaslight Boys knew where I was almost immediately. Their presence on the street told me. Lucy, and Mrs. Foster either knew or would soon know that I had been captured. I recognized some of the boys as those who had saved me from ruffians the week before. One of them was the boy named Rassie. If I could get him to take a message to Lucy, I'd sure feel better about my internment.

As the cell door clanked shut I began to wonder how I could escape. Having been aboard the ironclad *St. Louis,* I had information about the structure and design of the boats the Confederate army would be wishful to know. I may have been a prisoner, but I had done my share of studying them while aboard.

I settled into my bunk and began the long wait. I knew they would try me and probably sentence me to a hanging, but I had other plans. I knew for instance the man who built the Myrtle Street jail. He was a friend of my father. If there was a weak spot in the design of it he would know.

When I say I began the long wait I had no idea how long. It was late August when I entered the jail and almost late March before I knew anything of my fate. It came to me that I was to be transported to the Federal prison in Alton about fifty miles upriver. I had done everything possible to figure a way out of that jail, but all of my calculations came to nothing. Then one day they opened my cell door and escorted me out into the street.

I was transported by wagon along with other prisoners and soon found myself down on the wharf awaiting orders to board the *City of Alton*. There were nine other men with me and the thing I couldn't get over was they hadn't put us in leg irons. When I asked about it, the sergeant explained.

"There's still ice floating down the river, Captain Grimes. If you feel like jumping in you just go ahead, but they'll be no need for a search party."

Being a riverboat pilot, I knew he was correct. He needn't explain anything at all. If I jumped into the icy water I would die before I could get out, let alone get myself dry. There was a chill in the air this morning anyway and I wanted a coat, something the Federal troops were quite stingy with.

It was not long before they removed us from the wagon and ushered us aboard. The captain and pilot were folks I knew and they gave me a funny look from the wheelhouse as we boarded. Suddenly, I had hope. The riverboat pilots I knew would not let a friend go down without knowing the reason why. I saw Beaumont talking to the sergeant and a few minutes later he came over to where I was.

"Captain Grimes, does your father know what you're up to?"

"Captain Beaumont, it's good to see you. How's the wife and family."

"Better than you I would venture. What have they got you for Ab?"

"For carrying mail to the troops in Mississippi."

Beaumont paused and studied me for a long moment. "You mean to tell me you were captured for delivering mail?"

"That's it, old friend."

"You didn't shoot anyone or weren't caught fighting?" he quizzed.

"All I was doing was taking the mail south. I don't carry any weapons because I'm not actually enlisted with either side. The only thing I carry is a spoon, fork, and knife, although the knife was a bit more than a butter knife."

"Captain, I'll see what I can do. I can't promise anything, but this is a travesty. How dare they lock up a fellow pilot for something as slight as delivering mail?"

He was off then, and I didn't see him for the rest of my trip, but he sent help in the form of one of his crew. It was full dark and getting colder. They had the ten of us laid out on deck where we were leaning against the inner wall of the boat. The sentry had gone to sleep and without warning a man appeared above me and pulled me to my feet. He motioned for me to follow him and I didn't hesitate.

We walked the gangway quietly as he took me down into the engine room where he showed me where to lay my wrist. The crank of the engine sheared off my handcuffs, leaving only a small scratch on my right hand. He picked them up and threw them into the boiler. Then he handed me a bag of filthy clothes.

"Get yourself outfitted young man, you have just been shanghaied. You now work for me in the engine room."

"Captain Grimes." I introduced myself.

"I'm Gus. I'm the engineer. Make sure you cover yourself real good with grease. I want you blacker than Tiny over there," he said pointing to a long, tall black man down in the hole. "You'll be working beside him for the night."

I got into the dirtiest clothes I could pull from the bag and then made myself extra dirty with grease. I knew what the men had in mind, but I wasn't so sure it would work. The boat was chugging upriver, but would the sergeant believe I had jumped? Certainly he would search the boat. I knew they would turn it upside down looking for me.

"Heave to, Grimes. I don't want you shirking your duties on the job. Pull your weight," Gus ordered.

I leaned into my work and began to toss wood into the catch. Tiny, my work partner, was anything but tiny. He was possibly the biggest black man I had ever seen. Keeping up with him was not easy. He looked as if he was moving in slow motion because of his size, but I soon discovered that to be a mirage. He was doing twice the work I was capable of with less movement. If I had to match the man stride for stride, he was going to kill me.

Tiny was a free man and had been all his life. He worked hard, did his job and kept his mouth shut. I could use a few good men like him. I was not delivering mail for the south because I wanted every state to have its own stable of slaves. I was fighting for the Constitution and what it said about states rights. The sovereignty of the individual and the state is what I believed in. That's what I was fighting for. Slavery was not the issue, but becoming the issue all the same. If the Federal troops won, whatever the Federal government said from now on would trump any state law.

We had to be nearing Alton, but as yet there had been no effort to search the boat. Had the captain seen fit to replace me? I wished dearly to know what was going on, but kept my head down and tried to keep up with Tiny. He was tossing wood as if the chunks were twigs. If I survived the night I was going to be most surprised. What was it, three or four o'clock in the morning?

I heard the whistle sound and I knew we were getting ready to dock at Alton. It would be only a matter of minutes before the boat was swarming with troops looking for me.

The door to the engine room burst open and Gus yelled at the soldier.

"Here, here; what are you doing in my engine room?"

"Looking for an escaped prisoner, sir."

"There be no one down here but men what make the boat go. I have no room in here for a man to hide out, but search if you've a need to," Gus offered.

"No need sir, I can see from here there is no place for a man to hide."

"Then be off with you. I've work to do if we're fixing to dock."

The soldier backed out and I breathed a sigh of relief. For now I was safe, but I knew they would look again. The sergeant could not afford to lose a prisoner.

Thirty minutes later the door was thrown open again and Sergeant Evans stood there flanked by two soldiers. Tiny and I looked up long enough to see what was happening and then returned to throwing our wood. We weren't stuffing the boilers, but restacking the wood so it would be easier to retrieve when we moved out. Our job was not done.

"What gives, sergeant?" Gus asked.

"We're missing a prisoner."

"There's no one in this room but working men. Ain't no room for nothing else, but like I told your man earlier, you can search if you want to. I'll not stand in your way."

I never looked up, not wanting to make eye contact for fear I would betray myself. I leaned into my work and grew my wood pile all the more.

Hearing the door close, I looked up and wiped my brow. They had overlooked me again. Gus was smiling and said, "What are you looking at? Get back to work."

I wasn't one to second guess success, so I dug in and kept stacking wood. A few minutes later the door opened again but I never lifted my head. If they wanted me they were going to have to come in here and get me. As it was, they didn't recognize me in grimy clothes, and I wasn't about to go waving a flag at them. I was in good hands and I intended to stay right there. I heard the door close and looked up, but Gus was pressing to chide me.

"Quit looking around and do your job," he ordered playfully.

I smiled and picked up another chunk of wood.

"And wipe that smile off your face or I'll keep you down here," Gus warned.

I quit smiling after a minute because I began to wonder if the man wouldn't do just that. My arms were fatigued, but I kept throwing wood. Tiny looked as if he could go all day. I wilted at his strength.

"Don't worry, captain. I dare say you could keep up with a bit of practice." It was the first thing Tiny had said all night. I was taken aback by the man's perception of my thoughts. He had known exactly what I was thinking.

A moment later the door opened and Captain Beaumont stepped in. "You can come out now, Grimes, they're gone."

I started to step out of the hole but before I could make a move Tiny stuck his big black hand out for me to shake.

"Good luck, captain," he said as we shook hands.

I went with Captain Beaumont. Another man, the one I had relieved, entered the engine room and took his place beside Tiny as I was exiting. The sun was up and it must have been around eight thirty. I had been working a full shift and because of my condition, I was never recognized.

Captain Beaumont escorted me to his private quarters and provided me with clean clothes along with soap and water.

"When you're all cleaned up, captain, come on up to the wheelhouse for some breakfast. Usually I eat in the dining room, but this morning we're taking our breakfast upstairs in order to keep an eye out for those troops, just in case they decide to return."

"Thank you."

I was ready for sleep, I can tell you that much. But I cleaned myself and put on clean clothes. They were half mine to begin with, only they had been cleaned.

Making my way up to the wheelhouse I entered the room with a table already set. The pilot was Van Dorn and he paid me little mind.

"The *Omaha* will be in shortly. You can cross over to her deck and head back downriver to St. Louis if you've a mind to," Beaumont said as he buttered some toast.

"That would be right nice. Give me a chance to ride my old man's boat."

"You're pappy will hardly recognize you."

"Is Dad still on board?"

"He was the last time she came by. I suspect he's still doing what comes natural."

"Nearly thirty years he's been on the river."

I thought about it for a minute and corrected the captain. "Thirty two. He's been on the river for thirty two years now."

"You don't say. I guess I miscounted in there somewhere."

"Easy enough to do," I added as I ate. "Captain Beaumont, I don't know how to thank you for what you've done."

"You can thank me by not getting caught again."

"Now getting caught sir, is something I can promise you I will try not to do."

We heard the whistle as the *Omaha* came in to tie off next to the *City of Alton*. I could see Dad standing in the wheelhouse giving orders and I knew what he was saying, although I couldn't hear him from such a distance.

Dad had his run from St. Louis to Omaha and the packet was still running a regular schedule with one stop in Alton. The Federal troops weren't worried about river traffic going north or west from St. Louis, only the traffic which tried to head south.

Omaha, Nebraska was as far from the war a man could get and in the other direction. I never considered my dad to be a very smart man until that moment. Suddenly as I watched him bring the *Omaha* alongside I realized just how wrong I had been.

Being a pilot and a captain I had free passage on any boat, but the *Omaha* was special. She was the boat my father had educated me on. When most riverboats had a life expectancy of two years good service, Dad was still rolling down the river in a fifteen-year-old boat that looked as new as anything on the river. As I watched the roustabouts tie off on the mooring, I suddenly felt a deep respect for my father which had not been there before.

Maybe it was because I hadn't seen him in over a year, or maybe it was the war, but whatever it was, I was looking at the old man in a new light. I suddenly understood his hard-nosed discipline, his inability to put up with child's play. He was a stern father, and unforgiving when you made a mistake. I now knew the reason why.

In his world there was no room for a mistake. If he made a mistake peoples lives were in danger. He had no intention of becoming washed up. He would pilot a riverboat as long as he had his faculties. He might even be walking with a cane eventually, but he would still run a boat. I understood him now. The elder Grimes would not go quietly into retirement.

If I could only master his resolve I would be able to handle my mission with greater ease. So it was I hung on every word he said as we headed downriver later that morning. He didn't say much, but what he said I could put in my pipe and smoke.

"Nothing ventured, nothing gained," he said when I told him what I was doing. I could see he respected the idea. He kept his hands on the wheel and stared out the window the entire time.

"That's how you grow, son. You must first put something into life if you want to get something out of it."

I sat in the wheelhouse beside him as we made our way downriver and the room was quiet mostly. Every once in a while he would have another thought and he would voice it. The last I'll never forget.

"Some folks are always waiting for an external situation to change their lives. They're waiting for someone else to do for them what they could do themselves. It's those folks who'll never amount to anything. People who wait for external circumstances to change before they make an internal decision will be losers their entire lives. They'll never be happy, son.

"Can you imagine the cook saying, give me a good meal Lord and I promise to prepare it later. No, you've got to prepare for a good meal before you can have one.

"I used to wonder if you'd be all right, but I've no need to wonder any longer. You'll be just fine," my father said.

I wish I could be as sure as my father, considering the assignment I had given myself. He let me bring the old steamboat into dock and then we parted ways. I turned around and saluted him as I stepped off the *Omaha* deck and onto the dock. Suddenly my mother was there beside my father to wave goodbye and my heart pounded regret. I had missed a chance to visit with her. The war was beginning to mess with my head. I had forgotten my mother was onboard.

Federal troops were everywhere, but they weren't looking for me. I had been in jail for six months and transferred to Alton the previous day. I walked up Washington Street and headed toward Mammie King's boarding house. If the women were still there they would know what was in the wind.

They were there and in good spirits too, although worried about me. I told them of my escape from the Federal troops at Alton and how I had gotten home. I asked about the mail run.

"Bobby has been doing it in your absence," Lucy said.

I sat there in the parlor with my mouth agape.

"You shouldn't be so surprised, Ab. He knows what to do. You have shown him everything. He recovered *Jokers Wild* and patched the boat up. He's been running the blockades for the last six months. He should be in any day now, and then on the first he'll be off again."

"Bobby Louden has been running the mail all of this time?"

"Bobby has been doing a splendid job since you got locked up. He gets by the Yankee's with little to no trouble at all."

Well, if Bobby had been doing so well all this time, I was going to have to ride along and observe. I thought I knew a thing or two, but the way Bobby was being talked about gave me hesitation. Maybe the boy didn't need my help at all.

Chapter 15

Bobby and Mickey came in the next day and they had some stories to tell. Being kids, the Yankee's weren't so watchful of them, but they had to be careful just the same. The young river pirate was telling me how he solved the problem of the blockade at Belmont. I listened as he enlightened me.

"Them ironclads can't move like a regular steamboat," he said. "Once they're anchored it takes them a while to get up a head of steam. I just waited for a dark night and paddled right by them. I'm not running in the moonlight anymore."

"That makes plenty sense. I wouldn't have been caught had it been darker."

"There's a new general at Corinth who's wishful to meet you," Bobby said.

"Then I'm wishful to meet him."

I learned that my friend Mark Twain had headed upriver on a steamboat to try to pass the fort at Jefferson Barracks, and was fired on. The Yankee's had managed to dismantle one of the smoke stacks with one shot from their guns, and Mark turned back southward. Where he might be now was anybody's guess. No one had seen or heard from him since the incident.

Bobby had already dropped the return mail at the cemetery, so I let him pick up the mail headed south since he had been doing so nonstop for the last six months. I went along with Mickey to see where they were meeting now that the Federal troops solidly controlled everything in the area. My idea was to ease back into my mission without being caught again. What the boys had learned would be invaluable to me.

They had the Gaslight Boys watching the streets and keeping an eye out for troop movements, informing them of any danger areas. I had promised to pay for such information and according to Bobby I owed the boys a good deal already. In the last six months they'd created a detailed map of where the Yankee's were and what they were up to. That was a map I wanted to see. In fact, I wanted a copy for myself.

One thing that had happened while I was incarcerated was an unprecedented number of police officers dying on duty in St. Louis. One of the men killed recently had been a friend of mine. His name was Jim Wallace. He had been stabbed while on the wharf. That particular killer was still on the loose. The cauldron down by the water was getting nastier by the day. It was certainly no place for a woman alone or a man either, but I had to take my chances.

I wasn't sure who was in more danger of dying, the police officers working the wharf or the soldiers fighting the war. One thing was indisputable; I didn't want to add my name to the list of the dead.

We met Bobby behind the Hudson Bay Co. tanning works on Broadway and then mounted up and rode out. He had the mail bag and we didn't waste any time talking about the last six months. We got on the road and headed south for the newly restored *Jokers Wild.*

The boat was covered up in a small inlet off the Mississippi river. It was too early to row out and risk being seen, so we waited in the woods until dark.

At dusk Bobby untied to skiff and we pushed off, easing out into the Mississippi. Mickey took the horses on south. It was a dark night and the moon was not up yet, although it would be later.

We rowed hard to make time. All night we guided our boat downriver and saw no one. We put in at Cairo Island as the sun was coming up and covered the skiff. Making a small fire we ate and rested. Ice was still on the river, but I had noticed a rise in temperature as we headed south. There was still a chill in the air, but with the sun, it subsided and the air around us grew warm. We rested, waiting for nightfall.

There was still ice working its way downriver in March 1863, meandering to warmer climates. Cloaking the blackened skiff with an abundance of tree limbs and tying them off, I made certain the dinghy would appear as floating debris on the water and not the seaworthy vessel she was. Bobby and I shoved off and began to float the seven mile stretch where we would once again be under the Yankee guns.

The night was dark with the moon delaying its arrival. Time was of the essence, for if the moon should rise while we were on this stretch of water, we would no doubt be seen and Bobby had learned recently the Yankee guns mounted on the bluff would not hesitate to fire on floating debris. Whether they had figured out our scheme or they were only engaged in target practice I had no idea, but the effect would be the same if struck.

This was a slow quiet process with fog beginning to appear in spots on the water. Rowing could be heard for a good distance in the dark of night along with any small movement in our little boat. The sound would be magnified by the fog so we held perfectly still and let the current take us downstream.

As we neared the first boat we could hear soldiers talking and laughing on deck and although our first instinct was to get away, we could do nothing. To do anything this close in was to be captured once again. I kept my eyes on my young friend making sure he didn't move as much as a finger or whisper a sound. The mail bag lay between us in which I had placed rocks so we could sink it if we were caught.

It was now that I felt the most helpless, now when I could do nothing. How far had we drifted? One mile? I refused to look as we were still within hearing and sight of the *Carondelet*. Too close to breathe, I thought.

As the minutes slowly ticked away we began to relax. We had made it past the first Yankee gunboat, but there were three more ironclads up ahead that I could see in the distance, their lighted decks reflecting in the fog. It was taking too long. The moon would surely be lifting its light over the southern portion of the river by the time we floated the entire seven mile stretch.

"We've got to row the distance between the boats," I whispered to Bobby. "Leave the oars in the water as we get near them," I added.

We pulled out our oars and began to row. Quietly as possible we dipped water and pulled. If the other ironclads were like the first, the soldiers would be engaged in conversation and wouldn't hear our efforts. It was a gamble of sorts but one we had to take.

Steadily we made our way downriver and then we were too close to row anymore. The next boat was on us and we held perfectly still, although I could now hear my own breathing from the rowing I had been doing.

"Hey Barney, come here a minute," someone said onboard the *Cincinnati*.

"What is it, Dobbs?"

"I thought I heard something out in the water."

"What did you hear?"

"I'm not sure, but there's something or someone out there."

"There's nothing out there but ice. That's what you're hearing.

"No, this sounded different, but I can't put my finger on it."

Silence overtook us, for the men on the *Cincinnati* were listening with pricked ears. I held my eyes on Bobby and he on me. Neither of us moved. The fog had cloaked us but sound was magnified in the fog. If we gave ourselves away, it would be by moving or saying something and neither of us wanted to suffer the consequences.

After a few minutes we were away, but I still heard Barney reply. "There's nothing out there Dobbs, you're just hearing things."

The last two boats were on shore so we only had to worry about one of them and it turned out to be the *St. Louis*. I knew the captain and he knew me, but could he see us? We remained unmoving as a corpse while our castle of debris floated near the ironclad. Chills ran down my spine as we approached within twenty feet of her hull, but the fog shielded us as we drifted her length. Forever was the length of her it seemed and as we cleared the bow the moon began to lift itself on the eastern horizon.

We were by her then, but we were going to be visible to the guns up on the cliffs if we encountered any thin areas of fog. As our distance from the *St. Louis* increased to three hundred yards I began once again to row. We had been lucky to get by I thought, and then we were around the turn and headed west for New Madrid.

I saw the flash of light on the bluff overlooking the river and a moment later the river exploded around us, splashing cold water into our boat alerting me to the fact we were not yet clear of the Yankee cannons. The sound reached us a couple seconds later. I grabbed my oars tight and began to pull in the direction of the north bank. That cannon ball had been all too close. If they were firing on us, there was no doubt we would soon be followed by one of the Yankee ironclads. It would take a few minutes for the boat to get up steam, but it would be coming. I rowed as if my life depended on it, which, of course, it did.

Another flash a moment later and the river exploded again, followed by the report of the cannon. This time the ball landed farther behind us. I had to get us out of sight and soon. The fog was too thin at the point where the river turned west. I turned the boat again and headed downstream as hard as I could paddle. They were not done and I suddenly wanted off the river. We had to find a good place to hide, somewhere the Yankee ironclads could not get to.

"You've been coming this way Bobby, is there an inlet anywhere nearby that no ironclad can get into?"

"About two miles farther along there's an island with a cave on the back side. I put in there one time, but I didn't have no Yankee's after me."

"It'll have to do. We'll be lucky to get to it before they see us. Start cutting the tree limbs loose, they're slowing us down. They've seen us anyway," I added.

Bobby went to work cutting the tree limbs loose and I made haste for the island in the middle of the river. I couldn't see it, but I believed I knew the island he referred to. If my memory served me, the landmass was left over from the 1811 earthquake and stood directly in the path of any boat coming downstream. It was a small beachhead with a dozen trees rising from the topmost part of the marooned forest, the rest no doubt had been taken down to size by the erosion caused by the overflowing water during flood season.

The cave was there and we made haste to pull our little boat into the small opening on the back side of the island. We pulled, pushed and shoved to get the boat out of sight and covered our tracks that were clearly visible up close. Bobby found a hollowed out log and drug it in front of the opening. I added a few tree limbs and then we ducked out of sight just as the *St. Louis* rounded the island. There were soldiers on deck looking high and low for the skiff, but we were now out of sight in the black hole that was the cave.

We held still as we watched the boat half circle the island and head on downstream. They were searching for us, and we held right still, going nowhere.

Once they were out of sight I relaxed, but I knew they would be back. The captain commanding the *St. Louis* was no pushover. He had captured me once and if I made the wrong move he would have me again.

"If he doesn't come back upriver before daylight we're going to be in trouble," I said.

"Do we have to wait here?"

"It's best we do. If we pull out now there's no telling what kind of fog we're going to encounter downriver, if any at all. I don't want to get caught needing a hiding place. We've got one right here."

"That makes sense, but what if they see our cave on the way back upriver."

"That's a chance we'll have to take. If we're caught out on the open water, they'll have us for sure."

We only had to wait thirty minutes for the boat to come steaming back upriver. It was moving slowly and from deep in our cave we could see soldiers on deck sweeping back and forth with their eyes trying to see what was not on the river. We held ourselves motionless and waited for the boat to clear the island. The behemoth disappeared around the bend. I listened as the captain barked orders to his men, but they were too far away for me to make out what he was saying.

I was racking my brain thinking what I would do in his place. He was afraid of running the boat aground if he got too close to the island. He would keep her in the open water, but he would make a complete circle of any island such as we were on. He was not a cruel man, therefore he would not send his soldiers into such frigid water to swim ashore and search our small oasis. However, he would do a complete and thorough search from the deck of his ironclad.

"If we stay back and don't move there's no way they can see us," I whispered to Bobby. "Just let them search. They won't come ashore."

"My feet are freezing," Bobby said.

"So are mine, but we can't risk a fire until they're gone."

They were coming back around from the north side of the island like they had earlier. They looked, and they saw a dark spot on the cliff wall, but there was nothing for them to see. As they were about to round the corner of our island oasis and steam out of sight I heard the captain shout. "Drop anchor!" Then, "All engines stop!"

Their boat was lit inside by gas lanterns, but we could chance no such thing. I could sense Bobby's worry as the anchor made a splash in the night and sank to the bottom of the river. The *St. Louis* couldn't be more than fifty yards from us, the fog our only keeper.

I now had to turn to my faith in God. We were in need of a miracle, and I only knew one way to get something like that. Silently I began to call on the Lord for an answer to our dilemma. I had found at times in my life when man can't see the tip of his nose, God could perform miracles. I needed one of them now. If the *St. Louis* was still anchored outside our cave when the fog cleared or the sun came up in the morning, we were going to be captured.

The last thing I wanted was to endure the humiliation of another capture by the same captain. It had taken me six months to escape the clutches of the Federal Army the last time, and I didn't believe I could handle a repeat performance.

I knelt beside our little boat and began to pray in earnest. Bobby must have figured out what I was up to because after a few minutes he was kneeling beside me doing the same thing. We prayed together for an answer to the problem at hand. There was nothing else we could do.

When we had said our request and gotten up I felt better. Even if I was to be captured again, I understood it to be God's will. How does a man of faith survive a war such as the one we were now engaged in? There was only one way, and that was to spend a lot of time on your knees.

The fact I carried no weapon was on my mind. I needed God's protection for that very reason. War had a funny way of making a man pray more often. I was learning this from experience.

We could see the glare of the lamps from their boat, but there seemed to be little to no movement aboard. What were they up to? Why weren't they doing something—anything? Had they bedded down for the night? The only place to sleep on one of those things was on deck or on shore. They weren't designed for sleeping quarters like a riverboat. When Eads had built the boats for the Federal Armies he had not worried about where a soldier would lay his head, only how the ship would be used in an engagement.

It was too quiet. Did they know where we were? Had they spotted something and even now they were sneaking up on us?

We had effectively blocked ourselves in on purpose. Could our ploy have been a mistake? There was no way to get the boat out of the cave without making all kinds of noise, but what about us? Could we slip out and sneak to another position? What if we did? Wouldn't they hear us? We had to remain quiet and still. In this regard Bobby was very efficient. He could sit still longer than I could. Given half a chance I believe he could outwait an Indian.

The fog appeared as if it was going to lift at any moment, but instead rose so thickly we could no longer see the lights onboard the ironclad. Or had they been extinguished? I was wishful to know. All this waiting was nerve wracking, but what are nerves if you can't exercise them once in a while? The moon was growing full, but the light was defused by the thick fog which the icy river now brought to life.

This was no good. We had to move, to get away, but how? The river was too cold to swim, the moon, although weak, was too bright to chance anything and the fog was so thick you couldn't see your hand in front of your face. On top of that it was impossible to rest such as the Yankee's were now doing. We needed to do something.

We heard a whistle of sorts, and the steam blow off a boat and the *Jessie K Bell* was paddling by on the north side of the island having given the Yankee's the slip in the thick fog. Captain August Bryant had made a mistake. He had believed all the ironclads were back upriver around the bend. The *Jessie K Bell* was our savior as the soldiers aboard the *St. Louis* scrambled from their slumber and pulled anchor. I wondered what Captain Bryant's solution had been for the cannons at Belmont, but it seemed fog was the answer.

As the *St. Louis* drifted away, I knew it would take her a while to gather a head of steam, and while they were floating downriver we would be right behind them paddling to clear the ironclad while she was engaged in enforcing her will on the steamboat *Jessie K Bell*. Using the *Bell* for a distraction was the perfect answer to our prayers. Still, I was puzzled about how the captain had managed to get a steamer through several miles of Yankee stronghold.

Three miles downriver we neared the two boats which were causing all kinds of commotion on the water and as we listened, we heard gunshots, some yelling, and for a few minutes I was confused. Had they shot the captain? Why had they put up a fight? I wanted to step aboard and ensure justice was being done, but I was in no position to do anything but surrender, and I would not, for there was no justice in surrendering.

I said a small prayer for Captain Bryant and then we floated downriver in the eerie fog which had engulfed the Mississippi.

We were on the dangerous part of the river now, the part which wound around and twisted and turned in all sorts of fanatical ways. This section was full of snags and sand bars, any of which would ground our boat, but still we couldn't see for the fog. We had been delivered, but into what? I didn't like floating blindly down the most dangerous part of the river, yet we had to gain more distance.

As the sky began to gray we were still enveloped by fog and I made haste to row toward shore. Having no idea which bank we might be closest to I made for the Tennessee shoreline. By the time we tied off, I was certain we had been closer to the west bank.

The heavy fog had not dissipated, and I didn't want to go downriver any farther without being able to see. We had a few hours between us and the *St. Louis,* so I was confident of our safety.

The Federal Army had control of St. Louis and New Orleans along with the seven mile stretch of river just before Belmont which they had taken from the south, but other than that they had control of nothing. Rebels were thick in the woods on either side of the river and all the way south to New Orleans. With any luck Bobby and I would be among them by tomorrow.

It was late in the evening the same day when we spotted Butcher's Landing. I breathed a sigh of relief and made for it. Riley was there and waved at us as we paddled up to the dock.

"I figured them Yankee's had you done in by now," my old friend greeted me.

"You ought to know they can't keep me locked up. It took a while, but I got shut of them and here I am."

"Lieutenant Twain left a message for you."

"What is it?"

"It's been several months ago, but it was something along the lines that if you get yourself killed he was going to court your fiancée. So you'd better not get killed for her sake."

"That's Mark for you. Did he say anything else?"

"Nope, just that he was going to sit this one out."

"Now what does he mean by that?"

"I think he intends not to fight. He's done deserted."

"Mark Twain a deserter? Why that's impossible. I know him too well. He'd never do such a thing."

"Like it or not captain, he's gone and done it. He was already dressed in civilian clothes when he left here," Riley said.

"If he's deserted, he's putting an awful strain on our friendship," I said.

We camped in the woods near the dock that evening and the following morning we rode for Corinth, once again borrowing Riley's mounts. The first thing we encountered as we left the dock was a thunderstorm. I had seen the rain coming, but I had not expected a storm like this.

Lightning struck a tree in the road beside us and the horses reared straight up taking off at a dead run. A moment later the rain dropped from the sky in buckets. We had our hands full holding on. I looked over my shoulder and Bobby was still in the saddle behind me. There was nothing to do except let the horses run themselves out.

The road was clear ahead and then suddenly lightning struck a tree next to the road and I saw a huge limb coming down across our path. As the limb struck the road my horse jumped and came down on the other side. I looked back to see Bobby's horse follow suit, jumping the tree limb as well. We were lighting a shuck I guess you could say, but to my way of thinking there was no way to outrun lightning.

Slowly the horses began to put some distance between us and the storm. They ran, showing no sign of letting up. I reckon they had never been so close to a lightning strike before, but I had seen them up close. Wherever lightning struck it had a tendency to leave the ground burning. A good strike at just the right spot would uproot a tree and kill it, then later a good wind would finish it off by blowing it over.

It was nearing ten o'clock when we brought the horses to a stop. I was getting worried about them. I knew horses could run, but these two wanted to keep running. I choked mine off and brought him up short waiting to see of Bobby could rein his mount in. He got it stopped but the horse was still pitching and fussing, wanting no part of the storm which lay behind.

"Easy boy," Bobby said. "We need shelter. There's an abandoned farm house about two miles to our south."

"Let's go. We need to beat the storm," I said as I followed Bobby into the foreboding forest.

He led us about a hundred yards to a wagon trail. No doubt Bobby had found this place on a previous trip. As we rode on the house came into view and I saw a barn which would shelter the horses from the oncoming storm.

The horses were our first priority and we got them settled in the barn before making our way to the house. This was an old farmhouse all right, though it was a small home when measured against many houses in the south. It was quite good enough for us. There was wood stacked on the porch and Bobby brought some in along with kindling and lit a fire in the hearth. As the fire got going I began to relax. I must have been tired because I fell asleep as I dried myself beside the fire.

"Captain, there's someone outside," I heard Bobby say.

I sat straight up and took a look around. All was dark.

"Who is it?" I asked.

"I don't have any idea, but I think they're waiting for us to come out."

"Why would anybody be laying for us?"

"I don't know."

I listened for a moment. "Stoke the fire, Bobby," I said. Outside the rain came down in a steady downpour. Whoever was out there was wet and getting wetter.

"Go ahead and stoke the fire some more. If they're wishful to come in out of the rain maybe a good warm fire will convince them, but keep ready. We may have to abandon our comfortable dwelling for a cold night out."

Bobby stoked the fire, and I moved back into the corner where I could watch the front porch better. It was a few minutes only before I recognized movement. Whoever was out there seemed to be alone. Taking a chance I got up and opened the front door stepping out onto the front porch. Looking about I saw nothing out of place.

"You might as well come inside and get warm," I said. "There's coffee and jerked beef. We even have grits for breakfast if you're hungry."

Slowly in the rain darkened night I saw the head of a young kid peep around the corner of the house. I mistakenly believed Bobby was still in the old house minding the fire, but at that very moment he tackled the kid from behind. Dressed in a man's hand-me-downs, it was hard to tell how old.

A scuffle ensued and I wondered over to see how Bobby was doing. He must have been expecting little to no resistance, but he had his hands full of a high-spirited young person who was letting him have some dog ear slaps to wake him up. It was obvious by now that the kid was a young girl and that Bobby had realized it. He was doing his best to hold back from hitting her while taking it on the chin. Finally he got control of her flailing arms and pinned her to the ground.

"If I were you, Bobby, I'd let her up. She doesn't look any too happy about you overpowering her like you did."

"I'll let her up if she'll quit slapping me!" Bobby insisted.

Still squirming, the girl muttered through clenched teeth, "If'n you don't let me up this very minute, I'm gonna claw your eyes out."

I stepped down from the front porch and offered Bobby a hand. Taking it, I lifted him away from the girl and offered my hand to her. She took it and once on her feet she began to brush herself off.

"You're welcome at our fire, young lady. We sure didn't intend you any harm."

"If'n you can keep yonder swine off'n me, I'll be glad to accept your hospitality," she said.

"Just who are you calling swine," Bobby said.

"Who do you think?"

"Now children, let's control those tempers. Little lady, you're safe here. No one will bother you as long as you're with us. Now come in out of the rain," I said as I headed back into the house.

The girl turned out to be another orphan who was wondering about the countryside lost and tormented by her newfound situation. She couldn't talk much without crying about her new lot in life. The more she talked about what had happened to her home, the madder I got at the Federal troops. They were supposed to be fighting a gentlemen's war, not terrorizing young girls and killing entire families for no reason.

Mona Freedman was her name and she had been devastated. Her parents had been killed execution style because they wouldn't take the oath of allegiance to the Federal cause. For that reason alone, her family had been murdered, and she would have died with them had she not been off picking berries for supper. She had heard the entire exchange while hiding in the woods near the house and she had witnessed the executions of everyone on the premises. Once everyone was dead, the soldiers burned the plantation, stole the animals, and headed east. That had been two weeks ago and now Mona just wanted rest.

Bobby stared while she slept on our blankets.

"What are you thinking about, Bobby?"

"I'm thinking how much I'm beginning to hate those Federal soldiers."

"What're you going to do about them?"

"I have an idea for a coal bomb, one I can toss into the coal pits at the dock. Once that one piece of coal is shoveled into the boiler, the boat will explode."

"What are you going to make it out of? It's got to look like coal."

"I was thinking about a hollow piece of iron filled with gunpowder then capped. It would look just like coal if it was shaped right."

"That might just work. Maybe Tucker can fix us up with something when we see him on the return trip."

"That's what I was wondering. Would he help?"

"Tucker's a man who'll do anything if the price is right."

The girl stirred, turned over, and looked across the room at me. She rolled her eyes back in their sockets, going right back to sleep.

"We'd better get some sleep if we're going to deliver our mail in the morning," I said.

Chapter 16

When we rode into the camp in Corinth Mississippi the following morning the men were just setting up to breakfast. I handed out a good portion of the mail then handed the reins over to Bobby who completed mail call.

Shelby was there and I gave him the letter from his wife. The man had acquired another stripe since I last saw him, this one a rocker. Evidently Shelby Foster was becoming a top-notch soldier. We stayed on for two days. I noticed Bobby was spending a good deal of time with Mona and the two were becoming close.

I received permission from Colonel Elijah Gates to head north with my parcel and the three of us rode out swiftly on that third morning. By the time we left camp my right arm was almost paralyzed from shaking so many hands. My intention was to bring down another mail run for those lonely men from Missouri.

We returned to the dock and launched our wheeled contraption onto the decks of the *Belle Creole* then started downriver to the plantation Belle Grove. Captain Joseph Compton catered to our every need until he had safely deposited us on the docks at Belle Grove.

It seemed I was to be traveling with a complete entourage if things continued in their current state, as I now had Bobby, Mona, and Mickey. Suddenly it occurred to me that all three of my traveling companions were orphans created by the Civil War. I don't know why I hadn't realized this sooner. Not that it meant anything, but the observation tugged at my heart.

Tucker provided Bobby with three coal-shaped pieces of iron molded into capsule's with caps. Bobby then set out to fill them with gunpowder while Mickey harnessed our team to the boat and we were soon underway.

I saw a new respect in Mona's eyes for my young companion, Bobby Louden, and she seemed to want to stay by his side where she could lean on his shoulder. Mickey was spending an inordinate amount of time plying me with questions and while I'm sure the couple was listening, they were also engaged in their own communication.

I didn't see where it would be conducive to our good health to come on the Yankee's unexpectedly in our travels for we were riding an amphibious wagon and they would want answers. Such a contraption could be used for no other purpose than what we're using the skiff for and the Yankee's would be quick to grasp the situation.

On our return to St. Louis, three days were required for the ladies to get the mail out and return. There was a knock on Miss Lizzie Pickering's door the third day, and since I was the only one present, I proceeded to answer the door on my own. I was greeted by Colonel Leighton.

"Greetings, captain. May I come in?"

I didn't know what to say or whether I should run.

"Come, come now, captain surely you're not going to be inhospitable."

I gathered my wits about me and let Colonel Leighton in. We returned to the parlor where I had been sitting. I offered the Yankee soldier a seat.

"I assure you, captain, you have nothing to fear from me," he said as he peeled off his gloves.

"How long have you known I was here?"

"Just since this morning. We both know you're not really Harvey Shively, so I'll get right to the point. My brother is fighting for the Confederacy. I only want to make certain he is well. Can you deliver a letter for me?"

"You know that I'm Absalom Grimes, the mail runner?"

"I do."

"And you're not going to arrest me?"

"I promised my Jennie that I would do nothing to harm you, captain. I don't care to elaborate on the circumstances as to how."

"Then you're not here to arrest me?"

"I will tell no one what I know. I have a letter for you to take south if you would do me the honor."

I sat in my chair stunned at the prospect of this Federal asking me to deliver a letter for him. I had envisioned many things in my daydreaming ways that called for many scenarios to be played out, but nothing along these lines.

"Captain, this war's of the devil's making. I should not wish ill on anyone no matter which side they represent for we're pitted brother against brother. No good can come of such a circumstance."

"I believe I understand, although I never expected to see the like.

"Captain Grimes, I understand your mission is a peaceful one. In another time or another place I might undertake to do the same. I no longer perceive you as a threat."

"What about the reward on my head?"

"I have no need of money, captain and I, nor Jennie, will ever betray you."

I heard footsteps on the front porch and three of the women returned with Lizzie Pickering in tow. When they stepped into the parlor the women's chattering stopped and they froze dead still. All eyes locked on the Yankee colonel sitting across from me.

"I will be glad to deliver the letter for you, Colonel Leighton," I said as I got up and met him in the middle of the room. He handed me the letter, then bid the ladies good day.

"Miss Pickering," he said as he let himself out of the front door.

"Ab, what does this mean?" Lizzie asked in confusion.

"It means that nothing has changed. The colonel will say nothing nor will he do anything to stop us. In fact, I believe he'd help us if he was forced by the army to make a choice."

They began to chatter in the language of women, which most men find intolerable. The height of their voices reached mind-searing proportions before they settled down again. I waited the ordeal out simply because I had nowhere else to go.

One hour later there was another knock on the door. Lizzie answered it to find two Yankee soldiers guarding two female prisoners.

"May I help you, gentlemen?"

"Yes, ma'am. We have been directed by Colonel Leighton to turn these prisoners over to you."

"I don't understand."

"They're being released into your custody, ma'am."

Lizzie swung the door all the way open and allowed the two young ladies to enter. "Would you please tell the colonel, thank you," she said as she closed the door behind them. She led them into the parlor where I was waiting along with the other three women.

"Ladies, this is Captain Grimes," Lizzie introduced.

"I remember you, captain. You were in the Myrtle Street jail with us."

"I do seem to remember a couple of young ladies down the hall from my quarters, but there were only two."

"You're correct. We were the only two female prisoners and you gained our release. Thank you, Captain Grimes."

I didn't know what to say. I was having things attributed to me that I had nothing to do with, or did I?

"Miss Marsha Sanford?" I guessed.

"That would be me," the shy one insisted.

"Then you must be Ruthie Dalton," I said to the other.

"I'm Ruthie," the other girl stated. "We don't know where to begin to thank you, captain."

"You can thank me by not getting caught again," I said.

"Colonel Leighton said that you would see us to safety."

"He did? He must figure me for some kind of hero. Do those guards know of my presence in the Pickering house?"

"They do know, but Colonel Leighton said in front of us that he would have them both court marshaled and shot if either of them mentioned a word to anyone."

"Lizzie, can you put our guests up for the night?"

"Certainly, captain. Ladies if you'll accompany me I'll show you where you can sleep."

"I guess we'll test the good colonel's word," I mumbled to no one in particular.

My mail was getting more dangerous to carry as I was now expected to deliver living breathing females who had sympathies which lay with the south. This was an extra burden I hadn't counted on. Going through the enemy lines with mail was one thing, but with human cargo quite another.

We now had it arranged that the friends of soldiers throughout Missouri should address their mail to various trustworthy persons in St. Louis. The ladies would then gather them up and have them ready for when I returned. In order to facilitate a reputable standard if detained and questioned, the ladies had arranged with various corset and hosiery houses to act as drummers for them so that they could refer the Federal soldiers to those places of business to verify their employment. This technique saved my most mysterious ladies bacon on more than one occasion.

On this trip my lady friends had gathered quite a large number of letters for me to carry, but all was well, for I had plenty of help. Bobby and Mona had stayed with a friend of Mona's until I called for them. I had learned that the railroads east of the river were still running a regular schedule so I decided to make this trip the easy way. Marsha and Ruthie were desirous to return to Louisville and I had agreed to escort them to safety.

Five of us crossed the river by ferry and then boarded the southbound train from St. Louis to Cairo where we boarded the steamboat *De Soto* for Louisville. Mickey had stayed behind to guard our launch and the horses. In all, we carried four carpetbags full of correspondence, and I wondered how I could do this alone. There was no feasible way that I could see. The mail had already outgrown my ability to carry it. I said as much to Bobby and he agreed with me, something was going to have to be done.

After dropping Ruthie and Marsha in Louisville the rest of us headed south to Memphis by train. From there we took a train to Holly Springs and then borrowed horses overland to Corinth.

Again we gave out mail call and the men liked the fact Mona was handing them their mail. Well, she was a mite prettier than any of us. In my haste to leave St. Louis I had forgotten to deliver my letter from Shelby to Mrs. Foster. I told him of my error but insisted I would not forget on my return. He sat down and wrote out another one for me to give her and again we left on the third morning.

Mona enjoyed her stay so much that she decided to stay on and assist with the cooking chores for the soldiers. This was a sad parting for Bobby, but he understood.

Returning the horses, we caught the train at Holly Springs and were back in St. Louis in two days. This had been my easiest trip to date and unbeknownst to me, it was to remain so.

General John C. Moore was wishful of me to report on the Yankee progress taking place on the river which meant my next trip would be in the skiff. I preferred the train ride, but I had a job to do. It would be necessary of me at this time to do some private investigating of the Union forces so that I could make a detailed report on their progress when I returned to Mississippi.

I decided to make an attempt to navigate the river as far as Fort Pillow which was in Confederate territory for the time being. Island Number Ten was also in Confederate hands, but the Federal gunboats were attempting to annihilate the position and rectify the situation.

If I could spy on the enemy progress, I was to drift all the way downstream to Vicksburg and report to General Pemberton. The general was to give me a dispatch to carry back to General Moore at Corinth. This was the plan, but I had misgivings for the first time. I would have to float past the Yankee gunboats once again and I was not thrilled with the prospect, but being a trooper I knew what to expect. In essence, I was to give my report at Fort Pillow and continue downriver to repeat it at Vicksburg.

Back in St. Louis the women delivered the mail and picked up the return parcel while I rested at the Pickering house. I had no justification for the feeling, but I felt as if the Yankee noose was tightening around my neck. Reading the *St. Louis Post* I waited. According to what Dutch had written, the Yankee's under General Grant were attempting to dig a channel across land from Island Number Ten, thereby eliminating the need to engage the Rebel location on their way south. This is what I needed to see for myself.

I was curious to see how this was being done as the river was at flood stage and the bottom lands were all of eight to ten feet deep up and down the Mississippi. Knowing this did nothing to make me feel confident about my upcoming trip. Bobby would be with me but he was all the help I could risk at the moment. Mickey would still take our team south to Belle Grove but other than that I had all the help I wanted. Bobby had yet to use his first coal bomb, but on this trip we figured we'd get our chance.

After spending a week in St. Louis, Bobby and I took our launch down to Nealy's landing and waited on the steamer *Far West* whose captain was William Blake, an old friend of mine. We boarded our wheeled skiff to the captain scratching his bearded jaw. Mr. Hogan was happy to see we were still free and walking about, but we didn't have the time to visit on this trip.

As things were, Bobby's bombs were riding one per carpetbag of mail. We had three bags and three bombs. Their weight would help sink the bags if we ran into any trouble and if we didn't they would be ready to use on short notice.

Captain Blake dropped us off near a small tributary north of Cairo and waved goodbye. We made our way up the creek to a house owned by another old friend of mine, a retired riverboat pilot, John Graham. Here we acquired rations for four days and shoved off for Dixie, or so I believed.

As Cairo came into sight we went ashore and began to cut willow branches, tying them to our skiff for cover in the night. The last thing I wanted was the Yankee garrison at Cairo firing on my boat as we had no wiggle room. If a shell hit us we would likely be killed.

I was amazed at how far Bobby had come in so short a time. My young companion was adept at thinking strategically and sharper than any casual observer would expect for his age, which was now seventeen. Once we had the boat covered and darkness had descended, we pushed off once again hugging the west bank, but the current got hold of the boat and began to pull us all the way back across the river where we would be right in front of the garrison as we passed by.

We dared not use the oars and so we settled low and out of sight. As we were about to clear the garrison a few soldiers who were bored from nothing to shoot at began to use our floating debris for target practice and bullets began to prick and punch holes in our skiff. The two of us hid behind our mail bags and hunkered down as low as possible to get out of the line of fire. I was worried about those holes though, if the water should get rough the boat would take on water and we would be bailing, with what I don't know, just to stay afloat.

About four miles below Cairo we came to Bird's Point and lost no time in removing the willow branches and putting distance between us and those trigger happy soldiers. The Federal fleet of ironclads lay anchored about Island Number Nine which is where the Confederates had placed the chain across the river so that no big boats could pass. The chain was gone. General Grant had seen to it that the cumbersome infrastructure was removed so that his boats could float easily up and down that part of the river.

Island Number Nine seemed to be as far as they had gotten though, because the entire mosquito fleet was anchored there. The Rebels still held Island Number Ten a little farther downriver, and were letting nothing with a stars and stripes pass. The mosquito fleet consisted of sternwheelers and other vessels covered in iron two inches thick. They still presented a good target, but most times a cannon ball would just bounce off the iron and land helplessly in the water.

I made note, as we floated past, of the boats which had been covered in iron by James Eads. There were eight transports and as we floated near one of them, the *Jessie K Bell*, Bobby tossed the first of his bombs on board into the coal chute. The gunpowder filled canister of iron landed with a thud, but after several alert soldiers shuffled about searching in the darkness for they knew not what, things settled down and we were well under way again. I felt safe executing this little maneuver simply because I knew the Federals had confiscated her, and my friend the captain was in the Myrtle Street jail safe and sound.

Not wanting to press our luck, we steered away from the rest of the fleet around Island Number Nine and headed farther south. It was then we came upon the next Yankee position and I was surprised as to what I found. There were four boats equipped with upright steam engines used to operate saws much like the snag boats used to clear the Red River snag a few years before. This had been done by Captain Henry Miller Shreve at a total cost of about three hundred thousand dollars, but he had done it and cleared four miles of log jams in the process.

As I witnessed the four flatboats I knew the Yankees would soon be around Island Number Ten and well out of range of any gunfire from that position. Like the stubborn ant hill that never goes away, those Yankee's were moving about in our Confederate backyard making a nuisance of themselves and a bother to every man wearing a grey uniform.

The Yankee saws were about eight to ten feet long and so arranged as to be able to saw the largest of trees in twain a dozen feet below the surface of the water. They could be adjusted to remove trees out in front of the boat on land with grappling to lay the tree over away from the boat so as not to damage the boat or injure any of the men. The stumps whether below water or on land would then be sawed up and dragged out of the way by steam tugs. It was about two and a half miles across the point and from the looks of things those Yankee beavers were only about two or three days from completing the pass around Island Number Ten to New Madrid.

The Confederate guns on Island Number Ten would be cut off. There would be no way for our side to remove them once the Yankee's had control of this part of the river. The result would be that the guns would have to be spiked to prevent the Yankee's from using them against us and the island would have to be abandoned. This was not the kind of report I wanted to give our commanders in Mississippi. At this rate, the Yankee's would be in Vicksburg by fall.

It was early morning hours by the time we rowed back to Island Number Ten and put ashore. There we were greeted by well wishers, but I had bad news to deliver them. The captain in charge was Captain Bradley Eckert. He was none too pleased with my report on the Yankee's, but to have gone on without coming back to tell him would not have been in good character. It might have been weeks before he knew that his position had been outflanked.

These men were in good spirits and in good shape. They welcomed us with excitement and then cooled down as I gave my report. Such a report meant they were out of a job and the subordinates watched their captain closely to see how he would react to the news.

"If that's their doing, we've been out-foxed," their captain allowed.

"They have bypassed you completely, and in no less than three days, they will have the canal open to come and go as they please."

"Well, we gave them hell while we could."

"I'd say so. They were afraid to confront this position. So much so they've been digging a canal two and a half miles around."

"Why don't you join us for breakfast, Captain Grimes, we do manage to eat pretty good."

"Now you're talking. We won't put back into the river until this evening."

"You're welcome to share with us as long as we're here."

"We'll pull out at dusk. Mostly we'll want rest."

"Looks like we all get to rest," Captain Eckert said.

Once Bobby and I had eaten we made ourselves comfortable on blankets offered by the soldiers of Island Number Ten who were now up and awake. Bobby and I went to sleep.

There was no shade as the sun ascended high overhead but the two of us slept like babies anyway. At noon I awakened to the sound of banging, and looked over my shoulder to see soldiers taking cannons apart. Once aroused I was unable to return to my slumber so I got up and visited with Captain Eckert.

"We're spiking the guns," he informed me as I approached.

"I figured as much."

"We'll miss them dearly, but this way the Yankee's won't be able to use them against us."

"Where will you and the men go when you leave here?"

"We'll make for Fort Pillow, and if the Yank's are there we'll go farther south."

Bobby showed signs of life so we ate with the men once again and then rowed them back and forth to the eastern shore of the Mississippi until all were safely away from the island. We waved goodbye and started downriver as the sun was setting in the western sky.

Chapter 17

The Federal mosquito fleet had not ventured south of Island Number Nine and we didn't want them to. Sooner or later they would risk another assault on Island Number Ten to test the defenses of the Rebels, but there was no need to alert them ahead of time that the island had been abandoned. If they wanted to waste the next three days digging a canal they no longer needed, I was of no mind to tell them any different. Soldiers occupied dredging and creating a new canal meant less soldiers picking up arms and shooting, but what would they do once they completed their canal?

There was no question as to why they were engaged in the earth moving exercise. Vicksburg lay to the south and as long as the Confederate army held her, there was a supply line from Texas all the way to the Carolina's and Virginia. They had to take Vicksburg, but all odds were against them. Had they moved at the beginning they might already have the town which sat on a bluff overlooking the Mississippi, but having missed their chance the Rebels had now dug in and were twenty thousand strong. That number was growing daily. Vicksburg was the key to Yankee victory in the west, but they were still six hundred miles away if you figured every mile that the Mississippi twisted and turned. Four hundred if you didn't.

New Orleans had been one of the first cities taken in the south, and Baton Rouge had recently surrendered without firing a shot, but Vicksburg would be a different story. The mayor of Vicksburg had told Admiral Farragut just where he could stick his

Yankee fleet, that the people of Mississippi didn't know how to surrender and refused to learn. He would have to teach them.

His response would mean an all out battle for the town, but I knew the Vicksburg area well and the land about the bluff was swamp. There was nowhere to put an army ashore on the east bank. If the Yankee's wanted Vicksburg they were going to have to pay a dear price for her.

The Forked Deer River was a tributary which emptied into the Mississippi just north of Fort Pillow and this is where I chose to lie in wait for the Federal fleet. A delay of a couple of days would not hinder our mission, and if the Federals got this far south, which I suspected they would, I wanted to be able to make an intelligent report on the matter to include troop strength and vessels.

There was a farm house on stilts about two miles north of this position so Bobby and I rowed in that direction and tied our skiff off on the front porch. Like I said earlier, the entire region was under water as the river was at flood stage. Around the house the water was approximately four foot deep. We had debated hiding our mail in the swamp across the river before rowing up to the house. Not knowing the owner, I was uncertain as to whether the place would be friendly or hostile.

As it turned out this was another retired riverboat pilot whom I knew. This elevated home was owned by Herval Scruggs and he was relaxing, waiting for the river to recede and the land to dry out before he began planting. Like I mentioned, he was retired and I don't believe he cared one wit about planting as he had built his home on this spot knowing full well the land would be submerged and under water every spring.

We sat down on his front porch to watch the river roll by and watch the Federal troops arrive. We had a drink from his wine cellar, which was anchored beneath the house in the water.

He kept his wine in the river so that the contents in the bottle would remain cool. This seemed unorthodox to me, but who was I to judge someone thirty years my elder.

When I took my first sip of his own grape wine I knew him to be a wise man. Where he managed to come up with such a flavor got me to wondering what else Scruggs was concealing in his cabin on stilts.

"You certainly know how to care for your guests," I said as I adjusted my chair on the front porch.

"I do what I have to, Little Grimes."

I didn't say anything because the codger had always called me Little Grimes. I don't go around correcting folks thirty years my elder like I mentioned. He had earned his place and I could only hope to do the same. We talked of the river, the coming changes and what it would all mean if the south lost. Bobby never said a word, he just listened. The wine turned out to be a nondescript dark bottle of brew from a place called Poeschel and Scherer known today as the Stone Hill Winery upriver at Hermann.

I had originally thought the bottle to be his own brew, but he corrected me later saying, "I'll never be able to make wine this good, but I can buy."

About noon the following day the first ironclad appeared and as she steamed into view, the *Jessie K Bell* came around the horn behind her. Just as the *Bell* cleared the bend an explosion ripped her asunder and the boat sank within two minutes. Although most of the burning upper deck was still above water as she had been in a shallow bend to begin with. Bobby and I looked at one another and wondered immediately if this was his coal bomb. All evidence seemed to point in that general direction. We sat our perch and watched as the boat burned and eventually crumbled into the water.

Other boats from the Yankee fleet appeared within minutes and began to rescue the soldiers who were still living, but as they were a good mile from us on the other side of the Mississippi we didn't bother to move. We had a good spot from which to watch the comings and goings of the Yankee fleet and were content to rest while sipping more wine from Stone Hill.

Later in the afternoon as the sun was setting, a launch with a half-dozen marines came around the corner of the house and tied off on the front porch. The commander of this little expedition was one Lionel Harris, a fellow I knew from St. Louis. He looked at me rather oddly and then said, "Captain Grimes, what are you doing in these parts?"

"I'm just resting, lieutenant."

"I have it on good authority that you're with the Rebel army."

"I've quit the Rebels and taken the oath of allegiance, sir. I'm learning the lower Mississippi under the tutelage of Captain Ben Greene of the *Wisconsin*," I lied. Both my companions knew I was lying, but I was counting on the fact my friends wouldn't give me up.

"The officer you mention just burned to death on board the *Jessie K Bell*. How is it you escaped unharmed?"

"Captain Greene was on the *Bell*?" I said.

"He most certainly was. Captain Grimes, I find it odd that you're here watching the *Bell* burn to the water line and that you've done nothing to help aid or recover your wounded friends."

I didn't wait to see what was going to be said next. The thought of getting my cipher book wet never entered my mind. I took a dive off the porch and swam under the house before coming up for air. Bullets were piercing the muddy water around me, so I quickly hid myself behind the center beam of the home and kept it between me and the marines. There was only about a foot of air between the swollen river and the bottom of the house so I was well concealed right up to the point that Lieutenant Harris ordered his men into the water to retrieve me. At this point I knew my efforts to be useless so I surrendered.

Bobby had done the smart thing and hadn't moved a wink. His guilt and complicity in the matter was well-masked by my own actions.

When I came out from under the house the lieutenant asked me, "Why did you risk being shot?"

"It just seemed like the thing to do, lieutenant."

"Well, you'd better get in the boat. I'll have to take you in with me for questioning."

"I don't have anything to say to those fellows," I said from my position in the chest deep water.

"Humor me, Captain Grimes. They might believe otherwise."

I climbed onto the porch and into their boat. Their attention turned to our blackened skiff the *Jokers Wild*.

"That's a very odd looking boat, Captain Grimes. Just what are you using such a craft for?"

"I decline to answer."

"Private Hobbs, tie a rope onto it. That skiff's going with us."

"There's no need to go to those kinds of lengths," I insisted.

"Actually, Captain Grimes I know you, remember? I think we'll drag the boat along so we can get to the bottom of things. If you had anything to do with the *Jessie K* blowing up, you'll no doubt be hanged."

"No doubt be hanged?" As Harris said those words my heart skipped a beat. Our carpetbags were still in the skiff with the mail and they contained two as yet unused coal bombs which would go a long way towards convicting me. I looked at Bobby and he knew exactly what was running through my mind but I couldn't say a word without incriminating the young man or myself. How could I get those bags out of the boat?

"Lieutenant, can I get my things out of the man's boat?" Bobby said thinking on his feet, "I was just hitching a ride with him. I didn't know he was knee deep in waging a war against y'all."

"Who are you?" Lieutenant Harris asked.

"My name is Bobby Louden, sir. I was just trying to get to St. Louis so I could go on west. This Grimes fellow said he knew a better way to get there and so I went with him, I didn't know he was in any trouble."

"Go ahead kid. I won't begrudge you what's yours."

Bobby stepped into the *Jokers Wild* and removed our carpetbags of mail. Then he stepped back on the front porch and said, "That's all that belongs to me, lieutenant."

For a long minute, the officer in charge was deep in thought, and I expected him, at any moment, to order his men to look into the contents of those bags, but at what seemed the last second I was spared.

"All right, let's go, men."

Lieutenant Harris was sitting in the back of the boat eying me as I rested in the bow and I could well imagine just what he was thinking. He was thinking I had blown up the Federal troop transport the *Jessie K Bell* and while I had knowledge of how the destruction of the ship had occurred, I was not the guilty party. I did have what I considered plausible deniability. I could deny my involvement completely and I would not be lying one bit.

As we docked against the flag ship *Benton*, I was ushered on board and greeted by Captain Bixby, another old friend who knew me from my now distant piloting days.

"Captain Grimes, I'm hoping you had nothing to do with what just happened out there. I'd hate to see an old friend hang," he added.

"Captain Bixby, I assure you I had nothing to do with that disaster. I was across the way visiting an old friend, Herval Scruggs, a man you well know."

"But you're known to be running the mail," he accused.

"I have run mail to Mississippi and back but I have not done so for a good while. I was simply vacationing with Captain Scruggs when this unfortunate incident happened."

"I hope you're telling the truth, captain. Admiral Foote is not an amused man right now. Come with me," he said and we entered the hull of the ironclad.

The interior was dark and drab, nothing like the riverboats I was used to riding. Gaslights lit the way down the hall to Admiral Foote's quarters. How these men could live in such an environment was beyond my comprehension. I was fairly caught for the moment, but in my mind I was watching for an opportunity to escape.

Bixby knocked on the admiral's door and a voice came from within.

"Who is it?"

"Bixby sir, we have Captain Grimes."

"The hell you say," I heard from behind the door.

The door opened and a short but, well-dressed man greeted us. "Captain Grimes, it's a pleasure to make your acquaintance. Come in gentlemen, please come in," the admiral insisted.

I heard the door close behind me before I actually realized I was in close quarters with two of the Union's best and brightest. I could kill them both with no one the wiser, but I was not a murderer. I would see what they wanted and give them nothing they could use.

"Your coat, captain," Bixby said as he held out his hand.

I pulled off my coat and handed it to Bixby, having forgotten that my cipher book was in my lapel pocket and not in its normal hiding place. He then proceeded to rummage through the pockets looking for anything which might convict me. When he pulled out my notebook I stood prepared to do battle—with my wits that is. The notebook was unintelligible to anyone but me as everything I had written in it was in cipher, which only I could understand. Bixby handed the book over to Admiral Foote who looked at the document while the good captain kept fishing in my coat pockets for more evidence which might convict me.

Finally Admiral Foote held the book out to me and said, "Please tell us what it says, captain."

"I'm sorry sir, but I will not," I replied.

"You'll talk soon enough, Captain Grimes. Captain Bixby, I want this man placed in irons and put in the hold."

"Yes, sir. What do we do with this?" Bixby asked as he held up my counterfeit greenbacks waving them before the admiral.

"Let him keep his money. I don't care about that."

"Yes, sir. Captain, if you will come with me?"

The two of us left the admiral and I was happy to be away. I would like my book back, but if I never saw my log again, I knew they couldn't read it. The captain took a good deal of my newly printed Yankee money and stuffed it into his own pockets, saying I wouldn't need so much where I was going. I was thankful to have been allowed to keep even a small portion of my counterfeit and the fact Captain Bixby had not found my jackknife which was sewn into the inside liner.

Presently, he locked me in a small dark room behind the stern wheel down in the hold below deck. It was so dark once he closed the door, I couldn't see my hands in front of my face. He'd handed me my coat before locking me in, so I at least had something to cover up with. I had glanced about while entering the room and well knew that I had no bed or chair.

Moving into the corner I made myself as comfortable as possible and began to think about my plight. They had no evidence I had blown up the *Jessie K Bell* and in fact I hadn't, although I knew of a little fellow who had. The fact that the Federals had decided to commission the boat as a troop ship was unfortunate. I had liked the boat and ridden on her decks many times. What boat would be next, I wondered.

This bunch of Federal troops on the river seemed to be about seven thousand strong and they would be looking to link up with others somewhere, but where? They had troops in New Orleans and Baton Rouge, but there was no way they could get troops safely past Vicksburg. Not now. They had missed their chance and I knew the Confederate soldiers had dug in to the tune of twenty thousand strong around the town with no end to the build up.

Time passed and I was left to starve in my little room on the *Benton*. Eventually the door was opened and I could hardly see from the shock of light having entered my room from the hallway. As I shielded my eyes from the sudden intrusion, I was grabbed by a soldier on either side before I could focus.

I was hustled out the door and down the hall to the exit where under heavy guard I was put in a skiff and rowed to the steamer *De Soto*. Once aboard I was escorted to Cairo. Here I was placed in jail. My cell was upstairs simply because the flood water was less than a foot from the second floor. All prisoners and the guards were living upstairs for the time being and I settled in to make myself comfortable. There was an old empty whisky barrel in the hallway and I convinced the guards on duty to let me have it in my room so I might be able to rest my chin on it or use it as a desk to write on.

I sent out for pen and paper and began writing a letter to Lucy to let her know that I was all right, and that I wouldn't be home on time. While I was engaged in this endeavor the guards brought in five young ladies and put them in the room next to me. Apparently they had sympathies for the south and were told to leave town, even given a small boat and sent away. Their boat had hit a snag downriver and sank, leaving all of them wet and irritable.

Having been rescued by Yankee's they were returned to Cairo and placed under guard. It sounded as though a party was taking place in the cell next to mine and I was severely distracted. Eventually I got up and conversed with them. Their names were Gretchen Anderson, Samantha Wilson, Christy Streeter, Vivian Chapman and Mrs. Reanna Loughridge who was down from St. Louis and had been visiting family.

While the guards were away eating, we devised a strategy of escape. I told them of my intentions and they squealed with delight. Of course, we still had to come up with a boat once we were out of the building. The walls between us were paper thin so getting the ladies out with me wouldn't be a problem.

I sat down, taking my jackknife from my coat pocket where it had been sewn into the liner. I cut a hole in the floor underneath where the barrel usually sat next to my bed. I worked at this slowly all afternoon and soon had the first two boards removed. The next morning there was water on my floor as the river had risen some more. There was no way I could enlarge my opening without getting my feet wet, so by the second afternoon I had very cold feet. Later that evening I finished my opening and informed the guests' next door of my success.

Unexpectedly I was sent for by the guards and escorted to the office of Commodore A.N. Pennock who was commander of the Union Naval Forces at Cairo. Once in his office, he, like

Admiral Foote, asked me to decipher the diary which they had found on me earlier.

"Sir, I am not disposed to read it to you or anyone else," I said.

"You'll tell me soon enough, young man. Sergeant, I want you to take this man down to the whipping post and have him secured. I'll get to the bottom of this matter one way or another."

To this day I don't know why the guard returned me to my cell first, but I didn't wait around for him to come back with help. I told the ladies of my plight and went to work to get the key out of my handcuffs and shackles while no one was looking. As the task was accomplished in record time with only a slight cut on my left wrist, I lowered myself through my prearranged escape hatch. I didn't like leaving the ladies behind, but they understood. I promised them I would return for them if at all possible and dropped myself into the cold dark water below.

The water was only about six inches above the floor in my cell, so air was at a premium once I was in the hole. If I had to go back to my opening, I had torn one of my bed sheets as well as one from next door, into long pieces. I had a length of about fifty feet which would be better than guessing as to the whereabouts of the freshly carved hole in the muddy water which I had to navigate if I had to come up for air before I found a way out. I didn't know if I could find an exit or not, or if the window or door would be locked, boarded up or barred, but I had to escape. I didn't want to feel the lash on my back as I had a unique aversion to pain. Much like exercise, I didn't see any need for it.

I had practiced holding my breath of late and I knew I could count to eighty-five before I had to come up for air. At first I had only been able to hold my lungs in check for thirty-two seconds, but practice had me in better shape. I searched in the darkness of the cell below for an escape and feeling my way around to where I thought a door would be, I found a window. Kicking out the window, I hoped not to encounter any bars on the other side. I was lucky, and as I came up out of the water I was outside of the building. I let go of my homemade rope and pushed for the surface.

I gasped for air as I had counted to seventy nine, almost at my limit, yet not quite. I bobbed up and down in the current a couple of times and settled in to drift on downriver. I knew I had to get out of the water soon and get myself dry, but I also needed distance between me and them Yankee's.

The clock was striking nine when I came up out of the water. It was dark and raining again, which didn't matter any to me for I was as wet as the water could possibly make me. Being a good swimmer had its rewards for I was soon in the turbulent water of the Ohio and Mississippi River bend. The two rivers merged at Cairo and had I not been a good swimmer the current would have drowned me for sure. I eventually found a good log to hang onto and continued to slip by the Federals in the dark of night. I saw a home in the distance and letting loose of my companion, I began to swim toward the lighted house.

I crawled out of the flooded waters about three hundred yards south of where I had tried to land and made my way back to the home on the hillside. Here I encountered an empty house and all light had been suddenly extinguished. This caused me to become guarded as the home had shown evidence of recent living and I knew I had seen a light emanating from the windows, but on my arrival there was no light and no one in sight. There was no sound and I thought this to be very odd, but I settled in to get as warm as possible for the night, so I got out of my clothes and hung them up to dry, crawled into the waiting bed naked and covered up with blankets, knowing I would awaken at the slightest sound.

I was feverish and came in and out of consciousness unwillingly. I never knew for several days that I was being cared for, but my good fortune had been to pick the home I had seen sitting on the bluff in the distance.

I didn't find out until later I was being cared for by a widow who wanted to be left alone. I had shown up and unintentionally laid claim to her sleeping quarters, so out of duty or compassion, she had brought me out of my fever by crawling naked into bed with me curling her warm body next to mine.

This was something I didn't want to have to explain to my fiancée as I didn't expect she would understand. As I regained my senses, I began to look at my surroundings and realized I was still naked underneath my blankets. I also realized how precarious a position I had found myself in.

A woman of uncommon beauty stood in the bedroom doorway eyeing me. She had been working in the kitchen and although I seemed to be aware that I was no longer alone, I had not expected this. Her beauty was by far the most unlikely I had ever encountered and her dress did nothing to hide her endowment.

"Where have you been sleeping," I asked as I became aware of my circumstance and the fact I was in her bed.

"I've been sleeping with you, but I don't even know your name," she responded with a mischievous smile and a wink.

I was taken back at her statement and didn't know how to respond to her. I didn't know if she was serious or if she was playing games with me, but I soon learned to respect her handling of affairs.

"I didn't take any liberties which were not due me. I simply did what was necessary to bring you back to reality."

"Can I have my clothes," I asked sheepishly.

"They are outside hanging on the clothes line."

"You mean they're still wet?"

"They wouldn't still be on the line if they were dry. I washed them for you."

"Can I ask the name of the fair maiden who has nursed me back to health?"

"My name is Beulah Ragsdale. May I ask yours?"

"Captain Absalom Grimes," I said respectfully.

"Well, captain, your virginity is intact if you must know, and should you remain another night or another month you're safe in my arms," she grinned.

At her statement I locked eyes with my tormentor and she smiled wider.

"I can see we're going to get along fabulously. Do you want cornpone with your stew or do you want it without," she asked.

"I would like some cornpone."

I watched through the bedroom door as my new captor swayed about in her kitchen dancing between the stove and counter. I knew there would be no end of trouble with this woman if things were allowed to go too far.

"Where's your husband?" I asked from my fluffed pillow cell.

"My husband was killed two years ago on the train to St. Joe."

"How did he die?"

"The train left the tracks and somehow landed on top of him."

"I'm sorry. No man should have to go like that."

"He was the engineer. He loved his run from Cairo to Chicago and back. When they offered him the chance to make the run from St. Louis to Hannibal and St. Joe he took the position and we planned to move the following month, but he never reached home."

"I'm still sorry."

"There's no need. He died doing what he loved. The railroad takes good care of me and intends to until I remarry."

"You have someone then?"

"I have no one, captain. I will find the right man sooner or later," she said.

She was a very attractive widow and I couldn't help but conjure up images of her bite being the death of me, much like a black widow spider. Her jaw was square but with high cheek bones, which gave her a beauty all her own. Her figure was shapely and the homemade dress she wore did nothing to hide her womanly body. I was mystified and wondered what I was doing talking to her when she knew I was laying in her bed naked as a jay bird.

Presently she brought me a hot bowl of stew from the kitchen. It was a mix I hadn't encountered before, but the taste was excellent.

"Do you approve?"

Sitting up in bed eating her concoction was very pleasing to an empty stomach of several days. I dipped my cornpone and ate until the bowl was completely devoid of food. Beulah sat across from me watching me eat until I was finished.

"Well, you certainly have an appetite."

Without thinking, I blurted out, "I should tell you I have a fiancée."

"How very nice," she said as she took my bowl and sashayed back into the kitchen. I didn't know what to think. I was being held captive by this woman until I had my clothes back. Did she have no shame? She came back into the bedroom empty handed.

"I'm sorry, did you want some more?"

"Actually, I was wondering if my clothes were dry yet."

"I'll go have a look-see."

She went out the front door swishing her long blue skirt, and a minute later she returned with nothing in her hands. "They're still wet, captain. You'll just have to wait a little longer."

"If we wait any longer it's going to be dark."

"If they have to hang there all night they're going to get dry before you get dressed. You wearing wet clothes got you in this fix in the first place."

"You have me at a clear disadvantage, dear lady," I mumbled.

"Is that what you think? You believe I want to take advantage of you? I'll have you know, Captain Grimes that I am a lady and I would never consider such a disgraceful encounter."

"Yes ma'am, but you have me wondering about my own constitution."

"I see. Well, I won't do anything which either of us might regret. You see to it that you do the same."

"That's impossible."

"Excuse me?"

"You're doing things to me just by holding me hostage."

"I'm not holding you hostage, but you needn't leave here in wet clothes. Just relax," she said as she left the doorway and entered her kitchen. She stayed in the other room doing who knows what for the longest time and left me to stew over my predicament. A man has his limits and Mrs. Ragsdale was tempting mine whether she knew of my pretty state of affairs or not. Pretty. There was a word I should have left elsewhere. She was all the beauty and then some. One thing was quite certain; there was no shortage of beauty in this part of the country. I was in a quandary of life changing proportions and could see no graceful mode of departure. She was here in her own home and I was still naked under her blankets, the very ones she would sleep under tonight? Suddenly I began to panic and squirm over the prospect of the sobering night ahead.

I thought back to what had happened recently and attempted to take my mind off of my current state of affairs. There had been no less then twenty steamers being used by the Federals which were docked at Cairo when I'd arrived. I would have written this into my cipher book, but they had confiscated my information. No need to worry though, as I could not forget such a sight.

General Moore would want to know about this little detail. There were other things too, but how much could I remember? I had been tracking Yankee movements for months, and now all of the information was lost unless I could remember what I had written in cipher, and then how much of the gathered information would still be pertinent?

I had to get to Corinth, but I had also promised five prisoners back at Cairo I would be back to help them. Could I do it? Could I really commandeer a boat and spirit them away from the grasp of the Federals? This was something to think about. I would do good to trek up the Ohio and get a boat to return downstream. Everyone on the Mississippi seemed to know me or know of me by now and I was clearly a wanted man based on the welcome I'd received from Admiral Foote and Commodore Pennock. Even Lieutenant Harris knew of my recent history and I had done nothing to fool him or Captain Bixby.

I could do much worse than to realize I was a wanted man and the Federals seemed to know of me. My, how much difference a year can make. I was quite happy a year ago with the way things were going, but for the plight of my lifelong friend Samuel Clemens or Mark Twain as he now preferred to be called. I had managed to get out of jail and float downriver from Cairo, but how far? How far south had I drifted? This had to be Kentucky, but where?

"Can I ask where I am?"

"You're in Kentucky."

"Yes ma'am, but where in Kentucky?"

"The nearest big town is Paducah, but the streets of Wickliffe are the closest if you can call Wickliffe a town."

"Is that where you were when I let myself into your home?"

"No, I had gone to the neighbor's house down the road. Well, it's more like a path, but I call it a road."

"Does anyone else know I'm here?"

"Only I and the good Lord know of your whereabouts, captain."

"Do you think my clothes might be dry yet?"

"I can only guess, but I'd say not. They were still pretty damp the last I checked. I don't 'spect they'll be dry till the sun gets a good hold of them, and I haven't seen the sun now for three or four days."

I cringed at the prospect of having to spend a wide-awake sober night with such a beauty of a woman in her bed with no clothes. It seemed my sentence was pronounced whether I could endure the suffering or not. I once again let my thoughts get me riled just before Beulah walked into the room and said, "I guess I'd better turn in."

She put out the light and began to get undressed. I knew this because I could sense her whereabouts and I could hear the rustling of clothes slipping off of her body. I also realized I could see slightly in the dark as my eyes adjusted to the pitch black room. She was getting out of her clothes and I could see her silhouette, though I knew better than to watch. Would her eyes adjust as quickly as mine? Dear God, was she going to take off all of her clothes? I was vexed as I watched the woman peel off layer after layer of undergarments until I was unsure if she had on anything or not.

Finally as she seemed to be nearing the end of her ritual, I turned my back to her and faced the wall, expecting any moment for her to lift the blankets and put her naked body next to mine. My heart was in my throat. I was never going to be able to get through this ordeal unscathed. If anything at all happened between me and Beulah Ragsdale, I was still going to carry a scar to my wedding day.

The sheets lifted and I could feel the bed move as she got into bed beneath the blankets beside me. My mind began to spin in all directions wondering how I could have gotten into this unprecedented situation.

I had never been more uncomfortable than I was that night. My jail cells had offered more comfort, if you understand my meaning. At least I wasn't being tempted beyond my ability to overcome my own depraved mind. Torture would have been better, or so I thought at the time. In fact, what was happening was certain torture.

She settled in and her moving stopped without warning. I hadn't been touched in any way either accidentally or on purpose. My blood was running to my head and my mind was spinning with unthinkable thoughts, although she never said a word or turned my way. I had to spare myself for Lucy, but this situation was so close to actually sleeping with another woman, I struggled for self-control.

When I awoke I was again in bed by myself. I must have laid awake half the night in torment wondering what she might do, for she was no doubt a woman with experience, but she never moved in my direction. It was mid-day and the sun was up when I sat bolt upright in bed.

"Your clothes are on the dresser if you would like to get dressed, Captain Grimes." She stuck her head inside the bedroom door and smiled, "I believe you'll want to get dressed before you come to the table for lunch, at least I would," then she pulled the door shut.

I jumped up and began to dress as quickly as was humanly possible, not wishing to offend the lady in any way. Here I was being silly, for she had no doubt seen me naked already, but I couldn't bring myself to accept the fact. I felt as if I was in enemy territory and ready to be hung.

Once I was dressed I opened the bedroom door and stepped into her small kitchen. There she had food prepared and I was famished. I was hoping to be able to eat without making a glutton of myself.

"Have a seat, unless you don't want to eat before you go."

"I could use a good meal, ma'am."

Pulling out a chair I took a seat at her table where she had placed two settings. Although her home was small she had set out her most beautiful wares for entertaining guests. I commented on her place setting and she smiled.

"I find that people are only poor in their own minds. It is a fairytale that some poor souls buy hook, line and sinker. No one is poor, unless he or she thinks so. I am far from poor and although I could have much more, it's not necessary. He who can endure with little to nothing is better off than he who has everything at his disposal."

"Your philosophy intrigues me, Mrs. Ragsdale."

"It shouldn't. It makes perfect sense. A woman cannot acquire her strength and devotion in the throws of luxury. Such a woman as has never suffered would be as useless as one who has never been tested and tried."

"You mean rich people are worse off."

"In many ways. Don't discount the fact that I am rich," she said as she spooned food onto our plates. "I am not poor, although my riches have nothing to do with money. The Yankee's could take everything I have and burn my home to the ground, but I would still be richer than they are."

We ate without saying much as I mulled over what she said. I understood her meaning, while as yet, I didn't exactly see her point. I had a view somewhat different, but I had something to think about. What was the difference between rich and poor? Who was really poor if they had a roof over their head and food to eat?

Chapter 18

I said my goodbye after eating lunch with the prettiest lady on the river and headed for the settlement of Wickliffe. I needed a boat and a way back to Cairo. The rivers were still up and flooding the bottom lands, but I had to get back and rescue the women who had been incarcerated for their sympathies. I wondered as I walked just what I was up against.

The word Federal was derived from the Christian use which meant a covenant with God. The Constitution of the United States was exactly that, a covenant or contract with God almighty. All of those men who had signed the Declaration of Independence had pledged their lives and fortunes in order to fulfill that contract with the most high, and several of them had paid in one way or another with one or both, but they had upheld their end of the bargain until death.

So why such barbarian practices on the field of battle? Most of the Yankee's I'd met had little to no understanding of their relationship to God. Their practice of filthy language and their willingness to destroy anything in their path was certainly a testament to their unruly manner and their drinking was beyond all expectations. So my question became; who was on the side of right?

The southerners were for the most part gentlemen, even those who had been brought up in the poorest of circumstances. Lincoln himself had been born into a poor family from Kentucky and no one in Lincoln's family or mine had ever owned a single slave. He was a southern gentleman, but he would not relent and leave the southern states alone. Lincoln was determined to enforce his will on the newly formed southern Union who no longer wanted to be part of the Union as it was now configured. I felt the southern states were justified, for all I had seen from northerners thus far indicated we would be set back many years by their primitive heathenish ways if we merged two such incompatible societies. A way of life would cease to exist, and what of the new way? Where would it lead? Would the heathens bring down our genteel and respectful ways, or would they step up and learn the ways of southern politeness. My fear was the issue would be decided by the victors and that would be fine as long as the south won, but if we lost, our days as a free and noble people would be over. This was a war for states to decide for themselves what freedom meant, or what would be left of our freedom would come directly from the bully pulpit that was Washington.

As I entered the town of Wickliffe I found the dock and borrowed a skiff along with two gentlemen, Rufus Holmes and Ernest Gatsby to help me do the rowing.

We set out to retrieve the distressed young maidens in the Cairo jail. No money was necessary to convince these two gentlemen I needed help. They volunteered at my description of the damsels in distress so away we went. We moved downstream quickly and soon sighted the jail. There were troop ships all about the wharf, but we weren't going anywhere near there. We swung the boat around to the back side of the long two story compound and I peeped into the window where the ladies were being held. They were there, so I alerted them of my presence.

They made such a racket the guards came to see what was wrong. Convincing the guards they were just laughing and having a good time, the men departed back down the hall and I set to work to get them out. Tying a rope to their window bars we strung it around a nearby tree and began to pull. As the rope grew taunt a crack appeared in the wall, then it gave way completely and suddenly there was a hole large enough to ride a horse through. We dropped the rope and rowed back to the building a few feet away and began to take on passengers. As the last lady, Mrs. Reanna Loughridge, stepped into the boat, a guard appeared at the door in the hallway and yelled for help. He was too late to stop us however, and we rowed vigorously until we were out of rifle shot range.

We turned the boat in the direction of Wickliffe and within two hours, completely exhausted from rowing, mostly against the current, we put in at the docks. Here we unloaded the ladies and they had no trouble finding sleeping quarters for the evening.

"You might as well stay the night, Captain Grimes. The hour is getting late," Ernest insisted.

"I deem you to be correct, sir. A good warm bed beats any other arrangements I might be able to make."

"Good. My wife will fix us something to eat and we can get some rest."

I followed Ernest Gatsby home and had a fine dinner with him and his wife. We talked of the war efforts for a few hours before going to bed. When I awoke the next morning I was in for a surprise. Federal troops were in town going through everyone's home looking for the escaped prisoners, especially the one named Captain Grimes. Someone in town had snitched on us.

Learning of this, I hastily dressed and dropped out my bedroom window after thanking the Gatsby's for their hospitality. I made my way down to the creek behind the town and away from the main dock where the launch was supposed to be waiting. The launch was there and so were the five women I had helped break out of prison the previous day. Having been tipped off as well, they hastened to the assigned rendezvous down by the creek while the Federals went house to house looking for us. We paddled away in our skiff out the back way and headed downstream. The ladies took turns helping me and we soon found ourselves on the Mississippi, then on the east fork rowing away from the river until we could return to the main artery after dark later that evening.

The area being overloaded with Yankee troops as it was did nothing to assist us in our travels. It would not do any good to try rowing south in broad daylight, and there was nowhere else to hide our boat but up the first creek we came to. The east fork presented itself and not being choosy, we took it to get out of sight of the Federal gunboats.

Another small creek branched off and we went around the bend to get out of sight completely then rowed ashore. Once we ran the boat aground, I helped the ladies out and napped in the woods about three hundred yards farther along. The women talked about where they could go that might be safe while I gathered firewood to make a warm fire. They finally came up with Memphis. I felt like a rooster with too many hens in the chicken house myself. There was nothing I could do about my circumstances though. I had chosen to run the mail, and I couldn't, in my heart, leave these prisoners behind. I did not agree with the Yankee's putting women in prison to begin with, for none of them had done anything to warrant their incarceration.

I built a small fire so we could get warm and pass the time with a bit of comfort. This was not easily done as the wood was wet from recent rains, but eventually I found a stash of dry kindling and dry logs which had been shielded from the precipitation. Constructing a small pile beneath a big oak tree I got a fire going and began to feed the flames, instructing my charges not to throw anything wet on the fire as this would cause smoke and might give us away. What little smoke the dry wood would create could be dissipated by the oak tree before rising into the atmosphere.

"We never would have thought of such a thing," Gretchen said.

"Ladies, I'll get you to Memphis by day after tomorrow provided you do as I say. We still have to get by the Yankee fleet in the dark of night," I said.

"What will that be like," Reanna asked.

"It may get tricky. The Yankee's have been rounding up boats from all over and placing them in the service of the Union. Those boats are on the river now. Some are covered in iron and some are not, but until we get south of Dyersburg we'll have to watch ourselves and that's especially true at New Madrid."

"How far is New Madrid?"

"It'll take us a couple of hours to get there once we're back in the main channel."

All was quiet and the women rested until I roused them. "Come on ladies, it's time to go."

They got up slowly, not being used to roughing it and we made our way back to the boat. Once back in the water we rowed cautiously out of the creek then into the main waters of the Mississippi. It was a very dark night so I hadn't bothered covering the skiff with tree branches. On such a night as this I would rather we maintain our speed and maneuverability.

At Island Number One there were three boats anchored on the east side and Fort Jefferson lined the east bank so we took to the west side and stayed as close to that shore as possible. About twenty minutes later we drifted near Islands Number Two, Three and Four. These islands were inundated with Union troops and at least a dozen boats to include the *Carondelet* and the *St. Louis*, so once again we stayed as close to the west bank as we could. There were men milling about on the banks of each island, but we posed no threat to them and I doubted if they were looking for us anyway.

As we cleared Island Number Four, we rowed to the center of the river and drifted some. We were coming to the position of the Columbus Belmont chain, the blockade which the Yankee's had taken from the Confederates. Since then Fort Henry and Donnellson had fallen into Yankee hands and they were steadily working their way south.

As we cleared the bluff overlooking the river at Columbus we neared Island Number Five, also infested with Union troops. Island Number Five was on the west side of the river so we hugged the east bank here. The women slumped lower in the boat with each position we passed, yet they remained silent overall sensing the necessity to remain calm.

The night was moonless and very dark, which went a long way toward aiding our cause. We started around the bend at Hickman and stayed to the east of Island Number Six. If we weren't careful the river would dump us out right into the Yankee's lap at Island Number Eight. This was the same spot where they had been cutting a canal across land to bypass Island Number Ten.

As the current carried us around the bend past Hickman the river shifted back to the north and west. Then Old Muddy dipped south and we cleared the deserted Island Number Ten, and started to snake around back to the north. Federal troops were everywhere on both banks and one boat after another lined the shores. The ladies became motionless as our craft stealthily threaded the eye of the enemy needle.

We slipped by the canal opening and then west by New Madrid. The river turned south again and two hours later we rowed around Kentucky Island into Tennessee.

"All right, ladies, you can breathe again," I said.

From behind me came a deep sigh that I realized came from Reanna. "Good Lord, I never considered something so dangerous could be so incredibly stimulating."

"Is that what you call it," I asked.

"Why Captain Grimes, you ought to be ashamed keeping something like this to yourself," Reanna accused.

"Aye, what's the idea?" Christine added.

"Ladies, I assure you this isn't something I do in order to conjure up emotion and get my heart racing. Rather I do it for the boys on our side who are in Mississippi fighting a thankless war."

"I know, but the exhilaration created by the situation at the moment when you don't know whether or not you are going to be caught is positively incredible."

"I don't think of things quite the way you do, young lady."

"I want to help in some way."

"What?"

For a moment she didn't respond. "I want to help you run the blockades and deliver the mail."

"Surely you can't be serious."

"One thing Reanna Loughridge is not, captain, is a jokester," Vivian informed me.

"I can't take you down river with me every time I head south."

"Why not," Reanna asked.

"Because it would never work, you'd get me caught for sure."

"How many times have you been caught already? Maybe I'd help throw the Yankee's off your trail."

"No, no, no, I could never entertain such a thing. Where I have to go is no place for a young lady."

"You mean the camps."

"Yes, but other places too. There are swamps I have to navigate, sometimes I have to dive into the river to get away, and there are snakes, mountain lions, and black bear. I can't be responsible for you with that kind of danger around every turn."

"I see. Then I'll find other ways to help. I'll return to St. Louis and stir up as much trouble for the Federals as I possibly can."

"That's entirely up to you."

"Who in St. Louis is helping you collect mail and get it out?"

"I'm not sure I should tell you."

"If you withhold the information, Captain Grimes, I'll find out anyway."

"I figured as much. How well do you know a young lady named Lizzie Pickering?"

"Everyone knows Lizzie Pickering."

"When you're able to get back to St. Louis look her up, she will be glad for the help," I said as I dipped my oar, wanting to be away, not only from the enemy boats but from the questions as well. The women began to talk amongst themselves about how and what they could do to help, but my mind was on other things. For instance where was Bobby right about now?

Suddenly we rounded the bend in the river and I saw the lights of a boat. I hushed the women, not knowing for sure if we had cleared all of Grant's forces or not. The boat seemed to be anchored on the east bank of the river so I eased our boat over to the west side. As I drew closer I recognized the boat to be the *Planet*.

"Ladies, I'll place odds that boat is a Yankee troop ship taking on wounded soldiers from the recently fought battle at Shiloh. I could possibly get you aboard her and you'd sail right by Cairo incognito if you were helping nurse the wounded. The authorities would never check that ship even if she stopped over in Cairo two days."

"Can you do that? Get us aboard I mean," Reanna asked.

"There's no way they would turn down help from five beautiful young ladies such as you," I asserted.

"Shall we, ladies?"

"I don't know," Samantha Wilson stated. "They're Yankees. What if I can't hide my feelings?"

"Samantha darling, they're all wounded men, some of them may be dying. They're no longer soldiers on the field of battle. As long as you think of them as wounded Americans you'll be fine," this time it was her friend Christine who came to my aid.

"Well, if you think that's the right thing to do."

"You'll do fine, come on," Gretchen added.

I started back across the river and guided our boat toward the troop ship. I was certain I could be off without going aboard, and that was my intention. The trek back through the current put us just past the bow and I had to row back upstream for a few minutes with the women's help, but as we came abreast a rope was tossed down to us and I tied it off.

"A boat load of refugee's and at such an unlikely hour," the man said who stood on the bow.

"Isn't this the troop ship the *Planet*?"

"It is."

"Do you have the injured onboard?"

"Indeed, we are taking on more every hour."

"I've just delivered into your hands five nurses. Will you inform the captain so they might come aboard?"

"You're not serious," the man said in surprise.

"Sir, I assure you we've never been more serious in our lives," Reanna insisted.

"You know what you're letting yourselves in for?"

"Sir, if you will inform the captain," Reanna repeated.

"You'll get little to no sleep until the boat is unloaded in St. Louis four days from now and I don't have to inform the captain to let you ladies aboard," he said as he reached out his hand to help the ladies over. "I am the captain."

"Who's in charge of the troops," Reanna questioned.

"If you mean who's the doctor on board, his name is William Walcott. Joe James is my pilot and my name is Sam Anderson," he said as he lifted the ladies onboard.

"Ladies, you are in good hands," I said and unhooked the rope I had tied off before and let it drop into the water. I waved goodbye and sat down. Picking up my oars, I put distance between me and the Federal troops. I heard the captain ask, "Who was the man who brought you?"

"Why, Captain Absalom Grimes. He was the only man we could find who was willing to navigate the Yankee fleet in order to get us here."

I couldn't see the captain's face or his reaction, but I heard him. "Captain Grimes, the mail runner?"

"The one and the same. Now, Captain Anderson if you don't mind, we nurses have work to do. Can you show us to Doctor Walcott?"

I was too far away to hear anything after that, but I smiled at the audacity of Reanna Loughridge. She was going to become a dangerous woman if I knew anything at all about the opposite sex.

For hours I rowed and when the sun came up I continued. I drifted when the situation allowed, but rowing was the order of the day. At noon I put into a creek near Memphis but on the Arkansas side of the river. For now everything seemed to be under water, but I needed rest and I wanted to lay in the sun without the chance of being disturbed. Finally I found a small hammock where I could lay out in the sun or in the shade if the sun grew too hot and here I made myself comfortable. My trip south was to catch up with Bobby if I could, providing he had gotten clean away.

As I lay back with my hands behind my head, I realized it had been an entire week since I'd been captured by Lieutenant Harris and taken aboard the Yankee flagship *Benton*. A week would see Bobby to Belle Grove if all had gone well. If he'd encountered any trouble he might still be with the troops near Corinth.

When I awoke all was dark and the swamp had come alive. I was surrounded by creatures of the night chirping and crooning their nightly serenade, the silence of the day now absent. A bobcat screeched its mating call and my hair stood on the back of my neck. I was in his territory for now.

Gathering my coat that I'd used for a pillow I stepped into the skiff and pushed out into the water. Using said coat for a cushion, I settled into the seat, picked up the oars and started rowing for the river. I headed south to wait for Bobby at Belle Grove. Any other destination could cause me to miss my young partner altogether.

Bobby had been a member of the old Liberty Volunteer Fire Company. Based on his discharge for being a pyromaniac, and the fact he was at least trying to do the right thing, I had taken him under my wing and developed a quite effective partner that demonstrated unconstrained courage and noteworthy judgment. Since joining me in my grapevine enterprise we had taken an oath and solemnly swore that if either of us was in trouble or in prison for any reason we would hasten to aid and rescue one another. So, if I were Bobby, I would be trying to break Captain Grimes out of the Cairo jail unless the captain had already broken out.

Having recently vacated my aquarian quarters in the Cairo city jail, my partner would go ahead and deliver the mail to Corinth and then head for Belle Grove. If I hastened downriver I could be there waiting when he arrived. The Clements family was not the kind of folks who would turn on anyone and our southern safe haven was buried deep in the swamp lands of Louisiana. Belle Grove would be the last place to fall into the hands of Grant's Yankees simply because the Federals would have to conquer Vicksburg, Port Hudson, and many other Rebel strongholds along the Mississippi River to get anywhere near the place.

There's a saying that everything must come to pass and shy of thirty years old I had not seen any evidence in the wisdom of the statement, but for purposes of being expedient I must now say it's correct. However at the time I am telling you of, I had not yet seen or experienced the like of the things which I must include in my story. Just short of thirty I was still quite the daredevil, but time and experience was about to change my thoughts on the subject.

I paddled on downriver toward the dock at Belle Grove knowing it would be well after dark before I'd arrive. About two in the afternoon I rounded a bend in the river and saw immediately that my trip was not to be quite so easy. I came unexpectedly on a Union reconnaissance patrol. There were seven soldiers and I had seen them. I didn't know it at the time, but part of their mission was to make sure no one lived who could make a report on them, no one who might report to the enemy they had been seen.

The first notice that my day was going to be interrupted was when a bullet punctured a hole in my skiff and the second did likewise. I was taking on water from the second hole when the third bullet split my right side oar. I was no longer able to row in a straight line. Shoving the damaged oar into the river I grabbed a spare and put it in place quickly. Four men rowed the other boat while three of them took aim at me. In no time, I would be overcome, so I ran the skiff aground on the western bank and jumped onto land.

With my feet under me I began to run west, tripping and falling several times along the way. A bullet tore at my coat but I kept running. Sooner or later one of the men would get lucky and score a hit, something I dearly wanted to prevent.

A bullet clipped a tree beside me and spat bark fragments into my face. I ducked around behind it and estimated my chances of escape at a glance. All I could do was try, so I ran, keeping the big oak tree between me and them as much as possible. Suddenly the land before me fell away and I was confronted by a large mass of water. Without thinking I dove headlong into the muddy liquid. I came up swimming, hoping I had enough distance to emerge on the other side fifty yards away before the enemy reached the edge of the bank.

As I was pulling myself up out of the water another shot spit mud from the embankment into my face and then I was away, dodging their attempts by weaving left and then right as I began to put more distance between us.

Another shot was fired, but the evidence indicated it had come nowhere near me. Pain exploded in my right shoulder, and the force of the blow knocked me into the mud.

"I got him!" I heard one of them shout.

I didn't get up to offer them another target. Hunching low to the ground I crawled until I was out of sight and deep into the woods. Looking back I could see they were tracking me so I doubled back and headed for my abandoned skiff. All seven of them were after me, which meant the boats would be unwatched.

Slipping back into the water I swam while the soldiers combed the small island for any sign. As the wound on my shoulder submerged I winced from the excruciating pain the injury was causing. At my gasp of shock one of the soldiers turned and saw me buoyed up and making my way back to the main channel.

"He's getting away!" the soldier yelled. Immediately all seven turned and ran toward me. They were wading in water so as not to get their gunpowder wet, but I carried no gun and didn't care about being wet or dry. I just wanted to get away. Two men stood on the bank and took aim, so I dove to get under water and as soon as I disappeared I turned right and downstream. When I came up it would be out of their line of fire.

I came up for air and went back down as fast as I had surfaced. I had slung my head back in the opposite direction long enough to see they were losing ground. Comforted by this fact and the fact that I was nearing the bank, I determined to swim harder. My shoulder stiffened making my strokes difficult. I suddenly felt the bottom and I had land beneath my feet and I arose to climb the bank and sprint the last few yards to the river. Shots rang out behind me but none of them were close, or should I say lucky.

I shoved my bullet riddled boat into the river then jumped into their craft and rowed. I knew this would make them mad, but I was in no position to let them have me. Their boat was better and lighter than mine so if they did manage to recover my old skiff, they wouldn't find the travel easy going. I rowed in earnest for the other side of the river.

Eventually one by one the soldiers appeared on the distant river bank and watched as I rowed away in their lighter faster boat. One raised his rifle and took aim, but when he squeezed the trigger the bullet fell way short of me. They were stranded in enemy territory and they would be mad as hornets, with good reason. They had been outsmarted by one lone river rat.

Rowing south I made my way to the docks at Belle Grove just after ten o'clock. Bobby was there and so was Mickey. I settled into a good hot bath and when I was done the servants of the house led me to a strange room where Mrs. Clements set to work on my wounded shoulder. Here they had clean clothes for me to put on. Coming back downstairs after being sewn up, I ate a late dinner and then retired to the parlor where Mr. William E. Clements and Mr. Tucker Deal were waiting with the boys.

"Well, captain, tell us how was your trip south," Tucker wanted to know.

"How long have you been here, Bobby," I asked.

"I came in yesterday."

"Gentlemen, I came in with a bullet in my shoulder so you already know how my trip was."

Bobby shifted in his chair. "I went to break you out of jail in Cairo, but you'd already escaped."

"They found my cipher book. I refused to translate it for them so they were going to beat it out of me. I thought it was time to leave. I parted company with my captors unexpectedly."

"How did things go with the money we gave you?" Deal wanted to know.

"I would say it couldn't have gone any better. Captain Bixby of the Union Fleet confiscated nearly all I had left on me thinking I wouldn't need it in jail. I spent the rest in St. Louis and other places. No one knows I'm handing them counterfeit."

"That's good. We can finance a lot of war effort if everyone believes the money is the real thing."

"The Yankee's sank *Jokers Wild*, filled her full of holes and dropped rocks into her in the middle of the river. We'll never see her again," Bobby said.

I could see this hurt Bobby because the idea for the boat had been his. It was as if they had slaughtered his first born son.

"I sank two more troop ships to get even."

"You mean you used the other two coal bombs?"

"Yes, captain and Mr. Deal intends on making more."

"Do you know the names of the boats you blew up?"

"One was the *Ruth*. I don't remember the name of the other one but it was loaded with Yankee troops headed downriver."

"You did good, Bobby. Yes indeed, you've done an excellent job." Then it hit me. The women had been on a Yankee troop ship. "The other one wasn't the *Planet* was it?"

"No sir, it had something to do with a person's name."

"What about the mail, did you get it through?"

"Yes sir. I have the return mail out in the barn."

"I am beginning to think you could do this without me, although I hope you won't have to. If I'm not with you, it means I've been caught again and I'm in jail somewhere."

"I'll get you out if that happens."

"I know you will, Bobby."

We talked and made plans while I looked around the room and took note of the architecture needed to create such an atmosphere, for this would be the kind of home I wanted after the war ended. The color of the room was the lightest of green. The entire room was bordered by a three foot white board and chair rail. Pictures of ancestors hung on the walls and there was a picture of a couple picnicking under a tree near a barn while their horses cropped grass. The young lady wore a green dress with gold lace and trim with brunette hair while the man was well dressed and leaning back against the tree playing a banjo and serenading the young lady.

Another picture was actually a mural painted directly onto the north wall and this picture was of the plantation itself, all six thousand acres painted to reflect all of the glory which was Belle Grove. A large stone fireplace accented the south wall with a long oak mantle on which sat three things—a clock, a vase with flowers fresh from the garden and a six-pack of matching dishes which were garnered with ivy.

Belle Grove Plantation was a tough act to follow for anyone. The expense which had gone into the home's construction left nothing to be desired. No expenditure had been spared. Artists on a given plantation oftentimes were slaves themselves. More often than not, a master would send a talented slave to school for the purpose of building, or artwork, or any number of talents the best and brightest of them might display, thus helping the plantation owner to have the best. What the north didn't understand was that many slaves were happy with their arrangement. They built and made things most white man could never achieve.

While talking in the room continued, I nodded off to sleep. I awoke as the mantle clock struck eleven, sounding its bells in my head. Servants helped me to bed and I slept soundly for a day and a half due mostly to my wounded shoulder. The bullet had only been a scratch and had not penetrated deeply, but I was fighting infection just the same.

Chapter 19

One week later after my shoulder wound had healed somewhat and there was no danger of infection, the boys and I departed with Belle Grove Plantation and her hospitality. Mickey was given a beautiful stallion by Clements for his help with our endeavors, while Bobby and I rode two beautiful mares. We stopped by the Renfroze to deliver a couple of letters on the way, for which we had to accept a fine dinner, and arrived back in St. Louis on June 4th with a large packet of mail for the ladies to distribute.

Bobby was given quarters at the Pickering house, Mickey at the home of Vivian Chapman and I took up residence at the Loughridge home on the corner of twelfth and Christy. Here we learned immediately that the women had a fine trip all the way back to St. Louis. Samantha Wilson had apparently fallen in love with one of the wounded soldiers on board the *Planet*. This I found to be strange as her and Christine had been unsure of even getting on the boat. War was making for some very unusual love affairs indeed.

Several days later, I was lying on the sofa in the parlor of the Loughridge home while the women got the mail out, when I noticed a young lady I didn't know coming around the house. I was by myself and wasn't sure if I should answer the door or not. The knock was rather loud and urgent so I went down the hallway and opened the front door to meet a young lady in distress.

"I have it from a man down at King's saloon that you're Captain Grimes, the Confederate mail runner and you're staying with my friend Reanna," she said.

"I can't deny a word of your accusation."

"Oh, when I see her I'm going to…"

"Why don't you come in? Surely I can help answer some of your questions."

"What do you mean you'll answer some of my questions? You've just answered them all."

She turned and as she started to take off, I grabbed her by the arm and pulled her into the house. It was clear to me she was a Yankee through and through and if she got word to the proper authorities where I was staying I would be removed to Uncle Sam's more romantic quarters at Gratoit Street or the Myrtle Street pen. Shoving her into the hallway, I closed the door behind us.

"What's the meaning of this? Take your hands off of me," she squealed.

"Young lady, I have no intention of hurting you, but I believe you need to stay right here until Mrs. Loughridge returns."

"You're every bit the scoundrel I've been told about!"

"Not once you get to know me, and you'll get your chance," I said as I pointed the way down the hall to the parlor. "Go on, I won't hurt you."

She walked down the hall to the parlor and took a seat in the corner chair, staring at me with cynical eyes. I took my seat on the sofa and leaned back to look at her.

"You're a very spirited young lady. What's your name?"

"Phoebe Cousins and you had better remember it because I'm going to turn you in for the reward."

Neither of us knew it at the time, but this young lady was going to become a noted reformer and politician in St. Louis. She possessed all those skills the day I met her, but I didn't recognize any of them, except those that might get me hung. Had the circumstances been different I might have noticed her exceptional talent for gaining the upper hand in any conversation. With Phoebe, the argument didn't matter, she somehow gained the upper hand on any subject and beat you over the head with her logic, even if said logic was faulty and she had picked the wrong side of the argument. Eventually, I was to learn that most any woman could do this, but Phoebe Cousins was the best I ever saw at it.

We stared at one another, engaged in mental warfare, her resolve against mine. For the longest time we said nothing, yet I seemed to know exactly what she was thinking, or so I told myself, and she seemed to know my mind. Suffrage was the word of the day. I was holding a woman hostage against her will until I knew whether or not it was safe to let her go.

"I wonder what you've heard about me, Miss Cousins?"

"You're the most wanted man in this part of the country. You're a traitor; you're a murderer, and a liar. Shall I go on?"

"Traitor, murderer, and liar? That's quite a lot for one man to be accused of all in one day."

"You don't deny any of these things?"

"I'm not a traitor. I simply believe the south is right. I've never killed a man in anger and as for being a liar, such a thing becomes necessary in war from time to time."

"You are a liar!"

"Miss Cousins, there's a time for everything under the heavens. I have whitewashed some situations to save my bacon or get through the Yankee lines, but that's all."

"You disgust me, Captain Grimes. What about kidnapping women? You seem to have a special talent for that one."

"Once again, the necessity of saving my bacon, Miss Cousins. If I were to let you go, I suppose you'd go straight to the Yankee commander and tell him of my whereabouts."

"As straight as I could fly!"

"Exactly. So can you please tell me, what am I supposed to do with you?"

"You could run."

"No, not in my own hometown," I stated flatly. "I may be behind enemy lines but I was raised here and I intend to walk freely among my own people."

We heard the front door open and Miss Cousins stood to greet the incoming party. Mrs. Reanna Loughridge was returning with special guests she was sure I'd want to see. Suddenly the parlor was full of women including Gretchen Anderson, Samantha Wilson, Christine Streeter, and Vivian Chapman. Silence befell them as they looked on Phoebe, for they knew as I did that she was a staunch Unionist.

"Well, what a surprise, I see the whole gang is here," Phoebe accused smartly.

"Phoebe, what are you doing here?" Reanna asked.

"Might I ask the same about your captain?"

A hush descended on the entire room. Reanna looked at me as if to say, what does this mean?

"Miss Phoebe Cousins heard that I was staying at your home while in town and she came to see if it was true. I had no option but to detain her. It wasn't kidnapping as she believes, for I did not abduct her. She came here of her own free will."

"You held me against my will!"

"Did I tie you up? Did I physically abuse you in any way?"

"You made me stay here with you."

"I insisted, that was all and to my knowledge that's not kidnapping," I said.

"Let's all calm down," Reanna said. "Phoebe who told you that Captain Grimes was staying here?"

"My own father heard your father telling someone at King's Saloon on the wharf. I just couldn't believe it so I came to see for myself."

"Well, now do you believe he's staying here?"

"I must say, Reanna, I knew you were a southern sympathizer, but to allow this scoundrel room and board while he's in town borders on treason."

"I thought you and I were best friends, Phoebe."

"We are and always shall be."

"Then let me explain some things to you. Captain Grimes, have you not carried mail for the Union?"

I was stunned at her question, "Well, yes as a matter of fact, I have."

"Did you not help five of us to escape prison and arrange transportation to get us home to St. Louis?"

"I most certainly did."

"How about your mail runs? Why do you do them?" Reanna asked point blank.

"Most of the men fighting in Mississippi are from this area and they can't get a letter home because home is behind enemy lines and vice versa."

"So what you're doing is a humanitarian effort. Do you carry a gun, Captain Grimes?"

"No, I do not."

"You see, Phoebe, this man is a legend, but as with most legends a lot of false information is credited to him. I would suspect he's never killed anyone, have you, captain?"

"I don't know, there was a lot of fighting at the beginning of the war and my unit was engaged in several battles, but I know for certain since I started running the mail I've not killed a soul."

"They say you're blowing up boats," Phoebe accused.

"I can assure you I'm not," I responded as I thought about Bobby and his coal bombs. Bobby, my seventeen-year-old partner was doing things which were being attributed to me. If the situation remained as it was the Federal authorities would never know the name Bobby Louden. On the other hand, I was going to have to watch my step more closely.

"Captain Grimes only works to help others and to help relieve the suffering caused by this insane war. That's why the Yankee's hate him so much, can't you see that?" Reanna asked her friend.

"He's escaped from prison."

"More than once and don't forget these five ladies were locked up with me. The Yankee's have a habit of locking up anyone who disagrees with them," I added.

"I guess you're right," Phoebe relented. "I believed the worst sort of rumors about you, captain, and for that I'm sorry."

"I don't hold a grudge, Miss Phoebe."

"And neither shall I."

"Friends," I asked as I held out my hand.

"Friends," she said as she took my hand.

"Well, now that's settled lets have some tea," Reanna said.

From this point forward, Phoebe Cousins became a noted reformer and politician from the St. Louis area. She had evidently learned that just because someone tells you something doesn't make it true. She looked for the truth in matters and was not so quick to judge another. This she told me herself many years later when we met at the World's Fair, which happened to be in St. Louis in 1904.

We had a good time that afternoon once we'd explained things to Miss Phoebe. It was here I learned of the love affair between Yankee and Southern Belle for which I was responsible. Samantha Wilson had fallen in love with a wounded soldier while caring for him on the *Planet*. His name was Cedric Macklin and he hailed from Naylor, Missouri. Naylor was a small community in the bootheel or right nearby. The next closest town and county seat was Donavan. I knew of this only because I had several family members who lived on farms in the area down that way. There were family members such as Aunt Esmeralda and Uncle Stanley, my Uncle Jim and Aunt Winona, Uncle Stewart, and Aunt Lynn, not to mention the fact we'd lived in the same area when I was just a little tyke. I didn't remember much from those days, but I did remember my family.

In fact, I had so much family in that part of Missouri I was surprised I wasn't related to Macklin in some way. Samantha spent all of an hour telling me about her new love while the other women listened.

She caught herself. "Oh, my goodness, I'm prattling on so. You must think I'm an idiot."

"No, I just see a woman in love," I said.

Everyone had a good laugh, including Phoebe Cousins. The staunch Unionist hung around until the other four women left later in the day. Reanna, Phoebe, and I were left to visit amongst ourselves. My suspicion was that Phoebe wasn't quite sure of my innocence just yet and she was spending the time with me to learn one way or the other what I was up to or capable of. She wasn't quite ready to give up on the idea that I was a perfect scoundrel.

"I'm wondering, captain, where do you plan to go from here?"

"I can't say as I am not sure I can fully trust you, dear Phoebe."

"I'll not turn you in."

"Then there is no reason for me to tell you, is there."

"Reanna, I have enjoyed the day and you have my word that I'll say nothing to the authorities," Phoebe said as she got up.

"Yes, but if you overheard your father talking, it's only a matter of time before Union soldiers arrive to search the house," Reanna said as if warning me it was time to go.

"I see. You're right of course," Phoebe said.

"What shall you do, captain?"

"I'll let Phoebe escort me to the edge of town. No one will suspect her of walking with the likes of me."

A peculiar light shone in Phoebe's eyes at the realization of my statement.

"Captain Grimes, I'll do so this once, but only because Reanna Loughridge is my best friend and I would do nothing to endanger our friendship."

While I was entertaining the finest ladies of St. Louis, Bobby Louden was gathering a large amount of medical supplies for our boys down south. In this endeavor, he had the help of Miss Lou Venable and Mrs. Dutch Welsh of the *St. Louis Post*. Other ladies were busy collecting mail from all over town while I had been resting.

As Phoebe and I reached the edge of town she paused for a moment then asked, "Captain, if I were to write a letter to a friend of mine down south could you get it through?"

"I believe I could, but who do you know down south?"

"I have a cousin in Vicksburg, Mississippi. I just want to make sure her and my aunt Ziggie are all right. Uncle Carol died last year and I haven't heard from them since the funeral."

"You were in Vicksburg last year?"

"Yes, captain. Last February before the war came to the river I sailed downriver with Mom and Dad for the funeral. Uncle Carol had been sick and was not expected to make it. He died the day before we arrived, so we stayed for the funeral and then returned home."

"If you'll prepare the letter, I'll see she gets it."

"How do I get the letter to you?"

"Just leave it with Reanna. She'll see I get it before I leave."

"Thank you, captain," she said then turned and walked away, leaving me on the outskirts of St. Louis. I walked around the corner and felt the letter in my lapel which Bobby had given me at Belle Grove. It was a letter for Mrs. Foster. I turned in the direction of the boarding house where she had been staying and started down the sidewalk. I was nearing Washington Street when I looked up to see a column of twelve Yankee soldiers headed up the sidewalk. I didn't recognize any of them, but they might have been coached to look for me so I stepped into the first yard I came to and walked up the steps to the front door as if I were going to knock.

As I reached the door I turned to look at the soldiers who were walking by and stopped just short of knocking. My boots must have made a good deal of noise as I ascended the steps because the door opened to my surprise anyway.

"May I help you," an elderly lady asked.

She was a small woman, dressed very well. In this case, however her stature was not measured by her size. As with most women who had been through much, her stature was measured more by what she knew and how she lived.

"I'm quite sorry, dear lady, but I must have the wrong house."

"You're one of them Rebels aren't you," she accused.

"Ma'am?"

"I can spot you grey belly sap suckers a mile away. Why are you on my front porch?"

"Ma'am...I..."

"No need to lie, I can see what you are up to. You figured them soldiers might recognize you so you turned your back to them, is that it?"

"Ma'am...you..."

"I know what you are up to you Yella-Belly!"

"Madam, I assure you I am up to no go...I mean...I..."

"I know what you mean."

"Guards, guards, over here!" she yelled at the passing soldiers.

I didn't wait around to see how they would react. I dove past her into her house running straight for the back door. Opening it, I ran down the stairs and went into the alley. I went twenty yards when I saw an opening onto the next street over so I took it and hurtled over a waist high fence. Rounding the corner I found myself on Christy Street and continued to run. Then I saw Miss Phoebe Cousins ascending the steps to what must be her place and I sprinted in her direction. She unlocked the door and as she pushed it open, I bounded up the steps and into her father's house.

In abject shock she removed her key and pushed the door closed behind her. She sat her purse down by the door, hung her shawl on a peg and turned to look at me.

I was still gasping for air as she said, "Well captain, I never expected to see you return this soon."

"There are soldiers after me."

"No kidding. I would never have guessed."

"You won't turn me in, will you?"

"No, I won't betray a friend such as Reanna Loughridge, but you can't stay here. Father will be home soon."

"I didn't have any intention of staying. I only needed a hiding place for a short time and when I saw you, I could think of nothing else."

"How flattering, can I get you some tea or something to eat?"

"It isn't necessary to feed me."

"If you're going to be my guest for the next little bit, I insist. Have a seat in the parlor. If the soldiers come here looking for you, I won't say anything. God forbid I would have to explain to Reanna how you were captured at my door."

She went into the kitchen and prepared something for us to eat. When she returned she was carrying a plate of pasta and beans for each of us. She placed the plates on the dining room table and bid me join her.

"Here you are, captain. I do hope you find our food satisfactory," she said.

I accepted the plate. "Thank you, Miss Phoebe."

I sat down and as I picked up my fork I suddenly dreaded having to eat in this house. What if the Yankee sympathizer had put something in my food to drug me into a sound stupor? She could then notify the authorities with no one the wiser. I hesitated long enough to draw her ire.

"Captain, whatever is the matter?"

I sat in silence not knowing how to respond. If I admitted my thoughts, I might offend an innocent young lady, if I did nothing I risked the same.

"Just what do you take me for, captain?"

"I'm that obvious, am I?"

"Here," she said as she switched our plates. "I understand you have no reason to trust me, but I can't be the cause of your undoing."

Sitting back down she began to eat from the plate that had been mine. This put me at ease and I dug in, not realizing how hungry I was. We ate in silence and I developed a new respect for Phoebe Cousins. She had no use for me, but her friendship with Reanna Loughridge was apparently more important than what might become of me. When I finished she got up and took my plate and went back into the kitchen.

When she returned to the dining room she suggested we retreat once again to the parlor and I followed her to more comfortable quarters.

"You may rest on the couch, captain, but I have things to do. Make yourself at home, but once it gets dark I must ask that you leave. It would not be good for either of us if my father were to find you here."

"I understand, Miss Phoebe and I wish not to cause you any harm."

She left the room and my thoughts began to wonder. My Lucy would be home now and I was wishful to see her, but had no idea if this was a safe thing to attempt as the Yankee's were looking for me at every turn. If they believed as Miss Phoebe had that I was knee deep in blowing up Federal troop ships, I was in more danger than I originally had thought.

I should have stayed with Lizzie Pickering, but Bobby was there for a reason. I wasn't sure I could withstand her advances toward me. She was a beautiful young lady and I needed to have my thoughts on Lucy, not some other woman. This was the only reason I hadn't asked for rest at her place. Bobby would do well in her home and I'm certain he was visiting Mona as much as possible while we tarried in St. Louis. Mrs. Foster and her children were still boarding with Mammie, so Mickey stayed with them while he was in town.

Three days later I stepped off the train in Centralia, Illinois. I was met by Bobby, Mickey, Miss Lou Venable, Mrs. Deborah A. Wilson, and Mrs. Marion Wall Vail, all of them carrying my mail and first aid supplies. I was learning that Widow Webster had developed an entire corps of lady assistants from all over Missouri to which they were eager to serve the troops.

I thanked the ladies for their help and assured them they could go no further in their endeavors. They were somewhat disappointed, but understood from here on south it was a game of cat and mouse which might be interrupted at any time by a vicious dog. We men went on to Louisville and I knocked on the door of Belle Shirley, where she was putting together a large mail sack from the families in Kentucky. Her house was full of guest mail carriers to include Mrs. Sudie Kendall, Johnson, Ferguson, and a few others with names I can't remember.

We ate dinner with these ladies who were full of questions and could hardly contain their excitement at meeting the infamous mail carrier Grimes. We took what they had and left that evening headed for Mississippi by train. To date there seemed to be no barrier when attempting train travel in the south. Just outside of Louisville the train was stopped and held by a large contingent of Yankee soldiers who began systematically searching the train for the outlaw mail carrier.

I slipped to the back of the car and waited for a chance, any chance to give them the slip before they arrived in the car in which I had been traveling. Someone had tipped the scoundrels as to my traveling plans and they were searching the train in earnest. Where the train had stopped left me in a good position as long as the rear guards didn't see me leaving the train. I felt this to be impossible so I settled in to reduce my risk of exposure when I did run.

I didn't wait long as the distance between front and back guard was closing ranks quickly. I watched as both guard details entered their next car and chose that moment to jump from the one I had been riding. I sprinted from the car and dove into the woods. However, I had been spotted. A yell went up and the cars emptied of soldiers who were all intent on one thing— capturing me.

A few shots parted leaves around me and I knew these fellows didn't care how they brought me in, so I made haste for the river as fast as I could. I was going to have to go wide of where these soldiers might be inclined to travel and the Mississippi River seemed my safest ally. The Ohio River valley was where I was, but the Ohio flowed downstream into the bigger river and would take me where I wanted to go.

As I ran through the woods, I was slapped in the face repeatedly by tree limbs which had grown over the small path I had found almost immediately upon leaving the train. I stuck to this path simply because it would lessen my chance of stepping into a hole and breaking a leg or worse.

The firing had ceased almost as fast as it had begun. No longer offering a target for my Yankee brethren to shoot at presented the soldiers with a problem of sorts. They would now have to follow me into the woods and they had no way of knowing if I was carrying a weapon or not. I didn't know if they knew about Bobby, however, I wasn't about to hang around and find out. Once again Bobby was on his own. Mickey was with him so the two of them had a good chance as long as they stayed together. Likely they would be completely ignored because I had been spotted and all efforts would be undertaken to capture me and bring me in.

Running through the woods wasn't my idea of delivering mail, but the chase to bring me in seemed to be a working diversion, allowing Bobby the chance to deliver the mail to the troops. In any case, that's how things were working out. I had captured the attention of the north and for reasons justified in their minds I was being hunted.

Eventually I came to a bluff overlooking a deep hole in a stream below, but I wasn't wishful to jump from so high a place. The sound of soldiers running through the wood behind me changed my mind. I didn't have the slightest idea where I was, other than the fact I was several miles south and west of

Louisville. The water looked deep enough, but I knew there was no such thing as a safe jump if you couldn't see into clear water. There might be a large rock just below the surface or a log, any number of things could entangle or snare a man jumping from as high as I was about to. Judging the distance the best I could, I backed up and got about ten paces from the edge of the cliff. I began to run just as a bullet impacted a tree beside me. I launched myself off the cliff and suddenly I was flailing in mid-air, watching below as the water came nearer and nearer.

With unexpected smoothness I parted the water and in a flash I was on the bottom. My legs folded naturally as my feet touched stone and then I pushed for all I was worth in order to get myself back to the surface as quickly as possible.

The water had been deep and I had to swim and struggle to reach the surface. The bend in the river had obviously cut a deep furrow in the land and I was glad for it. When I came up for air I swam as quickly as I could under the cliff overhang where I could not be seen by the soldiers from up above, pulling myself up tight against the stone wall of the bluff.

Would they follow me? Was there a soldier in that bunch crazy enough to take the leap? I held still and hoped for the best. I couldn't fight them, and I would be caught if they jumped, but what if they had rope?

They couldn't see me without leaning over too far and falling so I was out of sight, but what if they moved up or down river away from the bluff which I had used for escape. I looked east and west to recheck my position.

Once again I was wet, but I couldn't stay in this place. Pushing myself out into the water I began to swim downstream. I could hear soldiers yelling and bullets piercing the water around me, but none were really close. It seemed when aiming straight down, accuracy was affected and their good aim became erroneous.

I continued to swim until I was well downriver, although I was not certain as yet what river I was in. As it turned out I was in the Rolling Fork River not far from the place where Abraham Lincoln was born. I continued downstream until the river reached the Ohio where I crawled out.

I spent the night there and made a warm fire. My clothes hung up to dry, I settled in to get some sleep. I awoke in the middle of the night cold and shivering, but dry. Donning my clothes, I went back to sleep until sunrise.

The next morning I found myself being pursued by the same group of soldiers. Not willing to give up easily, they had traveled a good deal of the night to close the gap between us. Cursing my luck, I started through the woods once again. I didn't wait around for them to confirm the fact they had caught up with me. Actually, I traveled as much as possible without leaving any tracks, but still I couldn't completely erase my signature from the land.

About ten miles downriver below the Rolling Fork and the Ohio River Falls, I found a small boat that was still floatable and pushed out into the river. I had no oar and no other device available to help me row, but the swift downstream current was all I needed to put distance between me and the soldiers.

I spent a good part of the day drifting and playing dead in a boat which looked as if it had been sunk in a flood and had somehow been dislodged from its moors and was floating downstream as debris. There was a good bit of dried mud in the bottom and the way in which it had lay on the riverbank when the mud dried left the boat catawampus as it drifted down river. Adding my weight to that of the dried mud, the boat appeared inconsequential to anyone who happened to see it drifting by.

I fasted all that day and the next, letting myself drift right past most of the Yankee fleet between Cairo and New Madrid. Near Osceola, Arkansas, a nosy commander for the Union forces on the river ordered the boat sunk. The cannon ball which destroyed my boat also punctured holes in my nerves and I swam for the Arkansas bank on the west side of the river. Almost immediately, the Federals opened up with cannon fire from several ironclads, rifle fire, and there must have been other weapons because I was being bombarded with enough ammunition to lay the entire sector to ruin. How I was missed by that many men firing that much artillery is a miracle I still count today.

I knew by the time I reached shore I was going to die, but I kept running, and then I was away. How they'd missed that many times was unimaginable, but I was evermore grateful for their inaccuracy.

I turned north after a few miles and settled into walking. I needed my breath back and I needed to count my fingers and toes. My wits were missing altogether and the fact I was still able to breathe seemed a shock. I kept looking for blood stains on my clothing as I walked, but I was disappointed again and again. I was alive!

I walked until dark, and countless times I thanked the good Lord for my deliverance. I hadn't been praying much lately and why He saw fit to deliver me from the fires of hell was beyond my ability to understand. I'd been spared. This fact more than anything solidified in my mind I was supposed to be doing what I was doing. I'd been delivered from the hands of the enemy when I should have surely died.

I couldn't say why I was special. I didn't feel worthy of such attention from God, but as I walked on, I concluded that although I couldn't reason out my existence, God had something

else in store for my life, otherwise why was I protected and
spared?

Chapter 20

I was back in the swamp of southeast Missouri trudging through the liquid forest when I heard a faint groan. Unsure of what to think, I held still until I heard it again. Believing I knew the direction from which the sound had emanated, I headed east toward the river. As I moved cautiously and quietly, I found a young man who was obviously injured and needed help.

The boy was all of twelve or thirteen and not a big kid, but he had dried blood all over his clothes, leaving me unsure as to whether or not I could help him.[2] He'd been running from someone or something that much was obvious. The blood seemed to be confined to the upper area of his body so I kneeled down and took a look at him. He'd been shot and had lost a lot of blood. Fearful I couldn't save him, I picked him up and took him over to a small hammock that rose out of the swamp not too far distant. Laying him under a tree I began to assess the damage and pulled his shirt off to get a good look.

The boy needed a doctor and I was no saw bones. The bullet had gone through his upper torso and exited his back just beneath the shoulder blade. His own insides had plugged the wound in his back which meant he was all tangled up inside and was probably bleeding internally. The open hole in front had been stuffed with a piece of cloth torn from his shirt which was probably the only reason he was still breathing when I found him.

He was unconscious, delirious, moaning, and thrashing about at times. I had to find a way to hold him still. There was a good

---

2 Ol' Slantface,; Mockingbird Lane Press 2014

piece of rope he had managed to hang onto, but that was all. Putting together a couple of log poles I tied his hands and arms to them and then tied his feet. In this way he could not thrash about and tear the wound open again. There was little else I could do without operating tools which I wouldn't know how to use anyway.

I sat down under the tree after covering the boy with my coat and began to contemplate the situation. Now who was low enough to shoot an innocent boy? The young man had to have seen or witnessed some crime or maybe the bullet hole had been an accident of his own doing, but that was unlikely because he had sought refuge in the swamp.

"Preacher," the youngster mumbled.

Several times I had heard him trying to say something but I hadn't been able to make out what he was saying until now. Preacher, now what on earth could he mean by that? Did he want a preacher because he knew he wasn't going to live? Surely a twelve-year-old boy had nothing to confess which would keep him from the pearly gates. What could he possibly mean?

He didn't seem to be aware of what was happening so maybe he moaned in some sort of a dream state. It was a cinch that he couldn't eat anything, but he'd need fresh water and I only had a little. I opened my canteen and put the tip to his mouth. Surprisingly the boy took a swallow and then laid his head back.

"Preacher, watch out for the preacher."

"What do you mean boy, a preacher did this to you?"

"Yes, kid...kidnapped us all."

"You mean there are more of you?"

"Twenty boys, and more at my pa's cabin."

My instinct was to tell the boy to rest, but I didn't believe he was going to make it, so I let him tell me what he could.

"Where's your pa's cabin son?"

"Current River, Van Buren near the Split Rail."

He choked and seemed to stop breathing. He was gone, I thought, but a moment later his breathing picked up. He was still alive, although unconscious. I wasn't holding out much hope for the boy, but someone was kidnapping boys and holding them in a cabin on Current River if the boy was to be believed and I had no reason to doubt a dying kid. Why would a preacher be kidnapping boys and where was he getting them? St. Louis. The streets of St. Louis were overrun with orphans because of the war.

When the war had started there were only two orphanages in St. Louis, the Mullanphy orphanage and the St. Louis Protestant Orphan Asylum, both of which had been unable to handle the multiplying orphan population overtaking the streets of the city. The fire on the downtown riverfront in 1849 hadn't helped matters any, but in the last few years everything had been rebuilt. Those two orphanages were caring for as many as fifteen hundred souls when the war broke out and now the number had ballooned to anybody's guess. The boys he spoke of had to be coming from St. Louis. Boys like Mickey and Bobby.

I looked around surveying our surroundings just to make sure no one was sneaking up on us when he spoke again.

"Slantface," he muttered.

Now what on earth did he mean? Who was Slantface and who was the preacher? Were they one and the same? The boy needed to rest, so I didn't push him any further. He was fighting for his life and I was helpless to aid him.

Slantface. Surely he wasn't referring to the outlaw slave trader Lucifer Deal. He was the only person I could think of that had a face that was off-kilter and slanty.

Unless this boy got to a doctor and soon, he was going to die. How could I move him without injuring him more? I had never felt more helpless in my life. I knew a little about first aid but this boy needed surgery.

If the man or men who did this were still looking for him, we were not safe to remain in the area. I had to get him in a boat and across the river. There was the landing at Reelfoot Lake, Tennessee, or maybe I could get him on a troop ship if they had a doctor on board, but I needed a skiff of some sort. To leave him here was not an option. He would die and I would be digging a grave I didn't want to dig. I didn't even know the boy's name.

Untying the boy's arms and legs from the poles, I made a travois using the poles and my coat. Once I had him on it I tied him in place and proceeded to head for the river. This was not easy going and my efforts would have been useless had he been a full-grown man.

I left a trail anyone could follow, but the boy was in trouble. I had to get him to a doctor or die trying so my conscience would be clear.

There would be Federal troops all around New Madrid so going into town was not a good idea. However, if I could secure a boat, that's what I needed to do.

Late in the day I left the boy under a tree after making sure he was still among the living. Sneaking down to the river I found a worthy boat and slipped it loose from its mooring and rowed back. About a mile south of New Madrid I put ashore and went after my charge. He was still breathing and appeared to be resting easy, but now I was forced to move him again.

Picking up the travois I started for the boat about two hundred yards away. I lay the boy down in the skiff, wrapped him with my coat and pushed off. I wasn't sure if I would know the entrance to Reelfoot Lake when I saw it, but that was a chance I'd have to take. If I could get the boy to the landing at Reelfoot, he would have a chance. There would be a doctor somewhere close by.

A few hours later I pushed into the submerged tree quarter of Reelfoot Lake where spruce trees grew from the water. Old oak trees were submerged yet still growing as if nothing had happened. If I remembered correctly there was a dock to the south where I could land the boat and maybe, if I was lucky, find a doctor.

After rowing for about thirty minutes, I saw the dock to the south and made for the structure. There were people on the dock, fisherman who made their living from the lake. Now I would have the help the boy so desperately needed.

When we eased up to the structure several local men gathered around to witness the strange boat at their dock. These were feudal men, men who still disputed the rights of land ownership that was now under water. They were there to make sure no one took fish or game from their land, land submerged since the earthquake of 1811. When I eased up to the dock with the injured boy, their faces turned somber.

"What happened mister?" The man doing the asking was no doubt a pillar of this community. He wore fishermen knee high boots and raincoat, along with a matching hat.

"I found this boy in the swamp across the river, but I couldn't take him into town at New Madrid because I'm wanted by the Union. The young man's been shot and needs a doctor. I don't know his name," I added.

"Skip, Irving, get over here and help get this young man ashore," he called over his shoulder.

Two men stopped folding their nets and rushed down to us. They could see something was wrong, but were unable to understand until they actually set eyes on the victim.

"Take it easy with him, he's hurt bad," I said.

"Get him into my wagon and hitch up the mules. I'll drive him into town," the unidentified fisherman stated.

"Is there a doctor in town?"

"Nearest thing we have to a doctor. This silly war has called our normal doctor to duty elsewhere, but if anyone can save him, Nurse Chapin will."

"She any good?"

"She's better'n Doc Benson most times. Jump out and get some coffee," the old fisherman replied.

"I can't stay. I've got to go after the others," I said.

"What others?"

"The boy said someone is kidnapping boys and holding them in a cabin on Current River. I've got to go after them."

"Hold on mister, you'll not go alone."

Turning, the fisherman went up the dock and spoke with several men while Irvine and Skip loaded the young boy into a wagon normally used for transporting fish to market. While Skip harnessed the mules, three men grabbed up guns and knives and started down the dock. The dark looks on their faces didn't bode well for whoever had kidnapped those boys.

"I'm Roland Inman. This is James Lehman and Hamilton Payne," he said introducing the two men which flanked him. "We'd be obliged if you'd make room for us in your boat. We want a piece of the varmints who did this, and if they're kidnapping children we're fixing to fetch home some scalps."

I took a good look at the three men standing on the dock and I knew instantly I wanted them on my side. Roland Inman had used the word scalp and I believe he meant it.

"Hop in gentlemen. We'll see if we can disrupt their plans."

They stepped down into my stolen boat and I informed them where and how I had stolen it.

"If'n you did it to save the boy's life, we don't much care how you found it," Hamilton Payne said. "We plan on some shooting anyway," he said as he rubbed his gun barrel.

James Lehman and Roland Inman did the rowing on the first leg of our journey in order to give me a well-needed rest. We put in at a small inlet close to where I had commandeered the boat and made our way around New Madrid on foot.

By late evening we were maybe one third of the way to our destination. We made camp under a tree in the middle of a long meadow and rested. James went after dinner and returned with a large rabbit which he dressed quickly and roasted over the fire. It wasn't large fare, but the meat settled my stomach.

"Why don't you carry a gun?" Roland asked.

"I run the mail from St. Louis to our boys in Mississippi. I don't want to be armed in case I'm captured."

"You're not running the mail now."

"No, and just as soon as I can get my hands on a weapon I'll fill them." 2

"My uncle lives over near the Bluff. He'll have just what you need," Roland said.

"How far is it to Poplar Bluff?" Lehman asked.

"About fifty or sixty miles. We'll make it in the next two days," I said.

Just outside of Poplar Bluff we came to a small cabin owned by one Ezekiel Inman and to confirm what Roland had said, the man had a virtual armory of weapons. I borrowed a Remington double derringer which was still in the original box, an Adams .44 self-cocking revolver model 1851 and a Spencer repeating rifle model 1860. This amazing weapon held seven cartridges and would fire all seven without reloading. My companions loaded up on ammunition and guns as well. When we left that cabin the following morning, I was wondering if the Yankee's knew what

358

they were going to encounter as they migrated farther south. Some folks in the south were ready for whatever came down their road.

Two days later we neared the Current River area outside of Van Buren and found a spot with a water fall where we could have fresh water and set up camp. From the looks of things we weren't the first folks to ever camp here. We spread out in search of the cabin which was supposed to be near something called the Split Rail. I had no idea what the Split Rail was. I didn't know if it was a train track, a saloon, or a sawmill, so we asked questions of any local folks we happened to meet.

James Lehman came back with the first clue about two in the afternoon.

"The Split Rail is just what it sounds like. There's a fork in the tracks which allow a train to go either north or west from here. That's the Split Rail."

"How do we find the fork?"

"It's about four miles farther west from where we are now. If we stay near the river on both sides we might find the cabin we're looking for."

"Yah, and a pack of trouble if what happened to that boy is any clue."

"Look here, Grimes, we're all nightrider members of the Knights of the Golden Circle. We can handle whatever we find, but you've got to get them boys away from here and to safety as soon as you can."

"You're all what?"

"Nightriders, and there ain't nothing we can't handle. If we find the place, you get them boys out of here as soon as the shooting starts. We'll be along."

"I'm still trying to understand what you mean by nightriders."

"If you ever cross us, you'll find out fast enough," Payne said.

"I have no intention of doing such a thing."

"That's good, because we like you, and I sure wouldn't take to having to do you harm."

"Let's see if we can find that cabin and those boys," I said.

Late in the afternoon we found what we were looking for, a small cabin overlooking the river, with a good size barn off to one side. We scouted around and determined the place was being guarded by at least seven men. There were five varmints in the cabin and two standing guard outside. One of them was watching the barn closely.

"If the boys are being held in the barn, we'll have to eliminate the two guards first," Roland said.

"What if they're in irons," I asked.

"Surely they're not being treated as slaves," Lehman said.

"The boy said Slantface. The only Slantface I know is a slave trader, and although I've never met the man, I'll lay odds he's set in his ways."

"You mean he may have those boys secured with chain and ball?"

"I wouldn't put it past him, not if the boy's correct," I said

"Hamilton, do you think you can sneak around back of the barn and have a look inside. We need to know if those boys are chained up. We can't start a fight to get them away from here until we set them free."

"Consider it done."

Hamilton moved about with the prowess of an Indian stalking his prey. We watched as he moved only while the guards had their back to him. Eventually, he made his way to the barn and disappeared. A few minutes later he reappeared and again cloaked his movements behind the backs of the men on guard duty. When he returned, I realized what I had just learned from Hamilton Payne. You could be exposed in broad daylight right in front of an armed guard and he'd never see you as long as you didn't move. Movement drew their attention, not the fact you were there.

"They're chained," he reported. "What now?"

"I'll have to go in there after dark and free them. How many were there?" I asked.

"I couldn't see them all, but my guess is somewhere between twenty and thirty."

"How were they chained up?"

"Looks like regular irons," he said.

"We're going to need a blacksmith for that," Lehman insisted.

"No we won't," I said. "I can free them all once I'm in the barn."

"Now how in the devil can you do that?" Payne asked.

"I have my own technique. I'll have them free thirty minutes after I enter the barn."

"How do you get out of irons without a blacksmith?"

"I'll be glad to show you sometime, but tonight you're going to be busy handling the guards and the men inside the cabin. You give me thirty minutes to set them free and then you can open fire on those mongrels."

"All right Grimes, thirty minutes after you enter the barn we open fire," Roland confirmed.

We waited for night to fall before I made my way to the barn. The posted guards outside had switched an hour before so I was quiet and careful. Leaning my rifle against the back wall of the barn I tried the back door. The large double doors were secured from inside. I eased over to the window and looked in. I could see nothing. No one stirred and all was silent.

Walking around to the front, I slipped between the door opening, and was inside while the guards were looking the other way. There was no light and I couldn't see. I held very still.

"I'm here to help you boys," I said in a low voice. "We've got to be very quiet or else the guards will hear us."

"Mister, we're all chained up."

"That's the least of our worries," I said. "How many of you are there?"

"Twenty-seven," the same voice responded.

"What's your name, son?"

"Bud Woodford."

"All right Bud, I'm going to free you first, and then you make sure I don't miss anyone. I don't want to leave even one boy behind."

Chatter started among them then and I had to quiet them, "Shhhh, ya'll are going to spoil the rescue. Now be quiet."

I freed Bud first and he led me to the next boy. "Hold still," I said. "This won't hurt at all."

I pried another set of cuffs open and left them hanging on the wall. Only three boys had a ball attached to their ankles, boys who had tried to escape and were at risk of running. The rest were only handcuffed. Some were attached to the barn wall and some were walking around freely. In twenty minutes I had them free from their bonds and we set to work on opening the back door. By now my vision had adjusted, and I could make out vague shapes in the darkness.

Suddenly I felt the door swing free at my touch and I turned to the boys behind me. "No matter what you hear or what happens, you boys stay with me, do you hear?"

"Yes sir," they whispered in unison.

"All right, let's go."

I had freed the boys by wedge and lever, a reverse of the same method I generally used for my own escapes. While steel makes for an impenetrable fortress to keep one in, such metal is poorly suited for keeping one's hand and feet secured because a proper latch system had not yet been developed for such restraints. There was the screw in type which held better, but those were not in use here because anyone who wanted could simply unscrew them.

The boys followed me to the edge of the woods where we hunkered down and waited for what I knew was going to come. I heard one of the guards comment, "Them boys sure are awful quiet tonight. We'd better make sure they're all right."

Both men started for the barn. Just as they reached the door, two of the rescue party hiding in the woods opened fire. Roland was waiting for men to come running from the cabin, which one did and he immediately took a bullet in the chest. James and Hamilton retrained their gunfire as soon as the men at the barn were down and began to pepper the cabin.

The cabin had no back door and the only two windows were up high so the men inside were fairly trapped. I counted three down, which meant there were still about four men inside the dwelling. My question was which one was Slantface and who was the preacher? I voiced my question to the boys as soon as I thought of it.

"Where's Slantface?"

"He's not here. Preacher shot him a few days ago, then headed down south," Bud assured me.

"You mean they're not here?"

"No sir, neither one."

"What were they planning to do with you boys?"

"Sell us aboard ships as cabin boys."

"Well, you'd better come with me if you want to go home," I said.

I had emptied the barn. The boys were anxious to get away from their dark and musty prison.

We marched through the backwoods and made our way toward Poplar Bluff.

"If any one falls out for any reason, we all stop until the situation is corrected," I said over my shoulder. "I have the point because I'm armed, but I can't see everything going on behind me. You've got to tell me if something happens.

"We'll be sure and speak up, sir."

I continued through the woods heading south and east. The fellows who were helping me had some blood letting to do and I thought it was best these youngsters weren't around to see what happened to men who kidnapped little boys. Roland, James and Hamilton could handle themselves just fine, but these youngsters didn't need to witness such brutality.

We walked for thirty minutes before I got the first complaint that I was moving too fast. I held up and made sure I still had all of my charges before continuing on through the tick infested underbrush.

They stayed together and on my heels for the next few hours and then I came to a spot where we could make camp. We had a running creek, and building a fire would be an easy thing to do with all of the deadfall limbs lying around us. With help from the boys, we soon had plenty of firewood stacked close by.

I got some help moving stones into a large circle and dropped tree limbs and kindling into the middle of the pit. Lighting the fire was easy, controlling all the fresh fuel the boys kept tossing into the fire was another thing altogether.

"Settle down boys, we don't need to burn down the entire state of Missouri," I finally told them.

"Misery is what we call it," one of the boys spoke up.

I settled back and listened to the incessant chatter being created by the little fellows and lay my head back against the tree and closed my eyes. It seemed their biggest concern was running into the preacher. Ol' Slantface didn't really bother them too much, not like the preacher did. I was developing the opinion that the preacher was the devil himself listening to the boys talk. I overheard them as they wondered about a missing young lad by the name of Dillon. It seemed he actually owned the cabin the men were using to hold their hostages, a place to lay over until the proper transportation arrangements had been made to get them to New Orleans.

Was Dillon the name of the boy I had found left for dead in the swamp? If he'd been traveling with Ol' Slantface where was the slave trader now? It seemed to me after listening to the boys' chatter that the preacher was capable of anything, but Ol' Slantface was at least fair minded, and missing.

So who were they? Ol' Slantface had been dealing in human flesh for years. If I knew anything about buying and selling slaves, the war would make the slave trade non-existent. The Negro pen in St. Louis was closed down and converted to the Myrtle Street jail, as if I needed proof. My stay there had been evidence enough and things would be much the same all over the south. So Slantface being used to buying and selling human flesh was branching out and kidnapping youngsters who no one would miss. Orphans created by the same war which had cost him his trade.

"Where are you boys from?" I asked as I opened my eyes and surveyed my surroundings.

"We were all taken from the streets of St. Louis. The orphanages are full so some of us had to live on the street," Bud answered.

"All of you are from St. Louis?"

"Yes sir," several boys answered together.

"What's going to happen to us now," a small boy asked.

"What's your name, son?"

"Rassie Cohen."

"I've seen you before."

"Yes sir, in St. Louis."

"How old are you?"

"I'm thirteen."

"What happened to your mother and father?"

"Pa was killed last year and a Yankee soldier kil't my ma."

"I'm sorry. I don't know what's going to happen for now, but we'll do our best to see that you're taken to where you want to be."

"That would be St. Louis. I was doing all right there, even if I was living in a loft."

"Then we'll see to it you get passage back."

"What about Ol' Slantface and the preacher? What's to stop them from kidnapping us again?"

"I may have enough connections in St. Louis to keep them from ever showing their faces in town again. The folks I know can organize a campaign with wanted posters which will make them both think twice before entering town."

"What about the men at the cabin? They can still get us."

"No, I don't think there will be any of them left to come after you."

"You mean they'll be dead?" Bud asked.

"There won't be any of those men left alive come morning. Now let's get some rest. We need to have a good night's sleep behind us when my friends catch up."

There were no more questions, and we got a well-needed rest. When the sky began to grey in the east I opened my eyes and looked over to see my three adult companions making breakfast from a deer they had killed in the middle of the night.

"It's a good thing we're on the same side in this matter," Roland commented. "We could have slit your throat and you'd never have known what happened."

"Well I see you killed a deer instead, but in the middle of the night? How in the…" I started to ask.

"We startled a nest of them and they scared us, so we shot one for general purposes. Besides we figured these boys would need to eat. The only food we found on the place was being consumed by the men in the cabin. "

"I see. Well I'm certainly glad we're on the same side."

"We dug seven shallow graves last night and left a note," Roland said.

"You left a note?"

"We sort of told Ol' Slantface he wasn't welcome in this part of the country and that he'd better find other accommodations. We also told him the boy was still alive and that's how we knew where to find the others."

Roland walked over and handed me a piece of venison so I got up and ate with the boys. The meat wasn't dressed to my liking, but I wasn't about to complain.

There were plenty of boys to go around, but I didn't really know their names so I began to write them down in a new diary or cipher book as I called it. I took down their names and got their hometown information so that I could at least determine their origins. My belief was such information may be helpful in finding a relative to take them in at a later date.

After I had listed them all, I studied my tally for a short time and I couldn't help but feel sorry for the poor fellows. I still had my parents. Several of them had explained to me that they were calling themselves the "Gaslight Boys" a phrase the boy's helping me in St. Louis had used. Their home was on the streets of St. Louis underneath the gas lanterns which lit the roads by night.

The nightriders returned with another deer. We cooked and camped for another day before moving on, but move on we did. When we reached the river, we started crossing the boys with our small but worthy craft in the dark of night.

At this point in the war it was obvious that the Yankee's owned everything on the Mississippi except for the stronghold of Vicksburg. Navigation on the Mississippi was going to be more brutal from now on. How could we manage to continue our trips now that they owned the entire river? We would have to travel in the woods and swamplands of Arkansas and Louisiana in order to get through, and be very careful doing so. Such an idea did nothing to comfort me.

Chapter 21

One week was spent in Obion County, Tennessee with the boys. When it was time to leave, several of them stayed behind to learn the fishing trade on Reelfoot Lake. The remaining boys left with me. I had promised to get them back to St. Louis, but how I was going to get through all those Yankees with so many boys had me imagining just what the noose around my neck would feel like.

The good folks from Union City provided us with wagons enough to get us as far as Paducah, where we boarded a train for Mt. Vernon. I passed myself off as a schoolmaster and we made it safely back to St. Louis in only three days time. Once we crossed the Mississippi River by ferry I said my goodbye's to the boys, some of whom I was certain by now I had seen before. Then I made my way to Lizzie Pickering's home and knocked on her door.

"Captain Grimes, do come in."

"Am I still welcome," I asked.

"You know that you're always welcome in our home," Lizzie said. "Bobby is here with a large packet of mail and I was just about to go after the ladies so we can distribute it."

It dawned on me just how valuable I was to the cause. With so much effort being taken at every turn to bring me in, mail was getting through with little to no trouble, because no one had ever heard of Bobby Louden or Mickey. They were moving back and forth through the Yankee lines completely unnoticed and undetected by the soldiers because of their youth. I couldn't have planned a better distraction. Still I was uncomfortable with the fact my neck was the one hanging out.

We spent the week in St. Louis and I laid low for obvious reasons, yet it was now June 1863 and I was anxious to be moving. A couple of the boys had visited me on several occasions, including Rassie and Average Joe. They'd had questions for me the likes of which startled a veteran riverboat pilot.

"We were wondering, what system of communication you're using to let folks know whether or not a home is sympathetic to the Confederate cause?" Joe asked as we visited in Lizzie's parlor.

"Now there's something I hadn't thought about."

"I've given a bit of thought to it," Lizzie said.

"Then let's hear your thoughts on the subject," I said.

"It's in the way we hang our linens out to dry."

"What?" I asked, not understanding her meaning at all.

"We all have laundry, captain; all we need to do is arrange our sheets and clothing as a signal much like the navy and the way they signal one another with flags."

"Lizzie, I'm forevermore astounded with your extraordinary ability to provide solutions to uncommon problems. Why that's so simple it'll be overlooked by every Yankee I've ever met, unless someone tells them outright. Laundry is the perfect contrivance for underground signaling and communication. Why, we even load and unload boats on the waterfront by hanging out flags to tell the roustabouts which cargo to unload next."

We set to work immediately to identify the signal and arrangement of clothing to indicate when and where the mail was to be left. We spent time working out the problem of letting only Confederate's know of the signal arrangements and what they meant. Then we laid the groundwork for getting the word out.

Although we wanted our side to know, we didn't want the Yankee's to know the secret to our communication.

While Lizzie and I worked on our communication project, Bobby and Mickey were gathering the necessary iron for making more of Bobby's ingenious coal bombs. When the boys returned they told me that the ironclad *Essex* was docked down on the wharf and was taking on supplies. This convinced me to leave the Pickering home and secure my own fame in the form of blowing up troop boats. My reasoning for this was simple. If the Yankees who were already incensed at me, believed I was the responsible party when it came to blowing up troop ships, no one would be seeking Bobby and he could go about his business as usual.

I took a carpetbag with me and went down to the part of town most folks didn't go without an escort after dark. There I purchased six sticks of dynamite and a long fuse. Estimating I had five minutes, I lit the fuse and sealed up the carpetbag. I walked down to the dock where a guard was standing at the plank I needed to cross in order to board the vessel.

"I have urgent dispatch for the captain," I said.

"I'll have to find him. He's on board somewhere."

Executing an abrupt about face, the guard left the plank and I waited for his return. All the while I could hear the fuse in my carpetbag hissing. I waited and waited but no one came. My hair stood on end or so it seemed. Surrounded by people talking back and forth all up and down the street, all I could hear was my lit fuse. Still there was no sign of the captain.

My senses were crawling and I wondered how to undo what was about to happen. Bobby was blowing up boats, but he was not killing himself in the process. What kind of fool errand was I on anyway? Turning about I began to walk calmly toward the corner of First Street, crawling out of my skin with every step. How very far away it was, fifty yards, forty, thirty, twenty.

Suddenly I heard the guard yell at me from behind and I sprinted the last twenty yards until I was out of sight around the corner. Dropping the bag I opened it and extinguished the fuse which had only four inches to go. This was the moment I learned levitation could be achieved by simply lighting a stick of dynamite and placing the hissing time bomb near the victim.

I picked up my bag and sprinted back to the Pickering house, seeking to be with others and forget the pangs of my temporary insanity. While I still possessed the explosives, I made certain to yank the fuse from its binding and left said fuse lying in the street. Never had I been so stupid. I had done dangerous things, tried some things I shouldn't have, and acted with mindless abandon at times, but never before had my stupidity reached such disastrous proportions. Did I have a death wish?

I was sitting in the parlor reviewing my most ill-timed recent blunder when Lizzie walked into the room and stared at me, "Ab, are you all right?"

"I'll be fine."

"You look as if you've seen a ghost."

I looked up at her but failed to incriminate myself in any way.

"Can I get you a glass of tea?"

"Yes, that would be just what I need," I said.

A minute later she reappeared with a fresh glass of tea and placed it on the table beside me. "Bobby and Mickey will be back soon. Might we talk in private, captain?"

"Sure, what's on your mind," I said, yearning for any conversation which might relieve my consternation.

Lizzie sat down across from me and folded her hands in her lap. "I still desire you, captain. Time has only made matters worse for me. I'm afraid I need you."

I was taken back with her statement. My feeling was that she had gotten over our little excursion to Colonel Leighton's wedding, but evidently she was nursing her feelings into something I was going to have to deal with.

"Miss Lizzie you are needlessly torturing yourself. You know I'm to wed Lucy Glascock."

"I know that's what you say, but you haven't done anything about it."

"I'm currently fighting a war and I'll not be responsible for creating a widow. I don't imagine myself risking such a catastrophe of events. If I'm to die for what I believe I'll die without being distracted by what's taking place at home."

"You mean you would be thinking about home instead of what you're supposed to be doing?"

"People who engage in fantasy, allowing their minds to drift and wander about everything they could be doing somewhere else instead of focusing on the task at hand, are very dangerous to themselves and others around them."

"You mean such a distraction might lead to your death."

"Precisely, Lizzie. I'll not be one of them. If I die it won't be because I was distracted from my mission."

"Fair enough, captain, but when the war's over you're going to have a problem on your hands. I don't give up easily."

Getting up, Lizzie took my now empty glass of tea and left for the kitchen. A knock disrupted our silence and Lizzie opened the door to let in Bobby and Mickey. For this I was grateful. Another ten minutes alone with the likes of this woman and I would be mush.

Lizzie Pickering would present me with a problem if I wasn't married by the time the war ended. Her words had sounded very much like a threat. I could do much worse, but I was promised to Lucy, and my word had to be honored.

Bobby and Mickey came into the room and sat down across from me then.

"What have you boys been up to?"

"We've been gathering information."

"Anything useful," I asked, happy for the distraction.

"Someone tried to blow up the *Essex* this evening."

"Really, how do they know?"

"They found the snuffed out fuse in the middle of Main Street."

"They're saying it was you," Mickey said.

"Well, in that case I did what I set out to do."

The boys looked at me funny as did Lizzie who was now standing in the doorway observing, so I filled them in on my attempt to take the heat off of other not so innocent parties involved, and place it squarely on myself.

"No wonder you looked like you'd seen a ghost when you came back in," Lizzie chided me. "Is that really what you were up to?"

"I accomplished what I set out to do. Now Bobby can blow up Federal troop boats undisturbed. Every time a ship blows up, they'll be thinking I did it."

A frown knitted her brow. "You'll never make it out of town at this rate, let alone to the end of the war."

"Now Lizzie, I'll not be caught unless someone rats me out."

"Maybe we'd better find you somewhere else to stay. They'll be searching for you everywhere."

"Not tonight. It's getting late and the Yankee's don't want to upset the local population. They may be high-spirited, but they're not stupid."

Two days later we left St. Louis and headed south by way of Centralia, Illinois where we met Miss Lou Venable and Mrs. Marion Wall Vail who had brought with them another large packet of mail. The ladies went on to St. Louis to continue their organizing and gathering of medical supplies. I myself had never been happier to get out of St. Louis, not that I didn't like the town, but Miss Lizzie Pickering had nearly been too much temptation for any one man, namely me.

Stopping in Louisville, the underground postmen, Bobby, Mickey and I picked up yet another large packet of mail for the troops. This was too much for the three of us to carry and arrangements needed to be made for some way to transport our letters and care packages if we had any hope at all of reaching our destination without being caught.

I managed a wagon and two mules from the Smyth family and we loaded up. Wanting to complete the idea that I was just a lowly farmer with two sons, we got into overalls and the boys went barefoot, straw hats on their heads. We carried no weapons except for Bobby's coal bombs which were well hidden. Placing the mail on the floor of the wagon, we spread it out as evenly as possible stacking food supplies on top to cover it. This included flour, sugar, wheat, coffee, and beans. I knew we would receive a warm reception when we reached Priceville, but I was also concerned the Yankee's would find our supplies too tempting and commandeer them for themselves, thereby uncovering our true purpose, but chances had to be taken.

A week later we skirted La Grange, Tennessee for the Yankees were everywhere. Halting the wagon we sent Mickey into town to snoop around and see what was happening. The young man returned two hours later with a detailed report.

"The Yankees headed south into Mississippi, lead by a Colonel Grierson. He's got a total of a thousand seven hundred cavalry. Their mission is to destroy all communications, the railroad lines and telegraph wires, then burn anything in the way of supplies they don't need for themselves."

"Do you know where they are headed in Mississippi," I asked.

"Some place called Newton Station."

"We're in trouble boys. I know Grierson and we're going to have to watch ourselves every step of the way. He'll cut right through Priceville and we'll be looking for a new home to make our delivery. Get aboard Mickey. We've got to get away from this place."

Bobby gave Mickey a hand onto the wagon seat and I nudged the mules forward. We had to get shy of this place and fast. I knew Grant had been making steady progress while encroaching on southern lands, but I had no idea he had come this far from the Mississippi. It seemed while I was running for my life, the Yankees had made steady progress, and if I didn't get word to General Pemberton and his troops, they would quite possibly meet Grierson unexpectedly. Knowing what I did, Grierson was going to have to go through General Price's army to reach Newton Station. If he succeeded, where would he head next? He would have his entire force three hundred miles deep into enemy territory surrounded on all sides, but he will have outflanked Vicksburg.

Our side wouldn't be sleeping. They would know Grierson was making tracks through Mississippi in short order. Grierson was good, but was he so good he didn't have to run? No, he would be surrounded on all sides by as many as twenty thousand troops with no hope of winning. Was this considered a suicide mission? Had he already decided that when the time came for surrender he would surrender his men to the likes of Andersonville Prison? This didn't fit with the Grierson I knew. He was a fighter, a winner. Grierson would not quit if there was an ounce of hope that he would be able to complete his mission and return to safety. He was savvy and would not hesitate to take on a force three times the size of his own.

"Mickey, did you hear anything that would indicate Grierson had artillery with him?"

"He's pulling cannons, is that artillery?"

"Yes, it is. I meant cannons. Did you hear how many?"

"No, but I did hear someone say he had thirty supply wagons in tow."

"I wonder how much of that's food? No more than a week is my guess. He's going to have to live off of the land sooner or later and take what he needs from the people down here. That means he's packing quite a supply of ammunition. He's got enough to fight any war he wants," I surmised. "We're going to have to be very careful boys. If we run into Grierson we're going to be in big trouble."

"I can create a few distractions of my own," Bobby said.

"I don't doubt you, Bobby, but we're going to have to be cautious at every turn. Those soldiers won't want any prisoners to slow them down."

"You mean they'd shoot us?"

"That or a hanging," I said.

"Wouldn't we even get a fair trial?"

"About five minute's worth and no fairness."

We rode in silence, and the forlorn look on my companion's faces was almost enough to get me laughing. I could tell they were thinking the worst, so I let them. They needed to understand this was life or death, not a game as they had supposed. Still I was having a good deal of trouble not smiling at the boy's newfound demeanor and giving my self-serving humor away.

Now if the mail got through to General Pemberton's army, the morale of his men would be exceedingly heightened. This fact was not lost on me, and apparently it was not lost on the Yankees either. Therefore, if we were discovered by the Yankees floating around in the area, we'd be doing a great disservice to those fellows who needed us most.

That evening we stayed near Holly Springs and there were no Rebels to be found in the wake of Colonel Grierson's ride through Ripley in northern Mississippi. The Rebel forces had obviously closed ranks and were following him southward. This boosted my morale as I was less likely to be caught by the Yankees if the first troops I encountered were Rebels.

The next day as we rode toward Ripley I began to smell smoke and ash. The Yankees had been burning things. As of yet I couldn't tell exactly what, but while the ruins were still in the distance it suddenly occurred to me, while words could start wars, they would never win them. Where this thought came from, I'll never know, but it must have been hastened by the smell of ashes and burning embers.

How careless our leaders had been with their words, how immature and fictitious those men now seemed. Good people were dying on both sides and there was no end in sight. I was doing what I believed to be right, but even I was unsure why. All the practical reasons for joining the war effort now seemed fleeting, and only the satisfaction of delivering the correspondence I carried would get me through. There was a satisfaction I was learning to crave when handing out mail, one I could not live without.

As we topped a low hill I could see what was once someone's farm smoldering in the morning dew. The barn, the shed and the house were all destroyed, burned as if they had never been. All the animals were gone, the crops destroyed and no one left to witness but the vultures and worms. Two dogs lay dead near what had been the house, but there was no sign of people, and in my estimation that was a good thing. Whether they had taken the folks or let them leave in peace I had no idea, but either way the Yankees appeared not to have killed innocent civilians as they had been known to do.

We decided to follow the well-worn path indicating the direction in which Colonel Grierson and his command had headed. We nursed our wagon of correspondence, as the last thing we wanted to do was catch up with his command. About thirty minutes later it began to rain steadily.

As the clouds mounted and the downpour continued we hunkered together and pulled a dry canvas from the back of the wagon to spread it over our wet miserable team of mail carriers. Normally, we would by now, find ourselves south of the Yankee forces, but with Grierson's command prowling the area, our wagon was still at risk of capture. A section of woods opened to our left and I drove the team into the trees looking for shelter. Finding nothing that suited me, I drove down an old wagon road looking for a likely spot which would allow us shelter from Mother Nature.

About an hour later the road turned sharply back in the direction from which we had been traveling and swung around under a large overhanging rock formation which towered above a bend in the Tallahatchie River. I was unaware that the Tallahatchie ran this direction, but when out riding and exploring you do tend to learn new things.

I pulled our wagon and cargo under the overhanging rocks and told the boys to unhitch the mules while I prepared a fire to dry us out. Mickey wasted no time dropping a cane pole into the river and I soon had us a fire warming our cold, wet flesh.

The hill rose behind us almost straight, but a wagon could still get through between the river and the cliff. This area seemed more like places I had known in Missouri than it did Mississippi, yet I was glad for the shelter Mother Earth offered in a time of need.

Mickey jumped up from his sitting position under a large old oak tree and exclaimed, "I got one!"

Fresh fish was going to be on the menu if he held onto his catch. He lifted up a five or six pound mudcat, which promptly stuck him in the hand with its dorsal fin and he let go. Luckily he hadn't had the chance to remove the hook from the mouth of his catfish just yet and he recovered it just before it squirted back into the water.

If he caught nothing else the one fish was enough to feed the three of us. Bobby wanted a chance at his luck, so while I cleaned supper he sat under the tree, but didn't get a bite. When the fish was almost cooked, Mickey relieved Bobby of the pole and immediately pulled another fish from the river. I would have thought this dumb luck except no matter how hard Bobby tried he couldn't arouse a bite, yet as soon as Mickey took over he would pull another fish from the muddy water. This scenario repeated itself all afternoon until there was no uncertainty in the matter. Bobby Louden simply was not a fisherman.

By dark we had our fill of the three to five pound catfish, and no longer looked forward to hooking another. The rain continued to fall and we got out our sleeping blankets and placed them under the wagon. Nursing a recent newspaper I tried reading by the campfire light as the boys looked on, although I was not reading out loud. What had caught my attention was a statement by Senator Stephen Douglas: "Lincoln's policy would destroy the Union of the United States by forcing the south into secession." The article was based on a speech Douglas had made two years before Lincoln's election. I pondered how correct the man had been. Stowing my paper away I went to sleep on a full stomach for the first time in a long time and regretted it almost immediately. My nightmares included being shot and beaten half to death by Yankees and no end seemed to come of my torture.

Only when I awoke the following morning at dawn did the nightmares cease. I was visibly disturbed by them and the boys prodded me with questions which I wouldn't answer.

Having grown up on the river, I had a love for catfish battered and deep fried, but I had never had my favorite food producing such nightmares before. Were nightmares to become a recurring thing? If so, my love for eating catfish would surely wane.

My companions hitched up the mules and we rode out about ten o'clock just as the rain began to clear out of the area. The wooded area we had taken shelter in came to life as we rode away. The birds came out along with the squirrels and chipmunks. We saw a few deer deeper in the woods and the hills opened up into a large meadow. We continued to follow the river south.

Bobby had been awful quiet of late, quieter than usual yet suddenly his voice cut through the morning air like a knife. "Why did they sink the *Jokers Wild,* captain?"

"What?" I asked taken by surprise.

"Why did those Yankee's have to sink my boat?"

"I guess they saw the boat as a threat. Something they couldn't control, so they filled it with holes."

"They shouldn't ought to have done that," Bobby responded while shaking his head.

"No they shouldn't have, but this is a war Bobby. They didn't mean anything personal by it, they just didn't want us using that particular boat anymore."

"I'm going to make them pay." His statement was flat and to the point. So much so, I was without warning reminded by his threat of what I personally believed about revenge, yet I decided to save my thoughts on the subject for another time. Bobby was already making them pay by blowing up Yankee riverboats and becoming quite a menace. Did he have more than I was aware of in his bag of tricks? If there was more, the last thing I wanted to do was stifle his creative thinking ability, not when the young man's imagination knew no bounds and might change the outcome of the war.

Grierson's troops would be moving south along the river at least until it turned to the west. Likely they had already reached the point of crossing. I didn't want to encounter them as I needed to get around the colonel and his men to get word to General Pemberton at his southern command. Albany couldn't be very far to the south. Had the Yankees burned the town's stores and taken the supplies?

Two hours later I had my answer. Although the Yankees had been there, they had only taken what they needed and left the town folk alone. Grierson was keeping a very tight rein on his men. Why? Had General Sherman been in charge he would have let his men destroy everything. The man was heartless. Were the unexpected manners the difference in commanders or was there another reason? Was he keeping a lid on things until he reached his destination? This was the most likely reason, yet maybe the man was not the ruthless taskmaster which seemed to define the field commander General Sherman.

Colonel Grierson was a man I knew from my part of the country and he was not the type to maim and kill needlessly, not if I read him correctly. He was, however, cold and calculating in any task to which he might be assigned. Grant would not be disappointed unless the boys and I could intervene in some way.

Was there anything the three of us could do to disoblige the Yankees from completing their mission? If there was, we would have to act soon. The Yankees were already riding uncontested through Mississippi and if they made Newton Station troops would be diverted from Jackson and Vicksburg, weakening the stronghold we had on the river in that area. Did Pemberton know this? If he diverted troops from the hills of Vicksburg the damage might be irreparable.

Suddenly I knew the reason for Grierson's raid into Mississippi. The gulf state was a stronghold of Confederate sympathies. Grant would not be able to take Vicksburg as long as so many Confederate troops remained in the hills around the town. Grierson's raid was no more than a diversion from the main forces which would put in somewhere south of town. Grant would not be dissuaded by the present armies occupying the river fortress. He would do something to divide them, to draw them away, leaving the town insufficiently protected. This was Grierson's mission. Now the question was what to do about it?

"Boys, we've got to go right around Grierson's troops to reach General Pemberton's position. It won't be easy, but we have no choice," I informed them.

Four days out of La Grange, Tennessee we encountered our first problem. Grierson had been seen and his advanced scouts were involved in a short skirmish with Confederate scouts. This had blown his cover and unbeknownst to me, he had culled his men, removing the injured and wounded from among them. He sent those who might slow him down back north, about a hundred and fifty men in all in an attempt to make the Confederates believe the entire force had turned back.

We heard them before we saw anything and I hastily guided our wagon into the woods as deep as I possibly could before coming to a halt well off the trail. We held our position staying still as the cavalry rode northward. I watched from behind the trees as they neared the spot in the road where we turned off. One soldier in the lead and carrying the Union guide-on glanced down at the tracks which swung away from the road. I watched as his eyes followed them into the woods. The recent rains had made them much deeper than I wished.

The soldier rode on as if the tracks weren't of any importance and I breathed a deep sigh of relief. My concerns weren't over yet, but if they meant nothing to him, chances were no one else would say anything.

The three of us watched without moving as the column of mounted soldiers continued on. Remembering how Betsy had almost gotten me caught the year before I looked back over my shoulder to make certain the mules were in no danger of giving us away. They were fine and we held our position.

For an hour I refused to move in case there were more cavalry bringing up the rear. Mickey had said seventeen hundred horse soldiers, and in my estimation this outfit was a little shy of that number. We waited and soon we were rewarded with the sound of hoofs. Into the clearing from the south rode another bunch of horse mounted soldiers but these were wearing grey. At once I had the opportunity to meet Colonel Barteau and inform him of what was happening.

I walked out from the woods with Bobby and Mickey in tow in order to head them off. They pulled up short when they saw us and the colonel called a halt and with two men rode over to meet us. The evidence seemed to point to the fact Grierson's men had stirred up the Confederates in the area.

"Can you tell me what you're doing in this area, sir?"

"I've been dodging Federal troops, but colonel I must inform you the main body is headed south."

"They've turned back to the north, we're following them."

"No sir, you're not. What you're following seems to be the sick and wounded. The main force is headed for Newton Station."

"How do you know all of this and why should I believe anything you say?"

"My name is Captain Grimes, I am a Confederate soldier but I deliver mail, hence the get up," I said. "There's at least fifteen hundred Yankees headed for Newton Station. We'll head for Vicksburg to get word to Pemberton, but it'll be up to you to stop them. I believe this is a diversion to draw troops out."

"You're Absalom Grimes, the Confederate mail runner?"

"I am, and this is Bobby Louden. The other young man is Mickey and he's the one who overheard the Yankees talking."

"What can you tell me, son?"

"Noting much, but they plan to burn supplies they can't carry and they're to destroy train tracks, telegraph wires, anything we can use to communicate.

"Dear God. If they reach Newton Station, the south will effectively be split in two," Colonel Barteau said.

"I hadn't thought of that, but don't forget, colonel, I believe they're also a diversion meant to pull troops away from Vicksburg. If they succeed Vicksburg will be severely weakened, leaving the town open for attack."

"I can't believe I fell for this trick. I must be at least seven hours behind the main body by now."

"There were supposed to be seventeen hundred. There'll still be more than fifteen hundred Yankees south of here." Turning to Bobby I added, "Bobby, bring the wagon out of the woods, it's time for us to go."

"Captain Grimes, we're forever in your debt."

"You just make sure they don't reach Newton Station. By the way, the commander's name is Grierson."

"Colonel Benjamin H. Grierson?"

"Yes sir, he's the one."

"Of all people," he said.

"Is there something wrong?

"The man is married to my sister. Good day, captain."

Turning their mounts, Barteau rode away with his men and never looked back. It seemed I had confirmed what he already suspected, for he'd been riding slow, studying the ground with more care than someone who had his mind made up. These men would have to ride hard to catch Grierson.

We were in the heart of Dixie, but so were the Yankees. I feared the outcome of the war could turn on the events taking place right here in Mississippi. It seemed the state was in some sort of trance, waiting. They wouldn't have to wait long.

Chapter 22

The recent rains had turned this part of Mississippi into one humongous swamp. The going was slow and tedious but there was no other option.

"We've got to reach Jackson to get word to Pemberton. If we don't, they'll be pulling troops away from Vicksburg and weakening the forces entrenched around the town."

"Do you really think they have a chance of defeating the soldiers at Vicksburg," Mickey asked.

"Sherman's not leading this charge through Mississippi. If anyone should lead a real charge through any state, Sherman would be the man doing so. The fact they have Colonel Grierson conducting the raid means that Sherman is somewhere waiting with his troops. It's a feint."

"You mean they're pretending to be somewhere else when they're really setting up at Vicksburg?" Bobby inquired.

"Exactly. If they manage to fool our commanders, the entire south will be cut off from supplies and Vicksburg will be isolated."

I brought the mules to a halt as flood water was running swiftly before us through an open field. I didn't feel like getting wet, yet I saw no other option. The thing about muddy water was you couldn't see the bottom to determine if you were going to hit an obstruction, but a farmer's field usually held no such traps. I eased the mules forward and when the water reached their hocks they stopped dead still. No matter the command they would not respond.

Stepping down from the wagon I grabbed them by the bit and pushed them back. This they understood and offered no resistance to backing up. Apparently they wanted nothing to do with crossing the shallow river-like water. We'd have to go around. But how? Which way led to a road with a bridge which they would not protest? Taking stock of the area I decided the best direction was to go west.

We rode into the woods a little later at a spot where there were wagon tracks, yet we had no way of knowing what lay ahead. Eventually, the road turned southward and we came to the high water again. However, this time it was a run off bridge letting the water roll across into a waterfall on the other side. I saw no drawback to this arrangement and started the mules forward. The water was running more swiftly but nowhere near as deep as before, nor was it so wide.

About ten feet into the churning water the mules once again froze. This time I hopped down from the wagon and grabbed their bits pulling them forward. They refused to move. Letting go I started to walk across the bridge until I reached the other side then walked back to them and tried again. This time they moved a few steps before coming to a stop. I told Bobby to take the reins and while he gave the command I pulled on their harness. Again they took a few steps forward and stopped.

I was losing my patience and I yanked hard on the reins. Nothing. Letting go I again walked over to the other side and stood waiting on the bank.

"Bobby, see if you can get them to move while I watch from here," I shouted.

Bobby shook out the reins and they began to move ever so slowly, but they were moving. I didn't move until they stepped free of the running stream.

Climbing back into the wagon I grumbled, "If they do that again, I'm going to shoot them."

The boys just looked at me but said nothing. They understood my frustration. We had to reach Jackson before Grierson reached Newton Station. If we failed, a lot of boys on our side would die in vain.

We encountered more and more water as we headed south, yet nothing as deep as the creek we had crossed. Mostly it was standing water puddles on the road, but you could look into the woods and see the water around us getting deeper.

Out of curiosity I began to study the road we were on. Someone had moved a lot of earth to make this road passable during the wet season. Who had done such a thing and how? The why was obvious the farther I drove.

An hour later we came to a wooden bridge and a sign which read, "This is as far as you go!"

As I pondered the sign, trying to figure just what it meant, a bullet punctured the top of my straw hat and lifted it from my head. I raised my hands and the boys followed suit. Another bullet lifted the hat from Bobby's head and just to make their point understood, a third bullet took Mickey's straw hat.

"Just turn around, I know ye can read," someone hollered.

"That there's a girl," Bobby insisted excitedly.

"Yep, and she could have blown our heads off," I said.

"You can't come this way. Go back," she said.

"Ma'am, we've got to deliver this mail and there just ain't any other way south right now. Everything's flooded all around the countryside," I said.

"You still can't come this way."

"Why not?"

A bullet nicked one of the mules, and all hell broke loose. Amongst the confusion I heard her yell, "That's why not."

The trace was cut in two and one of the mules was bucking loose. A moment later he was free and running through the swamp, no matter the water was three to four feet deep. The other mule continued to buck and kick until it, too, broke loose and took off in the direction of the first. I sat there steaming because there was nothing I could do. As the swamp once again returned to silence in the wake of the bolting mules, I sat my seat wondering if she wasn't about to finish us off.

"Pa's going to whoop me good for doing that," she said as she stepped out from behind a big old elm tree. What I saw perplexed me. She was a stick of a girl no more than ten or eleven years old. The gun she was wielding stood two feet taller than her red hair and freckled face. She wore pants with a rope tied around her waist and a green flannel shirt. She was barefoot and her getup didn't offer much of a departure from our own wardrobes.

"I take it this has happened before," I said.

"Don't you go thinking I'm going to be the only one in trouble. Pa won't be happy no way no how about you varmints being here."

"Where is here?" I decided to invoke helplessness and sympathy as much as possible.

"I better let Pa do the telling. Come on, he'll want to know what all the shooting was about if he's back to the house."

"Can we gather our hats?" Bobby asked.

"Go ahead. I wouldn't want you to get sunstroke walking to the house," she said as she waved at the shade the forest offered all about us. We understood her point but gathered our hats anyway.

"How far is the house?"

"About a mile if you're a crow, two if'n you ain't."

She turned and walked in front of us as we approached and led us away from the bridge. Bobby and Mickey kept looking at me until she added, "I wouldn't do anything stupid 'cause Pa will hunt you down with bloodhounds and skin you alive if anything happens to me."

For some reason we believed her and we hadn't even met her pa. The little slip of a girl was right. The road was nowhere near straight once you were on the other side of the bridge. As for our mules, they were lost to the swamp by now. If we ever recovered them it would be a miracle.

Bullfrogs jumped from along the roadside as we wound deeper and deeper into the swamp known as Moccasin Gap. I wouldn't have known the name but the girl insisted we shouldn't have come to "Moccasin Gap."

"Pa's going to be fetching mad with me for bringing in strangers," she said over her shoulder.

"We're just lost. We didn't mean no harm," Mickey said.

"Makes no never mind to Pa, he's going to be some put out."

"Where is your pa if he's not at the house," I asked.

"He's out cat hunting if he's not back yet."

"By cat hunting you mean panther," I said.

"Ain't no other kind in the swamps around here, big and black they are. I seen one my own self one time and they're a sight to behold when those big yellow eyes look down on you."

I noticed the rifle she carried was a Henry repeating rifle which meant she still had a few shots left.

After about thirty minutes of silence she said, "There's the house yonder," and pointed into the woods to our right.

We would have ridden right by the place if we'd been left on our own. It was a rundown old shack, and the best I could tell the structure sat on stilts. A plank walkway led to the house and its surrounding porch. While we walked the boarded path she took occasion to swat at a water moccasin with the butt of her rifle.

The snake objected to being knocked into the surrounding water and took a stab at the intruder, but the attempt was a well-meaning miss. A moment later the snake splashed into the swamp and disappeared.

"You'll want to shake out your clothes, especially your shoes if you stay the night. Snakes and other critters here about like to crawl into them for some reason," she said.

She opened the front door and said, "Come on in. Make yourselves at home, Pa will be along shortly."

The inside of the shack was sparsely furnished but there was room for guests. An old wood stove served double duty for heat and cooking purposes, but this time of year no heat would be necessary. Standing the Henry rifle in the corner she went to a curtained pantry and took out a few jars of odds and ends and started fixing something to eat.

"Pa likes to eat when he gets home. Don't like waiting."

"Who is your pa?"

"His name is Redigger Howard. I'm called Sissy. Pa likes to be called Red for short."

"I take it your pa's hair is as red as your own."

"Even more so. I wouldn't mention it to him though. He's awful touchy about his hair."

"That sounds like good advice, young lady. If you're fixing to cook, maybe I can get some wood in for you. Where is it?"

"Pa would scold me sure if he knew I was putting you to work, I'll get it."

"You said to make ourselves at home. That's all I'm doing, Sissy. Now where is it?"

"The stockpile is on the back porch through there," she said pointing at the back door. I grabbed what we'd need and set out to start a fire in the stove. Bobby and Mickey just sat in silence and observed, although I knew they were wondering the same thing as I, where was the girl's mother? Neither of them was going to ask that question though because the answer was painfully obvious. If her mother was alive she would be right here in this cabin.

"You all can sit on the back porch while I do the cooking. The air gets awful stifled in here. Just prop the door open to let the heat out or nobody will get to sleep tonight," she said.

That evening, once the sun had gone down, and while waiting a good deal of time for Red to return, the first dog showed up shortly after we ate. This was a young bloodhound named Rudolf.

"That's Pa's favorite dog. Something's wrong," Sissy said.

"What makes you think so?"

"That dog never leaves Pa's sight."

"Come here, Rudolf," I said. Examining the dog I found marks what looked like a cat had torn his hide in a couple of places.

"You'd better let me take that rifle and go find your pa. I think you're right. Rudolf's been in a fight with a cat."

"Don't you shoot any of the dogs," she warned handing me the Henry.

"How many more are there?"

"There's two more, Dempsey and Honesty."

"You have a dog named Honesty?"

"Pa says it reminds him to always tell the truth. To be honest. I think he named her in such a way so I would always remember to tell the truth."

"You boys stay here and don't wonder off. I'm going to take Rudolf and see if he can lead me to Mr. Howard."

I left the house and started down the road behind the dog. Rudolf was howling and barking as we went. After about a mile he ducked into the woods on the left and took off. All I thought was Mr. Howard had found his cat, but maybe the cat had found him first. I wasn't holding out much hope for the man.

For thirty minutes I followed the bark of the dog and never got any closer. He got farther ahead, making it more difficult for me to establish what direction it was coming from. The dog was howling now, which meant he had likely stopped.

I continued to work deeper into the forest, wading at times in water three feet deep, but I was getting closer. It took me another hour to reach the dog and when I did the sight was not pretty. Bodies lay sprawled over the small hammock. Mr. Howard had found his panther and it lay dead at his feet, but the man known as Red was in bad shape. He had lost a lot of blood and was in fact unconscious, although still breathing.

Dempsey and Honesty lay dead not far away. I had no light to work by and cursed myself for not bringing a lantern from the cabin. I had to try and patch the man up, but wasn't sure how. I couldn't see very well and I was a good two hours from the cabin.

I needed a fire, so I gathered what wood I could find, which seemed plentiful on the small hammock and got one going. Just as the flames took, I heard a cat screech nearby and I knew this little fracas wasn't over. The cat had been close and the hair on the back of my neck stood on end as it wailed into the night. Another joined its song and I knew without question I had never been more scared in my life.

Red must have found their lair. Another one began to screech its objection to our presence and the dog Rudolf had become deathly silent. Right then, I knew fear. Nothing moved in the darkness, not even a cricket presented itself. No frogs chirped and no birds called, not even a hoot owl. I couldn't hear the dog breathing, but at times Mr. Howard sucked in air. His was the only sound in the night.

I could feel the cat's eyes on me, and suddenly I wished I knew what a cat would do. Were they drawn to fire or would they stay shy of such a thing? They were obviously not any more afraid of me than they had been Mr. Howard. I'd never expected to find myself is a situation such as this, and neither had Red obviously. I recalled the story of a man in Louisiana who shot a thirteen foot alligator, then waded out into the swamp to find him. He became lunch for the gator. I was beginning to think I would be supper for these cats.

Finally I got up enough nerve to lay down the rifle and see what I could do for the man. His shoulder was lacerated in four nice slices which had gone right through his shirt, but the bad wound was his stomach. It was torn open and I had no idea if I could fix it. It looked as though he had taken a direct hit by a cannon ball of some sort, but this wound was cleaner than that. These two were the only noticeable wounds I could find on him. His shoulder had stopped bleeding on its own, but the stomach wound seemed to be bleeding still, which meant if I was going to save him, I had to do something and fast.

I felt naked without the rifle in hand. I still felt the eyes on me and the dog was at my feet afraid to move away from the fire. I kept looking up into the trees surrounding me, knowing if an attack came it would come from on high. The cats were in the trees overhead now. How many were there, three, four or more? I could feel them closing and so could Rudolf. We were being silently stalked.

I saw something move in the tree above me and picked up the rifle again. I knew suddenly my vision was hampered for I had been looking into the fire off and on. I lay back on the ground beside Red and Rudolf lay down beside me quiet as a mouse. With rifle in hand, I scanned the area above where I thought I had seen movement a moment before.

Shooting a rifle while laying flat on my back was something I'd never attempted before and just pointing it upward was awkward. I picked up Red's pistol, which had been lying on the ground and checked the loads. Three rounds were left in the cylinder so I closed it and held on. I laid the rifle down knowing it was useless in my current situation. I was going to need the pistol for close quarters and hoped three rounds would be enough. I couldn't afford to miss, which meant I'd have to let them get close enough that I wouldn't. The thought of having to do such a thing scared the dickens out of me.

I didn't see the cat immediately because it was black as night, but when I did I only had time to react. I put the pistol directly in front of my face and took aim as it was falling fast. I aimed for his teeth which seemed the size of a pitch fork and squeezed the trigger just before three hundred pounds of black panther landed in a heap on my chest.

Warm blood spilled onto my face and neck while I had the breath knocked out of me. Rudolf was barking while I struggled to get the dead cat off me. I saw in the trees above me two more, but they were suddenly wary. Something had gone wrong. I was still struggling to get the dead weight off of me when they disappeared. The cat lying on my chest was not moving.

Finally after several minutes of struggle I was able to set myself free. Breaking out of prison was easier than this sort of thing, I thought to myself.

I went over to the water and washed the blood off my face and hands then dragged the cat over to the edge of the swamp. I drug the other one which had been lying at Red's feet to the other side of the hammock and placed it near the water. Rudolf did not move, but cowered beneath a large oak. I scanned the trees above but all seemed quiet for now. By that, I mean the critters were beginning to engage in their usual night song. My guess was the cats had for now moved out. If they returned, I would know by the deafening silence they would most assuredly arouse.

I set to work on Mr. Howard while I had a chance. I had no needle and thread and if I couldn't sew him up, how could I move him? Suddenly I realized I was being watched again, but this time it was Red doing the watching. He had come to.

"I wouldn't try to move if I were you."

"How bad is it?"

"You got the cat, but I ain't sure who got the better bargain. He's not feeling any pain right now. Your stomach is torn open, but that seems to be the worst of it," I said.

"Can we tie a shirt around it long enough to get me home," he asked as Rudolf licked at his face.

"Now that I can do," I said.

"You'll have to help me. I may need a shoulder to lean on, but if you'll get me on my feet, I'll get home."

"Captain Grimes is the name," I said, extending my hand.

"Red Howard."

"Let's see if we can get your shirt off and tie you back together."

I worked at it for a few minutes before I figured a way, but soon we had his stomach bound up tight and I helped him to his feet. Reaching down I picked up his pistol and handed it to him, then his rifle, which he recognized instantly. He shucked his pistol and pointed it right at my gizzard.

"Where'd you come by that rifle?"

"Your daughter sent me after you when Rudolf came home without you."

"How do you know my daughter?"

"I don't, she was holding me and the boys hostage with this here rifle when Rudolf showed up. The boys are back at the cabin with her and they'll not harm her. They're only kids themselves."

He holstered his pistol and smiled. "I had to make certain. She wouldn't let just any bloke carry her rifle. I got it for her Christmas and she sets store by that thing."

"Come on, Red. Let's see if we can get you home," I said as he wrapped his good arm around my shoulder. I started to move but he held us up. Looking at him I could see it was the first time he realized two of his dogs were dead.

A tear came to his eye and he said, "A man never had two better companions. Come on, Rudolf. Let's go."

We took off with Rudolf either swimming or walking beside us all the way back to the cabin. The going wasn't easy and we stumbled a few times, but we managed to keep him from getting his stomach below water level. The last thing we wanted was for an unnecessary infection to set in. The way back didn't seem to take as long.

Sissy met us at the door and helped me get him in bed. The boys were sound asleep evidently, and once I had Mr. Howard resting in his own bed I soon followed. I had been tired before, but never as tired as I was right then. I fell asleep just before sunup and slept all day. The sun was setting in the west when I awoke. Mr. Howard was evidently in the same shape as I and still resting. From across the room I heard Sissy speak.

"Thank you, captain for going after my pa," she said out of the blue.

"I'll tell you, young lady I was never more scared in my life. Your father found the cats, all of them," I said as I sat up in my blankets on the floor.

"You mean it wasn't just one?"

"No, it was closer to a dozen," I said, exaggerating, although I had no idea how many cats had been out there. "Your pa's lucky to be alive. That dog of his saved him, led me right to him."

Looking around I saw nothing of the boys.

"Where're the boys?"

"They went to see if they couldn't come up with some horses or mules for your wagon. I told them they wouldn't find any around here, but they insisted they'd get what they needed."

"They will."

She looked at me and I could tell she was wondering if they would they pay for them or steal them? I didn't have the heart to tell her the truth, so I changed the subject.

"May I ask what happened to your mother?"

"She died when I was seven trying to have another baby. I miss her still."

"I'm sorry, I didn't know. Missing loved ones never gets easier. All you can do is hold the fondest of memories in your heart for them and in that way you always carry them with you wherever you go."

"You're a funny man."

"I'm funny?"

"Not funny, funny. Strange."

I waited in silence for her to explain.

"You seem nice enough, but you've taught those boys some bad things. I heard them talking. They've blown up boats and killed people and they were laughing about it."

"Sissy, our country is at war right now. That's what war is."

"I don't like it. What are they going to do when the war is over? Will they be able to stop?"

"I hadn't given it much thought."

"I can't believe you're teaching boys how to do such things."

"Now hold on. Bobby is the one who figured out how to blow them up. Don't give me all the blame."

"You haven't done anything to stop him."

"And I'll not either."

"Why did you go and save my father? What's the difference between killing people and saving them?"

"I'm not sure I follow you."

"Why kill one person you've never met and save another you've never met? I'm guessing you done both."

"You sure are inquisitive. I suppose when someone's in trouble you help them instinctively. War is another matter altogether. Sometimes you have to kill to keep from being killed yourself, a sort of them or you situation. Nobody wants to kill, but sometimes killing's necessary if you want to live."

"When is it necessary?"

"Well, last night for example. I had to kill in order to live. It was the panther or me, but sometimes a man can be like a panther and the only way you can save yourself is to kill him. Your father had done the same thing before I got to him."

"I see, so it's all right to kill to save someone's life."

"Only if there's no other way," I told her.

"I think I understand."

"Well, before you complete your reasoning, talk to your father. He may have other ideas in mind for you. Young ladies should have a different understanding."

"Why?"

"I don't know, but they should simply because young ladies are different."

"You're a strange man, Captain Grimes, but I think I understand."

We heard the wagon and I stepped to the front door to see Bobby guiding the four wheeled contraption down the hard packed road behind two large horses. These horses seemed to be twice the size of the Missouri mules we'd been using. Their strength and size said everything. One was pure white and the other was white with a spot of grey on its right quarter. The boys had managed to acquire two strange looking horses, but strong and used to pulling no doubt. Bobby brought them to a halt at the edge of the walkway.

"Well now, where did you come up with that fine pair of horses?" I asked.

"He stole them from the Carvers," Sissy spoke up behind me.

"I didn't either," Bobby chimed. "I told them we needed help and they lent them to me."

"Mr. Carver don't lend those animals to nobody," she said.

"He lent them to us. All I did was mention Captain Grimes and the horses were ours to use as long as necessary," Bobby said.

"You're a liar," Sissy said.

"Hold on now, there is no need in arguing over something that doesn't matter one way or the other," I intervened. "Bobby has the horses. We'll use them and return them."

"I still say he stole them."

"You boys are going to have to go south without me," I said.

"You're not coming with us?"

"I've got to stay here and see that Sissy's father gets well. There doesn't seem to be a doctor within any reasonable distance and I can't just leave his wounds to chance."

"Where will the Confederates most likely be?"

"I suspect we need to get word to Jackson, and then to Vicksburg. That'll be your best bet. Mickey, you need to go on to wherever General Pemberton's headquarters are located and let him know what is going on. We can't afford to have him pull the troops out of Vicksburg on a wild goose chase."

"Yes sir."

"Bobby, you've delivered enough mail to know what to do."

"Yes sir."

"I'll be along as soon as I know Mr. Howard'll be okay."

"All right, captain. We shan't dally. Come on Mickey let's get rolling."

The boys jumped back into the wagon and soon were out of sight. They had a perilous task ahead of them with Yankees running all over Mississippi, but there was no other way. Someone had to deliver the mail, and someone had to get word to General Pemberton at Vicksburg. I had penned a dispatch for Pemberton which Mickey carried with him in case the youngster was not to be believed.

Chapter 23

One week later Bobby returned with the wagon while Mickey headed south on his own. Mr. Howard was feeling much better and his general condition had improved greatly. We had discussed the cats several times in the last few days and I was surprised to learn while at war, the state of Mississippi was paying Mr. Howard for eliminating these creatures from the swamps in this area. While cats are predatory in nature it seemed that these particular creatures had decided to venture out and were known to attack humans, hence the bounty.

While the plight of Mr. Howard and the cats was interesting, Bobby and I still had mail to deliver. The situation taking place in Mississippi at the current time was not favorable for delivering post and had not allowed Bobby to complete his mission, so he'd turned back.

Before I left, I turned to Red. "You see to it you don't let those cats catch you off guard again."

"I'll make certain I actually know how many there are from now on."

"Sissy, you see he doesn't do anything for at least two more days. He doesn't need to be up walking around just yet."

"Yes, Captain Grimes." She smiled.

Now a week behind, we bid the Howard's farewell and headed south with our Confederate mail. Bobby and I waved goodbye as we walked down the planked walkway from the cabin to the road.

"You think they'll be all right, captain?"

"They'll be fine. It's us I'm worried about."

I stepped into the driver's seat and made myself comfortable behind the borrowed horses. The horses were well adjusted to the idea of pulling a wagon so I settled in to guide them. Bobby had found it necessary to turn the wagon about near Palo Alto and West Point three days south of the cabin. Grierson was in the area and the chances of getting through were next to impossible. It was there that Mickey had seen the opportunity to mount up and ride for Vicksburg via a borrowed Yankee steed. By now Mickey should be reaching Jackson then heading for Vicksburg, providing he didn't run into any trouble. That message had to get through and I knew if anyone could get the job done Mickey could.

I brought the wagon to a halt that first evening near a place called Water Valley. Bobby saw to the horses while I constructed a good fire and cooked a hot meal. Then we settled down to rest and get some shuteye.

By dawn we were four miles south and heading into the Holly Springs forest. Following ancient roads, we navigated the forest as quickly as possible and soon found ourselves in Grenada. The folks there hadn't seen the first Yankee and I considered that a good sign. It meant they were off to the west which is where I preferred they stay. We spent the night with a family named Greeley and once again we were off before dawn. The lady of the house fixed us a fine traveling ration for breakfast.

All the next day we saw signs of activity stretching across the land to the south. By activity, I mean buzzards circling high above, waiting to be certain a body was actually dead. We came across several fallen soldiers from the south in grotesque and unlikely positions, their final resting. This could only mean we were getting uncomfortably close to Colonel Grierson and his horse soldiers.

We couldn't stop and bury the fallen, but every so often we would come across a small party of civilians putting the bodies in their final resting place. The carnage was becoming predictable as I guided the wagon south through the trail of dead bodies. What was becoming obvious was the fact that every so often a small patrol would engage Grierson's soldiers and pay the ultimate price. These were the dead bodies being left to the buzzards. As yet, there had been no major skirmish or battle, but why was he this far to the west? Had I lost my bearing?

The following day the same scenario replayed itself on the quiet foreboding lands of the Mississippi valley. Bodies left to bury themselves, buzzards circling high above the trees making certain they weren't caught in a trap. The Rebels were paying dearly for this Yankee incursion, for we had yet to see the first dead Yankee. No doubt they were taking their dead with them if they had any, or they were burying them in the woods well off the trail we were following.

We came down a long hill and rounded a turn to find Mickey laying face down in the roadway. His lifeless body was a shock to us both. We sat in the wagon for a moment, stunned. The horse he had acquired was nowhere in sight. From the looks of the tracks I could see he had caught up with the Yankees unexpectedly. Had they mistaken him for a grown man? Why hadn't they at least buried the boy? I was confounded. What had caused his demise? Had he said the wrong thing?

Stepping down from the wagon I unhinged a shovel from the side of the wagon and picked out a likely spot about forty yards from the base of a large tree. I began to dig and soon I was joined by Bobby who had taken another shovel from the wagon. We worked in silence for about an hour before either of us said a word.

"What happened here, captain?" Bobby wanted to know.

"I don't know, Bobby. I've got to study on this and study the ground around him. I think he rode up on them unexpectedly, but regardless of what happened they should have buried him. He was just a boy."

"They may be moving too fast to worry about such things."

"True. Anything that slows them down wouldn't be welcome."

Bobby went silent, and I noted with a hint of satisfaction the Yankees would certainly pay for this egregious unjust slaying of a young boy. I could see the determination mounting in Bobby Louden with each shovel of dirt he tossed. He set about to do something in his mind, and I believed I knew exactly what it was. He was going to blow up some more Yankee troop ships.

Before Bobby could do any damage to the Yankee fleet however, we had to get the mail to the troops in Mississippi without running into Grierson and his men. We stopped digging at about four feet and considered the grave deep enough for Mickey. With a heavy heart we wrapped him in a thick blanket and lowered him into the hole. I then tossed in a handful of dirt and Bobby did likewise.

"Lord, I know this young man was but a boy, but he was a man at heart. He never shied from a task or showed any fear that I'm aware of. He was a good young man and we pray you will receive him with open arms. Amen."

"Do you want to add anything, Bobby?"

"No, captain. I believe what you said was just fine."

"I'm going to miss that boy."

"Me too. The Yankees did this without question, didn't they?"

"I don't see any evidence to the contrary," I said.

"That tears it! They're sure enough going to rue the day they killed Mickey."

"You got something in mind?"

"You just get me near the river, captain. I'll do the rest."

"You mean you're not going to help me with the mail anymore?"

"I beg your pardon sir, but I've got other fish to fry."

"Well, let's get him covered up and mark the spot real good so we can come back and put a proper headstone on his grave later."

We went to work and filled in the grave with Bobby shoveling about twice the amount of dirt I was capable of. Not that I was slow or lazy, but his young body was showing signs of masculinity I would never equal and when he bent his back into his work he just naturally accomplished more than anyone else. Bobby's arms and bulging chest were becoming his most prominent features, the result of so much rowing on the Mississippi. In only a year he had grown nearly six inches and his upper chest and arm size had now become an intimidating factor I had not anticipated or expected. Men much older than him would back up or back down at the first sign of confrontation, not wanting to test the young man's fury.

I couldn't blame them, for although I'd not witnessed it myself I knew Bobby in any kind of fight would be overpowering. I excused myself while Bobby put the finishing touches on the mound and went to look for an adequate marker. I found two tree limbs I could fashion into a cross and stuck them into the ground at the head of Mickey's grave, and together we marked it with his name. We didn't know anything else so his name was all we carved into the wood.

By the time we finished, we were both tired and settled in for the night, heating salt pork over a shallow fire. Salt pork would keep when nothing else would, which made it a common item for traveling. The problem was, the ensuing aroma was known to attract wild animals. Some a man could deal with, some took a little more resourcefulness.

Having just buried our little friend, I looked around and determined to pick up a few guns. Dead bodies were here and there, so finding a gun would not be hard, but I needed a loaded one. Something was eating at me. We hadn't traveled all that far and there were still cats in the area. I needed a gun and so did Bobby if we could find one. It took only a few minutes for me to find a loaded pistol which I stuffed into my waistband. Finding another, I walked back to our wagon and handed Bobby one of his own.

"We'd better go armed for now. No telling what we'll find farther south," I advised.

When Davy Crocket encountered his first bear on the Natchez Trace he wasn't strolling along the lane whistling Dixie, he was cooking salt pork over an open flame. The bear wanted what he smelled and Davy wasn't of a mind to give up his meal so easily. When that bear came out of the woods and charged, the only weapon Davy had at his disposal was his knife. They fought for several minutes before Davy was able to add bear meat to his rations, but in the end I don't guess the bear had a choice in the matter.

We were just about to take our meat out of the fire when I heard a twig snap in the bushes behind me. Night had settled, and whatever the animal was, beast or human, a heavily planted foot had given me warning. I slowly reached under my coat and withdrew my pistol, cocking the hammer. Now the action on my pistol was not a quiet one and whatever was in the bushes behind the wagon ceased to move. My senses told me the truth about what we were dealing with.

"Bobby, don't move. There's a panther behind you," I whispered.

Bobby turned whiter than a ghost. My partner held still as I had instructed, but he was more scared than I had ever seen him.

He knew death at that moment. He realized the predicament he was in and he also knew if he was going to live, he'd better do as I said. I had just rescued Red Howard from such a situation and now the cats were evidently roaming the area gathering easy meat—the dead soldiers Grierson was leaving in his wake.

Suddenly I knew this was one of the black cats I had already encountered, and I knew we were being stalked. Anyone with me was in danger of dying by one of them. No wonder the state of Mississippi was so willing to pay for their extinction. They were getting a taste of human flesh and once they were used to human meat, there would be no stopping them.

Where was he? I had a good idea because I had heard the twig snap, yet I was at a loss, for several minutes had passed since we'd heard anything. I was covering Bobby with my pistol and trying to cover myself.

Then the worst thought I could have stampeded into my already fearful mind and almost set me to panic. What if there was more than one cat? I had handled them back in the swamp, but what about now? Could I handle two or three at once? I knew there to be several still on the loose. Surely they weren't traveling in a pack.

I began to tremble with fear. I was being stalked by a most cunning animal and I had no idea if this was one cat or five. I had read a book one time about Vampires, and while reading I became scared beyond all reason. The nightmares that book caused were nothing when compared to the fear I now felt. The book had been fantasy, a product of someone's vivid imagination, the cat or cats were not my imagination. They were real as real could get and a nightmare all at the same time.

I saw the movement of the canvas on the wagon, but at first thought it was the wind. Realization came to me as the black beast was in the air. I had misjudged the movement. The cat had been sitting in our wagon watching for the perfect opportunity to leap. He had timed the ambush perfectly. I might have had some warning, but the horses were tethered some distance away.

Before I could get my gun up I was hit and knocked rolling by the black beast in the night. The massive teeth of the panther clamped tight on my gun arm as we rolled backward away from the fire. I felt the gun slip from my grasp, the cat on top of me ripping and tearing at my flesh through my clothes.

The animal had been so intent on me, Bobby was free to act independently. He picked up my gun and just as the cat was about to clamp down on my neck I heard the gun go off almost in my face. Not willing to miss his only chance, Bobby had walked right into the fight and put the gun to the cat's head and pulled the trigger. The explosion of the pistol blinded me for a moment. The cat fell in a heap beside me. When my eyes cleared Bobby was standing over me smiling, holding my pistol.

"You all right, captain?"

"I think so," I said as I sat up and looked over at the dead panther.

"I was of a mind to let the two of you fight for a while, but I saw what he was about to do and figured I better end it." Extending his empty hand Bobby had little trouble lifting me from the ground. "I'd better have a look at that arm, captain."

We stepped over to the firelight and examined my arm. It was punctured deeply in a couple of places, but I wasn't bleeding much. Taking a handkerchief from my pocket, I handed it to my friend who proceeded to tie it tight around my arm. Once in place he stepped back and looked at the rest of me.

"We were lucky," Bobby stated. "I'd better go get the horses. They'll live longer if they're close by."

"They would have warned us sooner had they been up close."

"Here's your gun," Bobby said as he headed for the horses.

I stood there for a moment looking down at the dead cat, which weighed well over two hundred pounds. I shucked the spent bullet and reloaded. Dropping the colt into my holster I walked over to the wagon, took out a rag and wiped the blood off of my face. Not satisfied with the dry attempt I took out my canteen and doused the rag with water. This time I got the blood off of me, although I was going to have some blood stains on my clothes. I knew I would never see them before daylight.

I now had the blood stains of two cats on my clothing and if I wasn't careful I was going to end up as dinner for one of them. Bobby returned with the horses that shied at the smell and protested being anywhere near the dead cat. They pitched and fussed for a few minutes until Bobby got them reined in and tied off nearby.

I didn't want to spend the night here, but we had made camp and the thought of moving wasn't any better of a prospect. "You go ahead and sleep. I'll keep watch."

"Are you sure?"

"I'm sure."

"Might as well cut that cat up and take some fresh meat with us."

"I was planning on it. You get some sleep, I'll tend to the cat."

"Whatever you say, captain. Mind if I eat first?"

Bobby was no longer scared, but I hadn't revealed the thought there might be other predators lurking in the darkness. No need to worry him none. At least this way one of us would get some sleep.

As Bobby crawled into his blankets I took out my knife and checked it for sharpness. The blade was in fine shape as I expected and I slid the shaft back into the sheath. Bending down

I drug the cat over to a nearby tree then went back to the wagon for a rope.

While Bobby slept, I relieved the big cat of its fine coat and placed the pelt on one wagon wheel where the hide could dry. If I had time later, I would scrape the meat off and make myself a fine blanket. I then gutted the cat, threw some fuel on the fire so I could see better, and went to work cutting choice meat from the carcass. When I was finished I roasted a piece and laid the rest out to make jerky. This cat was going to be good eating for the next few days. All the while I watched for the possibility of another cat as fresh meat was on the menu and with their excellent sense of smell, every predator within five miles would be sniffing around.

By sunup I had found a nearby creek and was busy cleaning off my knife and washing up. Bobby awoke to the smell of steaks cooking over an open fire and hollered out for me.

"Where are you, captain?"

"I'm over here," I said.

He came down to the creek to see what I was doing and settled in beside me.

"Shall I hitch up the horses?"

"Might as well. I'll have finished with the meat by then."

"Aye, captain," Bobby said as he returned to camp.

I peeled off my shirt to check my wounds. The cat had gotten me good. I had bled some, but the bleeding had stopped. Only one puncture was of any depth and looked as though it might become infected. I bathed this one thoroughly with fresh clear running water from the stream.

Once I had finished with the cat, I waded into the creek to wash what blood off I didn't see last night. When I'd finished, I pulled my soaking shirt from the water and scrubbed what was left of the garment. My right sleeve and shoulder were torn through, but I'd have to wear it until I could get another.

From that point in my life, whenever I slept under the stars I made sure I had my coat on once the sun went down and a revolver close at hand. Some nights were practically unbearable because of the heat, but I had more fear of being eaten by a mountain lion than of sweating a little bit, or being captured with a pistol on me. After two life-threatening encounters with the blackest of cats, I would never take camping in the wilds lightly again. I wanted out of this part of Mississippi and fast.

Bobby knew of my desire to leave, and when I returned to camp he had everything packed and ready to go except for our breakfast. We squatted beside what remained of the fire and bit into our kill. The steak was very tasty and although slightly tough, there was a tender sweet taste which came with the satisfaction of knowing you were still alive.

We doused the fire with what remained of our coffee and stepped into the wagon. Bobby put away our cups and coffee pot and I got the horses moving. We made tracks, and I was never so glad to be away from a place as I was Mickey's final resting place.

Mickey had never gotten word to Pemberton or his forces so now the job fell to us. The question was, did we have enough time left to warn anyone? Near one o'clock that afternoon we guided our wagon into Pontotoc and I knew we were in trouble. The Yankees had been here and left the place in shambles. Three days ahead of us they were and I'd been well off track. Somehow this riverboat captain had gotten my direction confused and ended up off course while on land. I had suspected I was well west of my current location, but I had gotten turned around in the swamps and come out much farther east. This mistake bothered me to no end. I was a riverboat pilot and prided myself on knowing were I was at all times. Now I had encountered my first error in navigation and was irritated at my own shortcoming.

Only a few houses remained standing and most of the town folk were picking up the pieces. We rode on through after sharing our meat with those who had nothing left for the next day. The Yankees had cleaned them out. An army had to eat and they had spared nothing for those left behind in their wake.

After giving what food we could to those in need I pointed our wagon southwest and got those horses moving as fast as they could manage without exhausting them. I had to get to Vicksburg to warn Pemberton and Bobby would be back at the river once we arrived. Grierson was making a beeline for Newton Station which meant I'd have clear sailing from here on. My error in judgment having provided for me a clear picture of what the Yankee's were up to.

If I could move fast enough we just might make it in time, but if anything slowed us down we would be too late. No doubt Pemberton was already aware something was going on behind him. I had to warn his command Colonel Grierson's action was a feint. If I failed, the south would be split in two, her forces in effect cut off from one another.

I was heading for Yazoo City as fast as our horses could trot. I would have run them, but they had to last us all the way. If they stumbled I would wreck the wagon and our mission would be over. We camped that night beside the tracks of the Mississippi Central Railroad. If the train was still running, we might catch a ride and be in Vicksburg by tomorrow. That was my hope. The best possible scenario, yet I was to be disappointed. The Yankees had no doubt stopped the train from ever leaving Le Grange, Tennessee.

At sunrise we harnessed up and took off again. I was in a race against time and the horses had gotten a good night's rest so I pushed them. They ran whenever we came to a downhill stretch and sometimes I would push them on while the ground was yet flat, but on the uphill pulls I would slow them to a trot and then to a steady walk. At noon I gave them a breather while Bobby and I ate. We watered and fed them and were off again. We made Yazoo City the next day about ten in the morning and traded our horses for fresh steeds. Folks in the town were very gracious and sympathetic to our cause, feeding us and treating us like kings while we dined on the finest china.

The smithy checked our wagon over and greased the wheels while we were eating to make certain we didn't encounter any problems on our way to Vicksburg. As I said, the town folk in Yazoo City were very sympathetic to our cause and made certain both us and our equipment were in the best shape before leaving town. Instead of two horses the people in Yazoo City had set us up with four. By noon we had the fresh quartet running at full speed down Main Street headed south.

Grierson was no doubt raiding Newton Station by now. The question was where were the Confederate forces? Could we get to them in time? My lasso licked at the horses and they picked things up a notch. We had to make the last fifty miles to Vicksburg by nightfall. With a fresh set of four horses there was nothing to stop us. Nothing but fate.

We were on the main road from Vicksburg gassing our team of horses when the unexpected storm moved in. I could see lightning in the distance and the sky darkened, yet I kept the horses moving briskly, trying to outrun the worst. Rounding a bend in the road we took the full force of the storm unexpectedly and the horses pitched and tossed in complaint. Grinding to a halt I tried to get them under control but doing so from the wagon seat was impossible. Bobby jumped down and grabbed the lead horses by the harness and guided us off the roadway to a place under an old thick-leaved oak tree. Here the horses calmed down, but lightning was all around us.

Sitting down we took off our rain soaked boots and placed them inside the warm dry wagon so they wouldn't get any wetter. Then the hail fell.

There was simply nowhere to hide our team of horses. We did our best to get them up under the tree, but all we could do was watch in horror as the horses and wagon took the full brunt of the storm. Bobby and I tried to hold onto them, but one by one the horses broke free of harness and ran off in different directions, the falling hail stinging them as they ran. The hail stones effectively stripped the newly greened foliage off of every tree in the area leaving them bare as if it were winter once again. I looked at the wagon and realized we should have kept our boots on for the hail had shredded the wagon canvas, filling the wagon with hail stones.

With no warning everything fell silent and the sky turned a dark foreboding green. The storm was over, I thought. From out of the silence I heard the train coming down the track nearby and said to Bobby. "We've got to leave the mail and catch the train." But I was wrong. "Hold on." Abruptly I knew at once what I heard was not the train but the sound of an approaching tornado.

"There's nowhere to run," I said.

"What is it?"

"A tornado." I felt completely helpless.

"Can't we do something?"

"Lay down in the ditch, it's the lowest spot around."

"That's it?"

"That's all I can figure, Bobby."

We slid down into the ditch and held onto one another. Neither of us knew of anything to do but pray at that point. I closed my eyes, but Bobby kept his open the entire time and watched as the tornado tore through. The louder the roaring wind became the harder I prayed.

I could feel the hand of the grim reaper reaching down from inside the tornado and touching me at that moment when everything around me seemed to be crashing and howling but I continued to pray and slowly the deafening noise subsided. Finally, I opened my eyes and looked into those of Bobby who had a big smile plastered on his face.

"That was amazing, captain," he said as he jumped up and howled.

I looked into the tree above me and saw twigs stuck directly into tree branches which shouldn't be there. Where our wagon was supposed to be was nothing but empty space. Half the trees in the woods around us were uprooted and laid over, the other half still stood, but devoid of leaves.

"Where's the wagon," I asked, knowing Bobby hadn't closed his eyes.

"It got sucked up into the tornado, captain. We'll not be finding any sign of what happened to it or the mail. The wagon blew apart like a bomb went off the moment she lifted from the ground. The mail'll be spread over several miles of land if I'm not mistaken."

"You saw all of that?"

"I saw more. The ditch was the perfect place for us to hide."

"It was?"

"Yes sir. Anywhere else and we would be dead right now."

"You saw that much, did you?"

"Captain, I don't know what kind of relationship you have with the Lord, but it must be an almighty good one."

"Sometimes I'm not so sure I even have one. We're now stranded."

"Yes sir, but we are very much alive."

"We've lost everything, Bobby. I lost the mail, the horses ran off and the wagon is gone. We'll never reach Vicksburg in time. Our boots were in the wagon drying off."

"We'll never get there if we stand here talking."

"I can do a lot of things, Bobby, but covering fifty miles without a horse or a pair of boots and getting there in time is not one of them."

"We'll never know if we don't try."

"Let's try. What have we got to lose?"

"Not one dad blasted thing, captain."

We set out walking at a good distance-eating stride wondering what lay ahead. Our outfit now consisted of insufficient clothing and a battered will. Vicksburg was a good distance to the south and fully fortified. Twenty thousand troops were guarding her perimeters and the bluff overlooking the Mississippi River. General Pemberton would be there. The question was would he stay? Would he split his forces or stand pat? We could only hope for the latter.

Sometimes a man has to step back and take a look at who he is. I found myself engaged in this practice as we walked barefoot down the muddy Dixie Road. I was no different than many other men, or was I? Why was I engaged in such a hazardous pastime? Was I addicted to the thrill and excitement offered by tempting fate or was there some other reason which made sense of my daredevil approach to life?

I needed answers and I wanted them before I got myself killed. What good are the answers to life if you're dead when you get them?

Chapter 24

For twenty hours we walked nonstop until our heels were bruised and our pride was shell-shocked. Our feet were lacerated, cut, bruised, and bloody when we arrived on the outskirts of Vicksburg the following day. I hailed the lines and the Rebel reply came back. We were ushered to Pemberton's headquarters only to learn the awful truth from General John Moore.

"Pemberton has already dispatched forces to Jackson to intercept the Yankee intrusion, captain. He's leading the charge."

"You've got to call them back."

"What makes you so certain Grant is going to attack Vicksburg?"

"He has to. Grierson is only a feint intended to draw off soldiers from this position and knowing that, the rest of Grant's plan can be predicted."

"How do you know his action is only a feint?"

"Mickey overheard the Yankees in Le Grange discussing their plans."

"Who's Mickey and where is he?"

"He's dead, sir. He died trying to get here and warn you but he ran into Grierson's Calvary. He was an orphan from St. Louis, just a kid a few years younger than Bobby here."

"Captain Grimes, you're an outstanding soldier, you've risked everything to prevent what has already happened. I can no more get Pemberton's troops back than I could part the Mississippi River."

"Sergeant Major, see to it these men get proper medical treatment," General Moore said as he saluted me and exited Pemberton's headquarters.

I learned by nightfall General John C. Moore had been busy fortifying his positions all around Vicksburg and getting ready for the coming siege. Bobby had wasted no time in securing a skiff and by the dark of night we were rowing our way downriver toward Belle Grove Plantation. We might not be able to walk, but Bobby insisted we get into a boat and move downriver. I didn't argue and soon we were drifting by Natchez Under the Hill.

Two days later we drifted to the dock at Belle Grove Plantation. Mr. William E. Clements was eager to hear news of the war and Tucker Deal went to work immediately to build Bobby a better and more efficient coal bomb, not much larger than the originals, but just a smidgen. My feet were healing rather well and I slipped them into some new leather boots and tried on some new clothes, ones that had never been worn.

When finished I looked elegant and fashionable, but I knew such clothing was wasted on a man such as I, at least at this point in my life. I had to get back to St. Louis and get there fast. Bobby would do all he could to disrupt the Yankee plans, but I had to return and see to it help arrived in Vicksburg soon. You might say why go two days farther south to add four days to your trip, but I had good reason. I needed more money and counterfeit would do just fine. I needed to let my feet heal, and Bobby needed his bombs.

A good horse would be needed to make a return trip to St. Louis and where else could I get the best but Belle Grove Plantation. I wasn't expecting the nice clothes, but I should have known a man like Clements wouldn't let me go unkept. After gathering the necessary funds, Mr. Clements bid me farewell and I was off to the races.

I rode hard and lodged the first night in Baton Rouge where I rested much too long. At ten I traveled north away from the Yankee controlled city and stayed to the west of the Mississippi River. The second night was spent sleeping under an old cypress tree. I found myself moving before the sun tinted the eastern sky. At noon I crossed the Red River and continued north, crossing smaller rivers twice before I got into open country.

I didn't know this area of the country well, but I did know there were many waterways as I spent most of the day fording them. I stopped that evening near the west bank of the Mississippi River.

The following day I encountered no rivers and as a result made good time. The horse was game, one of the best in Mr. Clements stables. His gait was a long-distance eating one and the gelding knew all commands given by the strange and unfamiliar rider on his back. We made our best time that day, passing Natchez Under the Hill, Port Gibson, Grand Gulf, Vicksburg, and eventually putting in at Millken's Bend.

As the sun rose in the eastern sky the following morning I found myself crossing the southern Arkansas line headed north. The horse was game and seemed to want to run at times so I let him have his head and we did some running. The state of Arkansas was full of Confederate sympathizers, but I had to keep moving as I had envisioned a schedule which would get me back to St. Louis in a reasonable time.

I rode into St. Louis on the first day of June to discover the Yankees had learned of a regular Rebel mail packet making its way downriver to the troops in Mississippi and were engaged in turning every stone in the city looking for any evidence which might lend a hand in bringing the unauthorized enterprise to a screeching halt.

This put me on edge and I was required to change my lodging repeatedly until I could collect the mail from the oak tree at Lemay Ferry. Soldiers were throwing anyone in jail identified as a southern sympathizer, including women and children. This seemed a bit harsh I thought, but the Yankees deemed such tactics necessary for reasons unknown to me.

I managed to stay with the Little family my last evening in St. Louis and we discussed the ploy of taking Mrs. Little and her daughter through to Tupelo, Mississippi where General Henry Little was stationed, but the rest of the family nixed the idea immediately.

"It would be insane," they insisted, so I left St. Louis on my own accord the next day.

Bobby and I had agreed prior to my leaving Belle Grove Plantation to meet in Indiana for a short rest and vacation from our unlawful hobby. I wanted a vacation after the last few months, a rest from all the trials and tribulations, some time to think, to plan and let my weary bones recuperate, but rest it seemed, was not allowed.

Leaving St. Louis in mid-June I put my horse on the steamer *Empress* and rode downriver to Chester, Illinois where I debarked. Not recognized at any point since my departure, I saddled my mail bag and headed west for Indiana where I was to meet Bobby. This all went as planned and I met him at the New England Hotel where we checked in and caught up on the last two weeks.

With little else to do, we visited the local theatre that evening and this is where our rest escaped our grasp. A theatre is designed for entertainment and in this respect the building held true to its billing. However, the dance girls had been replaced by an unusual type of auction. As we entered the foyer we were greeted by Yankee soldiers who asked, "Buyers or sellers?"

"Excuse me?"

"Are you here to purchase a soldier's draft notice or are you his replacement?"

"I'm not quite sure I understand," I said.

"You mean you don't know what's going on?"

"We're businessmen traveling, sir and I assure you we have no idea to what you're referring."

"Men are inside who have been drafted and they're attempting to purchase replacements by auction. It seems they would rather stay home and sip wine or go to school."

"You're telling me they have enough money to buy off their draft notices by purchasing a replacement?"

"You are a businessman, sir."

"May we observe the auction?"

"Observation doesn't cost a thing. Help yourselves to a seat gentleman, and if you have any questions feel free to ask."

"Thank you, lieutenant."

Bobby and I opened the door and entered the theatre taking a seat in the back row much as if the bench were a church pew until we could at least get a handle on the proceedings, which didn't take long. There was a young man standing in front of the stage near a chair and the seventy-five or so men who were on stage were bidding on the young fellow, I thought. This seemed completely backwards to me, but what did I know? I felt they should've been parading the replacement specimen on stage while the bidders should be in the front row seats, but after further review I understood. Young men would stand up and claim a bid. When the bid got high enough they'd go down to the podium and give their name to the officer where they were instructed on the next step in the process, and escorted out of the building. The bidding men were not willing that any young able-bodied replacement be able to get up and walk out on the proceedings, so they were at the same time watching the back door for newcomers such as Bobby and I. They insisted no one should leave without declaring his intentions. This seemed logical, but where and when did the young man get paid?

Bobby and I sat and watched with much interest as one young man after another was purchased for just below or just above one thousand dollars in Yankee currency. One of the cowardly patriots signaled a bid of one thousand twenty-five dollars and my partner stood and said, "I'll take that!" He was heard plainly by every man in the hall. I tugged his shirt and tried to get him to return to his seat but Bobby had grown very strong of late and my hand was swatted away with the malice of swatting a fly. Whisking by me he went up to the podium and gave a false name, whereby he was given a card with the amount printed on it along with his fictitious address. When he returned to his seat, I asked him what on earth he was doing getting involved in such proceeding.

"Both sides of my wallet are rubbing together man, get a clue."

I had never been addressed by Bobby with such a disdainful approach and was surprised by his comments so soon after being swatted at as if I were a nuisance. The amazing thing was his comment sank in. I resolved to stay with him to the finish in case escape from the Federal stronghold was necessary. Shortly thereafter a young fellow reached a bid of nine hundred and seventy-five dollars and I stood to claim his ransom. This was necessary if I were going to be around to assist Bobby in case of unforeseen trouble.

I gave the name "James Ferguson, Zanesville, Ohio," and accepted my bid card along with instructions to report to the offices of Attorney Charles Moore for payment. Henry Meyers, or Bobby, had instructions to report to the same office the following morning at ten o'clock.

We returned to our motel room after having a bite to eat while sharing a few glasses of wine which I was glad to spring for, and laughed uncontrollably. We became as two hysterical laughing hyena's unable to stop. Eventually, this became painful and I wondered if the wine didn't have something to do with our jovial condition. Neither of us was used to wine. The walls were as most, thin beyond reproach and we took care not to say anything which might give us away, yet laughter told anyone who might be listening nothing.

The following morning there was a long line outside of the offices of Charles Moore, Attorney at Law. Both the buyers and sellers were present. We were called into Moore's office one by one and given our money along with a document which we presented to the buyer, absolving them of any responsibility to the Yankee draft. These men could care less who they had purchased, only that they themselves would not have to pick up arms or become a cushion for a Rebel bullet. Their sole distinguishing characteristic was the fact they cared not one wit what happened to us, the money or their precious Union.

When the last transaction had been completed, we substitutes were handed over to a squad of Federal soldiers, marched out of Indianapolis about four miles to Camp Morton, which covered about twenty acres, a stockade of sorts with a small creek running through the center. By the time we reached Camp Morton our stomachs were beginning to rub together in the middle and the Yankees wasted no time in feeding their new recruits a good hardy meal. This increased the standing of the Union army in my book, for our introductory meal lacked nothing in the way of satisfying elements.

We were called into formation after supper and Captain Jack Crowley took roll call, then explained how things would proceed.

"Gentlemen, you are now Union soldiers. You'll not sneeze or go to the bathroom without asking permission of your platoon sergeant. You'll be served a nourishing meal three times a day while training here at Camp Morton. Once on the front lines you will find food can be scarce. Often you must live off the land. You'll not speak unless spoken to. If you have a question you'll direct your query to Sergeant Mead who is your platoon sergeant from this moment forward. Do you understand?"

Here the captain received a lackluster response from some of the men and no response from many of them.

"You will answer the captain loud and clear with a hardy "yes, sir," whenever you're asked a question, do you understand?"

This time the sergeant got a better response than the captain, but the answer he received was still rather subdued.

"I said loud and clear. Do you understand?"

This time we seemed to offer the proper response as everyone in the newly drafted unit responded unequivocally, "Yes, sir!"

"That's more like it. Now when I give the order you'll fall out and these tents over here will be your quarters until further notice. You'll be divided into squads and tomorrow you'll be measured for uniforms. In the morning we'll begin drilling and learning the necessary discipline associated with becoming an excellent Federal soldier. Fall out!"

Now Bobby and I selected a comfortable cot in the tent closest to the perimeter of the camp and lay our heads down to rest. In no time we were snoring along with the other recruits who had managed to fall asleep as well. Well after dark I awoke to the sound of rain drops in our tent so I nudged Bobby and whispered, "Lets go, we're not here to make friends."

My partner rolled out of the sack and we stepped out of our tent into the light rain. Because Mr. Louden and I loathed the idea of drilling, we made our way to the fence where the creek came into the camp and slipped into the creek, exiting by the water gate, which was there to keep stock from escaping. Unfortunately for the Federals, they had not deemed any safeguard necessary to keep the new recruits from getting away.

We got wet and muddy but the walk back to town was enjoyable as our pockets were now lined with two thousand dollars of additional Yankee greenbacks.

"Do you think their tailor will appreciate the fact he'll have two less uniforms to make," Bobby asked out of the blue as we strolled down the lane.

"I hope so. Some men are addicted to work though, and he may be disappointed."

Just then we heard horses coming in the distance so we got into the nearby bushes and quietly sat tight. To our knowledge there were no southern gorilla's or Rebel soldiers raiding this far north so the precaution was reckoned a necessary measure, especially if the approaching riders were from Camp Morton, which they were.

We recognized Captain Jack Crowley along with two other Yankee soldiers whom we had not met. They made their way past and soon we resumed our trek toward Indianapolis and the hotel New England. Upon entering, the night clerk took one look at our disheveled appearance and commented. "How in tarnation did you boys get so muddy?"

"We've been on a bum with some of your young city friends and they've pickled us in grand fashion," I said.

He smiled. "Their favorite pastime. I should've known."

We mothballed our tired and aching bodies for the evening and sent our clothes out to be cleaned. Setting a wakeup call for seven we climbed into our soft comfortable four-posters and settled into a sudden inexhaustible and sound sleep.

Our newfound riches allowed us to order breakfast in our room and receive our clothes back good as new. We quietly talked and planned our next move as we ate a fine breakfast delivered on the hotel's finest trays. Hanging around Indianapolis was not a healthy proposition, so we made haste to put distance between us and our recently deserted Federal unit.

Our best option lay in waiting for dark, so about four in the afternoon we ordered dinner and waited. Once the sun went down we checked out of our room and started down to the train depot. As we were exiting the New England a soldier we'd met at Camp Morton cried, "Halt!" from down the street.

Turning we ran for our lives. We had been getting a good dose of physical exercise of late and the two of us spared no effort putting distance between us and the soldiers who had come to town looking for deserters.

We ducked into an open alleyway at full speed and didn't slow down. Running past lighted windows we scanned the gloomy backstreet for any opportunity to escape or hide under cover of darkness. Diving through an open backyard gate we sprinted to the front and right back out into the open. Gaslights lit our way and we were easier to see, but the front side of the street was also more wide open for unobstructed running. A shot suddenly parted the post beside me as we hurtled a picket fence at full speed, diving behind the house then out into another alley.

Directly across from us was a stable and we wasted not a second diving into the structure and out a side door into another street. We sprinted in the direction of the south edge of town where catching our breath was suddenly the most important assignment of the moment. We settled down to wait for the train we knew would be leaving for Louisville and while we had money to buy passage we were now forced to secure our transit illegally.

Once we had our breath back we decided the best thing to do would be to put more distance between us and the Yankee troops, so we walked along the railway until the train could catch up to us. This proved to be a mistake as the train had up a full head of steam by the time Engine number 102 reached our position. She was making all of fifty miles an hour while we stood by helplessly watching as the cars sped past.

"That's just great old man," Bobby retorted.

"Well, we could always find some horses. There were probably Federal troops on the train looking for us anyway," I comforted.

"There's one more southbound at one o'clock," Bobby reminded me.

"We'd better make our way back closer to town if we intend to ride."

We headed back for the edge of Indianapolis and waited for the one o'clock southbound. We thought about buying tickets at the depot, but thought better of the idea. The Yankee soldiers would certainly be waiting for us.

Presently the southbound engine was heard in the distance and we made ourselves ready to board. The conductor yelled, "All Aboard!" and the train picked up steam.

When the engine blew its whistle the train was nearing our hideout beside the tracks and when the passenger cars cleared, we came out of hiding and jogged beside the freight cars until we could gage their speed and swing ourselves up. Bobby went first and I threw my mail bag up to him, then he assisted what he had begun calling the old man as he lifted me bodily with only one hand into the open gondola.

Riding in the dark didn't set well with us and after thirty minutes we made our way to the passenger cars and found an unoccupied spot where we could rest in comfort. This went better than expected as I fully anticipated the conductor would spot us and remove the unpaid passengers from his car, but the man never showed until we were pulling into the station at Louisville. He looked directly at us but decided any effort to enforce his company policy on us now would be considered too little too late.

Stepping off of the train in Louisville we made our way to the Galt House and had a wonderful bout with our authentic Yankee greenbacks. We were in hiding for two days while the Yankees widened their search for the two deserters who'd left them at Indianapolis. Several times they came close, but we managed to stay one step ahead of them.

We thought we would stand less chance of being recognized if we split up, so Bobby headed back for St. Louis and I headed south to Memphis where I went to the home of Captain Dan Able and knocked on his door. Dan was a tall lanky man much like the president and reminded most folks of the politician from Illinois. Dan provided me with a mule and buggy to travel below Memphis anytime I needed to go south, as long as I would transport Mrs. Thomas Snead and her daughter south to General Price's outfit. Thomas Snead was the general's chief of staff.

"In case you're unaware, there's a two thousand dollar reward for one Captain Grimes, Confederate mail runner," Dan said as he hitched up the mule for us.

"Two thousand? Why that's an insult. I should command five at least," I said in jest.

"Have you thought about what you'll do if you're caught with Mr. Snead's family in tow? Such a catastrophe would be no laughing matter."

I looked over at my two charges and wondered what would I do if recognized? The ladies would surely not fare very well after being captured with the likes of me.

Mrs. Snead and her daughter were wearing their traveling dresses and each had a carpetbag in tow. They appeared somewhat disheveled but in good spirits. Both wore matching bonnets and the girl had a doll tucked under her right arm. She couldn't have been more than five in my estimation.

"I'll have to make a point of not getting caught," I suggested more soberly.

"You may do better if you leave out by the north road. The Yankees are watching the southern routes closely."

"Thanks Dan, the last thing I want is to alert them."

Dan finished hitching the mule and walked over to Mrs. Snead and her daughter. "You're ready to go ma'am," he said as he picked up their luggage.

I walked over to the front porch, lifted my mail bag and placed it in the back beneath their bags. Mine was no different, but I wanted the mail on the bottom in case we were stopped for any reason.

After proper introductions, Dan helped the ladies into their seats and I stepped up and took hold of the reins. What was I going to be transporting next I was curious to know, as there seemed to be no end of special requests of late.

Getting mail through the lines had become a fox and hound affair and adding charges such as Mrs. Snead and her daughter to my baggage did nothing to ease my nerves.

"Ma'am, if the Yankees stop us for any reason, let me do the talking. If they ask who you are, what your names are or make any other inquiries, your name is Tillman, Blanche Tillman and you're a widow. I am taking you and your daughter through to Tupelo for the funeral of your late husband, Captain Alex Tillman. Just about everyone knows he was killed recently in a raid conducted by the Yankees. Can you remember all that?"

"Yes, captain, but what of you? What if they recognize you?"

"There's not much I can do about that."

"I can."

"Ma'am?" I asked in surprise.

"When you find a likely place I want you to pull over. I've a few tricks of my own."

Well I was surprised. What kind of chicanery was Mrs. Snead referring to? I could envision no possibilities available for changing my appearance, but if you live long enough you learn and I was about to learn. I thought my appearance to be what it was, although my long bearded face depicted no doubt a character of moral bankruptcy. I tried daily to keep my moral self in line, yet like clockwork something always seemed to happen which would send my sense of moral justice careening over a long dark cliff. This in itself accounted for my moral bankruptcy as I saw matters. Never did I allow myself to accept the blame for my own actions. My lack of honesty was on account of the war. Had the war not been taking place, I should never have told the first fib or stolen the first horse, or so I believed.

I found a shade tree along the north road and pulled the wagon over. Mrs. Snead got a blanket and I sat down beside the wagon per her instructions. She trimmed my mustache and braided my woolly beard.

I never thought of such a thing and had never seen a beard braided, but like I said, if you live long enough you'll learn. The braiding of my beard took an hour and the lady capped her work off by adding a couple of beads to the end of my scraggly locks. She handed me a mirror to view her handiwork, and I failed to recognize myself.

"Well, I never dreamed," I said as I surveyed my new look in the mirror.

"Now Captain Grimes, there is less chance of you being caught or recognized. Do you think you can get us through enemy lines?"

"With all due respect ma'am, I believe our chances of success just went up immeasurably, but no one can guarantee anything in this crazy war."

"I'm not asking for a guarantee, I just want a fighting chance."

"You've given us that, ma'am. You surely have."

We folded up the blanket and put it away. A moment later we climbed back into the carriage and started the old mule down the north road. Now I had seen many mules in my time, mostly Missouri mules, but this thing we had pulling us was bigger than most horses, standing a good sixteen hands. This animal was without doubt the biggest mule I had ever seen or was likely ever to see. Along with the usual white snout he was sporting two white stockings above the front hooves.

I had taken the time to make up a bogus pass and after eight miles of travel on the north road we turned west. Two miles later we passed through the enemy lines with our counterfeit credentials and settled in to traveling, the worst behind us.

I had up to this point done most all of my traveling with Bobby and Mickey. The thought of having to look for accommodations for the women had never really occurred to me until I discovered getting adequate accommodations with women and children along to be quite a different matter. The part of the country we were passing through had been devastated by both armies, leaving in their wake little to no decent place for a lady and her child to lay their head for the night. I could sleep in the carriage, but the womenfolk needed a bit more care.

It was well after midnight the first night before I found a room for them, and consequently I searched in earnest earlier in the afternoon from then on in order to attain the necessary sleeping quarters for Mrs. Snead and her daughter.

Three days later I guided our carriage into General Price's headquarters at Tupelo, Mississippi where Mrs. Snead was reunited with her husband. After witnessing the happy reunion involving husband, mother and daughter, I was more thoroughly paid for the danger and trouble necessary to get my charges through the Yankee lines to Tupelo.

"Captain, please come into my office," General Price insisted.

I followed the general into his quarters and accepted a seat across from him.

"The war on our side has turned ugly. With Grierson's raid into Mississippi, Vicksburg is now in question. Nearly all supply lines have been cut off and we're in danger of losing the rest. I have a dispatch I want you to get through to General Pemberton at Vicksburg if you can still get through the enemy lines."

"The lines surrounding Vicksburg, sir?"

"I'm not referring to any other."

The door of General Price's office opened and General Henry Little walked in. He was quite happy to see the men out front getting their mail as Shelby Foster had taken charge and was handing out the correspondence in my absence. I noted with a heavy heart there were too many men not present or not responding when their name was called.

"Captain, this is General Little from St. Louis. He has a message for Pemberton also."

"General Henry Little?" I asked.

"Yes, captain," the general replied. "Henry Little. Is there a problem?"

"No sir, I was asking only because your wife and daughter wanted to come along with me when I left St. Louis and were desirous of coming here to be with you, but the rest of the family, namely General Morrison wouldn't hear of it."

"My father-in-law never has liked me. The General will most certainly marry his daughter to someone else as fast as they can shovel dirt on my grave."

"You're a general, I don't think this war is going to get you."

"This war has already claimed several generals fighting for the southern cause. I'm not exempt from the battlefield, captain. None of us are."

"Sir, your wife and child most certainly wanted to come but the decision was not mine," I said watching as a small tear trickled from his right eye. Having to watch Mr. and Mrs. Snead reunited was not helping matters any.

"Gentlemen, as much as I concur and would love to have my own family present, we must get down to business," General Price interrupted.

"General, my men are doing without. Since Grierson's raid they're finding little to eat," Little said.

"I'm well aware of that fact, general. My men are faring no better."

"We must get the supply lines open."

"Where? All the track engineers seem to have sided with the industrialized north. We've no one who knows how to lay track or replace what Grierson has destroyed."

"We can make an effort. To sit here and do nothing isn't the answer."

"No. If we do nothing, Vicksburg will surely fall," Price said.

"Sir, what of the Yankee supply ships? If they can ship rations downriver I can surely hijack their fare and deliver the rations directly to Vicksburg," I said.

"You can do that, captain?"

"If anyone can do such a thing, I can."

That would alleviate the need for repairing the train tracks between Vicksburg and Newton Station. The supply would have to be steady," Price said.

"With the right men I could steal their supply shipments and sail the rations right into Vicksburg."

"Who would your men be?"

"I can name two right off, Shelby Foster and Jessie White."

"Foster is a good man," General Price said.

"So is Jessie White. I'll need them both and one day to gather the rest."

"All right, they're yours. I'll give you twenty-four hours to come up with the rest. I want a list of names on my desk before you leave out."

"You'll have it, sir," I said as I departed General Price's office.

Chapter 25

I rounded up seven men in six hours. I left Shelby Foster in charge of collecting the return mail while I gathered men. The following morning our unit left Tupelo for Louisville.

We gathered at an old Indian mound which had been used by local Indians for ceremonies in north Mississippi many years ago. My best understanding of the mound put it somewhere between eight hundred and a thousand years old. The tribe who had inhabited the area was now long gone. They had not been Cherokee or Choctaw, Taposa maybe or even Chickasaw.

A few of us collected arrowheads as we rested. We set out for the Ohio River and Louisville, where most of our journey would be over land. The supplies we needed to commandeer would be loaded in St. Louis and shipped downstream.

I'd selected a rough and tumble crowd of men who knew how to handle a steamboat from stem to stern. Jeremiah Boudreau was a pilot from down New Orleans way. Since signing up to fight for the Confederacy, he'd not piloted anything, but once you knew how to handle a steamboat, you don't forget any time soon. For this reason I selected Jeremiah as second mate. If something were to happen to me he would take over and see the mission through.

Joseph Ezekiel Brown was known to everyone as Jeb and although small in stature he commanded a much greater presence when confronted. Jeb was from Baton Rouge and had at one time learned under the guiding hand of Captain Henry Miller Shreve. I placed Jeb third in command. If something happened to the first two pilots he would guide the boat to Vicksburg and through the Yankee positions.

Along with Shelby Foster and Jessie White I selected three men who had a good deal of experience in the engine room, capable of stoking the fire or oiling the doctor, a pumping engine for the boiler. Feeling quite capable of any incursion onto an enemy boat, the seven of us made haste, taking stock of our experience as we went.

Wilbur Vanderbilt was an engineer and capable of following any command the skipper might give. He had learned his trade over the last fifteen years on such boats as the *Kate Adams*, the *Tennessee*, and the *Bayou Sarah*. Vanderbilt was well qualified as engineer for any one of the pilots. He was a man of average size yet he always walked with a swinging style or happy demeanor. Never had the man succumbed to negative thoughts, even when losing in the heat of battle. In short Vanderbilt could be counted on.

Pierre Slaughter was an immigrant from France, but a fierce rival in any sort of skirmish and the reason I chose him. The oldest of the bunch he had a cool head in any fight.

Solomon Yoder was the son of an Amish furniture maker and the youngest of our group, although he possessed something unidentifiable which made him the most dangerous of the men I'd selected. He'd been chosen for his ability to kill the enemy in as a cold-blooded a fashion as possible without leaving a trace of evidence or making any sound. Whenever the enemy was close, he would slip out of camp and scalp a Yankee. When asked if he was part Indian he denied it vehemently.

In Louisville the seven of us stopped at the art gallery of Nicola Marschall, both designer of the Confederate uniform and the Confederate flag. Major Orren R. Smith had tried to claim himself as the rightful designer of the Confederate flag, but anyone who knew him knew also he was quite incapable of any imagination. Mr. Marschall was located in the building on the corner of Green and Fourth Streets.

What exactly it was that made us venture into his building is still unknown to me this day, but the fact remains each and every one of us was grateful for having met the Confederate flag's originator. He was a most gracious host and served each of us a hot cup of coffee. I learned afterward that shortly after we left his art gallery he went into hiding, fearful if we could find him the Yankee's were no doubt only a few steps behind. I discovered after the war was over he had quietly returned to Marion, Alabama a place he dearly loved and went back to teaching at a school for young ladies, his specialty being art and piano.

It should be noted here that a mail carrier does not know the contents of that which he is carrying, not if he's in the least bit honest. On my last trip through Louisville only a few days prior, I had delivered much correspondence and one of those letters was from the Confederate war department telling Mrs. White of Louisville that her son Jessie White had been killed in the battle of Missionary Ridge. We were completely unaware of this fact as the seven of us came strolling down the street to Jessie's mother's house. His two sisters were sitting on the front porch when we reached the stairs, dressed in black, the color of mourning.

"Who died," Jessie asked.

Helen the elder of Jessie's two sisters responded by standing straight up only to faint in a heap. Jessie's youngest sister Dora's eyes bulged out and she ran into the house screaming for her mother, stumbling over Helen as she went. A moment later Jessie's mother reached the front door. The instant she spied her son, she joined her daughter on the floor in a dead faint.

We watched as Jessie ran to his mother's side and asked, "Mother what's wrong? What's happening?" She looked into her son's eyes and threw her arms around him, putting him in a headlock and sobbed uncontrollably.

The two of them sat in the doorway holding one another for several minutes before the mother could talk. Helen had roused and she sat up while her sister stood inside the house overlooking the happy scene.

"I got a letter which said you were dead," Jesse's mother finally said.

I ducked my head a bit knowing I had something, if not everything, to do with such a letter being delivered.

"Mother, I assure you I'm alive and doing fine."

"I can see. I still have my eyes, young man."

"We were hoping to get a meal before train time," Jessie said.

"You mean you want me to cook for you and all your friends?"

"Not now. I was unaware the three of you were in mourning."

"We'll get shut of these clothes fast enough and we'll have a celebration for your homecoming. We'll cook. Boy, are we going to cook. You go ahead and make yourselves comfortable men, I've got to run down to the market but I'll be right back," Jessie's mother insisted. "You girls get upstairs and change your clothes. When you come down you get a fire going in the stove. Open the windows and let some air into the house and open the curtains."

Jessie's mother disappeared into her own bedroom and when she returned she had transformed herself from a widow in mourning as Jessie's father had been dead several years hence, to a bright jovial and happy woman wearing a bright green dress.

"Don't you go anywhere, young man," she told Jessie. "I'm going to cook that dinner and you'd better be here when I get back."

"Yes, ma'am."

I wanted to laugh at the insanity of it all, but I held my tongue and repressed any smile until Jessie's sisters returned to our midst. They hugged him until he was smothered, then set about getting the house ready for the coming celebration. The finest china came out of the cabinets, the best silverware, and a fresh tablecloth was brought out. The table was lengthened and chairs were added.

Mrs. White and the girls prepared a feast while we men milled about the front porch and backyard. By three in the afternoon the fresh beef aroma was wafting through the windows, and tempting our taste buds. Soon we found ourselves eating. A joyous time was had by all who were present, not the least of which was Jessie White.

Later the same evening as we waited beside the railroad tracks for the train to arrive, I noted the most troubling fact I had ever encountered as a man. I was in a struggle for good over evil, yet the struggle was going on inside of me.

I had always considered myself a good man, yet now I was walking a darkened path lit here and there by good deeds, but could my actions of late really be identified as good deeds? I brought many smiles to many faces whenever I delivered a mail packet, but I was also engaged in trying to kill the enemy, something I had not sought to do originally. Lying to get my way was becoming habit and deceit was becoming a way of life for me. Captain Absalom Grimes was a good man I supposed, but when was a good man justified in doing evil things?

I was suddenly stunned by my lack of faith, for had my faith been strong enough to win the day, I'd never found the first lie necessary. Had my faith carried the strength it should have I would never have assembled such a group of men, killers in their own right. I, Captain Absalom Grimes, was now the leader of a group of killers. I was torn by my allegiance to the south and the ability to do good works, and the evil that I must do in order to continue the southern cause was sickening my resolve.

I personally knew of men who were good in both blue and gray uniforms and I knew of evil men on both sides, yet what were we fighting for? Evil was rearing its ugly head in the north and south, just as it had taken hold in my life. The prevailing theme had always been good triumphs over evil because God was on the side of good, but what happens when good and evil are no longer clear? Both were living inside of me. Was this how I should now view the north and south?

I was a man of my word or had been until I began lying for the Confederate cause. I was now a spy, an underground mail carrier, a thief and a killer. Bobby may have been the one who actually blew up the troop ships, but I was responsible for steering him in such a direction in the first place and as such was culpable in the matter. How many deaths was I accountable to God for? I had killed on the battlefield at Pea Ridge, the German sergeant on the *City of Alton* and numerous others, but I was also setting prisoners free. Men the Yankees intended to hang I had returned to freedom.

My reasoning led me to discover both sides were on the side of right which only meant one thing. The outcome of this war would not be decided by the right side winning, but by the winners nevertheless. If, as I now suspected, both sides were partially correct in their assessment of freedom the only possible outcome would be decided by the victors. How such a scenario would shake out remained to be seen, but regardless which side won, the years immediately following the conflict would be brutal.

Then the question would become—how to undo what we have become in the name of winning a war? Men on both sides, winners and losers, would not simply go away into the night never to be heard from again. They were now trained killing machines. Where would they go, what would become of them?

Settling onto the northbound train we first put our horses in the cattle car and settled in to rest for a few hours. The train blew its lonely evening whistle and the wheels churned. The conductor yelled, "All Aboard," as the engine blew steam and the train picked up speed.

We spread ourselves out in the passenger car and took individual seats so that if one of us came under fire no one else would be likely to get hurt. This arrangement worked so well we made a promise to ensure we always traveled in such manner when riding the train.

Swapping trains in Centralia we found ourselves at the Mississippi River and ferried across on the *City of Alton*. This served only as a reminder of what had taken place on my escape from the troops during the prisoner transfer.

The seven of us were dressed as western men bound west. My own beard was still beaded and braided along with the fringe jacket I wore, which gave me the look of a buffalo hunter. For this no Yankees gave us any grief. We settled into the same barn I had stayed in before while breaking my own mother out of jail and here we planned our strategy.

I was happy to get busy with the planning for my mind was worrying about things I had no control over. I could no more control the evil which presented itself than I could control another's thoughts. Evil would do what evil would do even if it used me for its outcome. I could no longer control what I was doing or thinking.

About noon Vanderbilt came back into the barn and laid a document on the barrel I was using for a desk. It read as follows:

Wanted
Dead or Alive
Captain Absalom Grimes
The captain is wanted for treason, blowing up troop ships,
running unauthorized mail and murder!
A $5,000.00 reward is offered for his capture!

This was followed by an unmistakable picture of yours truly. My beard was not braided in the picture the Federals offered, but the facial features and my eyes were a dead giveaway. Unless I wanted to be hung, I was going to have to step carefully about St. Louis from this day forward.

The other piece of paper Vanderbilt delivered that he had laid under my wanted poster was a shipping list of supplies being loaded onto the *Lafourche*. I couldn't believe our luck. Everything our soldiers in Vicksburg would need was being loaded onto the southbound steamer to include weapons, ammunition, first aid supplies, and food.

All we had to do was get aboard and sail away. The question was how? I wasn't going to waltz down to the wharf and step aboard, not with a five thousand dollar reward being offered for my head. Anything I did would have to be incognito. The deed would have to be done under the cover of darkness and preferably out on the open water where no Yankee troops could come to her aid.

"Gentlemen, we'll need skiffs. Three should be sufficient. I want them placed in the water south of Jefferson Barracks. We'll not have a lot of time. Our boat is sailing tonight," I said. "Pierre and Solomon, I want you two to get them. Steal them or buy them but get them in place by sundown."

"Yes, sir."

"And gentlemen, report back to me when you've completed your mission."

"Yes, sir," they said and were gone.

About five minutes later the side door to our hideout was pushed open and in stepped a man I knew to be former Major John Wisner. His left arm was missing which now placed him among the injured or maimed, a group of men the Federals had not yet considered dangerous or whether they might still have some fight.

"I'm here to see you to the Sappington residence. There are men present who need your assistance, Captain Grimes."

"Men who need my assistance?"

"Yes, captain. They need you to get them through the enemy lines. They've just recently escaped Lynches Negro pen and sir, you know them all."

"All of them?"

"Yes, sir."

"How many are there?"

"Six in all."

Six more men would make our number an unlucky thirteen!

"They'd better be the right six men or else I'll leave them at the Sappington residence," I said quite clearly.

I got into the buggy with Major John M. Wisner and rode to the house of Dave Sappington. The residence was located on a hill not far from Jefferson Barracks, yet tucked away beneath the shade of old elm trees. The house was of marble and stonework commonly seen in the area, yet the Sappington home was set apart from the rest by a finely groomed lawn and garden. Bushes and trees were neatly trimmed as ornaments on display. Not one shrub was out of place.

Our buggy pulled up to the front steps, seventeen in all, which came down to a circular drive. Dismounting we ascended the staircase and knocked on the front door, which was quite literally two front doors. A butler soon opened it and led us to the back patio where quite a few men were gathered.

"Captain Grimes, how good of you to join us," Dave Sappington said as he offered his hand in friendship. "We've been eagerly awaiting your arrival."

Looking around I knew the major had been correct, I knew these men. Captain Hampton Boone, Walter Scott, Bob Steward and John Carlin had all been in the pen with me last year. Along with them were Mark Twain and Sam Bowen, my old steamboat pals from Hannibal.

"Mark, I thought you'd headed west."

"Sadly, old friend I was unexpectedly delayed by some nosey Yankees."

"These are the six men I'm to transport?" I asked.

"They are, besides Mark Twain we have..." Sappington began.

"I know them all, major. Introductions won't be necessary."

"I'll take you men south provided you listen to me and do exactly as I say. The first one who doesn't will be left on his own recognizance in the middle of nowhere, understood?" I shot a glare at Mark.

"You've nothing to worry about with me old pal," Mark said.

"Of all the men present, you'll be the most trouble," I snapped.

"That's a very distrustful way to start out," Mark complained.

"You've not given me reason to suspect anything different."

"Go on with you now, you've other fish to fry."

"I'll go when I am good and ready. Major, have these men down by the river at sundown one mile below Jefferson Barracks. I'll pick them up there."

"Shall I give you a ride back?"

"You shall," I said.

Getting back into the horse drawn carriage I soon found myself in the old barn downtown. Our steamboat crew had nearly doubled in size, yet the planning required for our mission was still the same. Three small boats would work as before only they would be required to carry more passengers.

I noted once again that we were steamboat pilot poor just as we had been before the war started. Each of us knew the code of the Old South and knew the southern gentlemen's code to be right, but was I the only one to recognize the north was also correct in her assessment of freedom for all? I cursed the revelation as presented to me and carried on.

By the dark of the moon thirteen fighting men pushed three small boats out into the river and prepared to board the coming steamer. None wore a Rebel uniform, but all wore a pistol. We drifted and waited for the vessel we knew would be along and just after midnight, well below any population, she came into view. We had to be nearing Chester by this point but the Illinois side didn't matter. Putting oar to water we rowed our skiffs in the direction of the *Lafourche*.

As all three skiffs neared her port side I saw ropes shoot out from all three boats and lasso the usually elusive mooring at the back. We heaved to and thirteen fighting men slithered aboard her decks.

Two of the skiffs bumped together before we could get them situated away from one another and one poor Yankee soul came aft to investigate. In the moment which followed, Jessie White slit his throat and laid the unfortunate soldier overboard.

Slowly and cautiously our Rebel band made its way forward and by the time we reached the pilot house, five Yankees had met a quiet demise, their bodies carried aft and dropped into the churning Mississippi River. We seized the pilot house and the engine room and from there we gathered the necessary information, namely that there were only seven more Yankees on board. White took care of them in their sleep.

It was grand to have my hand on the wheel again, but my jubilation was short lived. As the sun came up a few hours later another boat appeared on the horizon and as she sped past on her decks was noted the sign, "Vicksburg has fallen!"

End of Book 1
Captain Grimes, Unreconstructed.

Book 2 coming in 2016

About the Author

John T. Wayne was born in St. Louis, Missouri in August of 1958. He is the middle son of three boys. At seventeen he joined the United States Marines and served two honorable tours. After nearly seven years of service life he got out and attended the University of Oregon on a full G.I. scholarship. After only six months he realized the professors could not teach him what he wanted to know to become a great writer and set out to learn it on his own.

In 1985 he began writing after losing his daughter to cancer. He is a self-taught writer, looking to become the best of the best. Any story he writes will be steeped in history, usually facts omitted by current curriculum such as the orphan problem created by the Civil War.

In one hundred fifty years since the war, no one has written about the orphans until now. These very orphans became the cowboys of old. Prior to the war the term cowboy was not in use. It only became fashionable once the war was over. The reason being, the only thing ranches out west could hire once the war got up a full head of steam was the orphans being created by the war itself, boys with no experience handling cattle.

John T. Wayne now resides in Arkansas with his wife, his mother, Bonnie and, his Aunt Rose. John and his wife have three sons, seven grandchildren and are looking for a ranch in Northeast Arkansas. John rides horses as often as he can. A former ASE Certified mechanic he enjoys the hobby of Hot Rodding.

Other books form John T. Wayne include:

Catfish John
The Treasure of Del Diablo
Ol' Slantface
Blood Once Spilled
Cowboy Up! (a book of quotes)
Captain Grimes (Unreconstructed) *Part One*

About the Front Cover Artist

Whether working in his floating river studio the *River Rover* or in his home studio on the Missouri riverfront in Washington, Missouri, Gary Lucy captures the beauty and ruggedness of nature and river life.

In 1973, Lucy received his first taste of national exposure by winning second place in the Federal Duck Stamp Competition, and in 1977, he again received national exposure by placing third in the National Wild Turkey Federation stamp design competition. Only a few years later, in 1982, he placed first in the Missouri Duck Stamp Competition for his painting of *Bufflehead Ducks*. In 1977, Lucy was also commissioned to paint his first mural, *Missouri Wildlife* for the West Plains Bank in West Plains, Missouri. A second mural *Missouri Wildlife II,* followed the first in 1979, this time for the Washington Missouri Library. In 1980 and 1985, Lucy painted the *Missouri Trilogy* and the *Songbirds of Missouri* for the cover of Southwestern Bell's phonebooks. *Missouri Trilogy* now hangs in the governor's office in Jefferson City.